W9-AOE-838

Date: 1/11/12

LP FIC COULTER
Coulter, Catherine.
Split second

Split Second

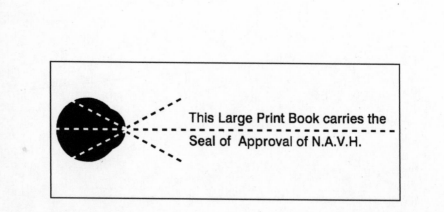

This Large Print Book carries the
Seal of Approval of N.A.V.H.

SPLIT SECOND

CATHERINE COULTER

THORNDIKE PRESS

A part of Gale, Cengage Learning

GALE
CENGAGE Learning™

Detroit • New York • San Francisco • New Haven, Conn • Waterville, Maine • London

GALE
CENGAGE Learning

Thorndike Press® Large Print Basic.
The text of this Large Print edition is unabridged.
Other aspects of the book may vary from the original edition.
Set in 16 pt. Plantin.

LIBRARY OF CONGRESS CATALOGING-IN-PUBLICATION DATA

Coulter, Catherine.
  Split second / by Catherine Coulter.
    p. cm. — (Thorndike Press large print basic)
  ISBN-13: 978-1-4104-3826-3 (hardcover)
  ISBN-10: 1-4104-3826-0 (hardcover)
    1. United States. Federal Bureau of Investigation—Fiction. 2. Savich, Dillon (Fictitious character)—Fiction. 3. Sherlock, Lacey (Fictitious character)—Fiction. 4. Large type books. I. Title.
  PS3553.O843S65 2011b
  813'.54—dc22   2011017785

Published in 2011 by arrangement with G. P. Putnam's Sons, a member of Penguin Group (USA) Inc.

Printed in the United States of America
1 2 3 4 5 6 7 15 14 13 12 11

To Anton,
my favorite guy in the whole universe.
A big thank-you, as always.

C.C.

CHAPTER 1

Georgetown, Washington, D.C.
Tuesday night
Nonfat milk, Fritos, and bananas, Savich repeated to himself as he pulled into the parking lot of Mr. Patil's Shop 'n Go. It was after eight o'clock, and Savich was on his way home from a hard workout at the gym. He felt good, his muscles relaxed and warm, and he looked forward to playing with Sean, maybe with his new video game, Wonky Wizards. He breathed in deeply, enjoying the bite of fall in the air. He looked up at the low-lying clouds that promised to bring a shower in the next couple of hours. Nonfat milk and Fritos and — what else?

There was only one car in the parking lot, which wasn't unusual at this time of the evening. A strange play of rapid movement behind the store's large glass window caught his eye. He pulled the Porsche to the far side of the parking lot, out of the line of sight, got out, quietly closed the car door, and walked to the edge of the window. He could see a man inside, his face flattened in a leg of pantyhose, standing in front of the counter, pointing a Saturday night special at Mr. Patil's chest. Mr. Patil, who wasn't more than five-five with lifts in his shoes and was at least seventy-five years old, looked petrified. Savich watched his hands shoot into the air above his head. He could hear the man yelling at him, but couldn't make out what he was saying. Then he saw a customer. At the end of the counter stood a man about his own age, wearing a bright red Redskins sweatshirt, jeans, and glasses.

Savich felt his heart seize.

Pressed against the man's legs were two small children, a boy and a girl. His hands were wrapped around their shoulders, hugging them tightly against him. Each child held an ice-cream bar, now forgotten.

Keep it together. He couldn't call 911, and take the chance of sirens freaking the guy out, not with the kids still in the line of fire. He quickly ran around to the back of the Shop 'n Go and heard the engine running before he saw the Chevy Impala, tucked in the shadows off the parking asphalt. He saw a woman in the driver's seat, leaning in toward the passenger's side to get a partial view inside the store. Since she wasn't wearing pantyhose on her head, she obviously wasn't slated to join the actual robbery; she was just there to drive the man in the store out of here. Savich couldn't see the license plate. No matter. She hadn't seen him. Good.

Forget her, let her get away. He crouched down and ran back around to the front of the store. He held his SIG at his side and began whistling. He opened the door and called out, "Good evening, Mr. Patil," and the man in the pantyhose whirled around, his gun leading, as the little girl yelled, "He'll hurt you!"

The man froze for the longest instant of time in Savich's memory. Savich saw the father grab the children and hurl them to the floor, and then he fell over them while Mr. Patil hefted a six-pack of beer the man had brought to the counter. Then Savich's SIG was up, and he fired. The rule was always to fire only when you intended to kill, but the bullet didn't go into the man's chest, it went into his shoulder. The man screamed, fell hard to his knees, clutching his shoulder, and the .22 went flying.

Savich listened for the Impala's engine to rev, for the car to roar out of there, but he didn't hear anything except a car door slamming shut. He yelled, "Mr. Patil, get down!" Savich dropped to the floor and was rolling when the door burst open and a submachine gun started blasting bullets. He heard Mr. Patil scream from behind the counter, knew he hadn't been fast enough and she'd hit him. He heard the kids screaming, heard the father's deep voice, hazed over with fear, saying, "It's all right, it will be all right." He came up and fired, hit the woman square between the eyes as she swung the gun around toward him. The submachine gun hit the linoleum floor and fetched hard against the counter.

Savich saw Mr. Patil leaning heavily on the counter, a bloom of red on his right arm. He jumped up and quickly checked the gunman, pulled the stocking off his face. He was white, about forty, heavyset, his light brown hair seriously thinning. He moaned, holding his shoulder, the bullet still in him. He was lucky the bullet hadn't hit an artery. He'd survive. Savich picked up the .22 and said, "Keep pressing down on that," and then he went down on his knees beside the woman. Like the man, she was white, fortyish, but she was dead. Her dark eyes were open. A dribble of blood came out of her mouth, and the hole between her eyes was a perfect red dot. Blood haloed her head.

Please keep their eyes covered.

He quickly pulled off his leather jacket and covered the woman's face. He ran back to Mr. Patil and examined the bullet wound. Through and through, thank God. "You did great, sir. You're going to be okay." Savich grabbed a wad of paper towels from next to the coffee machine and pressed them against Mr. Patil's arm. "Press as hard as you can, sir."

He called 911 and asked for two ambulances and the police. He looked over at the father, still covering his children on the floor. Both children were quiet now, their father murmuring against their heads, "It's okay, kids, everything's okay now —"

Savich looked back at the wounded man, saw he wasn't moving or making a sound. He came down on his haunches, laid his hand lightly on the man's shoulder. He was a big guy, pretty fit, his face less ashen now that he realized they'd all survived. "Don't worry, I'm FBI. You did great; you kept your kids safe. Everything's under control now. The police will be here soon. You're a very brave man; it's a pleasure to meet you," and Savich stuck out his hand. "I'm Dillon Savich."

The man slowly stood, bringing the children with him, still pressed against his legs.

He straightened his glasses and gave Savich a shaky grin. He started to say something, then lost the words, the wild adrenaline rush choking them off. He took Savich's hand, shook it really hard, and at last he managed to say, "I can hear my own heart beating so heavy, it's like it's going to fly out of my chest."

"It's the adrenaline. Believe me, in a couple of minutes you're going to crash."

"No, I can't do that, not with the kids here. Hey, I'm Dave Raditch. Thank you for coming in like that, so sharp and fast. I don't know what the guy was going to do; he might have shot all of us. It sure looked like he was going to kill Mr. Patil. Hush, Michael, everything's okay. Hold Crissy's hand, okay?"

Savich prayed Dave wouldn't bottom out completely after the adrenaline snapped out of him and fall over. He'd seen it before. He looked closely at Dave Raditch, saw he was occupied with stroking those small shuddering bodies, keeping them very close. Savich smiled at him. "You'll do fine," he said, and smiled down at Michael. Then, because it could have been Sean, Savich hugged him. As Savich pressed Michael's face against him, he thought, how would he deal with this violent terror? With the shock of sudden bloody death? As he rubbed his big hands up and down Michael's back, he said, "Michael, I really need your help. The police will be here soon, and I'll have to speak with them. I want you to hunker down with your dad and sister and talk about what happened, because the police will want to speak with you, too. Do you think you can keep them calm? Can you do that for me?"

Michael hiccuped, wiped the back of his hand over his running nose, and slowly pulled back in Savich's arms. He looked over at the man moaning on the floor, holding his shoulder, his blood everywhere. Then Michael looked at the woman Mr. Savich had covered with his leather jacket. Michael knew she was dead, knew dead meant she wouldn't wake up. And there was Mr. Patil, and he was hurt, too, that woman had shot him, but because he'd heard Mr. Savich tell Mr. Patil he was going to be okay, Michael didn't think he'd have to worry about him. He tried to straighten his shoulders and said, "I can do that, sir," in the most convincing imitation adult voice Savich had ever heard. What was he? Five years old? Sean's age. Thank God Sean hadn't been with him.

"Crissy, it's okay now," Michael said as he

patted his sister's back. "Dad, Mr. Savich said the police are coming and we've got to get our stories straight."

Well, close enough. Savich smiled.

Dave Raditch's left eyebrow shot up above his glasses. He didn't know where it came from, but when he met Savich's eyes, he grinned, nodded, but only for an instant, because Crissy's face was leached of color and she was shuddering like she had a fever. He cleared his throat. "Okay, Crissy, Michael's right, we've gotta tell the police exactly what happened before Mr. Savich came in. How about the three of us go over there by the potato chips and talk about how this went down, okay?"

Crissy Raditch turned to stare at the woman, and then licked her lips. "Did Mr. Savich shoot her dead?"

This is the big one. Savich said, "Yes, I had to, Crissy. I couldn't take the chance she would hurt any of us. Now go with your dad and Michael and work this all out."

Savich watched Dave Raditch herd his children behind the chip stand, out of sight of the devastation.

He looked at the dead woman, at the trail of blood seeping from beneath his leather jacket. Had she ever considered she might die at 8:27 on a Tuesday night?

He heard sirens.

He looked over at the kids' two ice-cream bars melting on the floor, and then at the big round clock behind Mr. Patil's counter. He watched the minute hand reach 8:28. Only a couple of minutes had passed, a couple of minutes that determined who would live and who would die.

CHAPTER 2

Cleveland, Ohio
Nielson's Bar & Grill
Tuesday night

He said his name was Thaddeus, and he was
sort of shy when he asked her if he could
buy her a Burning River Pale Ale. He really
liked it, he said, and it was brewed by Great
Lakes Brewing Co., so she would be help-
ing the local economy. While they sipped
their ale, they ate the really salty peanuts set
in bowls on the length of the bar. Alana Rafferty thought he was pretty cool with that
white face of his and longish black hair
topped with a black beret. She'd swear he
even used a black eyebrow pencil. His
clothes looked arty — black T-shirt and
baggy black jeans — and hung on him, since
he was so thin. Turned out he was also really
nice and funny, one-liners popping out of
his mouth. He was a nice change from her
younger brother, the jerk, who'd stolen two

16

hundred dollars from her wallet that morning when she'd visited her mother, then laughed at her when she accused him of it, because, the fact was, she always let him off the hook, just like her mother who always excused her loser father.

Thaddeus asked her questions about her job, and she opened up to him, even told him how she wanted to write a movie script for a new superhero she'd created. They drank two more Burning Rivers, and then he asked her if she'd like to drop in and see what was going on at Club Mephisto on Bradley Street, only two blocks over. Alana looked at his fine-boned face and long, thin fingers, those darkened eyebrows, the clever smile of his mouth. He seemed okay. She said yes, but she couldn't stay for long, she had to work tomorrow.

He helped her into her lightweight corduroy jacket, a gift from her mother on her birthday two weeks ago. She gave the bartender a big smile and a little half wave, and they walked out into the cool evening. It was clear, a half-moon overhead. She had a slight buzz going. Club Mephisto — it was a good place for dancing the calories off, but she really shouldn't go since it was a work night. She smiled at him and tried out his name. "Okay, Thaddeus, who stuck you with that name? Your mom or your dad?"

"My dad. He loved Thaddeus Klondike, you know, that old Wild West hero from Charles Haver's books?"

"Sorry, I've never heard of this Klondike or Haver. I remember eating Klondike bars. They're yummy. What else did Haver write?"

"I don't know. I've never read him."

"So here you are, stuck with Thaddeus and no context. No nickname? Like Thad or maybe Deus?" She was feeling more buzzed now than before, and that didn't make a whole lot of sense. Buzzed on three bottles of Burning River Pale Ale she'd nursed for more than two hours?

"Nope, it's always been Thaddeus." He stuck out his hand to wave down the taxi cruising by. "I kind of like it that way. With me, Alana, what you see is what you get."

The cabbie pulled to a stop and lowered the window a bit. "Sorry, buddy, I'm off duty for the night."

Thaddeus jumped forward and kicked his front tire. "Yeah, right, you morons are always off duty."

"Hey, dude!" The cabbie gave him the finger and peeled out.

Alana frowned at him. "Why'd you kick the tire?"

"Guy's a moron. I mean, look, you've got on high heels, and now we'll have to walk over to Club Mephisto."

"Nah, I think he's right. I'm feeling like going off duty myself, too. It's getting late. I think I should be getting on home now. Maybe we can go this weekend? You free?"

He lightly touched a long, thin white finger to her cheek. "I'll walk you home. You live close, right? That's what the bartender told me."

She nodded, smiling, and she stumbled. "Whoa, what's this? I only had three ales, and they weren't that strong."

"Maybe it was all those peanuts." He laughed, told her not to worry about it, pulled her closer, and walked her to her building on Hudson Avenue. He walked her up two flights of stairs, down a long, well-lit corridor. "Give me your key."

She knew you didn't give a guy your key, not a guy you'd just met, even though he was funny and really nice. It just wasn't smart. But wasn't he about her size? Didn't that make him safe enough? Alana was feeling really sick now, nausea churning in her stomach, sneaking up in her throat, and she swallowed, but it didn't help. She knew she was going to throw up, and she hated that. She tried to focus on getting inside and

19

popping two Alka-Seltzer tablets in a glass of water from her bathroom sink, watching them dissolve. She gave him her key.

When he helped her inside her apartment, she knew she wasn't going to make it to the Alka-Seltzer, she was going to throw up now. She pulled away from him, fell to her knees, and vomited on the highly polished oak floor of her small entry hall. She felt like her insides were churning backward, spewing out bile that would choke her. She huddled there, her knees drawn up to her chest.

He knelt down beside her, laid his palm on her forehead. His hand felt warm and soft. She whispered, "I'm sorry, Thaddeus, I'm feeling really sick."

He stroked her forehead. "That's all right, Alana. I'm the one who made you sick, and now it's time to end it."

"You made me sick? But how? Why?" She saw him twist a loop of wire in his hands, saw him reach down over her as she vomited again, beer and peanuts all over the front of him. She heard him curse as the wire went around her neck.

CHAPTER 3

Lucy Carlyle addressed the group of five agents seated with her around the CAU conference table. "Her name was Alana Rafferty, age thirty-one, divorced, no children. She was a graphic artist for Bloomfield Designs in Cleveland, Ohio. She was outgoing, loaded with talent, and just plain old nice, according to her coworkers and friends, and she met the wrong person at Nielson's Bar and Grill on West Blake Street Tuesday night. The bartender, who's also the owner, said she left with a guy all duded up in black, even a black beret, said he looked sort of gay, at about nine o'clock Tuesday night. Another couple saw the guy wave down a taxi, but the cabbie was off duty. Then the guy yelled out an insult, even kicked the tire. The couple said Alana

21

looked a bit tipsy, and when they walked away, the guy was holding her arm because she wasn't all that steady on her feet. They walked west, toward her apartment, two blocks farther on, at the corner of Hudson Avenue." She nodded a bit unwillingly at Agent Cooper McKnight, wanting to continue and not turn it over to him, but she said, "Coop."

Coop said, "Her body was found in her apartment at noon yesterday by the manager and a coworker from Bloomfield Designs. The Cleveland PD put a rush on the autopsy since the murder bore some similarities to four recent murders, two in San Francisco and two in Chicago. This was the first victim in Cleveland.

"The bartenders in all three cities describe the guy as looking arty, maybe gay, in his late twenties, early thirties, with longish black hair under a black beret, tall, thin to gaunt. Two of the bartenders said he looked like he'd dusted his face with white powder, and he had long white hands that he seemed to like to show off, you know, picking out individual pretzels or nuts from a bowl.

"The bartenders told police none of the women seemed to know him, but they all appeared to hit it off with him quickly. He always bought them beer or wine or whatever, and after about an hour or two, they all left with him.

"In each instance, the women were murdered in their apartments. Each had ketamine and Rohypnol in her bloodstream, probably due to spiked drinks. As you know, ketamine is an anesthetic and now a street drug known as Black Hole or Special K that's become popular at raves. Rohypnol is your classic roofie, the date-rape drug. Together, they're a potent cocktail. One Chicago detective said it looks like the guy uses a roll of common wire, impossible to trace, and he unrolls the length he wants and snips it off before strangling them."

Lucy said, "There's more information in the folders I handed out, photos of the crime scenes, copies of all the interviews, autopsy results, but those are the high points." She nodded to Savich.

Savich said to the group, "Mr. Maitland wants us to handle the case now that this guy's crossed state lines several times and is killing every few days.

"Look through the packets and familiarize yourselves with the cases in San Francisco and Chicago. All major police departments across the country have been alerted about this guy and are already on the lookout.

"Cleveland Police Chief Aaron Handler

has moved fast. He compared the sketch their own police artist made from the bartender's description to the other police sketches made in San Francisco and Chicago." He held up the sketch. "This is a composite sketch, based on the descriptions provided by the three bartenders. Chief Handler had the sketches posted prominently in every neighborhood bar in Cleveland, and they're running the sketch on local television channels. You can see the guy has a distinct look — dressed all in black, with his black beret and black jeans, boots, T-shirt, and leather jacket — and he's kept to his initial pattern — always a neighborhood bar, always choosing a young woman who's alone. He drugs her, and garrotes her in her own home or apartment, which means all of the women let him take them home."

Ruth Warnecki-Noble said, "Well, if they were all feeling ill from the drug he fed them, I guess it makes some sense they would accept some help. Plus, if they think the guy is gay, they probably wouldn't see him as a sexual threat."

Lacey Sherlock said, "I guess he drugs the women so they won't be able to fight him, either."

Lucy nodded. "The bartenders all said the

guy looks like a stereotypical artist type, white as a vampire with the white face powder, and bone thin, which means he does indeed need the drugs to make sure he can handle his victims. He looks harmless as a puppy, soft-spoken, real polite, attentive, a good listener. Another thing — Alana Rafferty didn't look dizzy or shaky on her feet when she left the bar, so he probably put the drug in her last —" Lucy looked down. "In her last Burning River Pale Ale."

There were a few more questions and comments, and then Savich brought things to a close. "Okay, Coop and Lucy are the leads on this case. Any of your specific input should go through them. I'd like each of you to think about this guy, about what makes him tick, and give all your ideas in writing to Lucy and Coop. Steve in Behavioral Analysis will get us a profile shortly.

"This police sketch and the local TV coverage might make the guy cut his losses and head out of Cleveland, or maybe he'll change his outfit and ditch the beret. We'll see.

"No matter what, this case is top priority. Whoever the guy is, we want to stop him before anyone else dies."

Lucy said, "This is really ugly, guys, and really sick. Dillon wonders if he'll realize he's a sitting duck and change his routine or his clothes — and that's my biggest worry. If he does change his routine and ditch the black, we'll lose any edge we have."

Sherlock said, "Whatever he decides to wear, I've got the weirdest feeling he's not afraid of the cops and he's not going to stop. He's arrogant."

Lucy nodded slowly. She agreed with Sherlock.

As Lucy and Coop walked back to their workstations, talking quietly, Sherlock said to Savich, "Why'd you put Lucy and Coop together? They don't care much for each other. You can tell that by their body language. Look at the distance between them."

"That's why I put them together," Savich said matter-of-factly. "They need to learn to get along. They're both excellent agents, and I wouldn't want to lose either of them. They've got to learn to respect each other, protect each other, or else one of them will have to go."

"I'd hate to lose either of them. I wonder why they don't get along well? They're the new guys in the unit; you'd think they'd have bonded simply because they're the rookies."

Savich said, "I asked Ruth what was going on between them, and she said she'd heard

Lucy call Coop a dickhead — quote/ unquote — because he dangles too many women on his string."

"Hmm, I hadn't heard that. Do you think it's true? You think he's some sort of idiot playboy?"

Savich shrugged, opened his office door, and ushered her in. "I've never seen anything in Coop's behavior that'd make me think so. He's got a good brain, he's committed, a good team player, and I can usually kick his butt at the gym." He grinned at her, flicked a finger over her cheek. "So, what's not to like?"

Sherlock laughed, hugged him a moment. She leaned back in his arms, studied his face. "It's only been two days since the shooting at Mr. Patil's Shop 'n Go. Are you all right, Dillon?"

"Mr. Patil will make a full recovery, Dave Raditch and his kids are dealing okay with the shock, and yes, I'm fine as well. Look, Sherlock, I'm handling things, okay?"

Mr. Hardnose. She looked at him for a long time, and finally she nodded slowly. "Yes. All right, then." She kissed him fast, then left his office to discuss with Ollie Hamish his bizarre case in Biloxi, Mississippi, where some shrimp fishermen seemed to be on a rampage, killing off their competition.

■ ■ ■

Lucy and Coop were studying the composite sketch of their murderer, tossing ideas back and forth, when Lucy's cell phone rang. It was a Dr. Antonio Pellotti at Washington Memorial Hospital. Her father had suffered a massive heart attack and wasn't expected to live.

CHAPTER 4

Washington Memorial Hospital
Thursday night

Lucy sat beside her father's bed in the CCU and counted each breath. Dr. Pellotti had told her when they wheeled him out of the cath lab, honest grief in his voice, since he'd known her father for years, "They managed to open up his left coronary artery and found a large part of his heart was beating very poorly. We're having to support his blood pressure with drugs. We're not sure how much longer he'll breathe on his own. We'll discuss options when and if a respirator is necessary." He'd taken her hands in his. "He may be in and out, Lucy, but I promise you he's in no distress. He's on morphine."

How did he know her father wasn't in distress? Lucy wondered now. Her father couldn't tell them anything one way or the other. And when someone wasn't conscious and was barely alive, where were they? Looking down at themselves lying there, helpless, wondering what was next? Praying they'd come back? Or were they asleep in the nether reaches of their mind, really unaware of anything at all?

Lucy stared at her father's face through the oxygen mask, all lean lines and seams and so much thick, dark hair, only streaks of white at his temples. She'd had dinner with him on Tuesday night, her vibrant, handsome father, laughing over a federal regulator who'd overdrawn his own personal account and was raising hell about it. But now he looked old, his flesh slack, as if his life itself was leaching out of his body.

But he wasn't old, he was only sixty-two, at the top of his banking game, he'd tell her, and it was true. But now he was still, as if his beloved face was a facade, as if he'd already left and was simply waiting for the door to close.

No, she couldn't — wouldn't — accept that. There was a chance he could come back; there was always a chance. If he was breathing, that meant his heart was pumping, and that meant — what?

It meant hope, at least to her.

"I told you to work out, Dad, or take a walk every evening; that would have done it." But he hadn't. He wasn't at all fat, but he spent most of his time either reading his favorite newspapers and mysteries or working on his endless deals and strategic loan plans for the bank. He always had something going on, something he was excited about. He'd always been involved and excited about his life, and that was a blessing.

Joshua Acker Carlyle was a very successful man and a loving father. Everyone she knew thought of him as smart and honest, a man to trust. He'd never dabbled in junk bonds or sub-prime mortgages or any of the other shenanigans so many banks had been involved with. His three banks were as solvent as most Canadian banks.

She caught herself already hearing his eulogy, delivered by his uncle, Alan Silverman, only ten years older than he was, a parental afterthought, he'd say, and laugh. He'd always banked his money with her dad and played golf with him most weekends. Uncle Alan and Aunt Jennifer, and their children, Court and Miranda, had been there all through the evening, but the doctors had asked them to leave. Only Lucy was allowed to stay with him. She'd turned off her cell phone because so many friends were calling and she simply couldn't deal with their sympathy and their endless questions.

31

"Can you hear me, Dad?" Lucy lightly squeezed his hand. The skin seemed slack, as if it were hanging off him. They said it was from the medicines, to help his lungs, but she hated it. He'd awakened earlier but hadn't said anything, simply looked at her through a veil of drugs and closed his eyes again. But maybe he could hear her. If he was hovering up there, looking down, of course he could hear her. Dr. Pellotti said he couldn't, but one of the nurses rolled her eyes behind the doctor's back and nodded.

And so Lucy talked. She told him about the case she was working on, the killer who targeted single women in neighborhood bars, and how he seemed to be coming this way, since he'd killed in San Francisco, Chicago, and now Cleveland. And why not Washington? There were so many single women here. She told him her partner on this case was Special Agent Cooper Mc-Knight, a man she didn't much like because he had the reputation of being a playboy. He always had a different woman on his arm, and he was too good-looking, and he knew it. She'd heard a couple of agents in the unit talking about all the women he dated, and they wondered, laughing in the way men did, about how he managed to keep them all straight. What did he think of her? She didn't have a clue. So far he was polite and attentive, maybe checking her out to put her in his line to take to bed. He'd said a couple of funny things, and wouldn't that make sense? Women tended to like guys who were funny. It fit with what she'd heard.

She talked and talked, and her father lay there, moving his legs now and then; sometimes, she'd swear, squeezing her hand. Once he'd mumbled words she couldn't understand before he lapsed again into that frozen silence. He was breathing, so she'd hang on to that. She told him about her boss's wild-hair adventure Tuesday night at his neighborhood convenience store, how he'd brought down two armed robbers with two children in the store. Dillon had said the kids were both champs, and their dad was a champ, too. "I wonder how I would have done if I'd seen that guy with a stocking on his face and a gun in his hand, while two kids were standing six feet away eating ice-cream bars."

She told her father all the rest of it before she paused for a moment, then rubbed her fingers over his knuckles, wishing he would squeeze her hand again, show her he knew she was here and recognized her. "I saw

Sherlock in Savich's office this morning, and she smacked him real hard on the arm, not that she could do much damage, he's hard as a brick outhouse, and then she kissed him. I know she must still be replaying what happened again and again in her mind. Can you imagine, Dad? Two innocent kids, and knowing all the way to your soul their lives were in the balance?

"Sherlock called the father and gave him the name of a shrink for the kids. I'll bet they're going to have nightmares for a while."

She smoothed her palm over her father's forehead, his cheeks. His skin felt clammy, and why was that? His leg jerked, then he was motionless again, and there was only the sound of his slow, difficult breathing. Lucy laid her cheek against his chest. "You're too young to leave me, Dad, please, you know it's always been just you and me, so you need to stay. You need to get better and tell Dr. Pellotti you're going to outlive him and his kids. Will you do that for me, Dad?"

She was crying silently when her father suddenly yelled, *"Mom, what did you do? Why did you stab Dad? Oh my God, he's not moving. There's so much blood. Why, Mom?"*

Lucy reared back, her mouth open to

shout for the nurses when she saw he was looking at her, recognized her. He squeezed her hand. "Lucy," he whispered, and then he closed his eyes and took in a hitching breath, and then he lay still.

She ran to the door to yell for the nurses, but she heard a nurse scream, "Code blue!" before she got there, and then the room filled up with men and women, and she stood by the lone window in the hospital room and watched them start to work frantically to save him, until she was ushered out.

Her father, Joshua Acker Carlyle, was pronounced dead by a young physician she'd never seen before, at 3:06 a.m.

Dawn was moments away when Lucy walked to the hospital parking lot. She realized she didn't feel much of anything. Her brain, her heart, felt empty. *But I'm really here,* she thought. *I've still got to put one foot in front of the other, walk to my car, get in, go home — and what?*

Lie in bed and plan Dad's memorial service — not a funeral, no, Dad told me often enough he never wanted to have his carcass stuffed in one of those high-shine coffins sitting on wheels in the front of a church with a big stupid photo of himself beside it that everyone had to look at. No, burn him up in private and spread a nice long trail of ashes into the Chesapeake, where he loved to sail, swim, and eat every crab he pulled out of it.

Lucy didn't cry until after she'd called her great-uncle, Alan Silverman, at seven o'clock a.m. and told him his nephew was dead.

Then the tears wouldn't stop. When she called Dillon at eight o'clock a.m., she sounded like a scratchy old record.

The worst of it was hearing her father's words again, sharp, clear, and panicked. *"Mom, what did you do? Why did you stab Dad? Oh my God, he's not moving. . . ."*

Special Agent Luciana Claudine Carlyle knew her father had witnessed his own mother murdering her husband, Milton, Lucy's grandfather, a man she'd been told had gone walkabout twenty-two years ago. Whenever she'd asked, that's what she'd been told — *Your grandfather left us, no word, no reason, just gone* — until she'd simply set him away in the back of her mind, and eventually stopped thinking much about him at all. As far as she knew, no one had ever heard from him again; he'd simply left one day and never come back.

Well, that was a lie. He hadn't just disappeared. Her grandmother had murdered him, stabbed him to death twenty-two years

36

ago, her own father a witness. That would have made her father forty years old when it happened, a grown man living with his parents, since his wife had died and he'd needed help with his small daughter, namely herself. Why hadn't he stopped it? Because he'd been too late to stop it, that's why. He'd never let on, never said a word to anyone, as far as she knew. Should she ask Uncle Alan? Would he know? She shook her head. She couldn't ask him that question, not without knowing more. Surely he didn't know, as she hadn't known.

Her father had seen his own father's murder again in the moments before he died.

Lucy couldn't get her mind around it, couldn't accept it. Her grandmother a murderer? Her grandmother, Helen Carlyle, had died peacefully in her bed at home three years ago. Both Lucy and her father were with her, and Lucy had kissed her good-bye on her forehead.

No, she couldn't believe it, not her grandmother.

Her grandmother was always fiercely contained, with something ramrod-straight about her. Lucy had sometimes wondered, though, in the deepest part of her, if there was a reason for that.

Lucy walked into her bathroom, sank to the floor, and leaned against the tub. She sat there for a very long time.

CHAPTER 5

Clayton Valley, Virginia
Blue Ridge Society auditorium
Sunday afternoon

Lucy couldn't seem to get warm. She was surrounded by her father's friends and business associates, by Uncle Alan and his family — her only remaining family. On Uncle Alan's face, she saw utter devastation. Beside him sat Aunt Jennifer, turned sixty-four the month before. Jennifer looked as stylish as she always did with her curve-brimmed black hat and Dior black suit. Lucy had always thought she was so like her sister-in-law, Lucy's grandmother — always self-possessed, always calm, always kind to Lucy. Her own children, Miranda and Court, who were both older than Lucy, sat stone-faced. Court was handsome and fit, a young aristocrat like his father, and Miranda looked like a bohemian wannabe, all dressed in drapey black, like a plump nun. Aunt Jennifer held Uncle Alan's hand tightly.

Out of the corner of her eye, Lucy saw the McGruders, her grandmother's long-time housekeeper and groundskeeper. They were both looking like devout missionaries, stout and somber, dressed in stiff, formal black, Mrs. McGruder's plain black hat pushing down her over-permed gray hair. Lucy nodded to them, tried to smile, but she was so cold she was afraid her teeth were going to start chattering, and that would be humiliating. Particularly since she had to walk about fifteen feet up to the small auditorium stage, look out over the hundred-plus people, and give her eulogy. *Eulogy,* she thought, *from the Greek* eulogia, *which meant to speak well of,* she remembered her father telling her before the memorial of one of his professors at Princeton.

At least there hadn't been a question about where to have his memorial service. Her father was an active member of the Blue Ridge Society for his entire adult life, a well-established group of like-minded people who wanted to preserve one of the nation's natural wonders.

Hold it together. She was surprised when Coop slid in beside her and closed his hand over hers. His flesh was wonderfully warm. He must have felt how cold she was, because he took both her hands in his and rubbed them until at last she got the signal from the minister. She rose and walked slowly to the lectern at the center of the stage. One of her father's bank managers and close friends had finished speaking. Mr. Lambert was a short man, which meant she had to raise the mike, and the simple act of twisting the mike upward made her brain blank out. She could see some of her friends, mostly lawyers she'd met through her roommates in college, and wasn't that strange? They were all here for her just as they'd all been at the hospital, and they'd called her constantly, as if they were on a schedule, until she'd asked them not to call so often, to give her some time on her own. She met the eyes of Mr. Bernard Claymore, the family's lawyer, for many years, not all that much younger than her grandmother. He was bent low, his old face weathered from spending so much of his life out-of-doors. Her father had said Bernie had all his wits and he was hard not to like even though he was a lawyer. That was good enough for Lucy, and so Mr. Claymore was dealing with her father's estate as well. She could see tears spilling out of his eyes and trailing down his seamed face from the lectern. It nearly broke her.

She was frozen to the spot, panic rising in her throat. She stood there, trying to center herself, and looked out again over the sea of faces, most familiar, some not. *So many people,* she thought, their lives intertwined with her father's, and how were each of them feeling about his sudden unexpected death? She saw shock and sadness and blankness and imagined all these expressions were on her own face as well. She met her Uncle Alan's dark eyes and remembered his telling her how he'd once fed her some strained peaches and she'd thrown up on him. And with that memory, Lucy realized she wasn't cold any longer. She said fully into the mike, "Thank you for coming to honor my father's life.

"My mother, Claudine, died when I was very young. I remember my father trying to explain to me that she wasn't coming home, and I remember he was crying but trying not to. I didn't understand and kept asking for her. Dad would always say my mom was in heaven and that God didn't want to let her go; she brought too much happiness and joy to those around her. And then he'd say, 'Do you know, Lucy, I bet your mom is making everyone in heaven laugh their heads off. If I were God, I wouldn't let her go, either.'

"I think God feels the same way about Dad. All of you know how he could make you laugh, even if you were in a big funk. He could throw out one-liners so fast it was hard sometimes to keep up with him. It was impossible not to wear a perpetual smile around my father, even when I was a teenager and my world was otherwise filled with angst.

"Another thing about my dad — I always knew he was in my corner. No one messed with me, ever, teenage boys in particular.

"When I told him I'd changed my mind and I didn't want to become a lawyer, that what I really wanted to do with my life was become part of the best cop shop in the world — the FBI — I'll never forget the look on his face. Surprise, and then tears filled his eyes. I asked him what was wrong, and he smiled at me and hugged me and said it must be fate. When I asked him what he meant, he told me my mother had applied to the FBI only a few weeks before her death. Then he laughed, said he would have to readjust his long-term plans since it didn't look like he would have a lawyer daughter to support him in his old age. In the FBI I'd do a whole lot more good than most lawyers ever do, but I wouldn't get paid much for it."

Lucy paused to let the burst of laughter wash over her. It was as if the entire audience sitting in front of her had drawn a collective breath, and let in some memories of their own.

"My dad loved his snifter of Hennessy Ellipse cognac every evening. He'd sit in his favorite chair, his head against the chair back, his eyes closed, and I'd know he was thinking about my mother. I know my mother and father are together now, and that all heaven laughs.

"My dad was the best of fathers. I will miss him forever."

When she relinquished the mike to her Uncle Alan and smelled his familiar bay-rum scent when he hugged her, she realized some of her deadening pain was gone. She felt warm again.

Alan Silverman didn't speak until Lucy was once again seated beside Coop. Alan smiled at her as he said in his deep, booming voice, "I am a lawyer, and Josh often told me the same thing."

And there was more laughter.

CHAPTER 6

"Please, Dillon, I can do my job. I want to work; I need to work."

Savich looked beyond Agent Lucy Carlyle's pale, composed face, beyond the misery sheening the air around her, to the fierce determination in her eyes. They were a darker blue than Sherlock's, the color of the Caribbean under a cloudy sky. She looked as neat and put-together as she always did, her chestnut hair, many different shades after the hot sun of summer, plaited neatly in a thick French braid, and her signature small silver hoops hanging from her ears. Her skin was so pale — was it whiter than usual? Grief, he knew, could leach the color out of you. She was wearing black boots and a white blouse and a black pants suit that looked to be a size too large for her. How much weight had she lost in five days?

He said, "What are you going to do with your dad's house, Lucy?"

Why did he care? "I'm going to sell it. I've decided to sell my condo, too." She drew a deep breath, spit it out. "I'm going to move into my grandmother's house."

This surprised him. Savich had heard about Helen Silverman Carlyle's huge mansion in Chevy Chase, Maryland, one of those fine old houses built at about the turn of the twentieth century, a barn of a place and a bear to heat, he imagined, in the Maryland winters. She'd been quite the philanthropist, a friend, in fact, of his own very famous grandmother, Sarah Elliott.

"Your grandmother died a while ago, didn't she?"

"Three years. My dad kept Mr. and Mrs. McGruder on to take care of the house and grounds after she died. They live in town, and checked in with my dad several times a month." She swallowed, looked down at her boots, frowned because she saw some mud on the toe, then looked up at him again.

"Why are you moving into her house, Lucy?"

Why does he want to know all this stuff? He can get the truth out of a stalk of asparagus, so keep it simple. "I don't know, it's just

46

something that feels right."

A black eyebrow shot up. "It feels right to you?"

Idiot. He can spot a lie even before it's out of your mouth. He was simply curious, but now you've got him focused on it.

She found a smile. "You're my boss, Dillon, but I know I can keep some things private; it's in my job description."

He smiled back at her. "Point taken. Are you going to need some help moving?"

She shook her head. "I'll take it slow and easy, move a bit at a time. Please, let me work while I'm doing it."

"Tell you what, why don't you work the Black Beret case with Coop in the mornings and take the afternoons off to get yourself moved. It's a big house, Lucy. Are you sure you want to rattle around in it alone?"

"I grew up in that house. I love it."

He frowned.

"What are you thinking, Dillon?"

"What? Oh, someone walked on my grave. I had this strange feeling someone else was outside Mr. Patil's Shop 'n Go when the cops started arriving, but that's impossible, the cops would have seen anyone out there.

"Now, Lucy, you promise me you'll holler loud if you need help? With anything?"

Savich watched her walk slowly from his office, after less resistance than he'd expected. It seemed she'd have agreed to anything just to get out of there. There was something going on with Lucy, and he'd bet some fresh grilled corn on the cob it was more than her grief for her father. No, this was something else, and it was connected, somehow, to her grandmother's house. Too bad his gut wasn't telling him any more than that. He'd have to keep a close eye on her.

Savich rose and walked to his one big window. It was a cool day, with lots of sun, and there were a good dozen people already eating an early lunch in the park across the street. He felt it again, someone walking on his grave, and he let his mind float back to that night, trying to focus on something or someone who didn't belong beyond that huge glass window at the Shop 'n Go just as the police arrived, but it was growing fainter in his mind.

CHAPTER 7

It was a glass half full, Lucy thought, but working a half day was better than nothing. She got out of Dillon's office as fast as she could. He always saw too much. She cleaned up some paperwork, humming to herself to keep focused, because her brain kept splintering off to her father, laughing or smiling, or to his face slack in death, and tears would clog her throat. An hour later, on her way out, Coop called her over. "I got a call from the Cleveland PD. A bartender notified the police department last night, said our guy came in the bar about nine o'clock, looked around, then left real fast when he saw the bartender looking hard at him. He said he ran outside and looked around for the guy, but he didn't see him. Then he called the police."

"So he's aware everyone's on the lookout for him."

Coop nodded.

"Same description?"

"He didn't even change his black socks."

"Do you think he will now?"

"He got a scare last night. I'm thinking he's gonna have to get out of Dodge, head to another big city, maybe Philadelphia or New York, and change his routine and color scheme.

"Hey, why don't I buy you some lunch — there's that new Moroccan restaurant over on Crowley. My friend at State says the couscous is pretty good."

She eyed him. He wasn't acting like a conceited jerk. In fact, she didn't ever recall his being anything but nice to her, and she realized she appreciated it. She didn't have to jump on his busy fishing line if he threw it her way. She started to say no, and then her stomach growled. When was the last time she'd eaten? She couldn't remember. Coop grinned. "Yep, it's that time. You got something heavier than that wimpy jacket? It's pretty chilly out there."

They stopped by Lucy's black Range Rover in the Hoover garage, and she shrugged into her leather jacket she kept in the backseat. She paused for a moment, eyeing the jacket. "I wonder if the cleaners can get blood out of leather?"

"What did you do?"

"Me? Nothing. I was thinking about Dillon's leather jacket, the one he put over the head of that woman robber at the Shop 'n Go."

"I don't think I'm going to ask him. How'd you come by that Range Rover?"

"My dad gave it to me when I graduated. He said an FBI agent couldn't have too much muscle, car included." Coop led her to his blue Corvette with its black-leather interior that smelled like a million bucks.

Lucy ran her fingers over the shining hood. "This is a very sexy car." *Not that I'm surprised; a cool car would be a must to maintain your rep.*

He lightly tapped his hand on the top of the car. "I had to put the top back on two weeks ago for the winter. In the summer, though, cruising around as a convertible, she's something else. The color is called jet stream blue."

"Not a girlie blue, yet not so dark it's nearly black. It's nice. The metallic finish gives it a kick. Jet stream blue? Neat name. Yep, very sexy, Coop." She couldn't help it, she smiled at him. Was she nuts?

"That's what my mother said. She presented her to me on my last birthday."

A laugh spurted out. *His mother gave him this car? What kind of line was this?* "Your baby is a her?" Well, why was she surprised?

"Her name is Gloria. The day after I got her, she was sitting here in my slot, singing out her name to me."

"And you're saying your mom gave Gloria to you?"

He nodded. "She said I was getting too staid, too set in my ways, and here I was thirty-one years old, and she wanted some grand-kids. When I told her she already had eight rugrats from my prolific siblings, and that I was only on the very first day of my thirty-first year, she said that wasn't the point. When I asked her what the point was, she smacked me, told me the point was I was to go cruising around D.C., looking hot, and getting myself some action. The salesman, she assured me, said the Corvette Grand Sport was just the ticket. She's got high hopes for Gloria."

Lucy eyed him. He sounded legitimate — self-deprecating, charming, really, not like the playboy of the Western world at all. She ran her hand over the hood. "Given Gloria's cost, your mom must *really* want a grandkid from you." Then she reached out and stroked his ego, to see what he'd do. "And, Coop, you already are hot. Everybody in the unit knows that."

He opened his mouth, stared at her, then

shook his head. "You've been listening to people you shouldn't, haven't you? There's nothing to it, just some of the guys pulling my chain. No, wait, it's Shirley, isn't it?"

"Come on, don't try to pretend you're some sort of hopeless nerd."

"I know it's Shirley. I heard her tell Ruth I had to add pages to my black book, it was so crammed. Then she was going on about Annette in the forensics lab and Glenis in personnel. They're friends of mine, that's all, just friends."

Lucy said, "Yeah, right, you're no philanderer, you've just got lots and lots of 'friends' who happen to be female."

"Shirley was looking over my shoulder when I was thumbing through my address book to find a sheriff's number in North Dakota. As for — well, both Annette and Glenis? They really are friends, nothing more."

Lucy laughed at him. It felt good, but it died quickly enough, and she swallowed and looked away. Her cell rang. It was one of her friends, Barb Dickens. Lucy knew if she answered it, she'd start crying at Barb's sweet concerned voice. She let it go to voice mail.

He said nothing more and helped her into the Corvette. Then, whistling, he walked around to the driver's side. He thought there was a bit of color in her thin face, at least until she felt guilt about laughing. Coop hoped she liked couscous.

CHAPTER 8

Chevy Chase, Maryland
The Carlyle Estate on Breckenridge Road
Tuesday

No time for another load; it would be dark in an hour. Lucy hefted the last cardboard box she'd brought over, this one filled with shoes and workout clothes, closed the door of her Range Rover with her hip, wondering idly if she should name him — or her? She didn't think so. *Gloria?* She was smiling as she walked up the elaborate flagstone pathway, lined with flowers that were fast closing down for the winter. Huge maples and oaks filled the front yard, and their colors were amazing, all oranges and reds and bright browns, happily tossing their leaves to the ground. Why hadn't Mr. McGruder cleaned up the leaves? She'd have to ask. Odd, she couldn't remember either of the McGruders' first names. They'd been a constant in her life until she'd left for college. Silent, for the most part — grim-looking, really, she'd always thought. Very proper, giving her a look whenever they believed she'd smart-mouthed her father or come in later than they'd thought proper from a date or made too much noise when her friends were over.

Lucy paused for a moment before climbing the six wide wooden steps up to the huge wraparound porch that encircled the entire house. Pots of flowers were scattered haphazardly along it, the plants beginning to lose hope now that winter was close. Hanging pots of ferns and ivy streamed down from the overhead porch beams. All this work to maintain a house that no one lives in? "Yes," her father had said, and laughed. "You never know." He'd been right.

Lucy loved that you could sit out on a spring day and watch the rain come down on all the beautiful flowers surrounding the house. It was only mid-October, still time for some more warm days, she hoped.

She realized she'd missed this house, missed the feel of it, the warmth of its memories, even though it was at least ten thousand square feet and the heating bills to keep it warm had to approach the national budget of some small countries. She'd lived here since her mom had died because, her dad told her, he'd needed help to raise her, and who better to help than her grandparents?

She'd lived here until she'd left for college at eighteen, and that was when her father had bought his own house and left as well.

She was twenty-seven years old, and here she was, moving back to the home of her childhood.

The main rooms were huge, with beautiful crown moldings and coffered ceilings, filled with Low Country antiques. The large Persian carpets sported lustrous blues and reds and yellows despite their age, or maybe because of their age. Everything felt settled and old and comforting.

All except the kitchen. It was brand-new, remodeled six years before by her grandmother, and so modern it was a shock walking into the room. There was a large island in the center, a breakfast section that could seat eight people, and enough sparkling high-tech appliances for a French restaurant. The walls and cabinets were painted a soft light yellow, the floors umber Italian tiles, and the tall ceiling was barreled, the beams a light ash.

Mrs. McGruder had stocked the pantry and refrigerator for her with lots of cold cuts and cheeses, a couple of casseroles, flavored water, vegetables — actually, anything she could wish for. She'd need to tell Mrs. McGruder she would see to things now, maybe ask if she could come to clean every couple of weeks.

She pulled out some ham, a slice of Swiss, and homemade rye bread, and ate standing at the island. After she washed up, she went upstairs. Her old bedroom simply hadn't felt right, and so she decided to take over her grandmother's huge suite. Along with updating the kitchen, her grandmother had redone her bathroom. It was an incredible space now, done in greens and cream, the tiles on the sink and floor green and yellow with splashes of pale blue, with matching towels and rugs. The Jacuzzi was nearly as large as her bed at the condo.

She sat in that humongous Jacuzzi, its jets going full blast, for a good long time. Afterward, she put on her pajamas, shrugged into a tatty chenille robe, and brought out the box with her workout clothes and shoes.

There were so many things to do that would take great gobs of time — clothing to unpack and arrange, books to go through, laundry — so much laundry to do — so many decisions to make. She held a pair of gym socks in her hand, simply stared down at them, not knowing where to put them, and began to cry. She was crying not only for her father but at the ending of a whole part of her life. There was no turning back, no changing what had happened. Life happened and would continue to happen. What would the rest of her life be like?

She didn't know, but she knew there had to be something in this house to give her a clue as to what had happened here. She would find out why her grandmother had murdered her husband. *And you saw it, Dad.*

She couldn't imagine it.

CHAPTER 9

Philadelphia
Chilly's Bar
Tuesday night

Ruley had served three tours of duty and been wounded twice in the Vietnam War, and come home to find that his four siblings and many of his friends despised him for fighting in an immoral war. A few days after his plane landed in Philadelphia, he bought a six-pack of Bud and a lottery ticket, the only one he'd ever bought in his life. He won a bucket load of money. His family and friends tried to do a one-eighty when they found out about it, but he decided he wanted new friends and he'd make his own family. He hung up on all the scammers who wanted to take good care of his winnings for him and bought lots of long-term bonds and a bar he named Chilly's, after a buddy of his who'd stepped on a mine in the war. He married and fathered four kids, all married with kids of their own now. He was set.

Chilly's Bar was a popular hangout with the young professional crowd in a neighborhood once filled with industrial buildings turned into lofts, artists of every medium imaginable, and run-down bistros. It had been gentrifying for more than fifteen years now, and the lofts were giving way to high-end apartments for account executives, and more coffeehouses than Seattle.

Chilly's had changed right along with the neighborhood. It was low-key now, a place to stop after a long day at the office. Ruley liked the pleasant hum of conversation, the good manners. He hadn't had to break up a fight in Chilly's for a good ten years now. He was looking complacently over the Tuesday-night crowd, most of them white wine drinkers. The wine from his top-end wine list made him lots of money, much more than he'd made years before when he'd had to push light beer. Chilly's, he thought complacently, no longer smelled like stale cigarette smoke, bless the lawmakers.

A young woman he'd never seen before came in alone. She was tall, pretty, and well dressed, and when she bellied up to the bar, she smiled at him. It was a beautiful smile, but it didn't reach her pretty brown eyes. There was some kind of trouble, he thought, behind those eyes of hers. She looked over his specialty Tuesday-night wine list and ordered a Peridot Vineyard chardonnay that cost twelve dollars a glass. Ruley asked her if she was new to the neighborhood. She'd been visiting the police station a block over, she told him, closed her eyes, and took a huge gulp of the very fine chardonnay. Not a happy camper, Ruley thought. He told her his name was Ruley and shook her hand when she said her name was Liz.

As the night wore on, Chilly's regulars sauntered in for their pre-bedtime drink. Ruley knew all their faces and most of their names. Lately he often heard them sharing horror stories about losing their credit lines or other business catastrophes, and he shook his head about it. Things never changed. Only the young sharks still talked urgently about their plans for expansion and higher market share. That never changed, either.

When he was finally ready to take a break at the bar, he asked Cindy, his second daughter, to take over. "Keep an eye on Liz," he told her. "She's in a funk." When he was walking toward his backroom office, he noticed a young man he'd never seen before come into the bar. He looked for the world like a throwback to the old neighborhood with his black beret, his black clothes on a rail-thin body, and his slouchy walk. Didn't this guy realize he was out of his time, that his effete look had been gone at this bar for more than ten years now? Ruley shook his head and walked into his office. Taxes, he thought. He was always paying some hand that was sticking in his face — city, state, feds, they all had lots of big hands.

Cindy was serving Liz her second glass of Peridot chardonnay when the guy next to her asked if he could buy it for her.

Liz Rogers looked the guy up and down and liked what she saw — namely, that she was bigger than he was and could beat him up if the need arose, which it probably wouldn't. She liked his thin white face, his dark eyes, and the beret that covered long black hair. It was a big plus that his hair didn't look greasy. Good hygiene in a guy was always a plus.

Cindy kept half an eye on the two, as she did everyone who sat at the bar. The young guy bought the woman a refill of the same fine chardonnay that made her dad's cash register cha-ching with pleasure. They chatted, Cindy saw, and looked rather cozy after about an hour.

Because this was a professional neighborhood, even the young people began to straggle out at about ten o'clock, some with a bit too much of Ruley's fine wine in their bloodstreams. A wine hangover isn't any big deal, Ruley always said, and besides, they were young, they could drink themselves stupid nightly for ten years and still get up with a smile the next morning and go to work. Hit forty and it's a different story. They'd learn.

Ruley was coming around the end of the bar when he saw the young man walking close beside Liz of the beautiful smile as she swayed out the front door.

She'd drunk only three glasses of wine; she shouldn't be weaving around like that. He frowned. Maybe she couldn't hold her drink, but still, something wasn't right. What was it?

Liz Rogers was happy, and that was good, even though she knew well enough life would be grim tomorrow morning when she had to face reality again, and that reality was her mother. She'd had to bail her mother out of jail yet again, this time for shoplifting at Marnie's, an upscale clothing boutique, and so she'd decided to stop at Chilly's Bar, only a block over from her mother's condo. Their wine was expensive, but then Todd — with two *d*'s — had come in and lightened her load and listened to all her woes, and paid for a glass of the swank white wine.

She had really dumped on him, bless him, and he'd told her he'd walk her home. She'd meant to tell him she didn't live in this neighborhood, that her mom did, but she forgot. When they stepped outside Chilly's, she took a breath of the cold night air and realized she had to cut this nice man loose and get a taxi.

She smiled up at Todd and pulled out her cell phone. "I've got to call a taxi."

"Why? You live right here in the neighborhood. I'd love to walk you home, Lizzie."

"Nope, this isn't my neighborhood; it's my mom who lives here."

There was a slight pause, then he said, "Then I'll take the taxi with you and walk you up."

"Nah, that's too much trouble; don't bother." No sooner had she spoken than she felt a wave of dizziness and a sudden sick feeling twist in her stomach. *Great,* this was all she needed after dealing with her mother and the cops and a low-life bail bondsman named Lucky Tasker.

"Are you okay, Liz?"

"Something hit me — I felt like I was going to fall over. Sorry, Todd, it's been a long day."

She dialed for a taxi. Ten minutes, she was told, and smiled up at Todd. "I think I'll go back into Chilly's and stay warm, wait there."

"Let's stay out here. I'll keep you warm."

She felt nausea roil in her stomach, threaten to come up into her throat. "I'm going to be sick, Todd. I've gotta get to the bathroom."

But he had his hand on her arm, pulling her back. The streetlight was ten feet away, and shadows were hanging long and deep, and as black as the lacy underwear she'd just bought on sale.

Why was she thinking about her underwear? She felt another wave of nausea and jerked as hard as she could, but he didn't let her go.

"Look, Todd —" Her words were loud and slurred. Clear as a bell, she heard her mother's dead-drunk voice slurring insults at her — mean, vicious insults — and it scared her so badly it gave her focus, sharpened her brain, and she saw everything very clearly. She said slowly, on eye level with him, "You son of a bitch, you drugged me." She slammed her fist into his face. He didn't have time to duck the blow, but it didn't have much punch because she was weaving around like a drunk, wanting to puke but too scared, too furious with this jerk, to get sick yet. Todd grabbed her hand and pulled her arm down to her side. "No, Lizzie, it'll be all right, you'll see. I wouldn't drug anybody. Let's walk, okay? You'll feel better, you'll see."

Not on your miserable life. She pulled her arm free and dug her nails in his cheek as he tried to jerk his head out of the way.

He yelled, stumbled back, and clapped his hand to his bleeding face. He screamed an obscenity at her and came toward her. What was he doing? She saw him pull a length of wire out of his jacket pocket. *Wire?* Liz threw back her head and screamed until she vomited. Then she swiped the vomit from her mouth and kept screaming. She felt like she was dying, her stomach twisting in on itself, and her head was spinning, but thank God, Todd was running away now, holding his hand to his face. She sank to her knees and saw the bartender from Chilly's running toward her and shouting, "Hey, what's going on? Liz, you all right? I knew it; I knew that guy wasn't right. I called the cops; they're on their way."

Liz didn't answer him. She fell onto her side, unconscious.

CHAPTER 10

Philadelphia
Sacred Heart Hospital
Wednesday

"Ms. Rogers, I'm Agent Lucy Carlyle and this is Agent Cooper McKnight, FBI. First I'd like to say you're a very smart woman."

Smart? Liz didn't feel smart, she felt like she'd had a boulder dropped on her. Her stomach felt like the lining was burned through, but hey, she was alive, and she'd hurt that creep who'd drugged her, sent him running, so maybe that was smart. She found herself smiling up at the woman with her gorgeous hair in a thick French braid. So many shades, what was the color? Chestnut, that was it.

"We'd like to hear exactly what happened, if you feel up to it."

"I already spoke to a police officer this morning."

They heard a man clear his throat in the

doorway. Coop looked over to see a guy about his own age, his dirty blond hair standing straight up, his light blue eyes bloodshot, but he looked near to snarling. Coop raised an eyebrow.

"I'm Dr. Medelin. I wasn't told Ms. Rogers had visitors. The police have already questioned her, so I don't see any reason for you to hassle her more, it's too soon, and she needs to rest."

Coop flipped out his creds. "We're FBI, not local police. We, ah, don't hassle people, and we only shoot them when we have to."

Lucy grinned, but Dr. Medelin didn't. "FBI? For a mugging? Come on now, give her a while, she needs rest after what she's been through."

Liz was appalled when her voice came out as a skinny little whisper. "Dr. Medelin, it's okay. I'm fine. I want to tell them what happened. Hey, they're federal, it must mean I'm really important."

Dr. Medelin paid no attention to either Lucy or Coop, simply walked to Ms. Rogers and examined her eyes, then laid two long thin fingers over her pulse, listened to her heart. "If you're sure, Ms. Rogers?"

"Oh, yes, I want this jerk nailed, and these guys look like they're the ones to do it."

Dr. Medelin left, saying over his shoulder

they could have five minutes, no longer. Lucy smiled. In her experience, doctors were more territorial than monkeys.

Liz looked up at Lucy. "I'm not all that smart. You want the truth? It was my mom's voice that saved me."

Lucy cocked her head to one side. "Tell us," she said.

". . . I was so appalled that I was slurring my words like my mother when she's drunk, which is usually every day, it snapped me back into my brain for a minute and I realized he'd drugged me. I went after him, got him good that second time and drew blood. I couldn't believe he came at me with some kind of wire. I screamed my head off." She gave them a big grin, then swallowed. "I was throwing up, and screaming. The bartender, Ruley, came running. Then I passed out."

Coop leaned over. "That was very well done of you. Not only did you save yourself, you're going to help us nail this guy when we catch him. You've given us DNA from the skin you scored off his face with your fingernails. You're a heroine, Ms. Rogers, a big whopping superstar."

Liz studied their faces. "Why? This wasn't a stupid mugging? Hey, you're FBI, and that means something really heavy is happening here. What?"

Coop said, "The man, Todd, who bought you the drinks and wanted to walk you home, has murdered five women that we know of to date. Have you heard the news stories?"

Liz swallowed, nodded. "But — that was him? Oh, my."

"But you saved yourself," Coop said, and patted her hand when it looked like her eyes were going to roll back in her head. "You're going to be okay."

After another fifteen minutes of running her through what had happened again, asking questions every way they could phrase them, asking them again, and waving away Dr. Medelin when he came back to the room and frowned at them, they knew her bucket was empty. Lucy said, "We understand you gave an excellent description of this guy to a police artist. We'll get back to you on that.

"You did really good, Liz. With the lovely DNA you got for us, we're closer to bringing this monster down."

"Weird thing is, like I told you, it was my mom who really saved my bacon. She's so messed up, and now — what's a daughter to do?"

"Keep bailing her out, I guess," Lucy said,

and smiled down at her.

"Nah," Coop said. "You owe her something better. It's time for some tough love. Send her to rehab, tell her it's that or jail time."

They left Liz Rogers humming in thought. They passed Dr. Medelin coming out of a patient's room on a dead run. A nurse, Nancy Conklin according to her name tag, said, "Poor Mark, the E.R. called a code. He's been on call for twenty-six hours now."

"I didn't know doctors still had such grueling schedules," Lucy said.

"He's a first-year resident," and Lucy supposed, that said it all.

"He looks sleep deprived," Coop said.

Nurse Conklin said, nodding, "Imagine how many patients suffer from that fact. Liz Rogers now, Mark's been hovering over her even though he knows now she's going to be okay. I think he's interested in her, not that he's got a second to spare away from this place. Sometimes life's a bummer."

Coop thought of Medelin's exhausted face and didn't hold out much hope for him.

CHAPTER 11

Hoover Building
Thursday afternoon

Savich handed a folder to each agent seated around the CAU conference, and walked back to the head of the table. He looked at each of them in turn, pausing at Lucy and Coop. "I have to say that what you have in front of you is about as unexpected as discovering that smoking cigarettes led to the extinction of the dinosaurs. As you know, Liz Rogers scraped her nails down our Black Beret's face. We've been waiting for the forensic genetics people to finish their DNA testing. They've turned around with the fastest prep and analysis time I've seen for DNA typing, and we've run the results against our national database." He paused for effect, and every agent at that table sat forward.

"The closest match is Ted Bundy's DNA."

Savich saw disbelief, astonishment, shaking heads, and heard snorts, gasps, and comments like "That's just plain crazy" and "You're making that up, Savich, to make sure we're on our toes."

Savich raised his hands, palms flat. "This isn't a joke. Incredible as it seems, Ted Bundy's DNA is the closest match."

Coop said, "*The* Ted Bundy? You're not putting us on?"

Savich smiled. "Yes, it's *the* Ted Bundy."

Coop sat forward in his chair. "But he's dead, Savich, electrocuted. Late eighties, wasn't it?"

Ruth said, "Yeah, he was electrocuted in Florida in 1989 for his last murder. He had more than ten years of appeals before they pulled the plug on him."

Jack Crowne, who studied serial killers, said, "He eventually confessed to more than thirty murders, but no one believes the number was that low. He was forty-two when he was electrocuted. They have his DNA profile?"

Savich said, "They typed him and entered him in the database, in case we found any more of his crime scenes after he died."

"So how can it be his DNA?" Dane Carver said, and smacked his forehead. "Well, hot diggity, it's an illegitimate son, right, Savich? Carrying on his daddy's fine work?"

"Nope."

Jack said, "But — no, you're kidding us, right?"

Lucy was staring at him, nearly *en pointe.*

Savich smiled at them. "It's no son. She's a woman. The statistical analysis they gave us shows she's almost certainly a first-degree relative, a mother or a sister or daughter. Given our perp's age, she's almost certainly his daughter."

Sherlock said, "Just a bit of background. Bundy had a girlfriend he met while enrolled at the University of Washington in 1967. She dumped him after she graduated, said he was too immature for her, and went home to California. Bundy looked her up in 1973, and showed her the new, improved package — law school, good attitude, the serious dedicated professional. He courted her, proposed marriage, but then two weeks later, shortly after New Year's 1974, he dumped her. No one knows why, but a couple of weeks later, he started his murder spree in Washington State.

"Obviously, something significant went down, but no one knows what it was. Regardless, it was the trigger.

"At that same time he was also dating a secretary. That lasted six years. There were other women as well, though we don't have many names. As you know, Bundy was quite good-looking and he could charm a lizard off a sunny rock. So it makes sense he would have had relationships with women. And one of these women birthed a daughter he never acknowledged. Or maybe she never told him she was pregnant. Again, we don't know."

Dane said slowly, "But maybe her mom told our killer who her monster of a daddy was, and the daughter realized Bundy's madness was flowing in her veins. Blood calling to blood, I guess you could say."

Lucy said, "Sherlock, when did Bundy go to jail for the last time?"

Sherlock shuffled through her notes. "He was apprehended February fifteenth, 1978, and remained in prison until his execution in 1989."

Lucy said, "Okay, that would make our Black Beret a minimum of thirty-three years old. Everybody thought he looked early thirties or late twenties, so this is in the ball-park."

Coop had a dark eyebrow up a good inch. "This is weird. Here I was, eating my sesame-seed bagel this morning, never thinking that during the course of this fine day I'd be dealing with Ted Bundy's daughter. I wonder why she is masquerading as a man?"

"Good question," Ruth said. "Maybe she'd rather be her father's son? More importance?"

Coop said, "Maybe being a guy makes her more like her father?"

Lucy leaned forward, leaned her chin on her folded hands. "I sure hope we'll have the opportunity to ask her when we get her."

Savich said, "Okay. Now, those of you who are familiar with Bundy know he had another daughter, this one born in the eighties during conjugal visits with his wife — yeah, the court let him marry — a former coworker. However, we've excluded her as being our Black Beret, because she has a very different body type and she is currently residing in Florence, Italy, and hasn't been back to the States in five years. So it's a daughter we know absolutely nothing about."

Ruth thought of her new husband and laughed. "I can't wait to tell Dix. He probably knows more than you do, Jack, since he was into Bundy's case big-time. He's going to freak. I bet he's going to call you, Dillon, beg to be in on the case."

Savich knew Dix Noble, sheriff of Maestro, Virginia, very well. "Dix is a smart man, Ruth. Maybe it'd be good to have his brain at work on this. I'll give him a call."

Sherlock said, "As I said, we don't know who her mom was or is. We don't know anything else about her."

"We do know she started killing in San Francisco eight months ago, and so I put MAX to work using Liz Rogers's description of him to the police artist. I got a call this morning from Police Chief Edmund Kreymer. He's plastering the sketch all over Philadelphia. He also sent the sketch to San Francisco and Chicago, and every other large-city cop shop in the country. This sketch is in your packet, along with the sketch the police artist in Cleveland put together.

"You'll see a lot of similarities, but Liz Rogers's description is the best, since she was up close and personal with Bundy's daughter for a good long while. I think she really nailed him, well, her. If you compare the Philadelphia police sketch with photos of Ted Bundy, you'll see there's more than a slight resemblance.

"Now, we could get lucky and identify her from the sketch. MAX is scanning all the photos we can access from records in San Francisco. If she was raised in the Bay Area, maybe he'll find her in a high-school yearbook or a juvie record.

"Shirley put together some of the info we have about Bundy in your folders with links to a good deal more, as well as the profilers' rundown on Bundy's daughter. Get back to me with anything you think would be helpful.

"There's no way Bundy's daughter can remain in Philadelphia unless she does a thorough makeover. And she's got a scratch on her face to hide. Liz Rogers thought she scratched her good, but she was nearly unconscious at the time."

Jack asked, "You really think she'll get back into skirts?"

Lucy said, "Why not? She's a killer, and that's what she does, so how is she going to do it without being caught and executed like Daddy was? I'm thinking maybe she'll go female but keep the arty look."

Coop was tapping his pen on the conference table. "It seems to me if she's following in her daddy's bloody ways, she must have killed before age thirty-three."

Savich said, "I know the profilers think she may have started late because her mother didn't tell her the identity of her father until she was older. Let's hope so, but we don't know that."

Ollie said, "She could have killed and

buried the bodies deep. But then, why is she coming out into the open now? Was there a specific trigger, like it appears there was with Bundy? Was she leading a fairly normal life until a few months ago?"

Everyone chewed this over.

Jack said, "I wonder if she visits her victims' graves, like Bundy did?"

"That's not all Bundy did to his dead victims," Lucy said, and shuddered.

Savich said, "Good points. Now, MAX is working on photos. We'll meet back here in a couple of hours."

Ten minutes later, Savich's cell blasted out George Thorogood's "Bad to the Bone."

"Ben Raven here, Savich. Remember your hairy shoot-out at Shop 'n Go last week? I've got some news for you."

"You put nail screws to the guy in the hospital, Ben, made him talk?"

"Nope, not yet. When you shot him in the shoulder, the bullet did more damage than expected. He's still in pretty bad shape. His name is Thomas Wenkel, and the Chevy Impala is registered to him, not to the woman, an Elsa Heinz.

"I called you because last night someone shot your Mr. Patil at the Shop 'n Go during what looks like another robbery. No witnesses, not a soul around, no one even heard the shot. Evidently he'd just turned off the lights and was locking the back door when someone simply walked up to him and shot him in the back. His wallet was missing, and the bank-deposit money bag was gone. A beat cop in Georgetown had been doing drive-bys past Shop 'n Go after the robbery attempt last week. The officer saw the store was closed, but he saw Mr. Patil's car was still there, and investigated.

"Mr. Patil is seventy-five years old, Savich, weighs maybe one hundred thirty pounds on a fat day. It's hard to believe, but he survived three hours of surgery. It's still no sure thing he'll survive, and the doctors don't want to commit. His condition's listed as critical."

Savich said, "And you're wondering why a robber would shoot an old man in the back when all he'd have to do is maybe tap his jaw with his fist and take the bank-deposit bag."

"Makes me wonder."

"I'm trying to remember Thomas Wenkel's exact behavior when he had the gun aimed at Mr. Patil that Tuesday night. Was he there to kill him, and just faked robbing the store? Hard to say. Of course, there was the woman — Elsa Heinz — waiting in the car. She sure came in fast, ready to kill everyone in sight. What do you have on her, Ben?"

"Elsa isn't what you'd call a nice person. She'd been in and out of jail all of her adult life — robbery, hijacking, all sorts of scams. I haven't found out how she and Wenkel got together."

"Okay, I'll think about it, Ben. Do you mind if I speak to Mr. Patil when he's cogent? Speak to his kids and his wife?"

"He might not make it, Savich, but if he does, have at it. I can use all the help I can get on this."

"I have this feeling Mr. Patil will pull through. I'll keep in touch, Ben."

"We can compare notes later."

"You've got a guard on Mr. Patil?"

"Yes, I got it approved for a couple of days, at least. Officer Horne's a young guy but smart, I've been told. He'll keep the old man safe."

Savich hoped very much that Mr. Patil, a nice man with photos of all his grand-children and great-grandchildren stuffing his wallet, would be ringing up beer sales again sometime soon.

What were the chances of another random robbery in that neighborhood if the first shooting really was a robbery? And only one week later? Savich thought about co-incidence. And he thought about death, always hovering close, and whoever knew when it would tap you on the shoulder?

It wasn't a second robbery; he knew it.

CHAPTER 12

Chevy Chase, Maryland
Thursday evening

Lucy fit her grandmother's beautifully carved key into the front door. It was a dark, cold night, winter making an early call, nearly midnight. She was tired and sad, and every couple of seconds she thought of her father and wanted to weep. At least she'd managed to get back to all her friends during the day, telling them she needed more time to herself, and moving herself into her grandmother's house was good for her. Did they believe her? She hoped so.

She, Coop, Jack, Dane, and Ruth had visited The Swarm, a bar not too far from the Hoover Building that catered to federal cops, and they'd talked about Bundy and speculated endlessly about his daughter — who she was, who her mother was, what it was about her terrifying father that could help with the case. So far, she hadn't tortured any of her victims, and there were other huge departures from Bundy Senior. The most important question was: *Had she killed when she was younger?* Dane had called Inspector Vincent Delion of the San Francisco PD, a homicide detective he knew personally, to see if they had any unsolveds, going back, say, fifteen years, that could possibly be her work.

Savich had told Lucy not to come in again until Friday afternoon. He said he wanted her to finish her moving, but what he really wanted was to give her more time on her own. All right, then, she could sleep in, and that meant she didn't need to go to bed yet. She wanted to keep going through every scrap of paper in her grandmother's study. Twenty-two years before, she wondered, had it been her grandfather's study? She couldn't remember.

At times she was tempted to convince herself that she'd misinterpreted what her father had said when he was dying, that it was a hallucination or a nightmare of some kind, and not a son witnessing his own father's murder, by his own mother, but she'd known instantly it was the truth. Had he kept it a secret until the last moments of his life, when that long-ago horror had blasted into his mind? Would he ever have told her? She didn't think so, despite the fact she was a cop, and maybe that was why — she was a cop. If he had told her, she would have had to decide whether to act on it, come what may. No, if he'd had final control of his mind, he'd have gone to his grave protecting his mother. And maybe himself? Had he agreed to keep quiet because he believed his mother was somehow justified in killing his father? Had her grandfather done something despicable? And did anyone else know? Her Uncle Alan, perhaps.

Lucy brewed herself some strong tea, swallowed two aspirin, a good way to prevent a hangover for her, and walked to the study, a large, high-ceilinged room with floor-to-ceiling bookshelves covering three walls. The fourth wall was a huge sliding door that opened onto a small enclosed garden where her grandmother had placed a small round table with a bright red umbrella, and a single cushioned chair. Lucy remembered she'd spent a good deal of time sitting beneath that red umbrella on nice days, simply sitting there alone, reading there sometimes, enjoying the beautiful flowers. It seemed very strange, somehow not right, that all of this was to be hers now, as her father's only heir.

She looked at the large desk. Three unexplored drawers to go, then she'd check again for any secret drawers or hidden spaces. The next drawers were filled with papers in neatly tabbed folders, just like the other drawers, but these tab names were very different from the banks, utilities, charities, and the like that had filled the others. No, these folder tabs read H. G. Wells, Tetra Time — whatever that was — and names of people she'd never heard of who turned out to be psychics, mystics, and science-fiction writers.

Lucy thumbed through the Tetra Time folder. It seemed her grandmother had culled a huge number of publications and books, from the conventional to the wild fringe, and thrown them all into these files. It was a surprise. Her grandmother had never spoken to her about an interest in such strange things. It didn't seem like her, not her self-contained, serene grandmother. *Were you a secret Trekkie, Grandmother?*

Get a move on, time's a-wasting. She couldn't find anything that gave a clue about why her grandmother had murdered her husband.

Lucy pulled open the last big drawer. On top was a thick folder, untabbed, filled with articles about ancient types of magic that supposedly affected the passage of time itself. *Magic? Time?* Where had her grandmother found these things? She leafed through folders about people bending spoons, about speaking to a loved one on the other side, interviews with people who'd seen the famous white light before returning from the brink. She quickly looked through more folders about extraterrestrials, alien abductions, experiences with ghosts, hair-raising tales of all kinds. She wondered if her grandmother was losing it at the end. She thought of her father and wondered if he'd seen the white light before he'd died. Lucy shook herself. She remembered the old movie *Ghost* with Patrick Swayze and felt gooseflesh rise on her arms. She remembered now that her grandmother had spoken to her once about psychic sorts of things. She had asked Lucy if she ever felt the slightest hint of anything unusual. "Like what?" Lucy had asked. And her grandmother had said, "Maybe seeing unusual sorts of things about the future?" Did she ever know what people were thinking before they said it? Lucy had thought it nothing more than a game, and after she'd said no, there'd been no more unusual conversations with her grandmother, so she'd forgotten about it.

She finished looking through the last

drawer, then searched behind each of them and under the desktop. Finally she sat back in the big desk chair. She'd found exactly nothing useful, only proof of her grandmother's obsession with nearly every insane theory under the sun, and she still had absolutely no clue what had happened between her grandmother and her grandfather.

No matter. This was a very big house, with lots of hiding places, and that was enough to give her a headache, and hope. She was decided on doing this, and doing it alone. She couldn't imagine telling any of her friends about this, or anyone else. She shuddered at the thought. If she found nothing, perhaps she could put it to rest. She yawned and looked at her watch, couldn't believe it was two a.m. Time to pack it in.

Tomorrow she'd start going through the books. She looked up at all of them and knew she'd need a break from this room. On Saturday, she'd start elsewhere.

CHAPTER 13

Washington Memorial Hospital
Friday morning
Savich left Sherlock with Coop, poring over possible matches to the sketch of Bundy's daughter that MAX had found in the San Francisco public records. He called Washington Memorial Hospital as he stepped from the elevator into the Hoover garage, and learned Mr. Patil's condition was no longer listed as critical. The nurse he talked to called it a minor miracle, given his age and the severity of the wound, and called him a tough old buzzard, something Savich was hoping to be called himself when he got to be Mr. Patil's age.

When Savich walked into the ICU on the third floor, he checked in with Nurse Alison Frye.

She said, "Here I am thirty years younger and twenty pounds heavier than Mr. Patil, and I have serious doubts I would have survived that bullet. I look at him breathing on his own, and I tell you, Agent Savich, I'm amazed. If he continues as he is now, he'll beat this." She laughed. "I wish we had more tough old buzzards like him."

She continued as she signed an order, "It's unusual to have a guard sitting right outside his door. No one understands why. I mean, wasn't it a robbery?"

Savich smiled at her. "Covering all the bases, Nurse Frye," he said, and knew she would think about that hint and probably give the once-over to every visitor who came to see Mr. Patil. That couldn't hurt.

Savich walked toward the small room with its glass window that gave directly onto the bed, and nodded to Officer Horne, who was young and had two shaving nicks on his chin. He was seated in front of that door, watching every step Savich took. Savich showed Horne his creds. "Any problems at all?"

Officer Andy Horne said, "Nothing suspicious, sir. I'll tell you, everyone wonders why I'm here, guarding this old geezer."

"Who's been here?"

Officer Horne pulled out his black book and carefully read, "His wife; all four of his children — two sons, two daughters — all four spouses; an old friend, Mr. Amal Urbi who looks older than Mr. Patil, uses a cane, belts his pants up to his neck; and his nephew, a Mr. Krishna Shama, a local businessman who dresses real sharp and looks successful; Detective Raven; and Ms. Martinez from the D.A.'s office."

"Very thorough. Thank you, Officer Horne. Keep a sharp eye out. I don't want anything else to happen to Mr. Patil."

"You really think he was shot on purpose, Agent Savich?"

"Yes, I do."

"But why would anyone want to shoot an old man?"

Savich only shook his head, then looked through the glass window to see Mr. Patil lying perfectly still in the narrow bed, IVs attached to each wrist. He was so slight, there was hardly a lump to see. He looked old and frail and insubstantial, but he was tough and he was alive, and Savich wanted very much for him to stay that way. He'd read the financial report Ben Raven had e-mailed to him, and then done a thorough check of his own. Mr. Patil had a fat portfolio, well diversified, and an excellent bank balance. He'd bought the Shop 'n Go fifteen years ago and had expanded to own four more stores spread throughout Washington, D.C., operated by members of his extended family. But the Georgetown store was his baby, and he insisted on managing it himself.

Savich remembered how Mr. Patil had welcomed him when he'd moved into his grandmother's beautiful house, telling him with a good deal of excitement that he'd known his grandmother, what a marvelous lady, and believed her paintings were admirable. *Admirable* sounded a bit like saying her paintings were interesting, and Savich could see his grandmother grinning at that. Savich walked in quietly and stood beside the bed.

Savich started to say Mr. Patil's name when he opened his eyes and looked up at him. There was only an instant of blankness before he smiled. "Hello, Agent Savich. It pleases me very much to see you."

Mr. Patil spoke English with the beautiful faintly sing-song accent of his native country. Besides English and Hindi, he also spoke French and Spanish. He'd come to the United States when he was twenty-four, too old to relearn English with an American accent, he'd told Savich. He spoke very formally, and his English was perfect.

Savich lightly touched his fingertips to Mr. Patil's forearm. "I'm very glad to see you, too, Mr. Patil. How are you feeling?"

"I am feeling quite pleasant, only I am tired, always tired. Sleep hovers over me, is always dragging at me."

"Then perhaps it would be best if I came back tomorrow."

Mr. Patil said, "Oh, no, it is very nice to see someone other than family. They all wring their hands and look at me like I'm already in my coffin. Detective Raven was here earlier, but I fell asleep in the middle of one of his questions. My arm is sore, but it doesn't bother me too much. I have heard the nurses call me a tough old buzzard. I like the sound of that."

Savich said, "I do, too. Your family is very worried about you, Mr. Patil, and your friends, Mr. Urbi and Mr. Shama."

"Oh, yes, and I love them, but after a while, they do grate on one's senses. Ah, but to see my very good friend Amal Urbi and his nephew Krishna, that was good. They do not hover. They act like sensible men and sit and speak to me until I fall asleep. They were here this morning.

"But then after they left, my wife came and stayed and stayed. Jasmine always asks questions — the nurses, every doctor who comes within twelve feet of me. She is not happy, she tells me over and over, not happy that I should be robbed two weeks in a row.

It makes no sense, she says, and asks more questions. She does not believe in co-incidence. The poor young police officer who is sitting outside this room, he does not have a chance against Jasmine. She tells me she hears that he is engaged and very possibly thinking of his fiancée and not really paying all that much attention to my safety. And then she shakes her finger in his face."

"I plan to speak to your wife myself. She can question me as much as she wishes to. Do you feel up to telling me what happened, Mr. Patil?"

"I would like to, yes, Agent Savich." He was silent, and Savich could practically see his brain weaving together the facts of what had happened Wednesday night, but it was difficult for him, even though he'd already told his story to Ben Raven. Savich waited. "There was not a great deal of business Wednesday evening, and so I decided to close thirty minutes earlier than I normally do. This was not unusual for me. I went through my same routine — straightening merchandise, making certain the refrigeration units were working properly, checking the locks, the lights, lowering the blinds over the front window, removing the cash from the register, counting it, preparing the deposit slip, and putting it in a deposit bag to take to the bank."

"Did you know the police found the empty deposit bag beside you?"

"That is what Detective Raven told me. It is odd, because many nights I leave the deposit bag in the safe for my son to deal with in the morning, but I decided to put the deposit bag into the business drop box at the bank myself."

"Tell me what you did then, sir."

"After I finished my routine, I let myself out of the back door. I was locking the door and setting the alarm when I heard someone breathing behind me. I was turning when I felt a very hard slap against my back, and it threw me against the door. And then I must have passed out, Agent Savich. I have no memory of anything else."

"Did you think it was a man you heard breathing behind you?"

Mr. Patil thought about that, slowly shook his head. "I do not know, I am sorry."

It was a thoughtful, cool recital. Savich asked him a couple more questions, got more information about Mr. Urbi and Mr. Shama, and said, "Mr. Patil, I plan to help Detective Raven find out who did this to you."

"Detective Raven told me the robber last

Tuesday night is just above my head on the fourth floor, recovering from the wound in his shoulder. He said there were complications following surgery but the man is doing better. Have you talked to him, Agent Savich?"

"I'm going up to talk to him now. You rest, sir. I will speak to you tomorrow."

"I remember that Mr. Raditch was there with Michael and Crissy on Tuesday evening, the night of the attempted robbery. I called him when I was able, and he said they were fine. Are they still all right? Do you know?"

"I spoke to Mr. Raditch two nights ago. There have been a couple of scary dreams for the kids, and one really bad one for him, he said. He and his wife are being very careful with them. My wife set them up with a child psychiatrist."

"That is good. I will tell you, Agent Savich, I was so scared for the children when that man walked in and pointed that gun at me. Now, you will tell me, Agent Savich, why is there a guard at my door?"

"What did Detective Raven tell you, sir?"

"Nothing at all, merely that since this was the second robbery so very soon after the first, there might be some connection between the two robberies, and that concerned

98

him. Like my wife, Detective Raven does not appear to like coincidences, either."

Mr. Patil looked very alert now, and there was such intelligence in his dark eyes that Savich pushed ahead. "Mr. Patil, think back to that Tuesday night. Do you believe the man with the stocking over his face was really there only to rob you?"

"You are thinking perhaps that he meant to kill me? And since he failed, another came to kill me two days ago?"

Savich said, "That is why the guard is outside your door."

"But who would want to kill me? I am an old man. I have no enemies that I am aware of. It is my wife who should be in danger, for she flays alive anyone who criticizes me or her children or her grandchildren. She is brutal. I am quite terrified of her." Mr. Patil shook his head, and Savich saw a small smile.

Minutes later, Savich went to the fourth floor to see Thomas Wenkel, a former resident of Ossining, in for ten years for armed robbery, paroled after eight years, and released eight months ago. He was a career felon. Did that include murder?

There was a guard outside his room as well. His name was Officer Ritter. No, Savich was told, no visitors, nothing out of the ordinary. Officer Ritter looked, frankly, bored. Ben had best change out the guard.

Savich paused in the doorway. Thomas Wenkel was watching TV, his eyes glued to the small set high on the opposite wall. It was a soap opera.

"Mr. Wenkel."

Thomas Wenkel brought his narrow, watery eyes to Savich. "You ain't my lawyer — go away."

When Savich stuck his creds under Wenkel's nose, he ignored them. Savich saw his long, thick fingers drum against the bedsheet. Then he turned to face Savich. "You're the guy who shot me."

"Yes. I could have killed you, but I didn't."

"Yeah, well, thanks for that, you bastard. Go away."

"Did you know Mr. Patil was shot this past Wednesday night, during another supposed robbery?"

"Stupid old fool. Did he bite the big one this time?"

"You know he didn't, since Detective Raven doubtless came to speak to you about it."

Wenkel shrugged, convulsively swallowed at a hit of pain in his shoulder, and concentrated on the soap opera.

"Were you going to kill Mr. Patil?"

"You ain't my lawyer — go away."

"Tell me, Mr. Wenkel, when you hooked up with Elsa Heinz."

"I don't know no Elsa Heinz." He shouted at the TV. "Hey, Erica, don't cheat on your husband with that yahoo! Don't you got no brain?"

Savich's eyes flicked to the soap opera, then back to Mr. Wenkel. "Elsa Heinz was forty-three years old, in and out of prison for years, just like you, Mr. Wenkel. Why did she come running in to save your bacon? Were you more than criminals together? Were you lovers, Mr. Wenkel?"

Wenkel started humming. There was a commercial on TV.

"She's dead. I had to kill her."

Wenkel never looked away from the television. He only shrugged, but Savich would swear he saw Wenkel's mouth tighten.

"Who hired the two of you to kill Mr. Patil?"

"You ain't my lawyer — go away."

The D.A. had offered Wenkel a deal to roll, but he'd said he didn't rat nobody out, ever.

Savich left. This was interesting indeed. Someone like Wenkel, he should have rolled. Something was wrong with that picture.

CHAPTER 14

Hoover Building
Late Friday morning

Coop said, "I gotta tell you, Savich, Inspector Delion was so excited this morning when I called San Francisco and told him the serial killer is Ted Bundy's daughter, he nearly hyperventilated. I gave him her probable age, sent him the most recent sketch, told him we were betting she lived and attended school in the San Francisco Bay Area since that's where the murders started. I told him we'd have a name for him soon. He'd already done some work on the first two murders committed in San Francisco, and he said a lot of people in the SFPD would be hyped with this news.

"He called me a couple of minutes ago, said they'd already looked through their unsolved murders but there weren't any good matches, but he found six unsolved missing persons — all women — who might fit the ticket. None of the six missing women have ever showed up, anywhere, and the young ones they didn't consider runaways."

Savich waved Coop to a seat. "Over what period of time?"

"He said the first one was a missing teenager, seventeen years ago, then another missing female every couple of years to the present, when the two women were murdered in their homes in San Francisco and, naturally, found pretty quickly. If Bundy's daughter is responsible for the missing women, she didn't want them found."

Savich punched a couple of keys on MAX, then frowned. "It seems to me if she killed those missing women, what she was doing was working all the kinks out, fine-tuning her craft. But why did she change everything when she took her show on the road?"

MAX beeped.

"Ah, here we go." Savich typed a couple more keys. "Come here, Coop, take a look at this."

Both men stared down at a series of high-school yearbook photos of three young women, sixteen or seventeen years old, at three different high schools in San Francisco, eighteen years ago. "Looks like that one, doesn't it?" Coop said, and pointed to a girl's photo in the Mount Elysium High School yearbook. "Look at that dead white face. The hair's blond and the clothes are red, but hair and clothing are easy to change. She's pretty, but there's a sort of indifference about her, maybe a remoteness, you know what I mean?"

Savich said, "As if she's not really plugged into this world, and she doesn't give a crap about any of its inhabitants." A couple more key taps and the screen filled with the face of the girl called Kirsten Bolger. Another couple of keys, and her hair became black. "Look at those eyes, Savich, dark as a pit. Black hair looks natural — bet she dyed her hair blond for the yearbook picture."

Savich made her clothes black, too, set a black beret on her head. "Okay, let's line her up with the sketch."

They studied them. "They're very close," Coop said.

"Now let's try her next to Ted Bundy." Two photos appeared side by side.

Coop whistled. "Would you look at that. Kirsten looks a lot like her daddy."

"Close enough. Okay, ask Delion to find Kirsten Bolger's mother." Savich paused for a moment, tapped his fingertips on his desk. "I want you and Lucy to go out to San Francisco, speak to her mother yourselves. I know it's the weekend, but ask Delion if he'll give you and Lucy some time this evening, maybe set something up so the three of you can meet the mother."

"You think the mom is in San Francisco, don't you?"

"Oh, yes."

"You know Delion will take the bait. Bundy's daughter — who could turn that down? The entire police department will want to come with us."

"I'll work with MAX to find out what I can about Kirsten Bolger and her family, and send the info on to Delion. He'll uncover more about Kirsten with some local phone calls, you can count on it. Vincent's smart, he's got a canny sort of intuition, though he likes to play gruff and tough. He's bald as a shiny egg, and you won't believe his mustache; it's his pride and joy. Say hello to him for Sherlock and me."

"You know the media's going to get hold of this and go wild with it. It'll be a sensation — Ted Bundy's daughter, another serial killer. It ain't going to be pretty. Every police department in the country is going to get flooded with calls claiming she bags groceries at Food Lion."

"There's nothing we can do about it, as

usual. We'll keep forging ahead until it happens, and then we'll deal with it when we have to."

When Lucy came into the CAU at noon on the dot, Coop said, "Tell me if this girl dyes her hair."

Lucy took the photo and looked down at the young face. "Yes," she said.

"Okay, now we've got the expert's opinion. You wanna go on a honeymoon trip with me?"

She cocked her head. "Don't you think we should get married first, Coop? Oh, wait, I bet you've used that line on a dozen women. Does that one work for you?"

"I should have said pre-honeymoon trip, and it isn't a line. It's business. We're going to San Francisco, Savich's orders. It could be a line, I guess, but I just made it up, actually. I repeat, Lucy, there aren't dozens of women waiting to jump me, okay? Interesting idea, though, taking a little trip to San Francisco as a trial run to see if we can last several stress-filled days in each other's company without physical violence on either side. Actually, a pre-honeymoon might save some parents a lot of money for a fancy wedding."

Lucy had to laugh, and it felt good for a

minute, but then she thought about the three hours she'd spent that morning going through a half dozen rooms at her grandmother's house, with nothing to show for it except, literally, an aching back. She said as she stretched a bit, "If I end up smacking you, I swear you'll deserve it."

"What's wrong?"

"Oh, my back. My grandmother's got so much stuff, it's taking me forever."

"You need some help with that?"

Are you nuts? Shut up, shut up. "No, that's not why I said it, merely an observation. The longer you live, the more stuff you collect, I guess."

Coop, who had grade-A cop radar, wondered why she was doing all that work by herself, but he let it go. The fact was she looked wrung out, not from a hangover from too much wine at The Swarm last night but from grief for her father. The last thing she needed was for him to start questioning her. At least he'd gotten a little laugh out of her, and maybe she didn't think he was such a loser playboy anymore. He heard himself say, "I told you I'm not a dog when it comes to women."

She didn't blink. "We'll see."

That was something, he thought. "Okay, like I said, we're going to San Francisco.

Here, let me show you the rest of the photos of Kirsten Bolger, then let's get packed. Shirley made reservations for the four-o'clock flight to SFO."

Lucy's heart leaped when she saw the photos side by side. Kirsten Bolger — was she really the killer? She thought briefly of all the thousands of square feet she still had to search in her grandmother's house, and the hundreds of books in the study. That all paled in comparison to this. Whatever was in her grandmother's house could wait. It had already waited twenty-two years; what was a couple more days? Nothing was going anywhere.

She asked, "So, where are we staying in San Francisco?"

"I'll go butter Shirley up, see if she can't get us an upgrade from the usual Motel Four and a Half. Hey, what's the matter?"

"I was thinking about the media."

"Try not to."

CHAPTER 15

San Francisco
Friday evening

It was a warm evening in San Francisco, and go figure, Coop thought as he shrugged off his leather jacket. He had to admit shirtsleeves felt nice after the near-freezing temperatures they'd left behind in Washington.

He hadn't visited San Francisco in four, five years, but he remembered the air, how it usually felt crisp and fresh, didn't matter if it was foggy or rainy or sunny. He breathed in deep, and the air was as he remembered it — fresh and a little exotic, with a touch of the ocean in it.

Both he and Lucy had brought single carry-ons, and both had their SIGs on belt clips after the usual involved paperwork with Dulles security.

The traffic was heavy on 101 into the city. Every once in a while, Coop leaned out the taxi window to look up at the bit of moon posing brighter in the sky with every minute as the sun was setting. Just beautiful. He and Lucy had plenty of time to discuss their plan of attack on the flight over, and were ready and anxious to get moving.

Coop dialed Inspector Vincent Delion's cell as Lucy tried to understand some of the Russian the taxi driver was speaking on his cell to his wife. Or girlfriend. She'd taken Russian in school, but it sure hadn't stuck.

"Yo, Delion here. That you, Agent McKnight?"

"That would be me," Coop said.

"You got an Agent Carlyle with you?"

"Indeed I do."

Delion said, "I sure hope you guys are hungry. I've gotten no calls from the media, which means no leaks yet, and believe me, that's a real pleasant surprise."

Thirty minutes later, Lucy and Coop walked into La Barca, a Mexican restaurant on Lombard Street, Delion's favorite Mexican restaurant in the city, he'd told Coop.

Coop recognized Inspector Vincent Delion immediately. He looked exactly how Savich had described him. "Hey," he said, "very fine mustache. I'll bet Hercule Poirot sends you hate mail."

Delion laughed and gave a loving little twist to the ends of his glistening black handlebar mustache. He knew it was magnificent, a work of art. It was polished to a high gloss, nearly as shiny as his bald head.

"Too bad Poirot's fiction, and Dame Agatha is dead, or I'll bet he would," Delion said with a good deal of satisfaction.

They all shook hands and sized one another up. Both Coop and Lucy recognized the cop in his eyes, eyes that looked ancient, filled with memories of stuff you really didn't want to know about, eyes that had seen too much over too many years.

And both of them wondered if their eyes held that same knowledge. No, not yet. Delion had twenty years on them.

Once they were seated, a young Latino set a basket of warm tortilla chips in front of them. All hands reached out at the same time, and everyone laughed, including the young guy, Carlos, who was pouring water into their glasses.

Delion said, "These are the best tortilla chips in town. Eat up, kids, the proud city of San Francisco is picking up the tab. When I told our lieutenant, Linda Bridges, you guys had info on the serial killer, and who you believed she was, she said to take you to my favorite place, on us. Then she told everyone to keep their fricking mouths shut, under pain of dismemberment, which never works but scares the rookies for maybe five minutes."

While they stuffed themselves on chips, salsa, and a bowl of guacamole, Delion talked about the case he'd worked with Dane Carver, and moved on to the continuing sorry saga of the 49ers. As he spoke, Lucy found herself thinking about her grandmother's attic, a massive open room that ran the full length of the house. She'd be busy for a week going through everything up there. Maybe she would start with the attic when she got back home. It beat searching through any more books.

When she heard Delion and Coop discussing the fate of football since Brett Favre had left the game, Lucy said, "Like Coop, I bow my head and weep when the Redskins lose, Inspector, but I can't stand it — tell us you've found Kirsten Bolger's mom."

Delion toasted her with a tortilla chip. "Yes, I found her. It's a good news, bad news sort of deal, though."

"What do you mean?"

Delion didn't answer her until their waitress, Cindy Lou, the archetypical California girl — blond, tanned, and gorgeous — had served their enchiladas and burritos.

"Well," Delion said, forking down a huge bite of beef enchilada, "her name isn't Bolger any longer, hasn't been for twelve years now. It's Lansford, as in Elizabeth Mary Lansford, wife of George Bentley Lansford, a big mover and shaker in Silicon Valley. He owns a big interfacing communications company that's international now, and he's using some of his millions to finance his run for Congress. He's got lots of juice, as you can imagine, lots of people who owe him favors. His rep is that you do not screw around with George Bentley Lansford around here. That's the bad news — we gotta be real careful when dealing with his family."

Lucy looked at the last dollop of guacamole, saw Coop had a chip at the ready, and struck first, saying as she chewed, "You gotta work on your speed, Coop. Inspector, that doesn't sound like bad news because we're not from around here and it'll be a treat to mix it up with him."

Delion laughed, scooped up some black beans on a tortilla chip. "When I met you, Lucy, I thought, *Now, here's a nice, quiet, kind of cerebral girl with her French braid and modest little silver earrings. She probably doesn't like to rock and roll all that much. I should've paid more attention to those shit-*

kicker boots you're wearing."

"Well, I don't know about all that," Lucy said, "but this poor boy over here would whimper if he had to face me in the gym."

Coop grinned at her. "I saw Sherlock clean up the floor with you, Lucy. As I recall, she had your legs tied behind your elbows."

"Sherlock's tough, I'll give you that, but Dillon holds back even though I tell him it really pisses me off."

"Good thing," Delion said. "Savich could break your neck while sipping his tea." Delion frowned. "Savich isn't a wild man, though. Only thing that would shake him is Sherlock getting herself hurt. I hear she got shot a couple of months ago."

Lucy said, "Jack, that's Agent Jackson Crowne, said when Savich saw her lying on the floor, he nearly lost it. She's fine now."

Delion polished off his enchilada, fastidiously patted his mustache with his napkin, and sat back, hands over his belly. He looked from one to the other. "You kids ready for the good news now? Like I told you, our girl's mother isn't Elizabeth Bolger any longer, she's Elizabeth Mary Lansford. She's an artist, does a kind of whimsical, fantasy sort of thing — elongated creatures with strange shapes and tentacles, and big eyes, like cartoon characters mixed with science fiction. She runs a local art gallery called Fantasia, over on Post Street. Here's your dessert — I called the gallery, and she's there this evening, some sort of showing for a local artist. If you children aren't too jet-lagged, we can go meet her after dinner."

Coop said, "Good news indeed; let's do it. Anything you can tell us about her?"

"Not much yet."

Lucy said, "Your mustache twitched, Inspector. Come on, what do you know about her?"

"All I'll tell you is that she's a local and she's never been in jail. As for anything else, I think it'd be good if you guys go in with no preconceptions. Then we'll compare notes."

Lucy said, "What about those unsolved missing persons you've been looking into?"

Delion pulled out his notebook, flipped a couple of pages. "The first two teenage girls simply went missing, both from Mount Elysium High School. We found out today both of them were in some of Kirsten's classes. The first girl was a junior, sixteen years old. She had biology with Kirsten. One day she's gone, no sign of her, nothing at all. Good family, reports that she was well adjusted, so probably not a runaway. It drove the police nuts, but there simply weren't any leads of any kind.

"Same with the second girl. She went missing a year and a half later, a senior. Here one day, and the next day, simply gone. Same good background, involved parents, no leads at all." He looked up at them. "She shared an English lit class with Kirsten.

"We found three other missing young women who knew Kirsten Bolger in some capacity, and they all simply disappeared, one every three years on average. There is another woman we haven't been able to connect to Kirsten yet, but I'll get to her in a minute.

"The last woman disappeared two years ago, a thirty-year-old woman named Elsa Cross who lived in Kirsten's apartment building on Dolores, south of Market. I started with her since she's the most recent. After her disappearance every eye was on her ex, but he was alibied up to his tonsils. I called her parents and asked them about a neighbor of their daughter's — namely, Kirsten Bolger. The mother remembered her daughter saying Kirsten wasn't very social, and she was always playing strange music in the middle of the night, but as far as she knew, there were no shouting

116

matches, no angry words between the two women, just mutual dislike. At the time, the police spoke to the manager and all the neighbors, and that had to include Kirsten Bolger, but there weren't any obvious red flags, so all I could find were a few notes about what Kirsten had to say when interviewed."

"And she said what?"

"She said she barely knew Elsa Cross, only said hi to her when their paths crossed, said she seemed nice enough. Nothing else. The case eventually went cold when no new information surfaced.

"I called the manager this afternoon, asked him what he remembered about Kirsten Bolger. He said she was a loner, always paid her rent on time, and always wore white, never a color for contrast, only white, head to foot. He said he never saw any visitors, guys or gals."

Coop said, "Bundy was a charmer, a real favorite at a party, evidently nonthreatening, given the number of women he got to leave willingly with him, yet his daughter is quiet, a loner, acts and dresses weird. But she doesn't wear white anymore; now it's black.

"There's another thing. From what the bartenders in Cleveland and Philadelphia tell us, she can be outgoing, charming, a mirror of her daddy."

Delion signaled to Cindy Lou for their check. After he set down his credit card, he said, "I wondered about that. I guess our girl's adaptable, has some talent."

Lucy said, "Sounds to me like she got into it with Elsa Cross, that or something around that time was the trigger that made her change her ways, and eventually set her out on her road trip. I wonder why she killed that first girl; she was only sixteen, you said?"

Delion nodded.

Coop said, "Maybe, like Elsa Cross, the girl made the mistake of criticizing her about something, and she found out about it."

Delion said, "Yeah, could be, but again, no one remembers any confrontation between the two of them. It was a long time ago, after all.

"Okay, now there's another woman — Arnette Carpenter — I went through her book but couldn't find she knew Kirsten Bolger at all. I've assigned a couple of guys to try to find a connection to Kirsten. They're going to be interviewing everyone involved again, all except for the husband." Delion gave them a placid smile. "I called Mr. Roy

Carpenter. We'll pay him a visit tomorrow morning ourselves."

"You're good," Lucy said, and grabbed the last broken tortilla chip before Carlos could take the basket away.

Delion signed the credit slip, picked up his notebook. "Roy Carpenter was the prime suspect at the time of Arnette's disappearance, but there was no body, no rumors of marital discord, no other woman lurking in the wings, so he got dropped and the case went cold. This was three years ago last May. He still lives in the same house in the Richmond District.

"Okay, kids, you ready for some modern art?"

CHAPTER 16

Post Street, San Francisco
Fantasia Gallery

Since it was a Friday evening and warm, always an unexpected treat in San Francisco, both natives and tourists swarmed the streets. There weren't as many panhandlers in Union Square anymore, Delion tolu them, as they made their way out of the underground garage. He missed Old Ducks, though, a Vietnam vet who used to play the harmonica over near Macy's, always with three blankets around his shoulders, a watering can to collect change from the tourists passing by, and a nice word for everybody. They walked over to Post Street, home to a good dozen art galleries.

There were more locals than tourists in Fantasia tonight, because the showing was for a local artist. The gallery lights were bright, and the mood was light with laughter, maybe because the paintings in the spotlights were filled with such outrageous colors and shapes, they made you want to smile. Whether or not you'd want to look at a creature with two heads and two matching tails every day of your life on your living-room wall was another matter entirely, Lucy thought. The artist getting all the attention was Exeter Land, a stylishly tall and skinny man, wearing perfectly wrinkled loose linen pants and a matching linen jacket. He held a glass of champagne between his long, thin fingers, and stood chatting in the middle of a group of admirers, flushed and happy.

They walked around the gallery, looking mostly at the people there, and spotted about a dozen of Mrs. Lansford's paintings, all hung on one wall and accented with the very best lighting. They were exuberant, Lucy thought, like Mr. Exeter Land's — in fact, like all the artists she carried, as if they all cheered at the same fantasy-land ball-park.

Delion walked toward a woman who stood at the far wall of the big open gallery floor, leaning against a small dark blue desk with white half-moons painted on it, a bottle of water in her hand. She was in her fifties, trim, with very long dark hair, not even a dash of gray, that she wore straight and pulled back with gold clips behind her ears.

Coop could easily picture her younger — she had a bit of the look of Bundy's onetime fiancée, as well as many of Bundy's victims. But she was older now, and carried a look of confidence, he thought, in herself, and in the scene unfolding around her. She was watching the crowd carefully, her eyes roving over each of the people in her gallery. Assessing the possible buyers? Surely she had to be pleased at the turnout for her artist.

Delion nodded to Coop and Lucy. The three of them formed a loose half circle around Mrs. Lansford.

Delion pulled out his badge, introduced himself, then introduced Agent Lucy Carlyle and Agent Cooper McKnight of the FBI. "We're here about the murder of five women in San Francisco, Chicago, and Cleveland, Mrs. Lansford."

She looked at the three of them in turn, nothing changing on her face, not even a small tic or an eyebrow going up, nothing at all. Her very dark eyes remained calm, only politely interested. "You want to speak to me about some murders? *Murders,* did you say? How can I possibly help you, Inspector? Agents?"

Delion brought out the driver's license photo of Kirsten Bolger, along with the police sketch and a photo of Ted Bundy. He spread them out on the desk behind her.

She took a quick look at the photos. Again, her expression did not change. "A moment, please. Let's go to my office." She said nothing to anyone, simply walked out of the main gallery, up a circular flight of steps, down a lovely rose carpeted hallway with more paintings for sale on the walls, and opened a door. She stepped back and waved them in.

Her office was a 3-D fantasy, Lucy thought, large and filled with color. The paintings, a sofa, four chairs, and a coffee table — everything was vivid, bold, and whimsical. There were large stuffed animals scattered about the room — a giraffe, a lion, a horse, and an anteater. The wall-to-wall carpeting was red, with big circles of white and yellow. You smiled, couldn't help your-self.

"Sit down, won't you?"

They didn't sit. Delion once again spread the photos on the desktop, a shiny black af-fair with a black computer on top and a black phone.

"Would you please look at these photos again, Mrs. Lansford."

She looked. "Yes?"

"You recognize your daughter, Kirsten?"

"Is that Kirsten? That looks like her driver's license, and the sketch resembles her, to be sure. Why, yes, I do believe it is."

"And you recognize your daughter's father. Ted Bundy?"

Still, there was no expression at all on her face. She was silent a moment, studying each of the photos now, then she said quietly, "What in the world would make you think such a thing, Inspector?"

Delion said, "One of the intended victims, a young woman in Philadelphia, scored her fingernails down Kirsten's face. We typed her DNA from the tissue and matched her to Ted Bundy."

"Imagine that. Is there no privacy of any kind anymore? I would very much appreciate it if you did not tell George that his stepdaughter's father was one of the most notorious serial killers of all time."

Lucy said, "You never told him? If he doesn't know, I imagine he will know very soon now, Mrs. Lansford. Unfortunately, we cannot control leaks, as much as we would want to. I'm sorry, but there's nothing to be done about it. I suggest you warn your husband. And when Kirsten comes to trial, every single thing everyone knows about her will come out."

"Well, then, I must trust you either don't

ever catch Kirsten or you kill her."

Hmmm. Coop said, "You saw the police sketch in the paper and on TV, didn't you, Mrs. Lansford? You recognized your daughter, didn't you?"

She shrugged. "No, the police sketches weren't at all like her, and so I dismissed it."

"But then other police sketches came out. You recognized those as Kirsten, didn't you, ma'am?"

"Perhaps I did notice a resemblance, perhaps it was niggling at the back of my mind, but I have a great talent for shutting out unpleasantness, and, believe me, there couldn't be anything more unpleasant than this creature murdering five women, let alone thinking that perhaps he was really a she, and that she was really Kirsten. I suppose I was afraid that sooner or later someone might come to see me. But I must admit, you're here much sooner than I expected. May I ask how you found me?"

Lucy said, "We had an excellent description and sketch of Kirsten. We narrowed down our search to the San Francisco area where the murders began and found her quickly enough from her senior yearbook photo at Mount Elysium High School."

Mrs. Lansford walked over to the giraffe

that was nearly as tall as she was, with an eye patch over one eye. Oddly, she lifted the eye patch, looked at the empty eye pit closely, then carefully laid the patch over it again and gave the giraffe an absent pat. "His name is Louie. Ah, so easy, it seems. I'm very glad one of the killer's victims managed to live through the attack.

"I don't know what I can tell you, since I haven't seen Kirsten in over a year. The last time was on her birthday, when I called to invite her to our house in Atherton to give her a special present."

"What was the present?" Lucy asked, seeing for the first time a fat pink hippo sitting beside a bright blue-and-orange chair. It should have been tacky but was, in fact, charming.

"A Porsche Nine-eleven, black, naturally, since she'd left her white period."

"Did her white period include blond hair?"

Mrs. Lansford nodded.

Coop said, "Did she favor a different color before then?"

"Red. That didn't last long. No, it was white for years. It was very unnerving to see her. And tedious. And weird. I told her so, but she ignored me, as usual."

"How does Kirsten earn a living, Mrs.

Lansford?"

"She went to law school — I know, I know, so did Ted Bundy for a while. She stopped going to classes, flunked out, just like her father. Despite all the white, all the bizarre outfits, she is very pretty, and very thin; she modeled for catalogs for a while, but she tired of that quickly enough. She really didn't need to work, since her step-father" — she paused for a moment, frowned at a small piece of paper sitting on the hoof of the blue horse, bent over and picked it off, rolled it into a ball, and gently placed it in the bright yellow sunflower wastebasket beside the desk — "since he gave her an allowance of five thousand dollars a month for many years. I told him he didn't need to do that, but he is a foolishly generous man."

Lucy said, "Mrs. Lansford, when did you tell your daughter her father was Ted Bundy?"

Elizabeth Mary Lansford laughed. "What mother would ever want to tell her daughter something like that? I never told her. But she found out, I have no idea how, and she wouldn't tell me how she knew. It was when she was twenty-five. She walked unexpectedly into the gallery, looked at the painting I had finished that morning, and she sneered

— she always sneered at my work — and she said, calm as you please, 'I know you hate me, Mother, like you hated my father. I could have visited my father in prison in Florida, met him before he died, but you never even told me who he was. You kept him from me; you *stole* my father from me. You're a bitch, a gold-plated bitch, and I wish he'd killed you.'

"Perhaps you wonder how I can remember her words so exactly, but I suspect Inspector Delion knows. You have children, do you not?"

Delion nodded. "I would remember, too, if one of them said that to me. What happened then, Mrs. Lansford?"

"She stalked out with me calling after her to wait, to let me explain, but she didn't even slow down. Of course, I couldn't say anything to George. The next time I saw her was on her birthday last year, when I think my husband tried to bribe her back with the gift of the black Porsche."

Coop said, "So you didn't even see your daughter or hear from her for — what? Six, seven years?"

"That's right, until her thirty-second birthday. She has since turned thirty-three."

"And you don't know how she found out about her father?"

"No. I asked her, but she refused to tell me."

Coop said, "How did she act at her birthday party?"

"It marked the one and only time Kirsten went out of her way to charm her stepfather. Because he gave her the Porsche first thing, I imagine. I listened to her laugh, watched her excitement when she saw the Porsche with a big red bow sitting squarely on the hood. George beamed at her, and she played up to him, still charming as could be, whooping and laughing with pleasure, flirting with him, truth be told. But before she drove off, she made sure to look at me, and there was such cold hatred in her eyes I wanted to cry. I knew I hadn't been forgiven for keeping the truth about her father from her, and I never would be." She turned away from them and walked to a window that gave onto the warm night and tourists and locals still thick on the street. When she turned back, her face was perfectly blank. "About six months ago someone broke into my studio at home and destroyed every painting I had there. It was Kirsten, of course. I — I never told George, merely locked the room until I could clean it out."

"*Sentra!* What are you doing here? Felipe told me you'd come into my office with three people; he didn't know who they were. *What is going on here?*"

Delion, Lucy, and Coop turned to the woman standing in the office doorway, the image of Mrs. Lansford, who was still leaning against the desk, only this woman was wearing a long bright yellow gown with diamonds at her neck, her thick black hair swept up in a French twist.

Sentra?

"Who are you, ma'am?" Delion asked, stepping toward her.

"Why, I'm Elizabeth Lansford, of course. This is my sister, Sentra Bolger. For heaven's sake, Sentra, have you been pretending to be me again?"

CHAPTER 17

Coop said, "I know, it's nearly one a.m. I was prowling around, saw the light under your door. You can't sleep either?"

Coop stood in Lucy's hotel-room doorway wearing black jeans, a black T-shirt, and boots. For an instant she didn't recognize him, since she was so used to seeing him in a suit, or a white shirt, the sleeves usually rolled up. Well, she wasn't in a suit, either, so who cared? She cleared her throat. "Good look — like a cat burglar," she said, and stepped back. "I did try to get some sleep, but it wasn't happening. I've been staring out toward the bay. You want a beer? We can play a game of Who's the Real Mother?"

Coop walked into a room the mirror image of his. "Sounds good." He sprawled on the sofa, accepted the beer, and clicked his can to hers.

"Hey, I like your sleep shirt. Red's a good

131

color on you."

"Ah, but that's not the best part." Lucy turned around. GIVE ME A REASON was written across the back, and beneath there was a squirrel on his hind legs, aiming a rifle outward.

He laughed, settled back. "I don't think Delion has ever been shut down so fast as we were by Mrs. Lansford. She practically shoved us out the door," he said, and sat forward again, staring down at the nondescript beige carpet beneath his booted feet. "So, let's play your game. Who do you think is Kirsten's mother, Sentra or her twin sister, Elizabeth?"

"My gut veers toward one, then the other. I thought Vincent was going to shoot both of them there for a while, what with that smug smile on Sentra's face, and Mrs. Lansford — that lady was extraordinarily pissed off. At us? Or at her sister?"

Coop said, "All of us. I Googled Sentra Bolger, found no mention at all of a twin sister, only that Sentra's an interior decorator, works out of her home on Russian Hill. There was a lot of stuff about her husband, Clifford Childs, and his family. You'd think there'd be more, but there wasn't.

"Elizabeth Mary Lansford has hundreds of links, of info about her husband and her

132

artwork, her gallery, and her charities —
but not a word about a twin sister. I did
find a mention of Kirsten, but only as a
daughter."

Lucy laughed as she set down her beer
can. "I did the same thing. I bet Vincent is
so hyped he's still up working on this."

Coop said, "He's a little like Savich, hap-
piest when he's got a trail to follow. A big
trail is that new Porsche Mr. Lansford gave
her for her birthday, and, of course, the
usual financial records and cell phone accounts. If she hasn't ditched them all, they
could lead us to her."

Lucy said, "I wouldn't be surprised if
Kirsten finds out we were here in San
Francisco, that we know now who she is. If
she does, she could disappear again." She
frowned for a moment, then walked to the
window and stared out again at the small
chunk of San Francisco Bay she could see
between two buildings opposite her room.
She looked down onto Bay Street, two
floors below. There were few streetlights,
and no people about. The entire wharf area
seemed quiet as a tomb.

"I wonder who named this hotel Edel-
weiss?"

He grinned at her back. "Hey, Shirley gave
it an eight on our short FBI-approved list of

hotels, so what's in a name?" It was late, and Coop was tired; he lost focus for a moment and found himself looking at her bare legs — nice, long legs, actually — and at the silver bracelet with a small dangling palm tree hanging from one of her ankles. He was smiling until she turned around and he saw misery in her eyes. She blanked it out in an instant and said, "When I look back on the interview, I can remember thinking some of the things she said were more than a bit odd. I wonder how much of it was true. Did you see her pull that piece of paper from the blue horse's hoof — she stared at it for the longest time. What was that all about?"

Coop said, "But the real question is: why was she pretending to be her sister?"

"The word *nuts* springs to mind. Maybe it was a game they played when they were younger, but —"

"Yeah, but this was nothing to joke about. Maybe Sentra Bolger was going for exactly the shock and rage we were treated to from her sister."

Lucy thought about that. "So, Coop, what do you think? Who is Kirsten's mother, Sentra or Mrs. Lansford?"

Coop sat forward, his hands clasped between his knees. "I'm thinking if Sentra is

Kirsten's mom, the women had to switch identities at the very beginning, even before Kirsten's birth, since there was never any question raised about maternity."

Lucy said, "It would be nice to have a DNA sample from one of them to really nail down Kirsten as the Black Beret, though I don't think these ladies are going to line up to give us one. But I wonder why Sentra would give her baby to her sister? It's true she appears to be several slices short of a loaf, and that throws even more doubt on Kirsten's mental health. Was she born crazy, a loaded gun?"

"No," Coop said slowly, "not crazy. I think Bundy was pure evil."

Was he evil? What did that make her grandmother, killing her own husband? She closed it off. "It's a pity Mrs. Lansford refused to talk to us at all."

Coop set his beer can down on the coffee table next to Lucy's. "It was more than anger. When she realized what it was about, she had to have time to think it over and talk with her husband, decide what to tell us."

Lucy nodded. "But if she'd had a gun, I do believe she'd have shot the lot of us, her sister first off. Her husband's going to go ballistic about what this is going to do to his run for Congress."

He nodded. "No way around it, he's screwed. When I called Savich before to tell him what happened, he was surprised, a hard thing to manage at the best of times, but the twin story did it. He said, 'Well, life never ceases to amaze, does it, Coop?' Then I heard him tell Sean not to feed Astro his apple pie; it was the last piece, and his mama wanted it if he didn't."

She gave a smile, a small one, but it still counted. Coop rose, pulled out a small bottle from his jeans pocket. "I brought some melatonin with me — it helps turn my brain off for a while. Want some?"

They washed down the tablets with the rest of the beer.

"Give it twenty minutes."

When she walked him to the door, he turned and looked at her. "Lucy, what are you up to at your grandmother's house?"

The smile fell away. For an instant, he would swear she looked panicked before she shook her head and said in a rock-hard voice, "Nothing, Coop. Forget it, okay? Breakfast is coming soon, so let's hope the melatonin does the trick."

He wanted to see her smile again. "What do you think of our pre-honeymoon so far?"

"I understand sleep deprivation is a common side effect of a pre-honeymoon. If you don't leave, we're going to qualify for that." She looked him up and down. "You might be an arrogant skirt-chaser, but again, you might not, so I'll ask it. Tell me, Coop, would you marry me if I had a kid whose father was Ted Bundy?"

"Not in a million years."

"Me, either."

"Good night, Lucy. I really do like your palm tree," he said as she closed the door. "See you in the coffee shop at eight a.m. sharp."

CHAPTER 18

Richmond District, San Francisco
Saturday morning

"It's the duplex on the right," Delion said, pointing, and pulled his Crown Vic into the only free spot on Clinton Street, a good half block away. "We're only a few blocks from the Golden Gate. If you guys like, I'll drive you through the park when we're done here. We can commune with the buffalo."

Delion had called ahead, and so he wasn't surprised when the door was opened immediately by a slight man with a receding hairline, stooped shoulders, and bright red sneakers on his feet.

"Mr. Carpenter? Roy Carpenter?"

The man nodded. "Inspector Delion?"

After introductions, Mr. Carpenter showed them into a long, narrow living room, the front window looking out over the cars on the other side of the street. Toys were scattered everywhere on small, colorful rugs. Lucy felt a lick of sadness. She hadn't known he had a child.

Mr. Carpenter said, "Forgive the mess. My sister and my nephew Kyle are living with me at the moment. She, ah, left her abusive husband last week, finally. She's staying with me until — well, I don't know how long. Please sit down. Coffee?"

Since the three of them were floating in Starbucks coffee, they turned it down. When they were all seated side by side on a nubby gold sofa, Mr. Carpenter said, "You're here about Arnette." He tried to keep his voice flat, devoid of hope, to prevent disappointment, Coop knew. It was hard, so very hard, since he knew, all of them knew, that even after three-plus years, a victim's family still held out hope that the missing loved one would once again, somehow, walk through the door and explain it all.

Delion pulled a small recorder from his jacket pocket. "Do you mind if we record this?"

"No, not at all."

"We believe we know what happened to your wife, Mr. Carpenter."

He jerked forward on his chair, and the naked hope in his voice was enough to break your heart. "You've found her? You know who took Arnette, what they did to her? Is she alive?"

"Mr. Carpenter, I'm sorry, sir, but we believe your wife was murdered. We also believe the person who killed her was named Kirsten Bolger. Do you know anyone by that name?"

Mr. Carpenter looked blank but only for a moment. Then he looked shell-shocked. "Kirsten Bolger? You think she murdered my wife? But why?"

Here was the link. Delion said, "We hope you'll be able to tell us that, Mr. Carpenter."

"But I didn't even meet Kirsten Bolger until maybe six months after Arnette went missing. She called me, said she modeled with my wife and did I want to get together to talk about her? I was wallowing in grief and questions, and so I said yes. I remember it clearly, because I wanted to hear someone talk about Arnette like she was somehow here, alive.

"I met her at McDuff's — that's a bar down in the financial district on Sansome Street. You really believe Kirsten Bolger murdered my wife?"

"Yes, sir."

"But that makes no sense, Inspector Delion. Why would you believe that?"

"We'll get to that in a moment, sir." Delion sat forward on the sofa. "I know it's been a long time, Mr. Carpenter, but do you remember any of your conversation with Kirsten Bolger?"

They heard a toddler scream out, "Mama, Cool Whip!"

"Oh, that's Kyle. He likes Cool Whip on his Cheerios. He's got a good set of lungs on him. Missy said she'd keep him out of our hair." He cleared his throat. "I remember Kirsten was glowing in her praise of Arnette. She never said she had a problem with her or anything bad, just told me how wonderful Arnette was."

Lucy said, "Can you describe Kirsten Bolger?"

"I remember she was something to behold. She was wearing black, nothing but black, all the way down to a small black pearl in her nose. She had really long straight black hair, parted in the middle, like Cher when she was young, and she looked like a model, so thin you knew she had to be starving, bony arms sticking out of a sleeveless black T-shirt. Arnette was never that thin, thank heaven; she always said she couldn't live without her peanut butter." His voice caught, and he looked down at his red sneakers. After a moment, he cleared his throat, met Delion's eyes.

"Kirsten's face, it was fascinating, not

beautiful, all angles and hollows, and very white, unnaturally white, I remember thinking, but still fascinating, and I thought the camera had to love her.

"I guess what I remember most is right before she left the bar, she said something like boy, was she ever hot, and I'll tell you, I blinked at that until she pulled off the black hair — a wig — and there was her own hair, blond fuzz, maybe two inches long, all over her head. I nearly fell off my chair, I was so surprised. And then I remember thinking that she shouldn't be a blonde, her eyes were too dark, her eyebrows, too. I wondered if she'd dyed all that blond frizz. But why?"

Delion said, "You said she was glowing in her praise of your wife. Do you remember exactly what she said?"

"She said Arnette was beautiful and kind and everyone had loved her, that when she disappeared no one could understand it. If you've read the interviews, you know this is what nearly everyone else said." Mr. Carpenter looked away from them for a moment, seemingly at a stuffed brown bear on the floor by a chair. He was struggling with himself, Lucy saw it plainly, but why? "Tell us, Mr. Carpenter, tell us what you're remembering. It's important. What did

Kirsten say that upset you?"

He looked like he was struggling not to cry. He drew a breath, and his words spilled out in a rush. "She said she was really sorry Arnette had left me, since I seemed like such a nice man. I tell you, I didn't know what to say. I stared at her. And I asked her why she believed Arnette had left me, since everyone was thinking it was a case of kidnapping. She leaned toward me, picked up one of my hands, and held it a moment between her own two dead-white hands. She said Arnette told her all about it, how she was sorry, but I just wasn't quite enough." He swallowed. "That's what she said — *I just wasn't quite enough.* When I asked her if she knew the man's name, she said all she'd heard Arnette say was the name Teddy."

Delion said, "No last name?"

"No, only Teddy. I called the police, told them about this, but nothing happened."

Delion said, "There was nothing about this in your wife's file, Mr. Carpenter. Did you also give the officer you spoke to Kirsten's name so there could be a follow-up with her?"

"Yes, of course."

"Do you remember the officer's name?"

"No, sorry, I don't. I do remember he had

to put me on hold a minute because there was a lot going on, a big drug bust, and I guess that meant lots of confusion. I could hear shouting and cursing in the background."

Both Coop and Lucy knew exactly what Delion was thinking: *I'm going to find and kill the idiot who took this call. Just a brief note or a couple of words to the lead — Inspector Driscol, now retired — and they might have caught Kirsten Bolger before she killed more women.*

Lucy said, "So, basically, she invited you for a drink to tell you Arnette had left you for another man, this Teddy?"

"Yeah, now that I think back on it, all the rest of it was window dressing; telling me about the other man, that was the bottom line."

"Did you believe her?"

"I believed her for maybe two seconds. I knew my wife, knew her as well as I knew myself. We'd been married for three years, not all that long, but we'd known each other since we were sixteen. I would have known if she'd met someone else. She would have told me. Whatever was in her head was out of her mouth in the next second.

"I wasn't enough? Arnette wouldn't say that, I know it to my soul." He paused, then tears swam in his eyes and he lowered his head. "We were trying to have a child, and I'll never know if she was pregnant when this Kirsten killed her." His head snapped back up, and now there was rage. "Why? Why did this woman kill her? And then she calls me and tells me Arnette left me for this Teddy? It makes no sense."

Coop said, "Your wife never mentioned Kirsten's name? Ever?"

"No. As I said, Arnette always said whatever was on her mind; sometimes that wasn't a good thing, but it was simply the way she was. If she'd had any kind of problem with Kirsten Bolger, she'd have told me. And who is Kirsten Bolger? All she ever told me was that she modeled, and that's how she knew Arnette."

Delion said, "Have you heard of the killer some of the media is now dubbing the Black Beret?"

"Of course. The guy who murdered two women here in the city — met them in bars, drugged them, took them home, and strangled them, right? No rape, which is why it's even stranger. Why are you asking?"

Delion said, "The Black Beret isn't a guy. She's a woman — Kirsten Bolger, to be exact."

Talk about a conversation stopper. Even

the air stilled. Roy Carpenter looked like someone had shot him. His breathing hitched, and he began shaking his head back and forth. "But these two women murdered right here in San Francisco, they were found right away. Not like Arnette; she's been gone three and a half years." He turned perfectly white. "Do you mean she didn't want Arnette found, and so she took Arnette someplace and buried her?"

"We believe so," Coop said. "I'm sorry, Mr. Carpenter."

"But why did she want to torment me? I didn't even know her."

She called you because she's an unbelievably cruel bitch. Lucy said aloud, "That's an excellent question." She sat forward. "Tell me, sir, was your wife by any chance an artist?"

"Why, yes, she was, but —" Roy Carpenter blinked. "She called it her hobby; she always laughed when I told her her paintings were good enough to sell. There, over the fireplace, that's one of Arnette's landscapes. Next to it is a portrait she did of her mother. They're acrylic; that was her favorite medium. I've got several dozen of her paintings. I change them out every couple of months. She was very good, don't you think?"

They rose to look at the paintings. Coop said, "Yes, she's very good, Mr. Carpenter, very good indeed." Coop supposed he'd call them neo-Impressionist, with their soft muted colors, the shapes slightly blurred, the trees a bit out of focus, but the colors were beautiful and deep. Her mother was a lovely woman, he thought, her face both haunting and beautiful. He saw hints of pain around her mouth and her eyes, a pain that seemed familiar and to have been with her for a very long time. It took talent to capture that.

Mr. Carpenter was staring at Lucy. "Why did you ask me if Arnette was an artist?"

"I think it might be our tie-in, Mr. Carpenter. Did Kirsten Bolger mention Arnette's art? Did she say she painted as well?"

"No, not that I remember. Wait, when she said good-bye to me, she said she was off to Post Street to visit the art galleries. I remember I was standing there on the sidewalk, not knowing what to say, and she patted my face and kissed my cheek. I was so surprised I didn't move. Then she gave me a little wave, pulled her black wig over her head, and sauntered off, whistling. I remember thinking she was crazy. I guess she is."

"Close enough," Lucy said.

CHAPTER 19

Washington, D.C.
Sunday afternoon

Savich gave Sean and Marty each a cup of cocoa, told them a third time not to spill it. He said to Sherlock, "That was Delion I was talking to in the kitchen. Kirsten's trail has gone cold. He said the Porsche Lansford gave her is long gone, no transfer of title, nothing, so she probably sold it for cash. She emptied out her bank accounts the week before the first murder in Chicago. Lots of cash, so it isn't difficult for her to survive. As for any credit cards, she must have also thrown them away. He can't find anyone in San Francisco who's seen her since then."

Sherlock said, "At least having her identity blared on every TV in the country can't send Kirsten Bolger any deeper underground."

"Let's hope not. There really isn't an option anymore, now that the *Drudge Report* posted that leak. No way to keep Ted Bundy out of it, either, too juicy. So now every talking head gets to rock and roll with this crazy killer. I need to get dressed if I'm going to make it to the news conference. Director Mueller wants me front and center when he releases her name to the media."

Sherlock felt a niggling fear at having Kirsten Bolger focus her mad attention on Dillon. "You want backup?"

Savich watched Sean very nearly tip his cocoa cup. "No, you don't have to come. Sean, don't wave your cocoa around while you chase Astro."

His cell sang out Sarah Brightman and Andrea Bocelli singing "Time to Say Goodbye," Sherlock's favorite song of all time. Savich didn't answer right away, because Sherlock and the two children seemed to be listening to it.

"Savich."

When he cut off his cell a few minutes later, he said, "That was Lucy. Mr. Maitland asked both her and Coop to be at the news conference."

"Go make yourself look tough and professional; I'll watch the cocoa." But Sherlock simply couldn't help worrying. That was part of her job description.

149

■ ■ ■ ■

The press conference was attended by every media hound inside the Beltway. Savich looked out over the media room, chaotic and noisy, with scores of reporters and TV people setting up their cameras.

Director Mueller outlined the process by which they'd discovered the real identity of the Black Beret. He closed, saying, "I cannot emphasize enough how dangerous this woman is. Just to remind yourself, simply think of her father, Ted Bundy. Being identified like this may make her even more ruthless and desperate. We know all of you will help with publicizing her photo. Please encourage your readers and your viewers to contact the FBI if they see her. No one but law enforcement should attempt any direct contact with her." He ended with the hotline number, and turned it over to Savich as the questions began.

Savich, as was his habit, said nothing at all, simply waited until there was silence again. He introduced Lucy and Coop, and paused again, focusing every face on him. He pushed a button on the lectern, projecting Kirsten's photo behind him. "Five days ago, Kirsten Bolger was in Philadelphia. We do not know if she is still there or has gone to another city. We do not know if she will continue to dress as you see her in this photo." He waited, then put up two more large photos of Kirsten Bolger. In one she had long blond hair and black clothes, and in the second, she was dressed like a man, with black hair and black clothes. "She has experience changing her appearance, from appearing as both a man and a woman, and this gives you an idea of some of the ways she's dressed in the past." He leaned forward, looked at them. "I want to emphasize along with Director Mueller that we appreciate your viewers' and your readers' help in contacting us if they see the woman in these photos. We don't know what she'll do now that her real identity and photos are public, but I am very concerned she may up the ante, as her father did. She is well aware that Ted Bundy was her father.

"I'll take questions now."

A tsunami of loud questions rolled toward him. He pointed toward Jumbo Hardy of *The Washington Post.*

Jumbo lumbered to his feet. He looked untidy and unwashed, as if he'd dressed to go out fishing on this fine Sunday morning, and had to hurry all the way back. "Is it true the mother of Bundy's daughter is an artist who is married to George Bentley Lansford, a candidate for Congress?"

It never failed — Jumbo always had the best sources. Savich saw Lucy was surprised this information was out already.

Savich said, "That appears to be the case, though we are awaiting final confirmation."

Jumbo said, right on the heels of Savich's comment, "You interview Mr. Lansford yet?"

"No," Savich said. "Not yet."

There were several dozen more questions, most of them about Ted Bundy, not his daughter, and Savich answered each one honestly, until Mr. Maitland shut it down. "Thank you, ladies and gentlemen, for your cooperation. We will keep you updated. Let me emphasize that Kirsten Bolger is a very dangerous woman. Ah, I hope all you bartenders out there keep a sharp eye out."

There was one lone laugh, a few more shouted questions, but there was no one to answer them. Coop said to Savich as they walked off the dais, "Are you going to ask Inspector Delion to interview Mr. Lansford?"

"Nope. You, Lucy, and I are going to do it. Turns out Mr. Lansford and two lawyers are here in Washington. I called. They grudgingly agreed to let us see him in a couple of hours."

Lucy said, "The lawyers'll hang over him like a couple of bats, won't let him help us."

Director Mueller nodded. "What about Lansford's wife, Kirsten's mother? What has she to say about her daughter being a serial killer?"

Lucy said, "We don't know, sir; she's refused to speak to us."

Director Mueller was shaking his head. "There's always something loony that finds you, whether you're looking or not. I expect all of you to be careful. Keep me in the loop." The director shook their hands, turned, and said, "Ted Bundy — I didn't think I'd ever hear that name again in the context of an investigation. This will keep all the TV shrinks in business for a good long time." He looked tired, Coop thought, watching him walk away surrounded by half a dozen agents and aides.

CHAPTER 20

Washington, D.C.
The Willard
Sunday afternoon

Coop thought the Abraham Lincoln Suite on the sixth floor of The Willard was a smart choice for a wannabe congressman. Was he sending the subliminal message that he was a trustworthy straight shooter? The Willard was only one block from the White House, another nice pointer.

A buff dark-haired thirtyish man in a dark blue suit, Lansford's aide, Coop supposed, answered their knock, gave the three of them an emotionless look from behind very cool aviator glasses, and, without a word, ushered them into the sitting room with its trademark Prussian-blue-and-gold color scheme. The suite was large, about the size of his condo, Coop thought, maybe fifteen hundred square feet of gracious luxury.

George Bentley Lansford was a tall man,

taller even than his aide, a nice plus for a budding politician. He was elegantly dressed in English bespoke that didn't look too expensive but that any donor worth his salt would recognize for what it was. He was healthy, fit, fifty-five, not as darkly tanned as his aide, and blessed with a full head of silver-black hair that would no doubt help him with some of his women voters. He looked, Coop thought, stalwart.

He stood between two men, both younger, probably the lawyers, both wearing severe black suits. They looked at Coop like rottweilers ready to go for a handy throat.

As for Mr. Lansford, Coop saw he was focused on Savich. He looked royally pissed, his hands in fists at his sides. He said from a distance of at least ten feet, "I assume you are all FBI agents and we can forgo the introductions. I recognize you, Agent Savich, from the FBI press conference on TV. I am very angry. You and that reporter from *The Washington Post* have destroyed my chances of being elected to Congress by releasing my name to the media. My lawyers tell me I cannot sue you, but let me tell you, I feel like hounding you until I die. I am innocent of any wrongdoing, but I am finished before I had scarcely begun my political career because of my connection to this —

this unfortunate young woman. Now, let's get this interview over with. I want all of you out of here as soon as possible. What exactly is it that you want?"

Savich said in his calm, deep voice, "You're right about a lot of that, of course, Mr. Lansford. Actually, your political career was over when your stepdaughter openly murdered a woman in San Francisco nearly six months ago. You just didn't know it yet. I agree it isn't fair, but there is nothing for me to apologize about. Once we had Kirsten's DNA, once we'd identified her, we were led inevitably to you, Kirsten's stepfather.

"I understand your anger, your sense of unfairness, but you're an experienced man, sir, a savvy man, and so you know there are always leaks, it doesn't matter the organization, whether it be a police department or a high-tech company like your own. Our news conference was a response to such a leak. Your relationship to Kirsten Bolger had to come out, it was inevitable, so I wasn't at all surprised when a reporter brought it up. It required only a modicum of research."

"It doesn't matter! It shouldn't have happened! It is not right that it should come out. Her mother and I are ruined, do you understand? Ruined!"

"May I remind you, sir, this isn't some sort of vendetta waged against you by the FBI or the San Francisco Police Department. Five innocent women are known dead at the hands of your stepdaughter. It is very likely Kirsten murdered another six women."

"But it isn't — yes, of course I'm distressed by the murders. Wait, what did you say? She killed before? Another six women? That's insane. I never heard such a thing. There was no news about it, nothing at all."

Lucy spoke for the first time, aware that Lansford's aide was standing six feet away, arms crossed over his chest, and he hadn't looked away from her. Why? "The reason you haven't heard of the other dead women is that Kirsten must have hidden the bodies of her early victims. It seems she was practicing, Mr. Lansford, honing her skills.

"Sooner or later the media will pick up on these other women we fear she murdered. You can count on it, since something this heinous can't be kept under wraps for long."

George Bentley Lansford looked like someone had punched a big hole in his elegant suit coat. They all saw that the murders were no longer an abstraction to him, that he'd finally realized to his bones that Kirsten had brought violent death to a dozen human beings, to people just like himself. He ran his tongue over his lips. "Practicing?"

Coop said, "Serial killers often refine their approach, discovering what sorts of killing methods give them the greatest satisfaction. Yes, we believe she murdered at least six more women, actually some of them young girls, and buried them deep so no one would ever find them."

Lansford looked sick, his anger defeated, and older than he had when they'd stepped through the door ten minutes before. "All right, I understand. I had no clue, none at all. I saw her very few times over the years. I thought she was sullen, indifferent to me, nothing more. You've got to believe me. If her mother had noticed anything, she would have said something to me. But, of course, her mother hadn't seen Kirsten for a very long time before her last birthday party; neither of us had. A dozen women? She's murdered a dozen women?"

Coop said, "When we catch her, we're hoping she will tell us where she buried them all."

Savich said, "Let me add that these six are the only ones we know about so far, all of them from the Bay Area. There could be more, out of the area, even out-of-state, but

I personally tend to doubt it, because we've discovered that each of the women who disappeared knew Kirsten. They weren't strangers to her.

"Mr. Lansford, as Agent McKnight said, not all of them were grown women. Annie Sparks was only sixteen years old when she went missing. She attended Mount Elysium High School in San Francisco, shared a biology class with Kirsten. Would you like to hear about the other five women who were almost certainly victims of your stepdaughter?"

"No! Listen, you can't be sure about these other missing women — girls — not really." There was no more heat in Mr. Lansford's words. He scrubbed his face with his hands. "I simply can't imagine that she would do such a thing, over and over — and enjoy it."

Coop had wanted to dislike this man, but the shock and despair he saw in his eyes was painfully real. Even the lawyers were trying hard not to show their horror. Mr. Lansford's aide, Mr. Buff Tan, hadn't moved an inch since assuming his nearby guard position. "You are in no way to blame, Mr. Lansford," Coop said. "We know you married her mother twelve years ago, which would have made Kirsten twenty-one years old, an adult. What would be helpful is if you would give us your impressions of Kirsten, any personal information you think could help us find her."

Lansford began to pace the suite's living room, his lawyers hovering close, wanting to object, but to what? Then, with perfect timing, one of the lawyers said, "There is nothing Mr. Lansford can tell you that would be of any assistance in finding her. After all, as you said, she was already an adult when he married her mother. As he has already said, he rarely saw her. She was nearly a stranger to him."

Lucy said, "Tell us about her birthday, Mr. Lansford — you gave her a black Porsche, right?"

Lansford stopped pacing and slowly turned to face her. "How do you know about that?"

Coop said, "Your sister-in-law, Sentra Bolger, told us."

He looked ready to spit. "Sentra? That idiot woman, you can't believe a word she says, she's nuts, and it's worse because she's good at it, she's very convincing."

Lucy said, "Yes, she is convincing. Surely your wife told you when we interviewed Sentra, we believed her to be Kirsten's mother and your wife, Elizabeth Mary Lansford?"

"Yes, yes, but she said Sentra refused to tell her anything about her conversation with you, only that Sentra had said she'd kissed you off." He nodded at Lucy and Coop. "You two were with her on Friday night?"

Lucy said, "Yes, we were, and believe me, Sentra was very up front, very believable at playing both your wife and Kirsten's mother. About Kirsten's birthday — Sentra told us Kirsten was charming to you, unusual for her, according to Sentra. She told us Kirsten was very pleased with your gift of the Porsche. Sentra was there, wasn't she, sir?"

"Yes, she was, not that I wanted her there, but Elizabeth believed it would be a good idea because she is, after all, Kirsten's aunt, and Elizabeth wanted Kirsten's family around her. Bruce" — Lansford nodded toward Mr. Buff Tan — "was there as well. Listen, Sentra loves to play roles. She could be Lady Macbeth one minute and then segue easily into Lady Gaga."

Coop asked, "Why did you buy her such an expensive present, Mr. Lansford?"

Again he ran his tongue over his lips.

One of the lawyers said, "A father's gift doesn't have to justify a price tag, Agent." Almost in the next breath, the lawyer cleared his throat. "Ah, what I meant to say is that even a stepfather, related only by marriage, a man who had nothing at all to do with any of her upbringing, can give a splendid gift, Agent McKnight, as a loving gesture to his wife."

Lansford said, not looking away from Coop, "Shut up, Cox. Listen, Agents, you want the truth? Here it is — I could barely tolerate Kirsten. She was cold and weird and generally unpleasant, and, as far as I could tell from all the years I knew her, she didn't have a single friend, didn't go on a single date with a man, and despised her mother. But then again, I rarely saw her; her mother, either. So was she always like this? A loner? Always creepy? I don't know, but it sounds right."

Lucy said, "Then why the Porsche, Mr. Lansford?"

He waved them over to one of the beautiful sofas. "Sit, all of you, sit."

Cox opened his mouth again, but Lansford waved him to silence. "I gave her the Porsche because her mother — although she didn't say anything about it to me — wanted desperately to see her daughter. I knew the only way to make Kirsten come over, the only way to make sure she'd be pleasant, was to do something big, like the

Porsche. That's why I gave it to her.

"Now, Elizabeth told me who Kirsten's father was when I asked her to marry me, when Kirsten was nineteen. Elizabeth didn't ever want me to question that she'd kept the truth from me on purpose if, somehow, I found out about Kirsten's parentage. I tell you, I couldn't believe it at first. I mean, Ted Bundy, that horrific monster — no, I couldn't believe it, didn't want to believe the woman I loved had actually slept with that psychopath. I didn't want to know any of the particulars, and that was fortunate, since she didn't want to talk about what had happened between the two of them.

"As I said, Kirsten was nineteen at the time. I'll tell you, even before I knew who Kirsten's father was, I didn't want to be around her. Like I told you, she was always sullen around me, obviously didn't want me near her mother, although she was just as sullen, just as unpleasant, to her mother. She obeyed her mother only when she felt like it. Then she'd turn on a dime — she'd become the nicest girl you can imagine, all smiles and hugs and charm, like at her birthday party. And yes, this was always connected to something her mother or I did for her. You can be sure I gave marrying Elizabeth a lot of thought after she told me about Kirsten.

"But you see, I loved Elizabeth, loved her to my bones, and she loved me. However, she put me off for another two years until Kirsten was twenty-one, out of the house, and on her own, and I wouldn't have to be around her. Then we finally married.

"I will be honest. I knew that if Kirsten's parentage ever came out, my businesses would suffer and we would be hounded by the media, but I didn't see how it ever would come out. Elizabeth told me Bundy never knew about the child, so who would tell?"

Lucy said, "Sentra told us you didn't know about Kirsten's parentage."

He snorted, a curiously charming sound. "I repeat, Sentra's nuts. She's a liar. She likes to cause problems, to give her sister grief. What if Elizabeth hadn't come in before you left? You'd still believe you'd spoken to Elizabeth, wouldn't you?"

"Very likely," Coop said.

Lucy asked, "Do you know who told Kirsten her father's identity?"

Lansford sighed. "It had to be Sentra. But why?" He snorted, waved a hand. "Am I an idiot, or what? It's Sentra we're talking about here, and that crazy witch would do anything, and for no good reason. I think it's only because they're twins that Elizabeth can't seem to distance herself from Sentra, once and for all.

"I know Elizabeth certainly never told Kirsten who her father was, though she told me Kirsten asked her often enough when she was a little girl. Elizabeth simply told her that her father was dead, and that came true, soon enough, in that Florida electric chair.

"Elizabeth said when Kirsten was twenty-five she became even more secretive from one day to the next, even more unpleasant to her — in fact, she simply cut her out of her life. Elizabeth wanted desperately to believe it was simply another phase, but she said she knew in her heart Kirsten had found out about Bundy.

"And then Elizabeth found the book on Ted Bundy, right on top of Kirsten's dresser, where she'd left it so her mother would know. As I said, we didn't see her again, until her birthday party, which was fine with me, but I know Elizabeth worried.

"Do you know, in that book on Bundy, Kirsten had drawn circles around her father's photos, yellow circles? And little hearts. I'm wondering now if she recognized herself."

CHAPTER 21

Little hearts. Savich could only imagine what Mrs. Lansford had thought when she'd seen that.

Mr. Lansford said, "When Elizabeth told me about Bundy being Kirsten's father, she admitted she hadn't had a clue what or who Kirsten was from the time Kirsten reached puberty. She didn't know what she would do or say or think about any particular subject from one minute to the next. She also admitted to me that Kirsten's strangeness had always frightened her, given who her father was. Elizabeth read every book she could find on whether psychopathic behavior could be inherited, but she simply couldn't be certain about Kirsten. She said she was afraid to even think about it; it was simply too upsetting.

"Because Kirsten hadn't been arrested by the age of twenty-one, Elizabeth told me she began to breathe more easily, finally admitted that was why she'd waited another two years to marry me. She hadn't wanted me near someone who could possibly harm me. I remember before she was twenty-five, Kirsten occasionally slept over, but let me tell you, I'd forget her for months at a time.

"That black Porsche." He dashed his fingers through his beautifully styled hair. It fell right back into place. "Do you know, I always liked black until Kirsten. But black was the only color I ever saw her wear. Fricking black. And so I bought her the black Porsche. I wanted to tie a black bow around the Porsche, but her mother said it wouldn't go over well, Kirsten would think I was making fun of her, and I confess, when she said that, I felt a chill run over me. So the bow was huge and red, and Kirsten smiled and patted me, told me thank you, and she kissed me maybe a dozen times. She even asked questions about my upcoming campaign. She was all interest, all sweetness — that day — and I'll confess, I wanted to believe she was simply a bit on the exotic side, that her weird behavior was mainly affectation. I never dreamed she was indeed a copy of her father. I mean, who could dream of such a thing? We never saw her again after that day."

Savich said, "You said she was unpredictable, Mr. Lansford. Could you give us an example?"

He walked over to the window and looked out onto the quiet courtyard. He said over his shoulder, "I remember once, she was maybe twenty-four, she waltzed into my office in Silicon Valley, completely unexpected, and told me she was taking me to lunch."

Coop said, "Did you go?"

Another moment of silence, then Lansford said, "I've never said this before, haven't, as a matter of fact, even let myself think it. But now that I remember that day, I realize I went to lunch with her for the simple reason that I was afraid of her. I tried to tell myself that I had no reason to be, but still — I'll never forget the first time I met her, this eighteen-year-old who was attending Berkeley, an art major, and she looked like she wanted to shoot me, sullen as a little kid — but much more than that. I saw something in her eyes when she looked at me, lurking there, if you will, something that alarmed me. I know that sounds melodramatic, as if I'm embellishing my reactions, since I now know who she is, but I'm not sure. That something I saw hiding in her eyes, it was this Kirsten — Ted Bundy's daughter. You know she also attended law school for a little while, like her father?"

"Yes," Savich said. "We know."

Lansford raised bleak eyes to Savich. "My poor wife is devastated. Can you imagine finding out your child has murdered five people?"

Lansford shook his head, trying to get his brain around the horror. "I remember Elizabeth told me once she must be the luckiest woman alive. I thought she was talking about meeting me, about our coming together, and my ego bounded to the stratosphere." He gave a sharp laugh, met Savich's eyes. "But what she meant was that she had survived Bundy, that he hadn't tortured her and murdered her — he only left her pregnant.

"She left yesterday to stay with her cousins in Seattle. Yes, I know, Ted Bundy lived there. Did she meet him in Seattle? I don't know, I didn't ask her, but I know it was her first home."

"What about Sentra?"

"I happened to go by the gallery Friday night and saw the two of them together. Elizabeth was furious, of course, and Sentra, well, she was laughing, talking about what an interesting evening it had been."

Coop said, "Mr. Lansford, do you think

it's possible Sentra is Kirsten's mother and not Elizabeth?"

"*What?* No, I have never thought that. What possible reason could they have had for a ruse like that?"

"Maybe your wife took the baby because, as you say, Sentra was nuts, not at all good mother material."

"No, Elizabeth would have told me."

"Has Sentra always been an interior decorator?"

Lansford laughed. "Oh, you can't know how rich that is. Sentra is the longtime mistress of Clifford Childs, an old-time San Francisco aristocrat with old-time money — actually, he has a vast reservoir of money. She's never earned a dime, never done a worthwhile thing in her life, even though she claims she's an interior decorator. She met Childs when she was all of twenty-two years old, and he was thirty, a recent widower with two sons. They've been together ever since, thirty-two years."

They all knew this, since a Google search had turned up dozens of society party photos. Lucy asked, "Why didn't they marry?"

"I don't know why, but the way Sentra tells it, she keeps turning him down. Why? Sentra says he's too possessive. He's always given her an outrageous allowance, treated her like a queen. They're quite the society couple. I believe he's even left her half his estate in his will. His two sons love her as much as Daddy, their wives as well — amazing, since I can't imagine her being able to hide what a loon she is for very long. Maybe it doesn't matter to any of them that she's crazy, or maybe this role is simply easy for her, and pleases her, and with them there is no pretense. Yes, one big happy family. It's all very odd. Do you know Childs came to my big fund-raiser in San Francisco and contributed huge bucks for my campaign?"

Lucy said, "Thirty-two years. That's almost exactly Kirsten's age. Excuse me for repeating this, but maybe you've given us the reason for Sentra giving up Kirsten as a baby — namely, Clifford Childs. What do you think? Sentra was twenty-two years old, had a baby, no means of support, and here comes her knight — namely, Clifford Childs."

Lansford said, "Sure, that could make sense, but like I already said, I know Elizabeth, and I know she would have told me if she weren't Kirsten's mother; there'd have been no reason for her not to. Actually, I think she would have been greatly relieved to be able to tell me that. No, there is no doubt in my mind that Elizabeth is Kirsten's mother."

"Did Sentra know Bundy personally?"

"Elizabeth never said one way or the other. But listen, I admire my wife for what she did. She was twenty-two years old, and she supported herself by selling her art, attended classes at Berkeley, and raised a child on her own."

Savich nodded. "Do you know how Clifford Childs has reacted to all this?"

Lansford gave a bark of laughter. "He called me an hour ago. True to form, Clifford and the family have closed ranks around Sentra. He sees her as a victim who needs his protection.

"Listen, Agents, do you think Elizabeth could be in any danger from Kirsten? The thought scares me stupid."

Savich said, "No, I don't think so, Mr. Lansford. If I were worried about one of you, I'd say it would be you. Take care in your daily routine, all right? Be aware of the people who come near you — until we catch Kirsten."

Lansford was staring down at his butter-soft black loafers. Then he looked up at all of them. "Agents, we will all be suffering until you do."

CHAPTER 22

Washington Memorial Hospital
Sunday afternoon

Mr. Patil had been transferred to a bed on a surgical floor, and his physicians were predicting a full recovery.

Savich was pleased to see Mrs. Patil standing next to her husband's bed, since he hadn't met her when he'd gone to the Patil home, and then Kirsten Bolger had come roaring into his life and he'd put off going back. But Ben had interviewed her and said he hadn't gotten any brilliant leads or insights from her.

She was leaning forward slightly, speaking quietly to Mr. Patil, her hand on his shoulder.

Mr. Patil looked over at him and smiled widely. "Ah, Agent Savich, you have not yet met my wife, Jasmine. She will not leave my room. She complains that I am not healing myself fast enough. When the doctors tell her I won't live, she tells them they are all worthless mongrels, but now that they tell her I will live, I hear her say to Dr. Pritchett that he is a miracle man, another Mother Teresa."

Mrs. Patil broke into rapid Hindi, none of which Savich understood. He waited until the woman was finished. Mr. Patil said, "She tells me you are very handsome, Agent Savich, that it is possible you would be worthy of our eldest granddaughter, Cynthia, who is as American as you are."

Savich smiled. "Thank you, Mrs. Patil, but I am already married."

"That is a great pity," Mrs. Patil said, and gave him a big smile. "But Cynthia, she is a silly girl. She would worship you, and you would probably scare her to death." Then she broke again into mile-a-minute Hindi to her husband. Why? She was as perfectly fluent in English as Mr. Patil. He looked at her while she spoke. She was younger than her husband by a good twenty years, putting her in her fifties, he thought, and she looked maybe in her late forties, the result of a couple of excellent face-lifts, most likely. She was a fine-looking woman, a spark in her dark eyes, and her hair was glossy black without a hint of gray, worn in a short swing around her cheeks. It seemed to him she was as Americanized as her granddaughter Cynthia.

When she ran down, Savich asked her, "Were you born in America, Mrs. Patil?"

"Oh, no, my parents moved here when I was seventeen, and that is why I have a bit of an accent," and she preened, patting her hair, and then her husband's veiny old hand.

Mr. Patil looked up at her, besotted.

Savich couldn't recall Mr. Patil's first name; then, in the next instant, Jasmine called him Nandi. This charming old man's name was Nandi. That name sounded so warm, so inviting, and it certainly fit him, Savich thought. They had four children, two sons and two daughters, and eight grand-children, the eldest twenty, the youngest two years old. Her precious husband had no enemies, Mrs. Patil told Savich, not a single one. It had been two robberies, nothing more, because who would hate a man who owned a Shop 'n Go? He made people happy. He sold them hot dogs and beer. He didn't lie or cheat or steal. Robbers, stupid, greedy robbers. Catch them.

In short, Mr. Patil was a saint, and Savich had better get on the stick. And she could be right. Could be, but something simply didn't feel right about a little old man like Mr. Patil getting shot in the dark.

Mr. Patil said, "Agent Savich, I find myself wondering also why you have not caught the man who shot me. A violent man who robs convenience stores, would he not be in your files, in your databases?"

"We're certainly checking that all out, Mr. Patil."

Jasmine said, "It has to be a robber, Agent Savich, not some evil archenemy who does not exist, out to murder my Nandi, because — well, because why? Yes, a robber, it simply must be."

Savich left five minutes later, thinking about Jasmine Patil, who'd given him a come-on sweep of her eyes before he'd left the hospital room.

CHAPTER 23

Chevy Chase, Maryland
Sunday afternoon

Lucy was opening the front doors when she heard Mrs. McGruder call out, "Lucy! Wait a moment!"

She turned, a smile on her face, to see Mrs. McGruder, dressed in her favorite dark purple, walking as quickly as her bulk would allow up the steps and onto the front porch, Mr. McGruder behind her, dressed in dark work clothes, heavy old work boots on his feet.

"How nice to see you both," Lucy said, and shook their hands. "I was very pleased you were at my dad's funeral." Her voice broke, and she held still, trying to get a hold on herself.

Mrs. McGruder took her hands, squeezed them. "I know, dear, I know. It's very difficult for all of us, but especially for you. You and Mr. Joshua were so very close. Isn't that right, Mr. McGruder?"

That nearly made Lucy smile. A wife calling her husband by his last name, something that was done maybe a hundred years ago. She'd always thought it was curiously charming.

Mr. McGruder scratched his forearm and allowed that it was right.

Lucy said, "I'm very pleased you came by, since I wanted to speak to you both. Thank you for filling the fridge, Mrs. McGruder, but I can do my own shopping now. But perhaps you could come by once a week and straighten up for me, do some general cleaning?"

"Well, naturally, but I can come every single day, if you would like, Lucy."

But Lucy didn't want anyone around. She wanted to be alone to search this barn of a house. No, she told Mrs. McGruder, that wasn't necessary. Before Mrs. McGruder could try to talk her around, Lucy turned to Mr. McGruder, complimented him on the nicely raked front lawn, done, he told her, that morning.

She didn't want to ask them in; she had too much to accomplish. But neither of the McGruders appeared to want to come in. Mrs. McGruder said, "How we miss Mr. Joshua. It was a lovely service, Lucy. Ah, and how we miss your grandmother. Such a gracious lady, she was, so interested in everything, and always seeing to her charities, always on the go, always reading and studying. A very sharp lady, she was. Isn't that right, Mr. McGruder?"

Mr. McGruder nodded, walked over to pick up a stray yellow oak leaf on the flagstone sidewalk.

Lucy said, "Do you remember my grandfather, Mrs. McGruder?"

"Well, that is a question for Mr. McGruder. He and Mr. Milton were great friends, weren't you, Mr. McGruder?"

"That we were," Mr. McGruder said, straightening, still holding that lone oak leaf in his hand. "A fine man; missed him sorely when he left. One day to the next, he was gone. I never could understand that." He shook his head. His gray hair didn't move, and Lucy realized he'd pomaded it down flat to his scalp.

"Did he seem unhappy before he left?"

"Mr. Milton? Oh, goodness, no," said Mrs. McGruder.

"Aye, he did," Mr. McGruder said right over her. "Maybe not exactly unhappy, but I remember he was all jumpy and distracted, I guess the word is, but when I asked him, I remember he wouldn't tell me what bothered him. And then he was gone, just like that." He snapped his fingers, then shook his head sadly. "So much trouble, so much death; it's enough to make a man wonder how much more time he's got left."

That was a cheery observation, Lucy thought, thanking the McGruders again and sending them on their way.

Not five minutes later, Lucy was zipping up her ancient jeans, then pulled a dark blue FBI sweatshirt over her turtleneck sweater and slipped sneakers over her thick socks. Out of habit she clipped her SIG to her jeans. She was hurrying because she didn't want to be searching the attic after dark — it was that simple. She didn't know why, but there was something about attics and basements after dark, when everything was quiet, that gave her the willies.

She needed to get a move on. The narrow door at the end of the corridor on the second floor had always been locked when she was a child, the attic out-of-bounds to her, and it still sported a Yale lock. She'd been in the attic only once, to see if she wanted any discarded furniture for her condo — three years ago, right after her grandmother had died. She pulled out her SIG and smacked the butt to the lock, once, twice, and it opened. She climbed the steps into the immense, shadowy attic. It seemed to Lucy that with every step she took, the air got colder and clammier. There was no heat up here, but why should it feel clammy? There'd been no rain for a while. She noticed the bare attic beams weren't insulated. It had to be roasting hot in the summer up here, and now in the late fall, it was as cold as the outside air.

She flipped the switch, and the long shadows of the huge open area gave way to a burst of light, not from a naked one-hundred-watt bulb hanging from the ceiling but from a bank of fluorescent lights. She immediately felt better, and wasn't that stupid and childish of her? *Stop it, get a grip. It's a ridiculous attic, and Ted Bundy doesn't live here.*

Lucy looked around and lost every drop of optimism she'd had about how easy looking through the attic might be. She'd forgotten how immense it was, overflowing with old furniture, a zillion taped boxes, and ancient luggage. She wondered if some of the stuff dated back even before her grandparents had bought the house fifty years ago. Well, it didn't matter. She'd have to dig in.

Yeah, but dig in to find what, exactly?

She didn't have a clue. Still, Lucy hoped

to her sneakered feet that when she found it, she'd know instantly.

Lucky her — all the boxes were beautifully labeled as everything from kitchenwares to master-bedroom linens to books.

She found a box labeled LUCY — TEENAGER and dug into it, unable to help herself. She'd pulled out her sophomore yearbook when her cell rang. "Yes?"

"Lucy, my angel, it's Uncle Alan. I'm downstairs, sitting on your doorbell, but you don't answer. Where are you, sweetheart?"

"I'm up in the attic, Uncle Alan. I'll be right down. Is Aunt Jennifer with you? Court and Miranda?"

"Nope, only me. Your Aunt Jennifer sends her love. Court and Miranda — well, it seems the less I know about what they're doing, the better. Your Aunt Jennifer, ah, hopes you're all right."

All right? How could she be all right? "I'll be right down, Uncle Alan."

Alan Silverman, her grandmother's youngest brother, was actually her great-uncle. He'd been in her life from her earliest memories. He was in his seventies now, having retired hurriedly after the bankers screwed the world, and she wondered cynically how many shaky derivatives and fancy bond packages he himself had conjured up.

He'd married late, produced two children, Court and Miranda, who were, actually, her first cousins once removed, many years older than Lucy. Neither of them had ever married, and that seemed a bit odd to Lucy, both of them, well into their thirties and still out dating. Court was a gym rat and liked to think of himself as a stud, and maybe that explained it — he was too focused on himself to consider letting another person in. He was a successful retailer, owner of three vitamin stores in the D.C. area — LIFE MAX Natural Supplements — that were doing very well.

As for Miranda, she was a wannabe hippie, something of a resurrected flower child but without the usual freshness or color. Her clothes were all long and too loose, too depressing, really, all browns and grays and blacks. She always wore her hair straight, parted in the middle, and Lucy wished she'd wash her hair a bit more often. She played the French horn quite beautifully, though as far as Lucy could tell, that was the only thing on which she expended much effort. Once, she remembered, Miranda invited her to a séance in her condo before she'd moved back to her parents' house some months before, after breaking it off with a guy her Aunt Jennifer had called The

Louse. Lucy had politely declined the invitation.

She opened the door and was immediately pulled into Uncle Alan's arms. He held her close and patted her back. "How are you, kiddo?"

She leaned back in his arms and smiled up at him. "I'm okay — well, as okay as can be expected. I miss Dad all the time, of course. But they've made me one of the leads on this whole deal with Ted Bundy's daughter; talk about a major-league distraction."

"But you're not in any danger from her, are you? I know, I saw you and Agent McKnight on TV at the news conference with your boss, Agent Savich. It's quite an accomplishment that they've made you such a big part of that, Lucy. If she was watching it, she knows who you are. You've got to promise me to be careful, sweetheart."

"That's a very easy promise to keep, Uncle Alan. Come in, come in."

She led him into the lovely big living room, then stopped in the middle of the room and sniffed. It smelled musty, she thought, like no one lived there. She'd hardly come into this room at all since she'd moved in. But she would have to, since there were plenty of hidey-holes here where something could be stashed. She felt a chill through her FBI sweatshirt. "It's too cold in here; let's go to the kitchen. I've got some fresh coffee."

Now, her kitchen smelled lived in, like a comfortable friend, in spite of all the intimidating stainless-steel gadgets, and she smiled as she bustled around to get milk and Splenda, both musts for Uncle Alan's wuss coffee.

She said over her shoulder as she reached into a cabinet, "How is Aunt Jennifer?"

"Sad, a bit depressed, as I am, as both Court and Miranda are. She loved your father as much as I did. We were all together for so very long." He fell silent, staring at nothing in particular on the opposite wall. "Josh was too young, Lucy, too young."

She felt tears sting her eyes and quickly handed him a cup of coffee. Thankfully, his tears receded as he went about his ritual of adding milk and two Splendas.

He took a sip, sat back, and smiled at her. "When I think back — do you know I met Jennifer when I was nearly thirty-five years old?" His eyes twinkled. "Jennifer admits only that she was much younger than I. And then we had Court and Miranda. We wanted more children, but it wasn't to be." He took another drink of coffee. "Life," he said. "It's so damned uncertain, you know?"

She nodded. Oh, yes, she knew, knew too well. And so did Mr. McGruder.

"Why did you move back in here, Lucy?"

Because of what my father yelled out right before he died. But she didn't say that; she couldn't; it wasn't fair to anyone if there was no proof, no reason for it. She said, "I always loved this house. I didn't want to see it go to strangers. At least not yet."

"Talk about rattling around. Your Aunt Jennifer doesn't think it's healthy for you, Lucy. She says too many ghosts live in the corners."

"Ghosts?" She smiled. "I haven't bumped shoulders with a single ghost yet. Listen, I'm fine. Do you know my old bedroom still looks like a teenage girl just walked out of it? Grandmother didn't change a thing, not that she'd need to, since there are — what? Ten bedrooms in this place?

"Everything's okay, Uncle Alan. Tell Aunt Jennifer not to worry. If a ghost turns up, why, then we'll have a nice chat and I'll offer it coffee with lots of Splenda. As for Bundy's daughter, I don't even live here officially, so she can't know my address, and don't forget, I'm always armed and dangerous."

"Even Court says he's impressed with

what you can do in the gym. He still spends much of his time there, you know."

Lucy thought again about her dashing, beautifully dressed cousin once removed, and that smirk he always wore. From their youngest years, Court had known he was hot. He'd hated his sister, Miranda, enough to make her hate him as much as she loved him. Lucy once saw Miranda haul off and punch him in the nose. He'd been so shocked, he hadn't retaliated. Lucy laughed. It felt good. She hadn't laughed since Coop had come to her hotel room in San Francisco. No, she'd also laughed when he'd patted her hand as they left Lansford's suite at the Willard early that afternoon, and Coop had remarked to no one in particular that anyone who told his lawyer to shut up without even sparing him a glance couldn't be all bad, and he'd given Lucy a blazing smile.

Uncle Alan drank more coffee, though it had to be lukewarm by now, with all the milk he'd added, and then drummed his fingertips on the table. There was something on his mind, Lucy realized, and he didn't know how to bring it up. So she patted his hand just as Coop had patted hers, and said, "Spill it, Uncle Alan. I can take it. What do you want to say?"

He took another sip of his coffee, carefully and studiously returned the mug to the middle of a napkin, then finally looked at her. "Your Aunt Jennifer and I want you to come stay with us for a while, Lucy. We're worried."

Worried? Why, for heaven's sake? She was shaking her head as she said, "I really appreciate your offer, but I need to stay here." She realized she might have sounded a bit cool, and added, "I can't, Uncle Alan. I've got so much on my plate right now, and I've got so much to do here —" She broke off, wondering how in the world she could be an FBI agent when things she wanted to keep buried insisted on popping right out of her mouth.

"Of course you've got lots to do. This is a very big house, too big for one single girl."

She ignored that. "I've got help. Mrs. McGruder cooked for me and stocked the whole kitchen, and Mr. McGruder takes care of the yard, of course. They were here a while ago. They'll continue coming. Everything will be fine."

"She's a lousy cook."

"Maybe not as good a cook as Aunt Jennifer, but I don't mind cooking for myself. I've done it for years now. Don't worry, Uncle Alan, everything's okay, I promise.

Thank you both for inviting me. But I'll be fine." And Lucy rose. There wasn't much daylight left. She had no intention of spending a single minute in the attic after dark, and she had to get back to it.

He didn't want to leave, she could see it on his face, a face that reminded her of his older sister, her grandmother, Helen. He was a lot younger than her grandmother — she could never remember how many years exactly. They hadn't been very warm toward each other much, she remembered, but Uncle Alan had loved his nephew — her father, Josh — very much. After her mother's death, when Lucy and her father had moved in, he used to visit them in the evenings several times a week. She stood there over him, smiling.

He rose slowly to his feet. He was taller than her father had been, and very proud of how fit he was. He worked hard on it with a program Court had designed for him. As far as she knew, Uncle Alan had only to deal with high cholesterol, and a bit of arthritis, nothing else — amazing, really, for someone in their seventies. Actually, she realized, he was on the thin side, even for him. Grief? She understood that; she'd dropped five pounds herself.

"Thanks for coming to see me, Uncle

Alan," she said, and walked with him to the front door. "Do give my love to Aunt Jennifer and to Court and Miranda. How is Miranda, by the way?"

He harrumphed. "The girl has taken to playing her French horn in her room at all hours. Drives me nuts. When she's not playing that blasted instrument, she's still hanging out at coffeehouses, probably meeting another loser like that last one who sent her running back home again."

Lucy had to laugh. "Ah, Uncle Alan, I meant to ask you: did you know Grandmother did a lot of reading about ESP, mystics, psychics, time travels, strange things like that?"

He stilled, never took his eyes from her face. Slowly, he nodded. "Yes, there was a time years ago when Helen was obsessed with odd things. The odder the better. She bought into all of it. What makes you ask, Lucy?"

"I was reading through some of the files in her desk. There's lots and lots about all of it. She never mentioned it to me, so I was surprised. I wondered if she talked with you about it."

"I didn't have much interest," he said. "Why should I? I was in the most mundane of fields, Lucy, banking, like your father.

That's as far away from magic as it gets. What do you think about it?"

Lucy shrugged. "Everyone's into something, I suppose. I have a friend who is perfectly nice but is up to his ears in astrology, won't begin his day unless he knows if Mercury is in retrograde, or whatever."

"She was your grandmother, not a friend. I'm not surprised she never spoke to you about any of the ESP stuff. Your father would not have approved." He lightly laid his hand on her shoulder. "Lucy, does this have anything to do with why you're living here in your grandmother's house? I mean, you have your own condo; you also have your father's house. Why this huge house?"

Did he have any idea? No, he couldn't.

She channeled herself back into a calm, reasoned FBI agent, who could always avoid being pinned down. "Why would you ask that, Uncle Alan?"

"You seem, well, preoccupied, I guess, like you'd really like to see me out of your hair."

"No, never that. Don't forget Kirsten Bolger. She's alive and well, and very likely regrouping as we speak. I've just got a lot on my mind."

"I wonder what your father would have thought about your moving in here."

"Dad knew I loved this house. It's why he

didn't sell after Grandmother died." *Now, that's a big whopping lie.* The reason he hadn't sold the house was because he was saving it for her; he probably believed it would be worth three fortunes in another ten years or so.

"It surprised me when he didn't sell it," Uncle Alan said. "You said you were looking through your grandmother's files? Have you found anything interesting?"

She shrugged, shook her head. "Perhaps in the future, when I've got some extra time, I'll go through her papers more thoroughly. Like I said, I read through some of her files because they were a surprise, but to be honest here, Uncle Alan, I'm really not all that interested in speaking to dead people or aliens right now. Do you know of something that's particularly interesting I should look at?"

"Well, I'm thinking lately that knowing more about those vampires on TV might put a spark in my marriage. What do you think?"

Lucy was smiling after she closed the front door until she walked back up the stairs to the attic. She'd give it maybe twenty more minutes of searching before she headed back down into the light.

CHAPTER 24

Lucy eyed the stacks of luggage in the far corner. Suitcases of all sizes and more than a dozen carry-ons, most of them older, without wheels, were all piled on top of one another in the front, the oversized luggage and duffel bags behind. Against the wall were a half dozen old-fashioned steamer trunks, all quite large, with an Art Deco feel of the twenties and thirties, looking like aging sentinels guarding all the assorted smaller pieces piled in front of them. She wasn't all that hopeful about finding anything that would shed light on her grandfather's death, but it sure beat going through boxes labeled OLD SILVERWARE, and besides, people always left stuff in suitcases. There was only one way to find out.

She lifted the first carry-on off the top of the pile, unzipped it, and found one stray safety pin, nothing else. The second carry-on was black, part of a set of luggage. She found an ancient toothbrush in a side pocket, and an old quarter. She flipped the quarter in the air and stuck it in her jeans pocket. She opened a dozen more of the small pieces and found nothing more than a dried-up bottle of red nail polish, an ancient hairnet that looked like a decaying spider-web, some more change, and two old Sidney Sheldon novels from the seventies. She still had hope when she moved to the larger luggage, the great bulk of it black. The first of the larger suitcases held nothing more than a single pair of women's cotton panties, a man's black sock, and a stick of old deodorant. Her hope was nearly gone when she reached the third suitcase from the bottom of the pile and nearly dropped it, it was so heavy. Her heart began to pound. She unzipped it, threw back the top, and stared down at neatly folded men's clothes — pants, shirts, suits, underwear, shoes, hand-kerchiefs, socks, belts. She picked up the handkerchief on top. It wasn't mono-grammed. Lucy looked over at the long clothes pole at the opposite end of the attic crammed with clothing in plastic bags. Why not hang these clothes as well? Why fold them in a suitcase? She'd seen a good half dozen boxes labeled MEN'S CLOTHES. Why were these clothes folded in a suitcase?

194

She opened the large suitcases that were left. More men's clothes, mostly vested suits and dress shirts but also a beautiful Burberry coat, gloves, several men's hats, three pairs of dress shoes. They were well made but hardly up-to-date — like clothes from an old movie set, in fact. She remembered her grandfather wearing clothes like this when she was a young child. Had his clothes been hidden away in these suitcases to make it appear he'd taken them with him?

She kept looking. The half dozen duffel bags were mostly empty, one holding ancient snorkel equipment, another holding a box of condoms, unopened, and that was interesting.

She'd finally worked her way back to the steamer trunks. She could hardly stop now — steamer trunks had lots of compartments, lots of little zippered pockets that could hide — what? She wished she had a clue. She'd probably find more safety pins and loose change. Best to begin with the largest trunk against the wall.

She studied the steamer trunk, a huge light brown leather affair with black leather bands, banged up but still as solid-looking as the day it was rolled aboard its first luxury liner. It was covered with travel stickers from how many years ago? Maybe ninety? The largest was an Art Deco drawing of three huge passenger ships steaming toward you. There was a globe showing the western hemisphere, the proportions way off, for effect, and decals showing a dozen faraway destinations, no doubt status symbols in their day. She lightly laid her hand on a sticker that had PARIS printed on it and let herself be drawn back for a moment. She could easily picture rich Americans who traveled from New York to London or Paris or Cairo on opulent ships before the war, uniformed porters hefting their trunks onto big wheeled trolleys. They evoked an image of full moons shimmering on the bare shoulders of women in satin gowns, of men with pencil mustaches, of attar-of-rose perfume and magnificent jewels. She slowly worked the largest steamer trunk away from the wall. It was very heavy. She managed to tilt a corner of it away from the wall, and used her legs to push it farther askew, enough to open the lid. It smelled musty, old. She unclicked the four sets of latches, but the top wouldn't open. She dragged the trunk out onto the open floor. Had someone not bothered to unpack, or forgotten to, just had the trunk dragged up here?

She saw a padlock tucked discreetly beneath a flap of leather at the very center of the trunk. Locked. She shook the padlock, but it was solid, didn't come free. Lucy looked at it more closely. The padlock certainly didn't date from the twenties; it was sturdy and pretty modern-looking. No way would she get that sucker open without the key.

She was suddenly aware that the fluorescent overheads were all the light there was, the windows completely dark. Full-on night had fallen, and she hadn't noticed. She'd been up here much longer than she'd intended, her allotted twenty minutes long past. As she stared at the dark windows, she was suddenly frightened. But of what exactly? She didn't understand it, but she was remembering something, something muffled and confused in her mind.

She saw herself, small, very small, crouched beside an ancient bureau, and there were voices. She couldn't see who was speaking, but somehow she knew who the voices were — *she knew* — and her heart was pounding loud and her mouth felt dry and she was afraid, just as she was now.

Lucy shook her head. What was happening? Her heart was pounding, and that was stupid, she told herself over and over, but it didn't stop her heart from galloping and her ears from listening to every creak and groan. She felt as if she were in a strange hollow of time where the past had superimposed itself over the present and brought her fear with it. She shook her head again. *It's simply dark, stupid. You are being ridiculous, remembering something out of context from when you were a really little girl. Get hold of yourself.*

She kicked the steamer trunk, which did precisely nothing at all, and that pissed her off because she was afraid simply because it was dark outside, and yes, there were these odd memories, no, not memories, something inexplicable that her brain had suddenly dredged up to scare the crap out of her. She pulled her SIG from the clip on her jeans, and just as she'd opened the lock on the attic door, she struck the padlock, once, twice. The third time, she really whacked it. The padlock flew apart.

She heard something, a small scratching sound, and turned into Lot's wife. Silence. She'd simply heard the house settle, maybe a mouse in the wall.

Stop being a wuss; open the blasted trunk. There aren't any bogeymen to leap out and cut off your head. Besides, you'd shoot them. You're frightened of a memory, but that was then, and everything here is now.

She looked away from the dark windows

and the shadowed corners of the attic, drew a deep breath, and pushed the steamer trunk's lid back. It hit with a sharp clunk against the trunk behind it.

An old musty smell welled out to hit her in the face. It wasn't overwhelming, but it was thick enough with a smell she recognized, something dead, and she sneezed as she lurched back. She sneezed again, wiped her nose, and leaned forward over the trunk, her hand over her nose. A thick white towel was spread over the top, and on top of the towel were at least a dozen room deodorizers, solid, giving off nothing now. She felt her heart began to hammer hard again.

Stop it; get it together. You're an investigator — investigate. But why the deodorizers?

She shoved the hard deodorant cakes away and lifted the edge of the white towel. Something caught on it, then broke free with a loud crack. She stared down at a hand, but there wasn't any flesh on it. It was a skeleton's hand, still attached, except the one finger that had snapped off when the towel caught it. She scuttled madly back on her hands, and barely managed to swallow the scream poised to burst from her throat. She sucked in her breath, swallowed a couple of times, trying to control her sudden terror.

You're FBI; you've seen bodies. Stop it.

She reached down, ripped the towel away, and looked at the skeleton that filled up the trunk. She couldn't recognize him, not anymore —

Lucy got to her feet, picked up her SIG, which was ridiculous, and forced herself to stand over the open trunk. She stared down at the skeleton of a man dressed in casual clothes nearly rotted through. She looked at the skull, at the empty eyeball sockets, at the rictus of shock on the skeleton's wide-open mouth.

The skeleton didn't date back to the twenties.

The skeleton dated back exactly twenty-two years.

Lucy backed away from the trunk as she pulled her cell from her shirt pocket and punched in Savich's number.

One ring, two, then, "Savich."

"Dillon, it's me, Lucy. I found a skeleton in a steamer trunk."

There was a beat of silence, then, "Where?"

"In my grandmother's attic."

"You okay?"

"No, but I'm able to function."

"Good. I want you to go downstairs immediately. I'm going to call a homicide detective I know in the Chevy Chase Police Department. I'll meet him and his people there at your grandmother's house. Go slug down a shot of brandy, Lucy. Everything will be all right."

"Well, actually, it won't be all right, Dillon. You see, I know it's my grandfather. Since I know his wife murdered him, we don't really need the police, do we?"

She could feel his surprise, though he tried not to let it sound in his voice. He calmly repeated, "Go downstairs. I'll see you in fifteen minutes."

Without thought, Lucy called Coop, said only, "Coop, please come right now to my grandmother's house. I need you."

"I'm close. I'll be there in a minute, Lucy."

Lucy didn't look back at the trunk; she simply hightailed it down the attic steps, flipped off the lights, closed the door, and stood there a moment in the carpeted corridor, still holding the knob, waiting for her heart to begin to slow. Of course it was her grandfather. Of course he hadn't gone walkabout as everyone had claimed. Nope, he'd been murdered by his own wife, just as her father had shouted before he'd died, his body laid to rest in a steamer trunk and covered with a white towel and cake deodorizers to mask the smell. Of course they'd locked the attic door. Of course they'd made the attic off limits to her. Of course.

A white towel — that was obscene. Her grandmother and her father hadn't buried him, they'd carried him up here to the attic. Is that why she'd been so afraid? Had some part of her known her grandfather was in one of those steamer trunks?

She leaned against the corridor wall and forced herself to breathe slowly, to shut the horror out, until her heartbeat slowed. She would deal with this; she really had no choice.

There were so many ways to identify the body, it wouldn't be hard. The suitcases filled with men's clothes would help. She'd known way down deep where fear and knowledge mingled that the clothes had to be her grandfather's, but the logical grounded part of her brain hadn't wanted to accept it yet, not until she'd opened the steamer trunk.

Step away from it. And so she did. She watched herself get her breathing to slow, to banish the fright and panic back up to the attic and the steamer trunk, her grandfather's body inside. It took a long time, but when her fear was gone, she was left with pain, and with anger. *Her grandfather.* He'd been in that steamer trunk for all the years she'd lived here, moldering, his flesh rotting away, leaving only that skeleton. There'd never been any justice for him, and no matter her anger now, there wouldn't ever be any, because her grandmother was dead. Her father had been part of it, and he was dead, too, and he'd kept the secret until the very end.

She was still breathing hard when she reached the front door. She couldn't stay inside the house any longer. No brandy for her; the mere thought of it made her want to throw up.

She saw Coop's Gloria pull into the driveway on screeching tires.

CHAPTER 25

Coop slammed out of Gloria and ran to her. He took one look at her white face and without hesitation pulled her against him. "It will be all right. I spoke to Savich, and he told me you'd found your grandfather's skeleton, that you'd said your grandmother had murdered him. He and Detective Horne will be here soon. I'm so sorry, Lucy, so very sorry." They stood beneath the porch light, silent, Coop simply holding her. She didn't cry. All her tears were frozen deep inside her.

He said against her hair, "You don't have to tell me what happened — we can wait until everyone arrives. Breathe deeply; that's right. Get yourself together. I'm here now, and we'll deal with this. Are you cold?"

She shook her head against his neck. "My dad helped her, Coop. After she murdered her husband, they carried him up to the attic and put him in a steamer trunk. My dad lived in this house twelve years, knowing his father was lying with a white towel spread over him in a trunk in the attic. And they spread lots of cake deodorizers on top to keep the smell down. How could he bear it? Do you know they locked the attic? I was never allowed to go up there. Come to think of it, I can't ever remember wanting to."

"I know, Lucy, I know. We'll get this all figured out. You'll see. Do you want to go inside? You're freezing."

"No, no, please, I don't want to, not yet, not until I have to."

Coop shrugged out of his shearling coat and wrapped it around her.

She hugged the big coat close. She was freezing. "I keep thinking that knowing all those years his own father was in the attic, murdered by his own mother — it must have driven my dad mad. But he protected her, kept quiet until the end. Do you think keeping this ghastly secret all these years, knowing what he'd done, feeling the guilt, the stress, the need to protect his mother — do you think it made him die too soon?" She didn't wait for him to say anything, which was good, since he had no idea what to say. "But why did he keep the body there after my grandmother died? Why didn't he move it, give his own father his own private burial?"

"We'll figure it all out, Lucy. Now, here's a cavalcade of cars coming, Savich's Porsche leading them in. Can you deal with this now?"

She raised her face. "Of course."

Detective Horne was new to the job, but he knew what to do. He was pleased Special Agent Savich didn't grind him under — indeed, deferred to him. He introduced himself to Lucy Carlyle and Cooper Mc-Knight. He asked a female officer to stay with Lucy while the rest of them trooped up to the attic. When Lucy shook her head and got to her feet, Detective Horne pointed a cop finger at her. "Stay."

Ten minutes later, Coop walked back into the library to see Lucy standing by a big burgundy leather easy chair, her hands clenched at her sides, the female officer in the kitchen, making coffee. She still had his shearling coat wrapped around her. He walked to her, took her hands. "We've seen everything. It will be all right, Lucy. We'll figure all this out."

"What's to figure?"

"Sorry, dumb question. Do you want me to call your aunt and uncle? Anyone else?"

She thought of Uncle Alan, Aunt Jennifer,

Court, and Miranda. She thought of her closest friends, all of them hanging back for the past week because she'd asked them to. No, she couldn't call them; they'd been overburdened already, what with seeing her through her father's funeral. She shook her head. "No, I'll call my uncle in the morning. You want some coffee, Coop?" *Uncle Alan, did you know what happened?*

He shook his head. "Lucy? Ah, crap, come here," and again he pulled her and his shearling coat against him.

He saw tears snake down her cheeks. She wasn't making a sound. He flicked them away with his fingers. "I'm very sorry, Lucy. Listen, did you find or remove any ID from the body to prove it was your grandfather?"

"No."

He said against her hair, "Savich has asked the autopsy be performed at Quantico. Detective Horne called his lieutenant, and she agreed but said they'd be sending along one of their medical examiners. The attic is a crime scene, of course, and the forensic team will be up there a good couple of days. There was dried blood on his shirt, over his chest, so we're probably talking a gun or a knife. That's all I can tell you right now. We won't know any more until the autopsy."

"It was a knife. Maybe it's still in one of

those steamer trunks I didn't open."

How could she be so sure it was a knife? Coop would get to that in a minute. She was speaking calmly, logically, and that was a relief.

"You know, Coop, there's no reason to expend all this manpower. It's my grandfather. I know his wife murdered him. It's over, case solved and closed."

He said, "I know, but there's a protocol that has to be followed, you know that. And you'll explain everything to us in a little while. It would be good to find the knife. I saw those suitcases full of men's clothing. We might find ID there."

Lucy felt herself finally getting back in control. "Coop, I want to go back outside now."

They walked side by side out of the house to stand on the top porch steps, watching two techs bring out a green body bag for her grandfather's remains. She said, "I can give them a swab from my cheek to check DNA, if they need it."

"They will," Coop said.

It was a dark night, only a sliver of moon and a long blaze of stars shining through the low-lying clouds. They heard techs talking by the van, heard voices from inside the house.

Lucy said, "Maybe it was too painful for Dad to think about touching his father's body again, stealing away with it. I can understand that, sure I can. Can you imagine, Coop, trying desperately to continue your routine, treating your little daughter — namely, me — calmly and naturally? And his own mother, being civil to her, not wanting to kill her for what she'd done. It always seemed to me he loved her, treated her courteously. But how could he? Did he ever find out why she killed him?"

He hugged her and his shearling coat, and realized he was getting a bit cold himself.

Savich came up, lightly placed his hand on her shoulder. "You're coming home with me, Lucy."

She turned to smile at her boss. "No, I want to stay here. I'll be fine; don't worry about me. I'll admit I was pretty freaked out —"

Detective Horne said from behind her, "I know, I know, you're FBI, you're tough, and you're nearly back to chewing nails again, right?"

Lucy was wrung out, but she managed a small smile. "Thank you for letting me stay in the loop, Detective."

Detective Horne hadn't intended she be anywhere near the loop, but since she was

209

in Savich's unit, and his lieutenant really admired Savich, he said easily, "Not a problem."

Coop said to her, "This is why you moved back here after your father's funeral, isn't it, Lucy? And why you were so mysterious about it? You wanted to find your grandfather?"

"No, it never occurred to me I'd find him. I was looking for something, anything, that would tell me why my grandmother murdered him in the first place." She shook her head. "I can't believe she stuffed him in a trunk in the attic."

Detective Horne blinked at that. "Your grandmother?"

"Yes, my grandmother."

"But how do you know your grandmother murdered her husband?"

Lucy pulled away from Coop to stand facing the three men, clutching that big, soft coat to her like it was her security blanket. "I'm not cold, but I'll bet Coop is. Let's go back inside."

When she was seated in a big green wing chair in the staid and formal living room, she drew in a deep breath. "My father had a heart attack. He was in and out of consciousness. Sometimes he recognized me, sometimes he simply looked at me and went under again.

"In the final moments before he died, he opened his eyes and yelled — it was terrifying because his voice was so frantic, panicked. He said very clearly, *'Mom, what did you do? Why did you stab Dad? Oh my God, he's not moving. There's so much blood. Why, Mom?'* She lowered her head. "I won't ever forget that for the rest of my life."

Coop wouldn't, either, he thought. What a load to carry — first for the father and now for the daughter. He studied her face. Smudges of dirt were stark against her pale cheeks. Hair was coming out of her French braid, tangling around her neck, but her hands were smoothed out and quiet on her lap. He knew she was calm again. He realized he admired her very much in that moment.

She looked at each of them in turn. "I knew I had to find out what happened."

Savich said, "So, this past week you've been looking for clues?"

"Yes. I'd already gone through my grandmother's study, all her desk drawers, some of her many books, but I didn't find anything, so I decided to try the attic. The door was locked — it always was, and now, of course, I know why — and it was easy to break open."

Savich said, "Lucy, what did your dad say when he told you to stay out of the attic?"

She looked blank. "Do you know, I don't remember. I just know I never wanted to disobey him and go up there." She paused for a moment, then said, "It was neat and organized, and as you saw, the boxes are all clearly marked; the old discarded clothes hung in plastic bags on wooden rods. The luggage was in neat stacks, too, at least before I went to work on it."

Detective Horne pulled out a small black book. "Let's back up a minute. You had no idea your grandfather was murdered until just before your father died? When was that?"

"My father died a little more than a week ago, Detective, and no, I didn't have a clue."

"Had you missed your grandfather? What happened?"

"I was nearly six years old when I was told my grandfather had simply left his family without a word. That was twenty-two years ago. My father and I already lived here then; we'd moved in with my grandparents after my mom died."

Detective Horne studied her face, his pen poised over his notebook. "So your father saw your grandmother murder her husband?"

"Yes. If he didn't see the murder itself, he walked in moments after she'd done it."

Detective Horne had heard so many outrageous stories happily recounted by veteran cops over beers, but he'd never heard a story like this. He said, "He never said a word about it to you, ever?"

"No."

"Do you think your father ever told anyone? A really close friend, or a relative he trusted?"

"My grandmother's youngest brother, Uncle Alan, has never let on that anything like that happened, so I'd have to say no one knew, only my father and my grandmother. We can ask Uncle Alan. I have to tell him about all this now, anyway. I think it will be as much of a shock to him as to me, especially so soon after my dad died."

Detective Horne said, "We'll be speaking to him and his family. You said you moved in here to look for clues why this happened."

Lucy gave him a twisted smile. "As I told you, Detective, I hadn't found anything yet that would tell me why, but I will keep looking. Surely something will turn up that will give me some idea of why this happened." She paused, looked down at her hands, now tightly clasped in her lap. She raised her head and looked at Coop, her face leached of color. "She covered him with an expensive white towel and deodorant cakes and closed the trunk lid on him." She paused for a moment, then said, "Dillon, I think I remembered something when I was in the attic, when I was looking at the padlock on the trunk. I was small and I was scared, but I saw —"

Lucy lowered her head and cried.

She felt arms go around her, and turned to lean into them. She pressed her face against a warm, soft neck and breathed in a floral scent. It was Sherlock. How long had she been here?

Sherlock whispered against her hair, "It will be all right, Lucy. We'll all figure this out. You're not alone with this any longer."

CHAPTER 26

Georgetown
Monday morning

Lucy was eating Cheerios along with Sean, both of their bowls heaped high with cereal and sliced bananas. She was hungry, and that surprised her a bit. She'd also slept pretty well the night before in Sherlock and Savich's very nice guest bedroom just down the hall from Sean's room. She'd heard him talking in his sleep a couple of times during the night, since she'd left her door open, something about King Neffer not playing fair. She was very grateful to them for bringing her home with them last night.

Savich said, "We need to leave soon for Quantico, Lucy, to see Dr. Hicks."

"I called Coop, asked him to meet us at Quantico. I'd really like him there, too, Dillon. Oh, dear, I forgot to call Uncle Alan. I'll be ready in —" Her cell phone rang. "Excuse me. Oh, it's Uncle Alan. Hello. I was going to call you."

Savich listened as he helped Sean wash his hands, and so did Sherlock as she put clean dishes back into the cabinets. Neither missed the devastation in the rise and fall of Alan Silverman's voice. Lucy's face was white and set.

Several minutes later, Lucy clicked off her cell. She patted Sean's clean hand as she said, "Uncle Alan said Detective Horne came by earlier, told them what had happened. He is understandably shocked and disbelieving. I suppose I would be, too, if I hadn't — well, he and Aunt Jennifer are very worried about me, want me to stay with them. I told them no, I can't. Then Uncle Alan told me he didn't think we should have a memorial, that if we did, everything would come out and my grandmother's name would become infamous. He wants to bury grandfather's remains privately. I suppose I agree. What good would it do to give the tabloids this kind of sick story?"

CHAPTER 27

An hour later, Coop, Savich, and Lucy walked into Dr. Emanuel Hicks's office in the Jefferson Dormitory at Quantico.

Dr. Emanuel Hicks, one of the FBI's top psychiatrists, was skinny as a knife blade, a problem for him only because he was known for impersonating Elvis, and a skinny Elvis was hard to pull off. He took Lucy's hand, looked her in the eyes, and said, "Lucy, I know it took courage for you to agree to come to see me, to let me help you try to go back and remember what you were so frightened of in that attic. I agree with Savich that something might have triggered actual fears from your childhood, memories that have been buried deep in your mind. Now, you were five years old?"

"Almost six. Dr. Hicks, I've been thinking about it, and now I simply can't imagine forgetting anything that important. I'm thinking those feelings weren't real."

Dr. Hicks said easily, "People do find that hard to believe; they want to dismiss feelings that suddenly surface, but I've seen it. Lucy, even before you opened that lid, you must have known, deep down, that something terrible was in that trunk. Do you prefer to think you simply manufactured the little girl — namely, yourself — to help you deal with what you were feeling, to explain your own fears?"

Lucy leaned toward him, hope in her voice. "Doesn't that make sense?"

No, not at all. Dr. Hicks said, patting her hand, "That's what we're here to find out, all right? Are you sure you want to go back, Lucy?"

"No, I'd rather not be frightened like that again, but I know it may be the only way to find out what really happened. So, I'm ready when you are, Dr. Hicks. I've never been hypnotized before. What if I don't go under?"

Dr. Hicks said, "I think you'll go under like a dream, Lucy. You're very intuitive. Isn't that what you told me, Savich?" At Savich's nod, he continued. "That always makes it easier."

Savich said, "Perhaps more than intuitive."

"Oh, no, surely not," Lucy said.

Coop was standing very quietly by the single window. "I remember that time in Kansas City when you just sat back and said you'd bet your knickers the old guy next door was the killer we were looking for. You said it was by looking at him, something in his eyes. Of course, it turned out it was that old man. Yes, I'd say you're more than intuitive, Lucy."

Dr. Hicks said, "Would you like to tell us how you came to that conclusion, Lucy?"

"Let's not go there, Dr. Hicks," Lucy said. "It was a onetime deal, nothing more than that. You know as well as I do that Dillon is the psychic one in this room, a regular FBI legend. Now, I appreciate your all being nice to me and trying to get me calm, but I want to get on with it."

Dr. Hicks looked down at her. "Perhaps you'll be more ready to deal with it now. As to the other, perhaps you're indeed more like Savich than you imagine."

Savich said, "On the other hand, I've learned that when something's bothering you, Lucy, it's all right there, on your face, an open book. Right, Coop?"

"Yeah, when she tries to bluff at our poker games, everyone laughs at her."

Dr. Hicks only smiled as he pulled an old gold watch on a golden chain out of his vest pocket. "This is my granddad's watch, nothing more than that. There's nothing to this, really. The most important thing is for you to relax, Lucy. Take some deep breaths, try to empty out all the stress, all the painful questions, from your mind. All you have to do is follow the watch with your eyes and listen to my voice. That's right, deep breaths. Sit back, relax, and look at the watch, all right?"

Slowly, he swung the watch in front of her eyes while speaking to her quietly. In less than two minutes, Dr. Hicks nodded. "Savich, do you want to question her?"

Savich nodded, sat forward, and took Lucy's limp right hand between his. "Lucy, do you remember you and your dad moving in with your grandparents?"

It wasn't Lucy's voice that spoke; it was a very small child's — high, soft, whispery. "I remember my birthday party."

"How old are you?'

"I'm two."

"Tell me about your birthday party."

She frowned. "There's a clown with giant feet, and he's making animals out of balloons, but I don't like him; he's big and scary."

"Do you remember anything else about your birthday party?"

"I went to the bathroom to get away from the clown, and my daddy was in there, and he was crying. He cried a lot. I hated that clown. Grandmother made chocolate cake for me. I love chocolate cake. Daddy said my mama loved chocolate cake, too."

"That's good, Lucy. Now I want you to move forward in time. You're five years old, nearly six. Are you going to have a sixth birthday party?"

She frowned again, but it wasn't Lucy frowning, it was a little girl's face scrunching up, no longer a toddler. She looked utterly lost and alone.

Savich squeezed her hand. "It's all right, Lucy. What are you seeing?"

"I'm wondering why I can't have a birthday party, and Daddy said it's because grandfather's gone. Gone where, to the store? He shook his head over and over, and I saw Grandmother and Daddy were really upset. I remember Uncle Alan was sitting at the kitchen table with his head down. He was real quiet, sitting there, and he said he didn't understand why Milton could leave. Why? He never gave any sign he wasn't happy. And why hadn't he said anything? Why? And then he didn't say anything else. Aunt Jennifer kept patting me. Everyone looked like they wanted to cry; they were always talking in whispers. And when I looked at them, they smiled — you know, fake smiles."

"Did you ask them why they were smiling fake smiles?"

"Sort of. They told me it wasn't anything at all, and I knew that wasn't true. Grandfather didn't come back from the store."

"How long was your grandfather gone before your birthday?"

They watched her count off on her fingers. "Nearly a week, I think."

"Okay, I want you to go back, Lucy, to nearly a week. Are you there? In the house?"

She nodded, a jerky sort of birdlike movement, like a child's.

"What do you see?"

"I don't see anything, but I hear Daddy yelling. He sounds really scared and mad at the same time. I'm scared now, but I don't want him to see me because I'm not supposed to be there."

"Where are you supposed to be?"

"At Marjorie's house, next door, but something broke in a bathroom and there was water everywhere, and so I left. Marjorie's mom didn't know I left."

"Where were your daddy and your grandmother when you heard them yelling?"

"Upstairs somewhere."

"And you want to know what's the matter, right? What do you do?"

She was shaking her head frantically, back and forth.

Dr. Hicks said, "It's okay, Lucy. We're right here to protect you. Nothing can hurt you. Do you believe me?"

Finally she nodded and expelled a shaky little girl's breath. "I walk up the stairs and hide. I look down the hall and see my daddy going up the attic stairs."

Savich said, "Do you see your grandmother?"

"No. She's already up there."

"Is your daddy carrying anything?"

"I don't know. He's crying. I think he's crying about Mama again."

"Do you go up the stairs to the attic?"

"No. I listen to them making noises, moving around in the attic, but I'm afraid to go up there, afraid they'll see me."

"Do you know what they're doing in the attic?"

"I don't see them, but they're arguing, and Daddy's crying again and yelling, and I'm afraid to move."

"Could you make out what they're saying to each other?"

"Grandmother keeps screaming about how she's sorry, how he ruined everything."

Lucy fell utterly silent, and her head fell to the side. Savich thought she'd come out of it and fallen asleep, but Dr. Hicks stayed his hand when he would have patted her shoulder. He shook his head to continue.

Savich said again, "Is your daddy saying anything to your grandmother you can understand?"

"My daddy's voice is shaking. He's yelling, and Grandmother's crying."

"What does your grandmother say?"

" 'I didn't mean to, Joshua' — Grandmother always calls Daddy Joshua even though Uncle Alan and Aunt Jennifer call him Josh."

"Do you hear your grandmother say what she didn't mean to do?"

"She just kept crying and saying over and over, 'He ruined everything, Joshua. My ring! He threw it out, said no one would ever find it. I couldn't bear it, I couldn't.' "

"What happened next?"

"They went to Grandmother's room, so I didn't have a chance to sneak out. Then they came back and they were both carrying lots of clothes and shoes and stuff. They went back and forth, and when they were in the attic I ran down to the kitchen."

"Did they ever know you were there, Lucy?"

"No. I went up later and saw my dad, and he was standing by his bedroom door, and he was crying. He saw me and called to me, and I ran to him, and he hugged me."

"You never said anything to your dad? To your grandmother?"

"No. I knew they'd be mad. I didn't want to get swatted."

"Lucy, tell me about your grandmother."

She looked confused. Savich realized she was only a kid and the question was far too complicated. "Do you love your grandmother?"

She nodded, another quick, jerky movement. "She makes me peanut-butter cookies; they're my favorite. She lets me sit beside her while she's reading. She's always reading. But she always sits in the living room. I hate the living room; it's like a dead room, and you can't breathe."

"Do you love your grandfather, Lucy?"

Her face lit up. "Grandfather likes me to sit on his leg, and he bounces up and down and says he's my horse. He always smells like beef jerky. I really liked jerky until —"

"Until?"

"Until he went away to the store and never came back. He worked real hard, and so did Daddy. He made lots of money, my daddy said that. One day before he went away, he came home from work and he was mad. I remember he shouted at Grandma and he said bad words. Daddy took me away. He bought me an ice cream and told me to forget it and never say those words."

"Do you know where he worked, Lucy?"

She looked thoughtful, but she shook her head.

Savich moved away to stand beside Coop while they listened to Dr. Hicks bring Lucy back. "You did very well, Lucy. Now I'm going to snap my fingers, right in front of your nose, and you're going to wake up. You're going to feel relaxed and settled, and you're going to remember everything we spoke about, all right?"

"Yes, Dr. Hicks."

Dr. Hicks snapped his fingers. From one instant to the next, Lucy was back, and she looked calm. She said, "I've got answers now."

"Yes," Savich said, "most of them. No doubt about what happened anymore."

Coop watched her face change. She looked ineffably sad. Slowly, tears began to stream down her face. "Can you imagine," she whispered, choking, "my dad saw his mother kill his father, and then he protected her, helped her shove Grandfather into a stupid trunk with a white towel over him?

226

It's too horrible, what he lived through, and he never told a single person, kept it all deep inside him, until he couldn't any longer. I wonder if that's why he never married again, because he could never tell anyone what happened. It was so vivid in his mind, still. In the last moments of his life he was reliving that horrible event."

Lucy put her face in her hands and cried, not for herself but for her father.

Coop laid his hand on her shoulder until she quieted. He said matter-of-factly, "Maybe that's why you stayed with your grandmother; your father was taking care of both of you."

Lucy raised her face to his. "Do you know, now that I remember back, my dad never left me alone with my grandmother. I remember now that when she read with me sitting next to her, Dad was always nearby."

Savich said, "At last you know. Now you have to let it go."

Dr. Hicks patted her arm. "You will be all right, Lucy Carlyle. You're a survivor, and you see things and people clearly. Yes, you will be fine."

Lucy gave him a twisted smile. "Me, see people clearly? I don't think so, sir. I really don't think so."

Dr. Hicks lightly squeezed her hand. "You

will come to see I am right. Now, why don't you let Agent Savich and Agent McKnight buy you a pizza in the boardroom, let your mind settle a bit?"

"It's been a long time since I was in the academy." But as she spoke, the words died in her throat. "How can things be all right?"

"I forbid you to worry about it right now, Lucy. It's too much to take in. That's what these two gentlemen are for. Let them stew and fret. Not you, all right?"

Lucy nodded finally, but Coop knew she couldn't help but stew about it.

Lucy turned to Savich. "Dillon, do you think they've completed the autopsy?"

"Let's see." When Savich slipped his cell back into his pocket a few seconds later, he said, "Dr. Judd will call you himself when they're finished, Lucy."

"She — she really stabbed him. It's still so difficult to imagine. And they were fighting over a ring? How could a ring be so important?"

"We may never know that, Lucy," Savich said. "You know that."

She nodded.

Coop raised her to her feet. "Let's go have that pizza."

CHAPTER 28

Wall Street, New York City
Enrico's Bar
Monday night
" 'It's a long, long way to Tipperary, but my heart's right there.' "

"I really like that song." Genevieve Connelly toasted Thomas, the young man she'd just met. He grinned at her; then, hearing some applause, he turned on his bar stool and bowed from the waist.

Genny took another sip of her mojito. "I don't even know where Tipperary is." She sounded too sharp, simply too sober, and took another drink. She wanted to get drunk, had to get drunk, even though it was Monday night, and a work night. She saw herself hugging the toilet bowl, but it didn't matter. She was too angry, too depressed, to worry about it. She took another drink and smiled at Thomas when he told the bartender, Big Ed, to serve her up another mojito. Before long, she knew Thomas was from Montreal, worked sixty hours a week as a waiter at the Fifth Wheel in the East 80s, and wrote poetry at night, a twenty-first-century e. e. cummings in the making, he told her, and he seemed perfectly serious.

She found herself telling him she'd very nearly been engaged, but that wasn't going to happen now, because Lenny was a jerk with an addiction she hadn't even known about. Yeah, a jerk who was in Atlantic City gambling right now.

Genny wanted to work up a mad, but the mojitos were making her mellow instead. "I trucked over to Morrie's after work to meet Lenny for dinner, only he never showed. I finally called his mother, and do you know what she said?" And Genny, an accomplished mimic, recited in a soft, sad voice, with a hint of a whine, 'Since he stole four hundred dollars out of my purse, dear, I'll bet he's in Atlantic City again. I guess he hasn't told you about his little problem?'

"His little problem? I mean, which one? He was a thief and a gambler, right? Well, I couldn't take it in, and so I hung up. I don't think she ever liked me much, and now it doesn't matter, does it? She calls it a little problem?"

"My brother gambles," Thomas said. "Our parents finally kicked him out."

"He never told me," Genny said, and stared into the mirror behind the bar, watching herself drink the rest of her third mojito. "Time to powder my nose, Thomas," she said, and headed off to the women's room.

Five minutes later, when she slid back onto her stool, her lipstick new and shiny, her hair freshly combed, Thomas said, "Okay, Genny, you know I'm a poet who's wasting his youth flinging high-priced spaghetti to yuppies on the Upper East Side. What do you do?"

She was staring at herself again in the mirror, but this time she saw only a distorted outline of her face. She raised her fingers to touch her cheek, to make sure it was really there. "What I do is financial analysis," she said. "I review companies' sales trends and projections, stuff so boring I bet I could out-scuttle a gerbil on a treadmill." She looked around. "I don't see anybody I know tonight, though Enrico's is a favorite booze trough for the financial crowd I'm in." He handed her another drink, and she took a gulp, hiccupped, and giggled. "Would you look at me — all pissy-faced, and I don't give a crap. The jerk — he wanted to gamble so much he totally forgot me."

Thomas eyed her, then broke into song again. "Do you know this one? 'From the halls of Montezuma to the shores of Tripoli —' "

Everyone joined in with him this time; even Big Ed sang along with them while he sparkled up a glass.

"I met Mr. Montezuma once, but I did lose ten pounds doing it." She didn't realize Thomas was more or less holding her up on her bar stool. He laughed. "You know, sweetie, it's late, and I'm thinking it's time for you to meet your date with destiny."

"What destiny?"

"Popping down a half dozen aspirin kind of destiny, but don't worry, I'll see you get home and leave you alone to enjoy your hangover all by yourself."

"With my luck, it's going to be bad." She realized she was slurring her words a bit. She sloshed around the mojito left in the glass, thought about a stranger walking her home — he seemed like a real sweetheart, but still, she'd met him only tonight. Genny pulled together arguments as clearly as she could, both pros and cons, and finally nodded. "Yeah, I guess I'd better hang it up." She gave him a sloppy hug. "Thanks for making me feel better, Thomas."

He patted her shoulder. "Anytime, babe."

There was applause for Thomas on their way out the door. He grinned, gave a little wave, and steered her outside. Once on the sidewalk, a cold wind whipped against her face and made her eyes tear up. That's all she needed was to cry, only these tears were just from the biting wind, thank heaven. She looked around for a taxi, slurred a couple of curses because there was nary a soul to be seen; everything was dead and empty and cold. Well, that was Wall Street at night, after all the hotshots left for the Upper East Side, or Connecticut, or the Hudson Valley, after the chicks flew the work coop. And Lenny was in Atlantic City, kissing dice and rolling them.

The jerk.

She stuck her hand through Thomas's arm and squeezed. He was a skinny dude, didn't have much muscle. "I've got a condo on Pine Street, only three blocks over."

A woman came dashing out of Enrico's, her long blond hair blowing wildly around her head, waving her hands at them. "Wait up!"

The blonde grabbed Genny's arm and tried to jerk her away from Thomas. "Are you all right?"

"Me? All right? Of course I'm all right;

I'm with Thomas. What do you want?"

"You won't be all right very soon now. I saw this creep slip something in your drink when you went to the restroom. I'll bet it's that rape drug, Rohypnol."

"What's Rohypnol?"

"You know, roofies, that date-rape drug. You've heard of roofies, haven't you?" The woman didn't take her eyes off Thomas.

"He gave me a roofie?"

"Yep, slipped it right into your mojito. I'll bet you're feeling pretty woozy about now, right?"

More betrayal. She couldn't take it. Genny erupted, whirled on Thomas, shoved him hard in the chest with the heels of her palms. He wheeled his arms to keep his balance. "You jerk!"

"Wait a minute!"

She slammed her foot in his stomach, and he fell onto his side and rolled off the curb to land on his back, trying to suck in air.

Genny stared down at her supposed friend and wanted to cry. She'd believed him — so cute, a really nice guy, and his singing voice was incredible. He'd listened, actually listened. "I'm sorry you did that, Thomas."

"I didn't!" he yelled at the blonde. "Who are you? Why are you doing this?"

"I'm Monica, you lowlife, and I saw you

do it! You're Genny, right? When I saw you come outside with him, I couldn't stand by, knowing he was going to do something bad to you."

Thomas was holding his stomach. "Genny, I swear I didn't put anything in your drink. I didn't. Why would I?"

Monica dove her hand into a huge black purse and pulled out her cell phone. "You lying pig. I'm going to get the cops here to take your sorry butt to jail."

Genny grabbed Monica's hand but missed because she was so drunk. Or was it the roofie? "No, don't call the cops, I only want to get out of here."

She looked at Thomas, on his knees now. "You did drug me," she said to him. "I feel really dizzy and sick, so you must have." She felt a bolt of rage and tried to kick him as he was getting to his feet, but she missed.

"Forget about him, Genny. Let's get out of here. If you're not better by the time we get to your place, I'll call the cops. Believe me, everyone got a good look at him, and he'll go to jail for it." She whirled around to Thomas, now leaning against a light post. "Don't you try to follow us, you got me, you creep?"

"Let's just go," Genny said as bile rose up into her throat. *Oh, no, please,* she didn't want to get sick.

There wasn't a taxi in sight. "Well, we're not far from your place, right, Genny?"

Genny couldn't answer, she was too busy simply keeping herself upright, putting one foot in front of the other.

It took a long time to get to her building on Pine Street, since every single step was a trial and error, but finally, with Monica supporting her, she managed to get her key into the outside lock.

It was past midnight. No one was around at that hour, certainly not the doorman, Sidney, who liked to snooze the night away in the storage room behind the counter.

Monica helped her onto the elevator. Genny studied the board, finally punched the button for the fourth floor. When the elevator doors opened, Genny was wheezing, barely able to walk. "I'm not going to make it."

"Sure you will. Hang in there, Genny, you're doing fine. Don't worry, I'm here."

Monica took the key out of Genny's hand when they reached her door at the end of the corridor, opened the door, and eased her inside.

"Yes, Genny, you made it. I'm proud of you. Now let's get you inside, and everything will be all right, I promise."

CHAPTER 29

Chevy Chase, Maryland
Tuesday morning

When her cell blasted out the horse-race trumpet call, Lucy's hand jerked, sloshing her coffee over the side of her Betty Boop mug.

"Hello, Lucy Carlyle here."

"Agent Carlyle, this is Dr. Amos Judd. I completed the autopsy on your grandfather's remains. Agent Savich asked me to call you directly."

She swallowed. "Yes, Dr. Judd, thank you. What can you tell me?" *Remains* — that's what her grandfather was now.

"I found scoring on two of the back ribs, consistent with a large smooth blade, such as a butcher knife, that penetrated the chest. There was also sharp scoring of a thoracic vertebra, indicating the thrust was deep, the blade headed straight for the heart. He died quickly, Agent Carlyle."

Lucy thanked Dr. Judd, punched off her cell, and poured more coffee into her mug. She didn't drink, just cupped the mug in her hands to warm them.

Her cell rang again.

It was their longtime family lawyer, Mr. Bernard Claymore.

His old voice sounded surprisingly strong and firm. He asked how she was doing, then immediately said, "I called, Lucy, to tell you I need to see you immediately. Your grandfather left me an envelope twenty-two years ago, told me to give it to you only after your own father died. This, unfortunately, happened much too soon. Come by and I will give it to you."

She stared at her cell phone. An envelope from her grandfather? Her heart began to pound. *Answers,* she thought, perhaps at last she would have answers.

An hour later, she walked out of Mr. Claymore's elegant suite of offices in the Claymore Building on M Street, an envelope clutched in her hand. Mr. Claymore told her he had no idea what was in the envelope; he'd simply kept it in his safe for the past twenty-two years. He assured her he had, indeed, followed her grandfather's instructions to the letter.

Another thirty-five minutes, and she was

maneuvering her Range Rover into a space that was really too small for her baby, but she was used to that, and she was good. She settled in with a few precious inches to spare. Her cell rang again, and she drummed her fingers on the steering wheel, sighed, and picked up. "Carlyle."

"Hi, Carlyle. It's McKnight." A brief pause, then, "Is something wrong?"

Why did everyone assume something was wrong? Surely she sounded fine and normal, thank you very much. Well, being hypnotized, remembering things that curled her toes whenever she thought too closely about it, that had been bizarre. She could picture Coop in her mind, an intense look on his lean face, focusing all his intelligence on the tone of her voice. This guy wasn't a dog, no doubt in her mind now. She knew to her bones that once Coop found someone, made a commitment, he'd stick. She smiled at that thought. Focus away, boyo, there's nothing for you to hear. "Not a thing, Coop, not a single thing's wrong. I've — well, I've got some stuff I have to do this morning. You know, concerning my grandfather. I'll be in about noon, okay?"

"Tell you what, why don't I meet you, help you take care of this stuff? Then you and I can talk a little about how you're really doing."

Yeah, right. Still, what could she say? Coop didn't have to know what was in the safe-deposit box; it wasn't his business. She could be silent as the Sphinx if she wanted to. She felt filled with energy, excited about what she would find in that box. But it was more than that. She felt revved, ready to take on the world, even Kirsten Bolger. "Sure, Coop, that'll be fine. I'm, ah, in front of the First National Bank here in Chevy Chase."

"Wait for me."

Lucy punched off her cell, sighed again, and closed her hands tightly around the steering wheel. Should she wait, or go into the bank? She saw there was a Starbucks across the street with not much of a line.

When Coop arrived in his blue Corvette, people rubbernecking to get a better look, she smiled. She stepped out of her Range Rover as he navigated his splendid machine into a parking space nearly as small as hers. She knew he was studying her face through his dark sunglasses as he walked toward her with that lazy walk of his. He was in his prized shearling coat, since it was chilly today. She gave him a big grin and handed him a covered cup of coffee —

black, the way he liked it. She saluted him. "Thanks for coming to me, Coop."

He slipped his sunglasses in his coat pocket. "Yeah, well, it's my pleasure, Agent Carlyle. If I hadn't, I wouldn't have seen you today. Sherlock and I are flying up to New York City in a couple of hours. There was another Black Beret killing up there last night, and we have a good witness — a guy who talked to her."

"Savich didn't call me. Why aren't I going?"

"Savich wants you here with him after what happened. Don't look blank, Lucy, you know exactly what I mean. You found your grandfather in a steamer trunk, and got yourself hypnotized. Dr. Hicks's orders, Savich said. He'll probably call you." He took a sip of the sinful coffee, gave a little shudder. "This perks my chest hair right up."

"I was just thinking that."

He eyed her. "I might need some clarification. You were thinking exactly that?"

She laughed. "I'm here to look in a safe-deposit box that belonged to my grandfather, Coop."

"Really? You're going in to see what's in the box? Right now?"

"You got it."

She was excited, nervous, he read it clearly on her face, and there was something else in her eyes as well. Was it fear? Fear of finding something else that would wreck her world, something about why her grandfather's body was in that steamer trunk?

She tried to leave him in the main lobby inside the bank, but he stuck with her. He said nothing at all when the bank employee looked up the box number on the computer and told her there was a note that she could be coming, even though this was the very first visit to this particular safe-deposit box in twenty-two years, and wasn't that a kick?

Yeah, Coop thought, *a real kick,* but then again, her grandfather had been dead for twenty-two years. He had a good dozen questions ready to trip off his tongue, but Lucy was doing her best to pretend he wasn't there. She followed the woman to the elevators, and disappeared.

Who had kept the box open, he wondered, standing against a wall with his arms crossed over his chest, and why hadn't she come to the bank before and opened the box rather than waiting until today? Had she just found out about it?

Coop waited for twenty minutes, until she walked out of the elevator, carrying only her purse. But her purse was huge. He found himself wondering how much bloody weight women could actually carry until their backs gave out.

"So, what was in the box?"

She pressed her purse against her chest. He was on full alert.

"Come on, Lucy, state secrets from World War Two? Something so classified you've got tucked in that purse that if you tell me, you'll have to either kill me or marry me?"

That brought an unwilling smile. "Well, we've already had the pre-honeymoon."

"It was too short. I'd like to see the squirrel nightshirt again."

"What was in the box is personal, so forget it," she said, and walked beside him out of the bank. He saw a glow in her eyes, no other word for it. She was ready to kick butt. She'd found something significant, something related to what had happened twenty-two years ago. He wanted to know; he wanted to protect her. But from what?

"You aren't going to tell me what your grandfather placed in that box?"

"No. Let it go, Coop."

"I want to help you, Lucy. Surely you know that."

She threw him a big, bright, utterly false smile. "Sure, Coop, but the thing is, I really don't need any help. Hey, don't you have to meet Sherlock, fly up to New York?"

CHAPTER 30

New York City
Tuesday afternoon

Detective Celinda Alba hated that the feds were coming, wished she could drop-kick them all in the Hudson, where she knew they'd all drown, weighted down by polluted muck or their egos. It was a homicide, and that was her business. But no, the feds had to stick their arrogant noses in it. Who cared if Bundy's daughter had killed before in San Francisco, Chicago, Cleveland, or wherever? No one had caught her, so it didn't matter. That woman was here in New York now, and they would deal with her, once and for all, if only the feds would let them.

Celinda knew she was good, a veteran cop with fifteen years under her belt. She had a feel for murderers, especially weird ones like Bundy's daughter. *Bundy's daughter* — now, that was amazing. As for her partner, Henry

245

Norris, he was still so new his cop shoes squeaked, but she knew in a couple of years his cop shoes would stomp on bad guys. People seemed to trust him immediately and trip over themselves spilling their guts to him. She'd see to it he got over this hero worship he appeared to have for the feds.

And here they were, right here on her turf, introduced to her and Henry by Captain Slaughter. As usual, her captain looked tired and harassed, and he was giving her his cold eye, its meaning clear: *Play nice. Cooperate, and don't make waves.* She'd heard it before. She shook the feds' hands, even managed a stingy smile. She saw Henry's mouth was open as he stared at the tall, slim woman with her curly red hair and ridiculous name. *I mean, give me a break — Sherlock —* and dressed all la-di-da in black pants, white shirt, black leather jacket, and black ankle boots. The dark guy standing beside her was taller than her captain, and he surely looked like he could kick your butt without breaking a sweat. She had to admit the boy was eye candy, no doubt about that, but so what? She wanted them gone. He wore black, too, as though he and the redhead were freaking twins or something, except his tie was red.

A fed rebelling? She wondered what color

246

his socks were. She said to her captain, "Sir, why aren't we dealing with the New York FBI?"

Captain Slaughter gave her a look because he knew she'd dated an agent at the New York office, and it hadn't ended well. He guessed she'd rather have the snake she knew than ones flown in. "This comes from the top, Detective Alba. You will give Agent Sherlock and Agent McKnight whatever assistance they need." And there was more cold eye; a buffalo wouldn't miss that warning. When Captain Slaughter left them, Detective Alba said, "Agent Sherlock, I hear you and Agent McKnight want to interview Thomas Hurley."

Sherlock could feel the wave of animosity rolling off Detective Alba, wondered which of the agents at the New York field office had put her nose out of joint, but knew they obviously had because those cowboys put everyone's nose out of joint, including their superiors in Washington. As for Captain Slaughter, he was wary, afraid they were going to treat him and his people the same way. Sherlock said, "Yes, Detective Alba, we'd like to see Mr. Hurley right away. We understand you're holding him as a material witness?"

Detective Henry Norris thought Agent

Sherlock was very cool, more than cool, and her name, it was perfect. He inched closer to her. "Yes, that's it. Celinda, you want me to take the FBI agents to see Mr. Hurley?"

Why don't you lick her boots, you little schmuck? No way would Celinda let the feds tromp all over the little puppy. She said, "No, Henry, you need to continue with your witness statements. I'll take them to see Hurley."

Sherlock and Coop felt the eyes of every detective and patrolman staring after them as Detective Alba walked them to an interview room down an institutional hallway with cracked linoleum and light green paint, an unfortunate color that had seen better days.

Sherlock said easily, "You know already that Kirsten Bolger has murdered six women. We're looking at another half dozen women we think she's murdered in the San Francisco area, which is where she grew up."

"Yeah, I know all about that. Captain Slaughter told us everything. Everyone around here will know everything soon, the media included. They'll be blaring this all over the place anytime now, probably on streamers across the bottom of TV sets. Then Bundy's daughter will dig herself a hole and we'll never find her."

"Nah," Coop said easily. "Kirsten Bolger won't ever run away and hide. It's not in her genes."

He had a bedroom voice, too, Celinda thought, and planted herself in front of the closed interview-room door, hands on her hips. "What do you think you can find out from Hurley that we couldn't? You read the interview transcript, didn't you? It was thorough, complete. There's not another drop of juice in him."

Sherlock didn't smile. "You never know what'll pop, do you, when he sees the FBI taking over the questioning?"

Coop was thinking Detective Alba looked like she wanted to belt Sherlock. She was a large woman, all muscle, and he'd bet she could give Sherlock a good go. It was too bad they wouldn't get any help from her. He wondered briefly why she disliked them, but he didn't really care. When he wasn't thinking about Kirsten Bolger, trying to figure out what she'd do next, he was thinking about Lucy, and worrying. He'd tried to call her a couple times, but she'd turned her cell off. He hated voice mail, hated it. He also believed she'd turned off her cell so she wouldn't have to speak to him. It had to do with what she found in that safe-deposit box, he knew it.

When Alba didn't move, Sherlock said, a hint of steel in her voice, "Thank you for showing us the way, Detective Alba. We'll take it from here."

And she simply took a step forward, forcing Alba to either step aside or the two of them would bump noses. Alba took a fast step to the left. Sherlock and Coop walked into the interview room and closed the door in Alba's face before she could do more than suck in her breath.

They looked at the young man sitting on the opposite side of a banged-up metal table. Thomas Hurley looked ill and wrung out, and scared.

"Mr. Hurley?"

Thomas nodded.

"No, don't get up. I'm Agent Sherlock, and this is Agent Mc Knight, FBI."

He perked up. "You're really FBI agents? Honestly? I've never seen an FBI agent." He rose to his feet, stuck out his hand. Sherlock, smiling at him, shook his hand, then Coop.

Sherlock motioned for him to be seated again, and she and Coop handed over their creds. They watched him study their IDs, but Sherlock didn't think he was really paying much attention, more like studying them to tell his friends what FBI shields looked like.

They sat down across from him and waited until he was done. Then Sherlock said, "Thank you for staying, Mr. Hurley. We need your help."

"That Detective Alba, she told me not to move." Thomas shrugged. "I'll tell you, I think she could make the mayor freeze in his tracks."

Coop sat forward. "From the transcript we've read, it seems to us you did everything right."

"Except belt the woman who supposedly wanted to save Genny." He sighed, fiddled with a pen. "If I'd done something, anything, Genny wouldn't be dead." Thomas Hurley gave Coop a weak smile. "You know what? It was Genny who hit me and knocked me down, not Monica. She was real strong, and she caught me off guard."

Sherlock said, "We know you're tired, Mr. Hurley, and sick over what happened to Genny Connelly last night. We know you've already recounted what happened a number of times, but we'd like you to talk us through it one more time, since you were up close and personal with her murderer — Monica, she called herself? She had long blond hair, you said?"

Thomas was staring at her. He felt punch-drunk, he was so tired. He heard himself say, "My sister has red hair, but it's nothing like yours, Agent Sherlock. Sherlock? That's really your name? Maybe I could fit it in a poem. That's what I am, you know, a poet, when I'm not a waiter."

He stopped talking, stared at her hard. Sherlock said, "Thank you, Mr. Hurley. You've never met an FBI agent, and I've never met a poet. Now, the woman said her name was Monica?"

Thomas leaned forward. "Yes. She accused me of putting a roofie in Genny's drink. I couldn't believe that. A *roofie!* It was a lie, you know that, don't you?"

"Yes, we know. She was the one who managed to drug Ms. Connelly's mojito without anyone noticing. Do you remember Monica coming close to where you were sitting? At the bar, right?"

"I swear I never saw her before she came running out of Enrico's, yelling for me to stop."

"How many times did you go to the men's room, Mr. Hurley?"

He thought for a moment. "Only once, I think, but Genny was there, so how could Monica — ?"

"Distraction, Mr. Hurley," Coop said. "Think about it. It's not hard to make people look away, focus on something else. You said Monica had very long blond hair. Think back now. Do you think it was a wig?"

"A wig? Detective Norris mentioned that, but I wasn't thinking about that at the time, so I can't be sure one way or the other. It all happened really fast, and Genny was hitting me, and I went down, and Monica was calling me a creep and a lowlife, and Genny wouldn't listen to me. Sweet Mary and Joseph, Genny's dead." He gulped back tears. After a moment, he said, "Do you know Genny was only at Enrico's because her boyfriend was gambling in Atlantic City, had a gambling problem she'd just found out about that night? Anyway, she was depressed and mad, and she wanted to get drunk, to forget the guy." He bowed his head, started clenching and unclenching his hands on the tabletop. "She was sweet, you know? I really liked her. If her idiot boyfriend had walked in the door, I swear I would have decked him." He looked at both of them, helpless, eyes blank. "And now she's dead, just dead. Gone, and nothing will ever matter to her again.

"Murdered by Ted Bundy's daughter, that's what Detective Alba told me. I think she believes I knew Monica, that maybe I helped her kill Genny, but that isn't true, it isn't."

"We know, Mr. Hurley," Coop said. "We know you didn't have anything to do with Genny's murder."

"Bundy's daughter — it's so hard to believe, to make yourself believe, you know? It's like it really can't be real; it's like something someone made up, like one of my poems. You're certain this Monica is really, truly Ted Bundy's daughter? I mean, *really*, Ted Bundy?"

CHAPTER 31

Coop nodded. "I'm afraid that's true, Mr. Hurley. I'd like to try jogging your memory a little differently. I'd like you to close your eyes and relax. Are you with me? Yes, that's right, lean back in that uncomfortable chair, take a couple of deep breaths, and picture Monica in your mind. When you've got her clear, tell us what you see."

Thomas kept his eyes closed and let his chin drop down, and for a moment, Coop and Sherlock thought he'd fallen asleep. Then his eyes popped open, and both Sherlock and Coop saw anger. Anger was good, it would help him focus. "She's thin, her chin's pointed, not as pointed as Reese Witherspoon's or Jennifer Aniston's, but sort of pointed. That hair of hers, it's really thick and blond, and it's hanging halfway down her back, more straight than not. Her face is white, like she uses face powder to make it even whiter. Her eyes are really dark. She's wearing lots of clothes, so I can't see any other part of her, except her legs. Thin legs, and tall black boots, the kind that fit really snug against your calf. Her eyes are set far apart, and her mouth's on the small side, sort of pinched. But still, she's somehow pretty. I'd look at her twice if I passed her in the street."

"Her daddy was good-looking, so why not?" Coop said as he took a photo of Kirsten Bolger out of his briefcase. "Is this Monica?"

"This is the same photo Detective Norris showed me. I told him at first I didn't think so, because this woman's hair is black."

Coop said, "But he told you to lose the hair, right?"

"Yes, he did. And yes, when I did that, I recognized her. Yes, that's Monica. I heard the other detectives talking about how she's killed lots of women before poor Genny."

Sherlock nodded. "Mr. Hurley, think back now. You're having fun, trying to cheer Genny up, singing, entertaining the crowd. You're sitting at the bar. When you turn out on your stool, you can see everyone in Enrico's, right?"

"Yes, just about."

"Look around the bar; look closely at the people. Do you see Monica? No, don't shake your head, keep looking. Scan the room slowly, the booths, the tables. Anybody dancing?"

"No, no dancing." Thomas fell quiet for a long time. He didn't move, not even his hands. Finally he looked her straight in the eye and said, "Yes, I remember now, I did see her. She was sitting in a booth against the far wall."

"Was she alone?"

He reared back in his chair a bit, looked surprised. "Well, wait, I don't know — no, she wasn't alone. There was a guy with her, kind of in the shadows, but I remember seeing him; he even sang along with me on a song. I don't think Monica ever sang."

"Describe what you see, Mr. Hurley."

"She's sitting at a table, a glass in front of her, but you know, it looks like plain old water to me. She's not even eating the peanuts Big Ed puts in these little bowls on all the tables. She's sitting there, her elbows on the table, her chin resting on her folded hands, and she's looking at me, watching me."

Sherlock lightly laid her hands over his. "Was she watching you or Genny?"

For a moment, Thomas simply couldn't deal with it. "Oh, sweet Mary and Joseph, she could be watching Genny."

She kept her voice smooth, infinitely calm. "You said her elbows are on the table, her chin's resting on her hands."

"Yes."

"I want you to close your eyes again. Yes, that's right. Good. Look at her hands, Thomas. Do you see any rings? Bracelets? A watch?"

Thomas's eyes were still closed when he said, "I can't make anything out — wait, she's waving at the waitress. She's probably going to order another beer for the guy."

"Which arm?"

"Her right arm."

Sherlock lightly rubbed her fingers over the backs of his hands. "Thomas, focus on her right hand. Do you see any jewelry?"

He shook his head, then, "Yes, there's a ring on her finger, a big silver ring; it looks kind of weird, because it's too big for her hand."

"Focus on the ring. Describe it to us."

After a couple of moments, Thomas opened his eyes. "You know, I saw a flash, so yes, there was some sort of stone on top of the ring. An emerald, I think, but that's only a feeling, I can't be one hundred percent sure."

"Did you see this ring again when she was shouting at you outside the bar? That's right, close your eyes, picture her."

"She's waving both arms around. She's wearing rings on both hands. Do you know, I think the rings are the same." He opened his eyes. "Why would she wear the same ring on both hands? I've got to be wrong."

Sherlock leaned over and patted his hand. "Maybe not, Thomas, maybe not. Do you think you could describe the guy sitting at her table to a police artist?"

"I can try, Agent Sherlock."

Detective Alba came in while Thomas Hurley was working with the police sketch artist, Daniel Gibbs. She stepped forward quietly to take a look over his shoulder.

Detective Alba said, "What's this? We already have a photo of Bundy's daughter. Why waste time with another sketch?"

Sherlock never looked away from the man's face that was slowly taking shape under Daniel's talented fingers. "This isn't Kirsten Bolger. This is a sketch of the guy who was sitting across from Monica in her booth at Enrico's."

Celinda felt a punch of surprise, followed quickly by an icy wave of rage. *"What?"* She looked ready to beat Thomas into the floor. "Hurley, you never bothered to tell us about any guy sitting with her? You made this up, didn't you, to impress her?"

Thomas shrank back. "No, I didn't make it up!"

Sherlock said easily, "Detective Alba, would you please step outside with me?"

Celinda didn't want to; she wanted to take a strip off the little twerp.

"Detective, now, if you please."

Once outside, Sherlock quietly closed the door behind her. "Did you ever ask him, Detective?"

"No, but he should have —"

"I've found — surely you have as well — that witnesses like Mr. Hurley who've been very close to violence are frankly traumatized, so much stuff swimming in their brains, it helps to guide them very slowly, very thoroughly. And in case you hadn't noticed, he's exhausted."

"Well, yeah, of course, he's a little tired, but that's not the point."

Sherlock cocked an eyebrow at her. "You know, Detective, I really don't know what the point is, except finding out as much as we can from this witness and catching this monster."

"Well, yes, of course —"

Sherlock paid her no more attention. She opened the interview-room door, stepped inside, and closed the door again. She wished there was a lock. She looked down at Mr. Gibbs's sketch. Nearly there.

A few more minutes passed, then Daniel Gibbs said, "Is this the guy, Mr. Hurley?"

Thomas Hurley studied the sketch, blinked, and said, "That's amazing what you did." He looked at Sherlock. "I really didn't think I'd paid that much attention to him, but — that's the guy. You believe me, don't you?"

Sherlock couldn't believe it, yet it made a weird sort of sense. The man staring up at her was George Lansford's aide. Dillon was thorough, never forgot to close the circle on anything, no matter how seemingly minor, and so he'd pulled up photos and names of all the participants in that meeting with George Lansford and passed them around the unit. This sketch was the aide who'd ushered Dillon, Lucy, and Coop into the suite, never saying a word, Dillon had told her. She'd swear this was the same guy, right down to the aviator glasses on his nose. What was his name? Something unusual, like that old movie *Coma,* but what? Then she had it — his name was Bruce Comafield. She couldn't wait to show the sketch to Coop. Talk about a surprise.

She smiled at Thomas Hurley, gave his hand a big shake. "I cannot emphasize what a great help you've been, Mr. Hurley. When we catch Monica, it will be in large part because of how good your visual memory is."

Celinda Alba walked in again, this time preceding her entrance with a little warning knock. She looked down at the sketch. "Who's this clown with the glasses?"

"Mr. Gibbs is very talented, Detective. They're aviator glasses; he must wear them all the time."

"How would you know that? Wait, you're saying you know this guy? There's no way, no way at all."

Sherlock gave her a really big smile. "As a matter of fact, Detective, I do know him; haven't met him, but I've seen his photo.

"Thank you, Mr. Gibbs, and thank you, Mr. Hurley; you've done a great job." She shook both their hands, gently laid the sketch flat in her briefcase, and walked past Detective Alba without a word.

"But wait, who is he? We've got a right to know, we've —"

"Later," Sherlock called over her shoulder.

CHAPTER 32

Sherlock took a taxi to meet Coop at Enrico's to talk to Big Ed. The driver gave her a look, shrugged. "Whatever you say, lady." Not three minutes later, he pulled up in front of Enrico's. She laughed, gave the driver a big tip.

When she stepped inside the dimly lit bar, she heard a man's voice. "You heard me, Agent McKnight, my real name is Eduardo Ribbins, and what kind of name is that? I hate giving it out, especially at the bar. I sure hate it that that sweet girl — Genny's her name? Yeah, Genny, tragic thing, horrible thing — nothing like that's ever happened here. You got that woman yet who killed her?"

He looked up to see Sherlock, didn't for a minute think she was a customer, and motioned her over. Sherlock introduced herself, sat down at the bar, motioned for him to continue. Big Ed said, "I've thought and thought about it, Agent McKnight, but I never got a good look at her. I remember once when I went on break for ten minutes, I happened to look back and saw her coming up to the bar. You've got to ask Bonnie; she took over for me." Big Ed turned and shouted, "Bonnie, get out here!"

Bonnie came out of the back, wiping her hands on an apron. When they asked about Monica, she said, "Yeah, I remember her. Thin as a stick, that one, and she was snooty to me. She had this long blond hair."

Coop said, "Do you think it was a wig?"

"Hmmm, you know, maybe so, yeah, I think you're right."

Coop pulled out the photo and showed it to both Big Ed and Bonnie. "Make her hair blond. Is this her?"

It took some lip chewing and lots of frowns, but Bonnie finally said, "Yeah, that's her. I'm sure." Big Ed nodded, eyes slitting as he stared down at Kirsten Bolger.

Coop said to Bonnie, "When she came to the bar, what did she do?"

"She gave me this look, like, you know, I'm some sort of rodent in her path, didn't order a single thing. She just stood there. Thomas was in the men's room, I think, but somebody else started singing at the top of his lungs, and everyone was singing along and clapping, and it was real loud and Genny was weaving around on her bar stool, and then I got real busy. When I looked back up, she'd gone back to her table, table seven by the wall." Bonnie frowned. "I wonder why she came up if she didn't want to order anything?"

Coop said, "Did you notice the guy she was with?"

Bonnie shook her head. "That's Ms. Darlene's section. Ms. Darlene! Come on out here."

And blessed be, Ms. Darlene, who was Big Ed's mother and pushing seventy, said, "I remember him. He was a young guy, good-looking, conservative dresser, like most of the yuppie Wall Street types we get in here. Looked real sexy in those aviator glasses of his. Oh, yes, he had some tan; he was really dark."

Sherlock pulled the sketch of Bruce Comafield out of her briefcase. "Ms. Darlene, is this the guy?"

Coop sucked in his breath but kept quiet as Ms. Darlene looked down and did a double take. "Yeah, that's him. What is he, a stockbroker?"

"Actually, he's an assistant to a very important man. Ms. Darlene, do you remember the blonde leaving Enrico's?"

"No, sorry. When I checked on the table a couple minutes later, she and the guy were both gone."

Bonnie said, "I saw her go out the front door to catch Genny, but the guy? I guess he could have gone out the emergency door, but there's a god-awful racket if anyone uses it."

Big Ed nodded to Ms. Darlene. "Mom's right, the guy couldn't have gone out the emergency door out back; everyone would have had their hands over their ears." Big Ed walked across the bar to a door with a red light over the lintel, next to the signs for the men's and women's rooms. He was shaking his head when he walked back to them. "The main alarm wire's been cut clean through. It had to be your guy who did that. Right, Mom? Otherwise, you'd have seen him."

Ms. Darlene's eyes shone with excitement. "Sure, he cut the wire, then it's a clean shot out the door into the alley. Do you think he hooked up with Monica and Genny? Maybe helped her kill Genny Connelly?" She turned on her son. "Eduardo, you always turn off the alarm when you come in. Didn't you realize it was off this morning? What happened?"

Big Ed suddenly looked like he was twelve

years old. "Ah, Ma, I just flipped the switch, didn't really look at it."

Ms. Darlene smacked him on the arm.

CHAPTER 33

As soon as they stepped outside Enrico's to walk back to the First Precinct, Sherlock gave Coop a huge smile and pulled out the sketch. "You remember him, don't you, Coop? His name is Bruce Comafield."

He studied it again, and said, "When you showed it to Ms. Darlene, I tell you, Sherlock, I couldn't believe it. You got this out of Thomas?"

She nodded.

"When you think about it, it's not so surprising Mr. Lansford's aide would know his stepdaughter. So he and Kirsten — do you think they're both involved in this killing spree?"

"No clue, but we're going to find out."

"So, he went out the back? Where did he go? Did he meet up with Kirsten, before or after she'd killed Genny Connelly?"

"Good questions. I could give Thomas Hurley a big kiss, but he might put me in one of his poems."

When they faced Captain Slaughter, at his request, ten minutes later, he said immediately, "Detective Alba here tells me you got Daniel Gibbs to do a sketch, supposedly of a guy sitting with Kirsten Bolger."

Detective Alba said, "We could have gotten that sketch, too, if Hurley had told us about the guy."

Captain Slaughter waved her away and looked down at the sketch Sherlock laid on his desktop.

Detective Alba jerked her head toward Sherlock. "She says she recognizes him, sir."

Captain Slaughter raised a salt-and-pepper eyebrow.

Sherlock handed him the sketch. "If you would make a copy of the sketch and fax it to the homicide divisions in San Francisco, Chicago, Cleveland, and Philadelphia, I'd appreciate it. Then we'll check it out. If it's really the guy we think it is, you'll know it right away." Captain Slaughter handed off the sketch.

Detective Henry Norris said, "At least we know for sure it isn't a sketch of Kirsten Bolger's daddy; we can all give thanks for that."

"Amen to that," Sherlock said, and smiled at Norris. "Thank you for your assistance.

Please send all your ideas and further interviews to us. We certainly appreciate it."

"Yes, indeed," Captain Slaughter said. "You're smiling, Agent Sherlock. You've got something up your sleeve?" He handed the sketch back to her and she gently laid it flat in her briefcase.

She patted his arm. "Yes, sir, I believe I do."

"You should tell us who you think this guy is," Detective Alba called after them. "I told you, we've got a right to know."

"Once we're certain," Sherlock said again, and finger-waved her good-bye, never looking back. She felt rather small about it, but Detective Alba was a pain. She'd been tempted for a moment to tell her they'd have gotten the same information at Enrico's Bar — if they'd thought to ask. She'd give Captain Slaughter a heads-up when she got back to Washington.

CHAPTER 34

Chevy Chase, Maryland
Tuesday afternoon

Lucy drove back toward Chevy Chase so excited she could practically fly. She hit traffic, and each time she stopped, she stared at the envelope on the passenger seat beside her, saw the bulging lump of the ring.

When she reached her grandmother's house, she carried the envelope into the library, as carefully as she would fine bone china. She set it atop the desk and stood there, looking at it. Slowly, she opened the envelope and turned it downward into her palm. A large, heavy gold ring fell out, pure gold, yes, and it was ugly and clumsy-looking. She looked closely, saw the top of it came to nearly a point in the very center. Three rubies formed a triangle around the crest. No, they weren't rubies, they were carnelians, flat, no luster at all. She rubbed them on her pants leg, but they still looked dull, no sparkle or shine. So this was the ring her grandfather had taken from her grandmother? This ring was why she'd stabbed him to death?

She took her grandfather's letter from the envelope and read it again.

My dearest Lucy,

I know, my darling, that you are grieving mightily as you read this, at your father's death. I am sure you know he loved you as much as is possible for a person to love, as do I, my dearest.

Forgive the shock of reading these words from my hand, no doubt a very long time since I held you last. I write after long thought and with your welfare in mind. You are probably reading this letter in your middle years, and wondering why I didn't tell you all of this when you were younger. It was for your own protection, and because of my respect for your father, and my only son. While he lived, I know he would not have approved of my writing to you, nor giving you this ring. This is why I instructed the ring and letter not to be given to you until after his death.

You are no doubt looking at or holding an old ring in your hand. It is an odd-looking ring, is it not? It is indeed very old and heavy — ugly, really — with its mysterious inscriptions and its few dull stones. But it is much more than that — it is your birthright.

I first saw it when you were about two years old, the night your mother, Claudine, was taken from us in that terrible auto accident. Your grandmother and I saw the accident because we were driving directly behind her, on our way to a Whistler showing at the Ralston Gallery. Your grandmother was devastated, and she was drunk, a nearly empty bottle of vodka sticking out from beneath her pillow. I had never seen her drink like that before.

She said over and over that she didn't deserve to be alive if our daughter-in-law, Claudine, was dead. She was suffering so much, I feared she would try to harm herself, but instead she started talking about the ring, how if she'd only been wearing it she could have stopped the accident and Claudine would still be alive. "A ring?" I asked her. "What difference could a ring have possibly made?" I asked her again when she didn't answer. She looked at me, her face blotched from her weeping, her eyes dead with despair, and then she took this strange old ring with the dull red stones wrapped in a sock out of the bottom drawer in her bedside table. I thought it was the ugliest ring I'd ever seen, and I asked her what it was. She said her own mother had given it to her before she died, and made her swear not to tell anyone about it except her own daughter, and that meant you, in this case — her granddaughter — when her time came to pass the ring along. Helen was crying, choking on her own words. She said the ring was magic. She said she'd always been afraid of it and had kept it hidden, and so Claudine's death was her fault, since if she'd been wearing it she could have saved Claudine. I thought she was having a breakdown, could no longer bear to be in touch with reality, but then, you see, she showed me what the ring can do.

Your grandmother never really recovered, was never herself again, at least to me, after that night. She kept the ring with her, wouldn't let it out of her sight, until she seemed obsessed with it, hardly talked to me of anything else. I grew to fear what she might try to do with it, fear who else she might tell and what would happen to her if she did. But I feared most of all for her sanity.

I thought I must get rid of the thing, but then I thought about how different our lives would be if she had managed to save Claudine. I thought of Josh, numb with grief that night, huddled next to you, Lucy. I thought of you, only two years old and destined to grow up without a mother because an idiot drunk had smashed his car into hers and killed her instantly.

And so, my dear Lucy, I waited four more years to decide that I must remove the ring from your grandmother. You are now only five years old, and you have no idea what awaits you in the future. The ring will be yours. It can be used for great good, but it is not my place to tell you how. You see, if you have your grandmother's gift, you will soon discover that for yourself, and if you do not, you will never believe me in any case. For your own safety, tell no one you would not trust with your very life. If anyone deserves this ring, it is you, my dear Lucy.

I find myself wondering as I write this letter to you how long I knew you before I went to my reward. I also find myself wondering how old you are as you read this. You see, my instructions were for you to be given this letter and ring upon the death of your father. I hope Josh lived a long, satisfying life and you, my dear, are middle-aged, and you have gained wisdom and insight into yourself and your fellow man. Do you yourself have a daughter?

I wish you joy, and love, and fulfillment in your life, Lucy. I will love you always.

Your Grandfather,
Milton Xavier Carlyle

Lucy laid the letter on the desk, picked up the ring, and laid it on her palm. She slowly closed her hand around it. To her surprise, she felt warmth from it, and more, the ring felt quite natural in her hand.

Without thinking, she slipped the ring onto her middle finger. Since it was so large, she curled her fingers to keep it on. She turned on the desk lamp and held it close to the light. She saw symbols etched beneath the three carnelians — a half circle, flat side up; a circle with an inverted cross coming out of it, like an incomplete symbol of Venus or woman; and two small isosceles triangles with nothing at all unusual about them. She had to concentrate to make the symbols out clearly, they were so shallow and faded in the gold. What did the symbols mean? Were they pictographs from a long-ago language? She looked on the inside of the ring. There, in letters large enough for her to see clearly, was a single word etched in black letters: SEFYLL.

Was that Welsh? She whispered the word aloud, stumbling over the sound.

She whispered the word again, changing how she said it until the word flowed more smoothly out of her mouth, as if she had the right pronunciation. She said the word aloud, and she would swear there was a gentle rippling in the light from the desk lamp. Strange, but simply a play of the light — nothing, really.

Her cell phone rang, once, twice, three times, but she ignored it, pressed speaker, and let it go to voice mail. She heard Dillon's deep voice speaking, but she paid no attention.

She stroked the ring with her thumb, then said the word again: "SEFYLL."

Dillon stopped speaking in mid-sentence. It seemed to Lucy that the very air stopped, but only for a moment, and then her cell blared out the racing trumpet call again, then rang — one ring, two rings, three rings.

And there was Dillon's voice, and he was repeating what he'd said before.

Like a rubber band snapping back. She fell into the big leather wing chair, heart pounding, too confused to be frightened. What had happened? Dillon was speaking the same words he'd been saying before. She blinked when she heard him say, "So, bottom line, it was Kirsten who struck on Wall Street last night, and she had an accomplice. Call me."

It was the oddest feeling, listening to him, knowing what he would say. Had he been cut off, called her twice, repeated the same message? She grabbed her cell. What had he said? "Dillon? Lucy here. Ah, you said there was an accomplice with Kirsten last night?"

There was a moment of silence, then, "Are you okay, Lucy?"

"What? Oh, yes, sure, I'm okay."

Another brief pause, then, "I know Dr. Judd contacted you about the findings of the autopsy. I'm sorry."

So, he'd called Dillon, too. Well, no surprise there. "Thank you, Dillon."

"Coop asked me to call you, said you weren't picking up. They've been interviewing Thomas Hurley, and they've got a police artist making a sketch."

But Lucy couldn't stop staring at the huge

ring still sitting comfortably on her middle finger.

"Lucy?"

"I'm sorry, Dillon. Would you tell me something? Did you call me twice just now, get cut off maybe, and called again, or did you call only once?"

"Just once, and you called me right back."

"I must have been mistaken, then. Don't worry about it. I guess it has been quite a week, Dillon. I'm okay, though."

Dillon wondered for an instant if Lucy was drunk, but no, that couldn't be right. She sounded like she wasn't really there, like she wasn't hearing him, or didn't care. Something was wrong.

"Lucy, is there something you want to tell me?"

Tell him? And look mad? Tell him this ring and this letter were scaring her to her toes? *Say something!*

"I'm fine, really. The house is no longer a crime scene, they cleared it this morning, but I'm not about to visit the attic, if that's what you're worried about."

"Tell you what, Lucy, you stay right there, and I'll be over with some takeout, all right? Sherlock and Coop won't be back until late, a flight delay. I'll call you later."

She scarcely heard him. She punched off

her cell and stared at the ring. That word — SEFYLL — when she'd said it aloud, when she'd said it correctly, time seemed to stop dead for a second or two, then replay itself. That sounded ridiculous. Was she being crazy? Maybe saying the word right on the ring conjured up some sort of weird hypnotic suggestion that made it appear that way.

Lucy took a deep breath, picked up the Chinese lamp that stood atop a side table, and flung it against the fireplace. As it shattered, she said clearly, "SEFYLL."

Everything stopped, and suddenly the lamp was back on the end table, whole, untouched. She saw what seemed to be a small shudder in time itself. Another couple of seconds passed — nothing happened. She ran to the lamp, put her hands on it, and waited. More seconds passed, and still nothing happened, nothing at all. The Chinese lamp she'd hurled against the fireplace and smashed into a gazillion pieces was sitting, solid and unharmed, on the tabletop. She sat down in the large leather chair at her grandmother's desk and stared in front of her. She wasn't crazy, and if something unbelievable was happening, something incredible, she wouldn't let it scare her stupid. She would understand it.

She began to experiment.

She held the ring — she learned she had to be holding it in her hand — and said the word clearly. Each time she did, the digital clock on her cell phone stopped, showed a time exactly eight seconds before, and with no pause, began to tick forward again. She hurled the lamp against the fireplace three more times just as she had before, and kept her eye on the second hand of her watch. As before, the lamp seemed to reassemble itself and the second hand on her watch always turned backward exactly eight seconds until it swept forward again.

Could she change anything she wanted in those eight seconds?

Lucy sat back down in the leather chair, her grandmother's ring still on her middle finger, her hand fisted to keep it in place. Her grandfather had stolen it, hidden it, so she couldn't use it again. Because he was afraid of what she would do with it? No, because she was going crazy, that was why. But her grandfather hadn't been sure Lucy could make it work. Did it work for her only because it had been her grandmother's? Evidently so.

Her father had seen his mother stab his father to death, but had he known about the ring? He must have known something about it; she'd heard her grandmother screaming about it to him the day her grandfather died.

The doorbell rang, but she ignored it, barely heard it.

Then someone was pounding on the door. She heard Dillon's voice calling out, "Lucy! Come, open the door!"

She looked over at the giant clock in the corner. It was well past six o'clock. It was dark.

She slid the ring off her finger and quickly slipped it onto the gold chain she wore about her neck, stuffed it into her shirt. She realized as she ran to the door that her middle finger, once warm where she'd worn the ring, now felt cold.

"Lucy, open this door or I'm breaking in."

"I'm coming, Dillon, I'm coming." And she thought, tears stinging her eyes, *Grandmother, if only you'd had the ring with you when my mother was hit by that drunk. If only.*

CHAPTER 35

Lucy finally opened the door, wondering whether Dillon would really have broken it down. He looked at the banked excitement in her eyes, watched her as she said in a voice as bright as a new penny, "Sorry, Dillon, I was washing up," and knew she was closed down tight. For the moment.

So he handed her the bag stuffed with Chinese takeout that included her favorite moo shu pork, and followed her to the bright kitchen to chow down on his own vegetarian delight. As they sipped the lovely hot tea that Sun Li, his and Sherlock's favorite waiter, had insisted he take with him, he told her about Sherlock and Coop's breakthrough in New York at the First Precinct, and showed her a printout of the sketch of Bruce Comafield that Sherlock had e-mailed to him.

Lucy bounced up and down, hooted. "Sherlock is unbelievable! Oh, yeah, it's him. This is incredible, Dillon. Can you believe he's wearing those same aviator glasses? Why don't we go get him right now? Let's grab him and haul him in."

"Sorry, but we already thought of that. According to Lansford, no one has seen his aide since the evening we visited him at the Willard. No word as to his whereabouts yet."

"We spooked him. I guess we should revisit all the witnesses in the other cities, see if anyone else saw this guy with her."

Savich nodded and took another bite of the vegetarian fried rice.

Bruce Comafield. They were nearly to home plate. Lucy looked over at Dillon, marveled at him. And at Sherlock. Would she have been good enough to get that information and sketch out of the witness, Thomas Hurley? She didn't know, but she'd missed out on an incredible find. She became suddenly aware of the ring pressing itself like a living thing against her skin, her incredible ring that had cost her grandfather his life. It was more than she could begin to understand, or begin to deal with at that moment. No, she had to focus here. She wanted more than anything to find Comafield, and she wanted Savich to trust her again with that assignment, rather than worry about her. She wanted to show him she was ready to throw herself back into the hunt for Kirsten Bolger. It hit her between the eyes that her boss was too perceptive, that any lie she told him, he'd recognize easily as a lie. Maybe he could help her.

"Lucy, you want some of this rice?"

She snapped back, fully aware he'd seen her distraction and known it for what it was.

She spooned up some rice and took a big bite, not caring if it was getting cold, because she hadn't eaten since that morning and she was starving. As she chewed, she felt the weight of her sins pushing down on her head. She swallowed the last bite, fanned her hands in front of her. "So much has happened. I didn't mean to worry you or alarm you. It was very nice of you to care enough about me to come over, and then you brought me dinner and told me about Bruce Comafield."

A black eyebrow went up. He said in that deep, calm voice of his, "It'd be nice if you'd talk to me, Lucy, if you'd tell me the truth about how you're feeling, and what you're thinking."

She looked guilty, she knew it to her heels, but she couldn't help it. She could keep her mouth shut, and so she did. She shook her head.

He searched her face, then nodded as if to say, *So be it.* "Coop will catch you up on everything. He and Sherlock will be back from New York later tonight. I'm thinking things will move smartly forward now that we know about Bruce Comafield. If he was her supply line from the real world, he can't be that any longer. Now he'll be with her full-time." He tapped his fingers on the tabletop. "I'm concerned about you, Lucy. Coop told me you visited a safe-deposit box today, picked up something that belonged to your grandfather?"

She nodded. "Yes, and it upset me, Dillon." She drew in a deep breath. "The box contained an old ring, but nothing more than that." She kept her head down so he couldn't see the lie in her eyes, and pulled the ring out of her shirt and showed it to him.

He held out his hand. He could tell she didn't want to, but she unfastened the gold chain, let the ring slide into her palm. She waited only a moment, then gave it to him. She watched him examine it. "Was there any explanation of this ring in the box?"

Lie, lie, no choice. "No, but I thought it could be the ring I remembered my grandmother screaming about, the ring she stabbed her husband to death over, when

286

he took it from her." Her words hung between them. He said, "And he left it in a safe-deposit box, specifically for you?"

"Yes."

He waited a beat, then, when she didn't say anything, he said, "What did you do this afternoon?"

He was giving her that steady sort of questioning look now, one that made her want to fling herself at his feet and confess every sin she could remember committing since the age of three. "I slept some. I didn't feel too well, and then I had bad dreams, about my grandfather."

Savich sat back, pushed away the remains of his dinner. He looked again at the ring on his palm. "This ring must have meant something significant to both of them. Isn't that ironic? She killed him, put him in that steamer trunk, covered him with a white towel, never imagining that he'd put this ring in a safe-deposit box for you. And that's a question, isn't it, Lucy? You weren't yet six years old when he went missing, yet what he'd done was save the ring for you. How did you discover it was there, waiting for you?"

"Our old family lawyer called me, told me my grandfather's instructions were to give it to me after the death of my father."

She knew this raised a lot more questions in his mind, but to her relief, he said, "The ring looks very old, doesn't it? Is that a triangle of dull rubies set on top of it?"

"It is very old, and yes, it's ugly, too, Dillon, not worth much, I don't think. The stones aren't rubies; I'm thinking carnelians. I have no clue why Grandfather bothered to save the ring for me."

Yeah, right. You're really a bad liar, Lucy. But what are you lying about? Savich wanted to shake her, but trust was a funny thing.

He said, "These symbols, I don't recognize them. Do you?"

"No. I've never seen them before."

"They could designate some society, or sect, or cult of some kind. And that inscription, 'SEFYLL.' "

Lucy froze. He was holding the ring when he said the word, but he had no reaction. He would have known, he would have been shocked, as she had been, if everything had happened again for him, starting eight seconds ago, or would all he feel be a shimmer in the light? Or was that what her grandfather meant by her having a *gift*? Could no one else experience what she had?

She had to ask, had to. "Do you know the word, Dillon?"

"Easy enough to find out." He pulled out

his cell phone.

A couple minutes later, they were reading that the word was Welsh.

He said, "It means to stand, to be or become stationary, to stop moving. Why inscribe that on a ring?"

She said absolutely nothing.

"If you don't mind, I'd like to take a couple of photos of it with my cell. MAX and I can do some research later, maybe make some phone calls."

Great, just great.

After he'd snapped his photos, he looked at her pale face. "You need to turn in now. Too much has happened in too short a time." He saw that she was holding out her hand, and so he gave her the ring, watched her thread it back onto the gold chain and put it inside her shirt again.

"Yes, I'm awfully tired, but I'd like to come back to work tomorrow, help set up the manhunt for Bruce Comafield with Coop. I don't want to get too far behind on Kirsten Bolger's case."

Savich gave her a long look, wondered what she hadn't told him, wondered what specifically she'd lied to him about, then nodded. "All right, I'll see you in the morning." He said good night, then returned to an empty house, which he hated. Sean and

Astro were doing a sleepover with Marty at the Perrys' house. He realized he missed Astro barking his head off as soon as he walked up the flagstone steps to his front door.

CHAPTER 36

Hoover Building
Wednesday morning

Lucy slipped into Gloria's passenger seat, waited for Coop to seat-belt himself in. "So, we're off to the Willard. I hope we can find out more about Bruce Comafield. Can you believe Dillon pulled ID photos of everyone in that meeting with Lansford and passed them around? Sometimes you want to punch him when he pulls tricks like that. And there was payoff — Sherlock recognized Comafield right away."

"We already know everything about him, from the mole behind his right knee to the C he got in poly sci — pretty funny for an aide to a wannabe lawmaker, or should I say *former* aide."

"Former wannabe lawmaker, too."

Coop looked over at her. "Do you mind if after we visit the Willard, we drive by my mom's so she can see what a hot tootsie I picked up in Gloria? Ah, you'd be the first hot tootsie I ever brought around, by the way."

"Yeah, yeah, I believe you. *Tootsie?*"

"All right, hot chick. That better?"

"Yeah, tons better. Now fill me in, Coop."

When they reached the Willard hotel, they learned Mr. Lansford had checked out a couple hours before, on his way to Dulles, to fly back to San Francisco to close down his campaign and officially withdraw from the congressional race. They tried to call him but were sent directly to voice mail.

Coop and Lucy spoke to the bellman, the waitstaff, the desk people, the housekeeper, all of whom had said they hadn't seen Bruce Comafield since early Monday. They found a confiding young woman in the gift shop who'd sold Comafield some shaving cream on Monday morning. He told her he'd been fired. It was weird, she said to them; he wasn't down about being fired, he seemed excited about something.

When Coop called Mr. Lansford's executive assistant in San Francisco, he confirmed that Mr. Comafield wasn't with Mr. Lansford; indeed, he'd been let go, since there was nothing more for him to do.

It appeared Bruce Comafield had fled right to Kirsten, to New York City. And he'd been excited about it. There was still no word on the APB out on him.

As Lucy and Coop rode the elevator back up to the CAU on the fifth floor of the Hoover Building, she found herself grinning at him. "Would you really have driven us to your mom's house if we hadn't been pressed for time?" She paused a beat. "Tootsie?"

"I'm now thinking chickie."

"That's sick. I like it."

"Tell you what, we'll go see my mom as soon as we can break free today. How about around seven o'clock this evening? I can try out both tootsie and chickie on her, see which she prefers."

He'd swear he saw disappointment in her eyes, but then it was gone, replaced by — what? Resignation? "I'm sorry, Coop, but I can't."

"That's okay. I can stick with you, see what you're up to, help out. I'm a pretty useful guy to have around, Lucy."

She lightly laid her hand on his arm. "Believe me, Coop, you don't want to be around me."

They weren't six feet from the CAU when Coop's cell rang. "McKnight here."

She watched his face as he listened. She saw ferocious delight. He'd scarcely rung off when she said, "What?"

"Savich got a call from a waitress in Baltimore at the Texas Range Bar and Grill. She swears she saw Ted Bundy's daughter in the bar last night."

"Hot diggity. I was hoping this would happen. Every worker in every bar in the U.S. must know Kirsten's face by now." Lucy high-fived Coop. "We're all heading to Baltimore, right?"

CHAPTER 37

Fairfax, Virginia
Wednesday afternoon

Savich settled his Porsche snugly against the curb in front of a very nice house in an upper-middle-class section of Fairfax. There were three high-priced cars in the driveway, two Beemers and a Lexus SUV. He knew Mrs. Patil was here; hers was the Beemer 750i Mr. Patil had bragged about to Savich, claiming it drove like a dream and felt like you were sitting on the living-room sofa when you rode in the backseat. Who owned the other two?

He looked around at the well-maintained front yard. Everything looked prosperous, well cared for.

His knock was answered by a small middle-aged Asian man wearing a Burberry coat, a small white bandana tied around his shaved head. He bowed to Savich.

"I'm Special Agent Dillon Savich, FBI, to

see Mrs. Patil. I called."

"Ah, yes, of course. Mrs. Patil asked me to answer the door on my way out. I have finished her jujitsu lesson. Please follow me, Agent Savich; she is in the living room, enjoying wine with Mr. Urbi and Mr. Shama."

Savich had believed Mrs. Patil looked fifty when he'd first seen her at the hospital. Now, she looked a laughing forty-five, in her white *gi* pants and shirt, and her feet bare, her toes painted a pale coral. She looked up to see him, and something passed over her face that made everything male in him come to full alert.

"Mrs. Patil," he said.

She was on her feet and lightly running across the living room to take his hand and draw him in. "Come, come, Agent Savich, I want you to meet Nandi's best friend, Mr. Amal Urbi, and his nephew, Mr. Krishna Shama. This is Special Agent Savich of the FBI."

She stood back and beamed while Mr. Shama and Savich shook hands. Savich knew Krishna Shama was forty-eight, very successful in the car-repair business, having expanded to six shops in the past four years. He had three grown children, a dead wife, and, Ben Raven had told him, lived with a twenty-three-year-old woman who worked for the State Department. He looked sharp, Savich thought, well dressed and lean, a runner, probably, and his dark eyes would do a shark proud. Officer Horne had described him well, too, like an ad for a successful businessman.

Officer Horne was also right about Mr. Amal Urbi, Savich thought. He looked older than Mr. Patil. He wanted to tell him not to rise, but Mr. Urbi got slowly to his feet and held out his hand to grasp Savich's. Savich noticed his belt was indeed fastened high on his chest. He was a pleasant-looking old gent, a bit desiccated, but his dark eyes were bright with intelligence. There were a total of six gray hairs sticking up at odd angles atop his head. Savich knew he was long retired, that his family's textile fortune went back several generations. He lived in one of the luxury condos in a complex he owned in Towson Corners. He'd known the Patils for a very long time, his friendship with Mr. Patil going back to childhood.

Both men seemed to care very much about Mr. Patil.

Once they were all seated, Jasmine Patil said, "I was telling our very good friends that Nandi was walking this morning. Can you believe that, Amal — Nandi was actually walking around! I heard several nurses cheering him on."

Who knew if Amal Urbi believed it or not, but still he nodded, adjusted his belt a bit higher, and looked pleased. Mr. Shama said in a smooth, deep voice, not a trace of an accent, "He is an amazing man, Jasmine. I remember thinking that when I was only six years old." He began tapping his fingertips on his knee. "My dear, is it possible to have some coffee?"

Mrs. Patil gave him a joyous smile, jumped to her feet, patted his face, grabbed a bright pink cell phone off an end table, punched one button, and said, "Eruska, please bring a carafe of coffee and your delicious *rasgulla* to the living room."

She beamed at all of them, fluttered her hands to great effect, Savich thought, watching Mr. Shama eyeing her like he would a particularly well-broiled hamburger. *"Rasgulla,"* she said to Savich, "are spongy cheese balls dipped in sugar syrup."

Not five minutes later, Savich accepted a cup of coffee, took a small sip and set it back on its saucer. It was thick, rich, dark as sin, and almost as good as his. He wished he'd asked for tea. He accepted a *rasgulla,* took a bite, complimented the cook. Too sweet for his taste, but there was an after-zing that was pleasing. "Mrs. Patil, when is Mr. Patil expected to come home?"

"Call me Jasmine, please, Agent Savich. Ah, the doctor tells me perhaps next Tuesday, if he continues to gain strength. But the thing is, I don't want him here. Mr. Urbi and Mr. Shama have convinced me he might be in danger at home, because why would he be robbed twice? Whoever tried to kill him might try again. He is safer in the hospital with that lovely young man sitting right outside his door, protecting him. You must catch whoever is out to kill my husband, Agent Savich. May I call you Dillon?"

Savich smiled at her. "How did you know my first name, ma'am?"

He saw the ma'am rankled, but her smile didn't slip.

"I asked Officer Horne — Dillon."

He nodded, and with apologies, asked where each of them was the night Mr. Patil was shot in the back. Nowhere near the Shop 'n Go, they each said, and offered witnesses.

Savich asked them about the first robbery attempt. Nowhere near, each said, and produced more alibis.

Savich backed off. Mr. Shama was looking at Savich like he'd like to shoot him. As for Mr. Urbi, he was smiling toward Jasmine Patil.

Savich said, "Gentlemen, do you know of any reason why someone would want to murder Mr. Patil?"

None of them knew who could possibly wish to harm a single hair on Nandi Patil's precious gray head, except, Mr. Urbi insisted, some madman who, for whatever reason, had a grudge against Nandi.

Savich needed to get them alone, but when? There was so much going on with Kirsten — he'd talk to Ben Raven about interviewing each of them. Savich rose, nodded to each of them. "Mr. Urbi, Mr. Shama, a pleasure to meet you gentlemen."

"I will show you out, Dillon."

She gave him that look again, a look that said she understood something very private about him, as a man. Yet she appeared to adore her old husband, and he was certainly besotted with her. Savich looked back at the two men, now speaking in low voices. Mr. Urbi looked up at that moment, met his eyes, and something moved in those dark eyes, something like understanding.

At the front door, Jasmine Patil rubbed her hand over his arm and moved closer. "It's truly a pity for my granddaughter, Cynthia, that you are married, Dillon."

He nodded. "Actually, ma'am, I don't

consider it a pity at all. My wife is very special. I will speak to you again, Mrs. Patil," he said, and left her very nice house in Fairfax, not looking back, because he knew she was standing in the open doorway, staring after him. One of these three had better answers for him, he was sure of it.

He called Ben Raven, got his voice mail, and left him a message.

Right now he had to focus on getting Ms. Kelly Spicer, veteran waitress at the Texas Range Bar & Grill in Baltimore, down for a field trip to the Hoover Building for an interview.

CHAPTER 38

Hoover Building
Wednesday, lunch

Kelly Spicer, longtime waitress at the Texas Range Bar & Grill in Baltimore and wife of the owner, Jonah Spicer, wasn't a perky twenty-two-year-old. She was flamboyant and fifty with a huge smile she liked to flash at her customers whenever she claimed she was "straight off the Texas range." It was a little fib, she told them, but God wouldn't care, now, would She? She laughed at her joke, shaking her big Texas hair, making the silver hoops dance in her ears, and drawing your eye to the awesome cleavage on display from three open buttons on her blouse.

Savich, Lucy, and Coop sat with her in the seventh-floor cafeteria of the Hoover Building.

Coop was very nearly vibrating, his eyes never leaving Kelly Spicer. He noticed her cleavage, sure — he was still breathing, after all — but he was so excited about her being here he wasn't even thinking of eating his bowl of turkey chili. He was leaning toward her, wanting to pull the words out of her mouth.

Lucy was as excited as Coop, and barely kept from dropping the beef taco off her tray.

Savich slid the roasted vegetables off his shish kebab as he asked Kelly what she thought of her sushi.

Lucy couldn't bear the idea of raw fish, and kept her head down and chowed on her taco. Coop was fiddling with a spoon, his bowl of chili still untouched as he waited for her to take two bites of her sushi. He took that as a signal to begin. "We know the Baltimore Police Department already showed you the pictures, Ms. Spicer. Are you absolutely sure the woman you saw last night is Kirsten Bolger?"

"Absolutely, Agent McKnight. By the way, I sure do like your name, like an Irish knight charging in on his horse. Odd duck, she was, that's what I told Gator. He's my husband; he went to Florida way back in the day. Football, football, that's what his life's about. Now that it's football season, he switches on the huge TVs and we turn into a regular sports bar."

Lucy said, "If he's from Florida, then why is it the *Texas* Range Bar and Grill? Why not something with Florida, like the Florida Swamp?"

"Now, aren't you the cleverest girl?" Kelly beamed her brilliant smile on Lucy. "I like that. The thing is, when Gator bought the place it was already named and famous for the Texas Espresso we serve. And we've still got Ivan the Bull for people to ride, so we gotta stay the Texas Range. Where was I? Oh, yes, last night — it was eight on the button when she waltzed in. She was alone at first, sat in a booth with a clear view of the bar and ordered fizzy mineral water. Then a guy came in and walked over to her, sat in the same booth, and they had their heads together, talking. I still wasn't sure, you know? But then Linda came in — she's a hairdresser from down the street, a really nice girl. She's a regular, in three or four nights a week, to socialize, you know? And that's when I really noticed her, because she was looking at Linda real close. Then she smiled, said something to the guy. She got up, ready to come over, I think, but Linda had to leave, had to get gas in her mama's car, and she was out the door. She sat back down, and the two of them talked some more. I remember they left at nine o'clock or thereabouts."

Coop said, "Mrs. Spicer, we brought you all the way here to Washington because of all the people who thought they've seen Kirsten, you were the only one who saw her in the company of a man, and described him."

Coop pulled out photos of Kirsten and Bruce Comafield, slid them in front of Kelly Spicer. "Are you sure these are the people you saw?" She looked down, then up at them, and beamed. "Yep, that's them, although, truth be told, I nearly didn't recognize her at first, since her hair was bright red, short as can be, and spiked up all over her head. But I knew she had to be Ted Bundy's daughter after the way she looked at Linda, knew it all the way to my stiletto heels. I can't wait to see what Gator will have to say about this. He didn't think you guys would take me seriously. He thought it was stupid to call you, but I didn't listen to him — a good thing, since I usually do. A smart boy, my Gator." She stuck a thick slice of raw tuna in her mouth, her smile never dimming as she chewed.

Lucy felt her stomach churn.

"You gonna come up and nail these two, right?"

"Yes," Savich said. "Tonight."

"Good. Imagine if Linda had settled in for a while. I'll betcha Ted Bundy's daughter would have been right over, buying her a drink."

When Ms. Spicer finished her sushi, she got her requested tour of the crime lab, charming every tech within distance of that huge smile of hers. Savich arranged to have her driven back to Baltimore. "Remember," he told her as he shook her hand, "you don't know any of us if you see us, all right? It's best if no one else in the bar knows about us, either. We'll let you know when to expect us."

"Zip my lips," Kelly said.

"Okay," Coop said a few minutes later in the CAU conference room. "We've got Kirsten's look du jour — red blazer; black jeans and black boots; short, spiky red hair. Practically an advertisement. I surely hate to say this, though. If Bruce Comafield is with her, none of us can be in the bar tonight. He'll recognize us, and that'll blow the deal."

"And that could lead to people getting hurt if they lose it," Lucy said. "That's our bigger problem — taking them down in a public place without anyone getting hurt."

Savich said, "The plan will be for you and Coop to take her down before she ever goes through the bar door. I'm thinking Sherlock will set up at the bar, nursing a beer, in case she makes it inside."

Lucy said, "We gotta hope for Comafield, too. What a piece of work he must be, Dillon, if he's not as insane as she is. Did you reach Lansford?"

"He's still in the air, but I was able to Skype him with the help of the flight crew. He was at first disbelieving, but once I convinced him on the phone, he nearly blew. He calmed down enough to say he'd believed Bruce hardly knew Kirsten. He admitted Bruce was gone many nights, and that was occasionally inconvenient, but he was smart and efficient, and so he let him get away with it. Bruce told him he had a sick mother and had to visit her whenever possible. Cancer, he said, terminal. I didn't bother to tell him that Bruce Comafield's mother is alive and well in Tulsa, Oklahoma, and owns two flower shops. I gave Mr. Lansford specific dates, the nights Kirsten murdered the five women. He said he'd have their employment records checked to see if Bruce was away on those nights.

"The rest we pretty much knew already. Bruce had been with him for four years, first as his executive assistant, and when Mr. Lansford decided to go into politics, Bruce flashed his political science degree, gave him a couple of recommendations, went right along with him. He said Bruce wasn't all that hot as a personal assistant, but he was an excellent aide, which is why he fired him when his political future tanked. Then he remembered it was Bruce who suggested he get Kirsten a black Porsche for her birthday, and that made him even madder. I was feeling a bit sorry for him. This was a big blow, after all. Then he lit into the FBI again. He'd been royally used and betrayed by Director Mueller leaking everything to the press."

"Did you hang up on him?"

"Tempted, but no. I'm convinced he had no clue about Bruce's relationship with Kirsten. Maybe he can still help us." Savich looked over at Lucy. She looked distracted, thinking about something else entirely, as she had at times last night. Of course, her grandfather, the ring. She'd been through a lot, and he knew she would work it out in her own way. The question was, could they count on her being all there tonight?

"Are you sure you're up for this trip to Baltimore with us tonight?"

"Of course I am. I'm revved about it."

"Lucy, I believe you told Coop he didn't

want to be around you. What did you mean?"

Savich imagined Lucy would take a strip off Coop when she was alone with him again. She looked past his left shoulder at Coop, fidgeted, finally said, "I, well, I told him I had stuff to do, Dillon, and I didn't need him hovering over me." Her chin went up, and she pushed a hank of hair back into her French braid. "I don't need or want anyone hovering over me, not Coop, not anybody."

She knew she looked miserable, knew she felt even more miserable. She was a liar — Coop knew it, Dillon knew it, probably the whole unit knew it. *Would she never be able to tell anyone about the ring?*

She said, "I'm fine. I can't wait to nail Kirsten and Bruce Comafield."

"Lucy, would you consider letting Dr. Hicks hypnotize you again? Maybe there's more you can find out about your grandfather that might help put this to rest."

She gave him a look. "Nice thought, Dillon, but I don't think so."

"Not really," Savich said. "Pretty lame, actually," and he stood, said over his shoulder, "We'll all meet in front of the Texas Range at six o'clock this evening, and get ourselves in place. We'll have plenty of backup, not to worry."

"You going to call the Baltimore Field Office in?"

"Not this time. We don't want to alert them by having too many agents hanging around, looking like they're pretending to be bored."

CHAPTER 39

Raven Street, Baltimore
The Texas Range Bar & Grill
Wednesday night

Over the wire, Sherlock wore a soft blue tunic with tight black jeans and black heels. She'd pulled her hair behind her ears, fastened with two gold clips. From her ears dangled gold hoops. There was no wedding ring on her finger.

She thought the wire was a waste of time. What were the odds Kirsten would get past Dillon and even make it inside? And even if she did, the other agents in the bar had eyes on her. As usual, Dillon had insisted, wanting to cover all the bases, anticipating every possible screwup.

She sipped the heavy dark Texas home brew, the specialty of the house called Texas Espresso, and tried to look depressed for the benefit of the four other agents she knew were watching her performance. She hadn't wanted to miss Lucy and Coop taking Kirsten Bolger and Bruce Comafield down outside the bar, but someone had to be in here, growing mold along with the home brew, just in case.

She hoped Ruth, Dane, Jack, and Ollie, scattered around the bar, were at least enjoying their drinks.

Stop your whining and look depressed. She'd nodded only once to Mrs. Spicer, saw she was lit up bright as a Christmas Santa. She was relieved Kirsten wouldn't ever get into the bar with Mrs. Spicer; she'd take one gander and know something was up. Sherlock studied the bartender, a thin-as-a-stick young woman with a chipped front tooth, who talked nonstop while she delivered drink orders to three waitresses and never got them wrong or spilled a drop.

She didn't appear to know who Sherlock really was, and that was a good thing, what with Mrs. Spicer looking fit to burst into song.

Mr. Gator Spicer hadn't shown himself yet, and that was also a good thing, since they didn't need a duet. They'd cautioned Mrs. Spicer to simply go about her business and not to pay any attention to Sherlock or the other FBI agents, assured her they would stop Kirsten before she ever got into the bar. She was trying, but they all knew she wouldn't manage to be discreet.

"You've never been in here before," the bartender said when there was a lull.

"Nope, first time." Sherlock looked at the faded name tag over the bartender's left breast — Trisha. Nope, Trisha didn't have a clue, thankfully. "I was out trying to walk off my mad at my jerk of an ex-boyfriend who stole my beautiful light blue Corvette. It was mine, and it was gorgeous, sexier than Brett Favre's butt in his Wranglers. I saw your sign and decided it was time for a beer. Or two. Wow, this Texas Espresso has hairy knuckles."

Trisha poured three more Texas Espressos, lightly shoved the big, thick beer glasses toward a waitress, who scooped them up onto her tray with no wasted motion. Trisha said to Sherlock, "This is a good place for beer, and that's a bummer for a bartender who lives off tips. I can make a mean martini, and there's not much call for martinis here. Nope, folk come here to gulp down beers by the dozen, listen to country/western music, and munch on peanuts that have enough salt in them to make you thirsty again. Later on, when they've had one too many, they try riding that mechanical bull — his name's Ivan — and I'll tell you, old Ivan's knocked many an urban cowboy on his behind."

"I can't believe you got that all out without a breath and still filled two more drink orders," Sherlock said, and raised her beer glass toward the bartender.

"Yeah, I'm good that way. They used to call it working the bar; now they call it multitasking."

"How old is Ivan?"

"He's been here longer than I have. What is that — nine years come December. You don't look like you're crazy enough to climb aboard."

"Give me two more shots of your Texas whoopee, and I might take a ride." Sherlock sighed. "What I really want to do is drink and mind my own business. Trisha, let me tell you, this beer not only has hairy knuckles, the freaking stuff has big hairy legs."

Trisha gave her a salute with a white towel. "I guess you're not used to real Texas beer. Actually, neither am I. When I'm forced to drink some, I drink it even slower than you. I tell Gator — he's the owner — he probably mixes the beer in his big Texas john."

"Now, there's a happy thought."

An hour passed while Sherlock pretended to sip her hairy beer and listen in on stories told at the bar, mostly by an old man in a cowboy hat who claimed to have lost his shirt in Reno and was living in the backseat of his Chevy Impala, waiting for Lady Luck to knock on his window again.

Kirsten had arrived at eight last night, and it was eight o'clock on the nose. Sherlock went on high alert, hoping she wouldn't hear gunfire, hoping Dillon would bring that psychopathic killer down hard and fast, without the need for violence, without anyone getting hurt.

Time passed slowly for her after that. Sherlock finally said quietly, "Another half hour gone, and still no Kirsten. Maybe she won't show tonight."

Of course, there wasn't an answer, since she could only transmit. She saw Trisha's hands flying. The crowd was two-deep now at the bar.

She'd forced herself to take the last drink of her first killer beer when she heard a mellow voice beside her right ear: "Hey, you all alone here?"

CHAPTER 40

Sherlock's heart kicked a high step in her chest. It was Kirsten, and she was here, not outside, facedown on the sidewalk, handcuffs being snapped on her bony wrists, being read her rights. How did she get past Dillon, Coop, and Lucy? Had Bruce Comafield gotten past them, too? She'd have bet Sean's favorite toy basketball Kirsten couldn't ever get past Dillon, that he could sniff her out from across town. So somehow Kirsten had come in through the back, even though Coop had checked the alley door, made sure it was locked. And that meant Bruce Comafield had gotten past Dillon without being recognized, and then he'd slipped back and simply opened the back door for Kirsten. Had they followed the same routine the previous night? It made sense they'd be careful. Too bad Mrs. Spicer hadn't noticed.

New ballgame, new rules; she hoped the

good guys would still win.

Sherlock turned to look up into Kirsten Bolger's thin, dead-white face, saw her dark eyes were glittering nearly as brightly as Mrs. Spicer's. Her hair was short, spiky, and tonight not red but black as Morticia Addams's. So she'd changed things up a bit. She was wearing a red blazer over a black turtleneck sweater with black jeans, and a red belt slung low. Kirsten had shoved her way through a dozen people to get to her.

"You're a girl," Sherlock said. "From your voice, I couldn't tell. Nice throaty sound. I hope you're not a smoker."

"Yep, I'm a girl, and thanks. Nope, never picked up that nasty habit. Hey, best thing about me is I'm all alone tonight. My guy kissed me off when my best friend stuck her hand down his pants and turned the key. The bitch."

Sherlock raised her empty beer glass. "Here's to the bitches of the world. May they join the bankers and the lawyers at the bottom of the ocean."

Kirsten laughed, leaned close, since the noise level had notched up even higher. So many people — too many, Sherlock thought, for much chance of taking Kirsten down without anyone getting hurt. Kirsten said, "Hey, what about ratty guys? Wait a sec."

317

She called to the bartender and asked for two beers.

Sherlock frowned up at her. "You want to buy me a beer?"

Kirsten laughed, waved that away with a very white hand, long, thin fingers and short, blunt nails. There was a big silver ring on her right hand. And the same ring on her left hand. "Hey, I'm not into girls. I wasn't lying about the boyfriend. I'm lonely. I figure one always has to pay for companionship, right?"

"I don't know. I've never been lonely until tonight. My ex-boyfriend, the chigger-brained moron, stole my car."

"What's a chigger?"

"You know, one of those nasty little spider things, bite you in tall grass in the summer."

"Why'd he do that?"

Trisha set the two beers in front of them, shoved over another bowl of peanuts. She gave Kirsten an appraising look before she bounded away to fill half a dozen more orders. The jukebox music was tuned really loud now, and voices shouted above the music. Sherlock wouldn't be surprised if they heard glass breaking soon. She took a lip-taste of the beer. "He took my car because the squat-brained dip likes my blue Corvette better than he likes that wimp-butt little white Miata of his. He said he was feeling insecure and figured the Corvette would impress his mama. Like I believed that. More like a dog-haired bimbo. Hey, thanks for the beer. Here's to all the tarts that my rutting goat of a boyfriend sleeps with; may they swim with the seaweed."

The two women clicked beer glasses and drank.

Kirsten tapped her fingers lightly against her glass, leaned close when someone bumped her, and gave the guy a killing look. "Hey, my name's Stephani — that's with an *i* at the end. My mom lost it there for a while, I guess, what with all the drugs they pumped into her. I was a C-section, as she told me every single day until I managed to get away from her the morning of my eighteenth birthday. Geez, nearly ten years ago next week." She fell silent a moment, looking into the depths of her beer.

Sherlock thought, *Why would you lie about your age when it doesn't matter?* She hoped the agent listening to them could hear Kirsten clearly in this noise.

Kirsten took another small taste of beer.

So you want to keep your mind clear so you can kill me with no muss or fuss.

Kirsten asked, "What's your name?"

Sherlock waggled her eyebrows. "Suzzie. With two *z*'s."

Kirsten grinned, showing straight white teeth.

Sherlock said, "I guess my mama kind of lost it, too. I sure wouldn't want to have a C-section." She looked briefly toward where she knew Dane Carver and Ruth were sitting in a side booth, but she couldn't see them through the crowd. Then she finally met Dane's eyes. He nodded toward a young man at the far end of the bar. Sherlock looked at the guy, then away. A minute later, she searched his face again, then stopped, didn't want to overdo. Did Dane think this guy was Comafield? The guy was young, sported a sad attempt at a goatee and a shaved head. He wore a nerdy tweed jacket with chinos, and thick black-rimmed glasses, not aviators. Could be him, could be. If it was, it was a good disguise. He was by himself, nursing what looked like straight vodka but was probably water. When he finally raised his head and turned to look at the jukebox, Sherlock's blood ran cold. It was Bruce Comafield.

That bald head got you past Dillon. I'll bet you even wove yourself into a crowd, used them as camouflage. Smart boy.

To be honest, she wouldn't have recognized him if Dane hadn't nodded toward him. One thing she knew for sure — Dillon wouldn't ever take the chance of coming in here to take Kirsten down; no way would he risk a shoot-out in the bar. Too many innocent people, and who knew if Kirsten or Comafield carried guns along with the wire tucked inside Kirsten's pocket? No, Dillon would take her down when she came outside with Sherlock weaving around like a drunk. But there were so many people, all of them talking, drinking, dancing, strolling in and out of the bar, always new people coming in. What if she pulled out her SIG and stuck it against Kirsten's ribs and simply walked her outside? She could manage that, but there sat Bruce Comafield, and he was the wild card in the mix. Still, if push came to shove, she knew she could take Kirsten easily, and she'd said so to Dillon. Too bad he'd placed his hands on her shoulders and said, "This is boss to subordinate, kiddo, a direct order, so pay attention. If by any wild chance you get close to her, you do not try to take her by yourself, do you understand me?"

And he'd had the nerve to wait until she'd finally nodded, as if he didn't trust her unless she did. *Smart man.* Sherlock sighed. Well, at least now she had a role to play —

she was center stage as the tethered goat.

Kirsten said, "There are worse things than a stupid C-section, the whining cow."

"Yeah? Like what?"

"Like seeing that cow all decked out in diamonds, prancing around on her new husband's arm, knowing she kept me from knowing my real father all my life."

Whoa.

"You never knew your daddy? Why'd your mama not tell you about him? But she finally told you? Well, that's good, isn't it?"

A woman tapped Kirsten's shoulder to squeeze past her to the bar. Kirsten tightened all over. Sherlock could practically see her black rage boiling up. Then Kirsten smiled, moved closer to Sherlock. "My daddy wasn't a nice man; that's what she finally told me."

"Well, then, it was good she didn't let you near him. He might have hurt you."

"Oh, no, he never would have hurt me. He would have loved me and admired me. Do you want to know what else? The bitch never even told him he had a kid — namely, me. He died without knowing I even existed."

Sherlock said, "He died? Your dad? How did that happen?"

Kirsten's eyes went dead, like frozen black

water. "Monsters killed him. He didn't have a chance."

Sherlock waited, but Kirsten said nothing more. She said easily, "Hey, you're wearing the same ring on both hands. Why's that?"

Kirsten looked down at her hands, seemed to study first the ring on her left hand, then the one on her right hand. "They're perfect, aren't they?"

"I don't know about that — but they're different-looking, unique. Someone special give them to you?"

"Yeah, someone real special. One of the rings belonged to my dad. The other one was made for me. So, now I wear them both. I'm never really alone, you know?"

"No, not really, but that's okay. I guess my own problem isn't in your league. I mean, ex-boyfriends litter the ground."

The frozen black water went liquid again. Kirsten smoothed herself out, gave her a smile. "Give it a try, Suzzie. The jerk stole your car, right?"

"Yeah, like I told you, that dog-breathed fool stole my Corvette."

"I can see how that could make the list, but he'll return it, right?"

"Probably. He's an idiot, but he's not stupid."

"Hey, you're funny. I'll have to try out

some of your descriptions. Dog-breathed fool, yeah, that'll make my boyfriend stand up and bark. Yeah, my girlfriend has him for a while, but I plan to take him back."

"You're pretty funny yourself. Hey, Stephani, I gotta hit the women's room. You wanna come with me?"

I can take you down in the women's room; it's nice and private. Dillon will understand, since I'd have you by yourself. Come on with me, come on.

"Nah, it's too crowded. I'll guard your beer," and Kirsten laughed, lightly laid her palm over the top of Sherlock's glass. "Good luck getting through the mob. Have at it, Suzzie Q with two *z*'s. Don't be long."

Bummer, Sherlock thought as she wove her way through the crowd, everyone so packed together the dancers could only sway in place. She passed Ollie and Jack seated across from each other, their beers on the small round table between them. She didn't look at them, simply kept walking. She waited until she got to the door with an exit sign and the unisex bathroom figure beneath it before she said out loud, "I'm on my way to the bathroom so Kirsten can spike my beer. Behavioral Science and Dr. Hicks are going to do back flips when they hear what she had to say. Don't worry, I'm not going

324

to drink any of the beer, I don't want to get sick. Dillon, you know I'm not flying solo, not with all of our people in here, so don't jump the gun."

When she headed back toward the bar, a guy tried to pull her into a dance. She pressed lightly on the nerve at his wrist, and he yipped and backed off.

Hey, Kirsten, you finished spiking my beer? I hope Ruth got a lovely pic of you doing it.

Sherlock felt her blood hum. She was so revved she felt ready to leap off a tall building and fly.

Time to play this out now.

CHAPTER 41

Sherlock squeezed in next to Kirsten at the bar. Kirsten was still standing, guarding both her beer and her bar stool. Sherlock couldn't help it, she gave a quick look at her new glass of Texas Espresso. Would she have to pretend to drink it? She felt Bruce Comafield's eyes, knew he was watching her. She'd considered dumping the drugged beer on the floor beside her, but she gave that idea up, what with both of them watching her.

Kirsten clicked her glass to Sherlock's. "Hear, hear, Suzzie, drink up."

He's watching; he's watching to see what I'll do. She didn't want to drink it, didn't want to, but she drew in a deep breath and took a small sip, then another. She didn't taste anything different, but she knew bad things were about to happen to her. A guy accidentally hit her arm, and she knew she could have let him knock the glass out of her hand, but what would be the point? She took another small sip.

Kirsten was so close to her now Sherlock could smell her perfume. She smelled like violets. "You know," Kirsten said, "I was thinking about moving. I'm getting real tired of Baltimore. Where do you live?"

"Two blocks over, off the Inner Harbor."

"What do you do to keep yourself in gold hoops?" She flicked a finger over one of Sherlock's earrings.

Sherlock forced herself to take another sip of beer. "I own one of those kitschy little tourist shops in the mall. I've got a great view of the boats in the harbor. It's kind of fun. You?"

"I live only a block away, in that big high-rise off Calvert. Cheap jerks, they haven't replaced the doorman yet, and he left four months ago. You got security?"

She saw Kirsten was eyeing her drugged beer, saw Bruce Comafield was watching her, and forced herself to drink some more. "No, I haven't got any security, either. What do you do for a living, Stephani?" Her words slurred a bit, and Sherlock was surprised at how fast the drug was acting, and she'd only drunk a little.

"I was selling art over in the Calliope Gallery. Do you know the place? Most of the paintings are dark, with old barns and graveyards and fluttering ghosts, you know, an Edgar Allan Poe theme, but that didn't work out."

"How come?"

Kirsten laughed. "I kept shooting all the freaking ravens off the tombstones. No, I'm kidding. I didn't like my boss. Now I'm currently assessing my employment situation, since my money's running pretty low. What do you think? Could I be an artist's model?" And even in the tight space, Kirsten managed to strike a professional pose.

"If I were an artist, I'd hire you in a minute."

Sherlock knew her words were frankly slurred now. She knew it was time to get moving, time to rock and roll out of the bar to Dillon waiting outside, before she fell over and puked all over her beautiful black heels.

She slid off the bar stool, staggered a bit, and grabbed the edge of the bar, none of it an act. She hated it, wished she'd managed to figure out how to dump the beer and fake the rest. She felt nausea pumping in her belly, felt her brain clouding over. "What's this? Three of these wonking Texas Espressos and I'm about ready to fall over?"

"They're pretty strong. How about I help

you home, Suzzie Q? No, it's okay, you're on my way. Hey, what about your skunk-brained ex-boyfriend? Do you think he'll be waiting for you?"

"That fat-fried jerk? He'll only show up to leave my car. He knows he'd better, or I'll call the cops on him."

Sherlock tried to take a step, slammed into a knot of people. Kirsten grabbed her arm, righted her. "Good for you, sweetcakes. Come on, now, Suzzie, let me walk you home. Wow, this crowd is as thick as that BP oil slick."

Sherlock gave her a sloppy grin she didn't fake. "Yeah, you're okay, Stephani with an *i*." She took a step and nearly fell over a big-haired woman at a table, but Stephani caught her arm again and pulled her back.

"You sure aren't much of a beer drinker. I'm glad you don't want to ride that mechanical bull. Look at all those yahoos hooting and hollering and getting tossed on their butts."

"No bull. I want to ride in my blue Corvette. I sure hope that dip-brain brought her back safe and sound."

Out of the corner of her eye, Sherlock saw Ruth, Dane right behind her. *Good,* they were following them. She heard a guy yell "Yahoo!" Then hoots of laughter and boos when he went flying off Ivan. The people at the bar looked like they were slowly moving toward the shows on Ivan. Sherlock saw Bruce Comafield toss a bill on the bar counter, force his way through the crowd toward the bathroom and the back door. Sherlock hoped Ollie and Jack were on him. She saw Mrs. Spicer standing frozen in the middle of the bar, a full tray in her hands, customers flowing around her, staring after Sherlock and Kirsten, her face wild with excitement. Thank God, Kirsten hadn't noticed.

And then Mrs. Spicer yelled over all the noise, "You have a nice evening, all right?"

Not good.

Kirsten froze, her hand tightened on Sherlock's arm.

Sherlock waggled her fingers in Mrs. Spicer's direction and said to Kirsten, "Next time maybe I'll give that mechanized bull a try." She beamed drunkenly up at Kirsten. She could feel Mrs. Spicer's eyes fastened on them, prayed Kirsten was too focused on killing her to pay any more attention to Mrs. Spicer.

Sherlock staggered out of the bar in lock-step with Kirsten. Four guys, all of them drunk and laughing and insulting one another, spilled out behind them. They were older, and one of them started singing "Good Night, Irene."

Sherlock knew she was going to throw up, and she had to act first. Had Kirsten's other victims felt this sick this fast? She had to hold on, had to. She couldn't believe it when a big black Pathfinder screeched up to the curb right in front of them and at least a half dozen guys and girls in their early twenties belched out of the behemoth and surrounded them on the sidewalk. *Oh, no. Dillon, you can't get to Kirsten, not with all these drunken happy people in the way.*

So it would be just her and Kirsten. Sherlock was leaning heavily on Kirsten's arm, her steps uneven and jerky. She wondered if she'd be able to take Kirsten down with the cramps coming in vicious waves that made her want to double over. She tasted bile in her throat, and swallowed, once, twice. Soon, she thought, she'd be throwing up her toenails, completely helpless. She knew what to expect, and she hated it.

Hold on; get yourself ready.

"We're getting there, sweetie. Don't worry, I'm with you, and I'll stay with you. Ignore all the drunk hee-haws. Maybe tomorrow you can take me for a nice long drive in that sexy Corvette of yours. Hey, sister, watch where you're going!"

Sherlock was nearly in Kirsten's arms, people forcing them closer. She managed to say, "Yeah, that's a plan. What's going on here? I can't believe it, three beers and I want to throw up on my expensive heels."

CHAPTER 42

The bar doors flew outward again, and more laughing, hooting drunk people spilled out. She didn't see Dillon or Lucy or Coop, but she couldn't really see much at all. She was surrounded by merry, mentally debilitated people who had no idea a monster was in their midst.

Sherlock felt her mind floating away, only to have it whip back when the cramps and the nausea struck harder. Through a haze, she saw Mr. Spicer come roaring out of the bar. What was he waving? Good Lord, it was a bat, and he was yelling something. She saw a blur of movement — Mr. Spicer was swinging the bat, mowing through the crowd like a berserker.

I've got to act; there's no more time. Where are you, Dillon? There was a space, and as she fought off a wave of nausea, Sherlock jerked away from Kirsten's grasp, whirled back, and struck her hard in the jaw. But there was no leverage behind it, because the world was spinning madly, and she was too close.

She saw Kirsten fall back, slam into a couple of people, who yelled in surprise as they leaped out of the way. She watched her trip and go down with a yell into a guy's legs.

She heard one of the older guys who'd been belting out Irene's name yell, "Hey, Redhead, what are you doing? Why'd you knock her down? You nuts?"

Sherlock fell to her knees beside her, managed to pull out her SIG and press the barrel to her mouth. "Hold it right there, Kirsten, party's over. You're under arrest." She knew her words were slurred, and though she wanted to tell her what she was under arrest for — how many women? — she barely managed to call over her shoulder, "Dillon, I'm here. I've got her down!"

Had anyone even heard her over the singing, the shouts, the laughter? If they had, had any of them even understood her words?

Kirsten came up on her elbows, stared up at Sherlock. "What? You're not —"

She knew she was going to heave, and yelled, "Dillon!"

She was weaving over Kirsten, unable to

334

control herself, her SIG a dead weight in her hand, all the people pressing closer. There were shouted questions, angry voices — she heard someone yell, "She's got a gun!" No more drunken laughter now.

Everything was happening so fast, all in an instant of time, and Kirsten was squirming wildly. Sherlock tried to hit her again, but it wasn't going to happen. She had to do something before she passed out, but her coordination was shot, the world and all its noise was fading in and out on her now. She managed to grab Kirsten's head between her hands and slam it against the sidewalk. Kirsten's eyes went blank; she was out. *Thank you, God.*

She heard Mrs. Spicer yell something about Billy — who was Billy? — to get back inside, and for Billy to stop. There was more, but Sherlock simply couldn't understand now; her mind wasn't working right, and she felt so sick and miserable, she simply wanted to roll under a car and die. Who was Billy?

Sherlock threw herself over Kirsten, her brain spinning, the din of people yelling, many screaming now, running to avoid Mr. Spicer's swinging bat. Billy, she knew it was Billy, she recognized his voice — he was yelling about Gator putting down the freaking bat.

Sherlock heard Dillon's beautiful voice over all the chaos. "All of you, quiet! We've got this under control. Go back inside, now! Take Mr. Spicer with you."

How much time had passed? Maybe an hour, maybe a minute, two seconds? She didn't know. Sherlock saw Billy shoving people aside like bowling pins until he came up to her and grabbed her shoulder. She very nearly threw up on him. His voice sounded like a foghorn, fading in and out. "What is this, you robbing her? You knocked her out cold?" He saw the gun and grabbed her arm. Sherlock, nearly gone now, made out the gun in his big hand — at least she thought it was a gun — and he pressed it against her head. "Listen up, sister, I'm a cop. I want you to step away from Ms. Spiked-up Hair. Drop that big-assed SIG, and get down on your stomach."

She was surprised her SIG was still in her hand. "Wait, wait —" Sherlock tried to reach under her tunic to her jeans pocket to pull out her creds, but it wasn't happening. Her jeans pocket seemed to be in a different universe, her hand floating all around it. She looked up at him, couldn't make out his face but felt anger pulsing off him —

and that was clear as day. She heard Dillon's voice but couldn't make out what he was saying. She knew she had to make this angry man understand, but her voice came out a blurred whisper, "FBI, I — I had to knock her out or she'd — kill me."

He was right next to her, and his hand clutched her hair, pulling her face back, "You, FBI? I'm a cop, and I say you're a drunk moron with a gun. Now, let go of it, you hear me, or I'll make you real sorry. As for you, buddy, you get your ass out of here or I'll knock your head off." Who was the buddy he was talking to?

Then Sherlock saw Dillon's legs. *Thank God, he'd finally gotten through.* She wanted to call out to him, but he was weaving now, his legs blurring with a dozen other legs as she gulped down the sickness. Billy was screaming, it hurt her ears it was so loud, and he was yanking on her hair, and she heard Kirsten groan. Billy let go of her hair and hit her shoulder hard. She thought she heard Dillon growl, like an animal ready to attack its prey, and that prey would be Billy.

"Dillon." Had she said his name aloud? She wasn't sure. Kirsten was grabbing her and shoving her off. No, she couldn't let her go, she couldn't. She heard Billy cursing, yelling, heard Dillon, but couldn't make out what they were saying. There was only noise.

Was that Mrs. Spicer yelling that the redhead was FBI and Billy was an idiot?

She was closing down fast. She heard Kirsten yell out Bruce Comafield's name. Was he here? She heard running, and then gunshots, lots of them, and they sounded like cannons firing in her face. She heard Comafield yell, "Run, Kirsten! Run!"

Sherlock tried to grab her, she really did, but it was a pathetic effort. Kirsten kicked her in the ribs, and when Sherlock grabbed her leg, Kirsten turned and slammed her other foot into Sherlock's face. Sherlock fell back onto the sidewalk. She saw bursts of white flare madly, then the dim streetlight was suddenly bright and looming, weaving around her, and all the people were shadows now, blurring into one another.

She heard running, screaming, more gunfire. Who was firing? *Everyone,* she thought. *Everyone, and Comafield. Kirsten?* Did she have a gun, too?

She tried to yell for Dillon to stop Kirsten, but nothing came out of her mouth. She rolled over, managed to come up onto her knees, and began to vomit.

Through the awful heaving, she heard Mrs. Spicer yelling at her husband.

There was gunfire still. She knew it was Comafield; he was firing to provide cover for Kirsten, that was it. Was he shooting at Dillon? Of course he was; he was shooting at everyone.

CHAPTER 43

Legs, all Sherlock could see were legs, a dozen or a hundred. She heard two people close to her yell and saw them fall. She heard Ollie shouting for people to get into the bar, and she saw his legs now, and he was shoving people, trying to get them to move.

She heard Lucy shouting at Comafield after a lull in the shooting. Was he out of bullets? She heard him curse, heard metal garbage cans clanking.

Another gunshot, a sharp, loud staccato. Was it Lucy, had she hit Comafield?

She was shutting down. Was she dying? She heard Coop shout, heard Lucy say something, then she heard more gunfire.

She smelled Dillon, and she smiled as she felt him kneel next to her, pulling her up against him, his hands on the pulse at her throat. "It'll be all right; it's over now, sweetheart; hang in there. The ambulance is on the way." He said it over and over, and she tried to smile up at him, tried to tell him she loved him, but the world was swimming away from her. "Dillon," she whispered, and then she was out.

Savich felt her pulse again. He lifted her away from the mess, and rose. He saw Lucy bent over Billy, pressing her hands down hard against the bullet wound in his shoulder. Ollie and Dane were seeing to the wounded civilians, and Ruth and Jack were still herding people back into the bar, trying to get everyone to calm down.

He couldn't believe it. What a debacle.

Bruce Comafield had two bullets in him. He saw Coop go down on his knees and apply pressure to his belly wound.

And Kirsten? Savich knew in his gut Kirsten was long gone.

He lightly shook Sherlock, but she didn't stir. He was so afraid he was ready to run to the nearest hospital himself. He saw people were beginning to come out of the bar again to see what was going on, but he didn't care enough to tell them to back off.

He heard Mrs. Spicer say with satisfaction, "You got the little pisser. And now look, he's shot. What happened to the girl, to Bundy's daughter?"

Savich began to rock Sherlock. Where

were the ambulances? He called out, "Mrs. Spicer, would you join Mr. Spicer and give everyone a free beer? That'd be nice, don't you think?"

Gator seemed to think about that. "Well, maybe you're right. I mean, Billy's my friend for a hundred years now, and he deserves one. Are you okay, buddy?"

Billy the Cop called out, "Yeah, Gator, give me a beer. That'd be good." And then he moaned real loud.

"Don't you dare die on me, Billy, you got that? Hey, I'll get you two beers. As for those stampeding yahoos, I'd like to take my bat to them." Still grumbling, Mr. Spicer walked back into his bar, his bat tucked under his arm.

Savich heard Billy the Cop say to Lucy, "Do you know, Agent, you have no idea how pissed off my guys in the BPD are going to be at you and your buddies. It might be best if you left right now, before they get here."

Ollie came down over Savich. "How is she?"

"Unconscious. At least she wasn't shot, but I'm worried she's overdosed. Where are the ambulances?"

Ollie dropped down on his haunches. "They'll get here soon. There's no sign of

Kirsten. What do you want me to do, Sav-ich?"

"Help Coop with Comafield. He's our only lead to Kirsten. I don't want him dying on us."

Coop looked over at Lucy when she said to Billy, "You're doing great, Billy. I gotta say, though, you've really got sucky luck. I mean, here you are out for a night of fun, and a maniac guns you down. Sorry about that."

"Ain't that the truth. Anyone dead?"

"No, thank heavens, just a couple of walking wounded."

"So why were all you FBI here?"

"I'll tell you something, Billy. The woman who got away?"

"Yeah?"

"She's Ted Bundy's daughter."

Billy cursed a blue streak, surprise mixing with pain. "We all knew she was out there, but not here, not in Baltimore. That was really her? Right here, at my neighborhood bar? I can't believe I missed that."

People being people, they began to slip out of the bar again once everything quieted down. They blocked the street, milling around when the ambulance sirens sounded in the distance, the cop sirens blending in. People who drove by slowed down to see what was going on, and others were hanging out of neighboring windows, asking what was happening. Even when the ambulances pulled close, few of them seemed to want to get out of the way.

It was a zoo until Ollie cupped his hands around his mouth and shouted, "Every one of you step back inside or I'm making arrests!"

Finally most people moved aside so the EMTs could get through.

Savich heard Coop call out, "Here first!" and saw Coop was pressing both palms hard on Comafield's belly.

Savich shouted, "How bad, Coop?"

"It's going to be close, Savich. He's shot in the abdomen, and there was blood and intestinal juice coming out. I can't control the bleeding; it's going to take an operation to do that. The other bullet went in and out of his arm, no big deal. Still, he's going to be luckier than most of God's creatures if he makes it. What about Sherlock?"

"She's in and out," Savich said, wiping her mouth.

And then she whispered, "Did she get away?"

"Yeah, but don't worry about it now. How are you feeling, sweetheart?"

"We screwed up." She pulled out of his

arms, doubled over again with cramps and dry heaves.

That was true enough, Savich thought, gathering Sherlock against him once her cramps had lessened. They'd held their fire because of the crowd, but it didn't matter, they all looked like incompetents.

Jack Crowne pushed through the crowd around them, saying, "FBI, let me through." He came down on his haunches. "How are you, Sherlock?"

She said, "I sure wish we could replay that whole deal."

"Ain't that the truth," Lucy said, still crouched beside Billy the Cop, and then she blinked. "Yes, I really wish we could." She raised her face to the sky. "Do you know a raindrop hit my nose. What more could we ask for?"

Coop was hovering next to the EMTs. "Take good care of him, we really need him. He's our spigot."

When the EMTs were ready to move Comafield, Coop stepped back, watched them slip a collapsible gurney under him, and lift him on its wheels and into the ambulance.

"Really, guys, take good care of him," Coop said to them. "We need that man."

Other ambulances had arrived, their EMTs spreading out to care for the other wounded.

It started raining hard.

And Savich prayed no one would die as a result of this fiasco. He huddled over Sherlock while they lifted her onto a gurney and put her in an ambulance. They said nothing at all when he jumped in after her.

Chapter 44

Savich stood over his sleeping wife. He hated her pallor, hated that her eyelids looked bruised. He knew intellectually she was going to be all right; the doctors had assured him of that at least three times. But that assurance didn't seem to matter to that place deep inside him that knew he would curl up and die if something happened to her. A nurse appeared at his elbow, lightly touched his arm. "You look worse than she does, Agent Savich. I swear to you, your wife will be fine. Her throat is going to feel a bit bludgeoned, but that won't last long, maybe a day or two."

He nodded. What had she seen on his face? Fear? All right, Sherlock would be fine, no reason for her not to be. The nurse wouldn't lie, would she? They'd pumped her stomach, and her blood pressure was

347

back to normal. They said the drugs were short-acting, and their effects were wearing off.

They'd soon know for sure if Kirsten had used the same drugs on Sherlock as she had on her other victims. The symptoms were right. He wondered if Kirsten had given Sherlock an extra-large dose.

Ruth walked into the room, handed Savich a cup of hot tea, a cup of coffee in her other hand. *Good old hospital cafeteria Lipton,* he thought, savoring the hot, bitter taste. He saluted her with his cup. They both looked down at Sherlock, her glorious hair, clips removed, now a wild nimbus around her pale face. He pulled the sheet over the green hospital gown to Sherlock's shoulders, smoothed it out. "She'll be okay," he said, more to himself than to Ruth. Then he said it again. "She'll be okay, Ruth."

Ruth touched her fingers to his forearm. "Yes, she will, Dillon. The nurse told me to repeat that to you myself until you believe it. Sherlock's a trouper, she's got a gold-plated engine of a heart. She'll be okay, so stop worrying." But Ruth knew he couldn't help but worry; she was worried herself, impossible not to be, as she looked down at her. Sherlock was always so full of energy; she radiated a kind of life force you could practically reach out and touch. But lying here now, she looked almost insubstantial, like a pale copy of herself.

Ruth said, "I nabbed a nurse as she came out of the OR. She said Comafield's intestines are a mess but that his surgeon is the best they've got, and that was all she could tell me. She looked worried, Dillon."

"He'll make it," Coop said from the doorway. "People like him always make it." He walked to the bed and stared down at Sherlock for a moment, touched her hand, then nodded at both Ruth and Savich and walked back to the surgical waiting room. He looked for Lucy, but she wasn't in the waiting room; she'd moved away to sit off by herself halfway down the hall where there was another small grouping of chairs. Her head was down. It looked to him like she was staring at her sneakers.

He went down on his knees in front of her, took her hands in his. Her skin felt clammy. "Hey, Lucy, what's going on?"

Her head jerked up, but she wasn't there, she looked as though she were a million miles away, and where she was, he thought, was a mad and lonely place — and where was this place? He couldn't stand to see that look, couldn't stand that she was so far apart from everyone. From him. He'd known her for only six and a half months, not long at all in the scheme of things, but he realized at that moment he didn't want her to hide herself from him. He realized in that moment that she was perhaps the one human being with whom he wanted to share his life. He rocked back on his heels. How had this happened? It didn't matter; it had happened, and he accepted it, relished it. He waited, said nothing.

He was right about the place Lucy was. Nothing around her could take her mind away from the ring for very long. But she hadn't even thought of the ring during the shoot-out at the Texas Range Bar & Grill, only afterward. Would she have used it to stop Comafield and Kirsten? Was it her duty as an FBI agent to do whatever she could to stop people from getting hurt, getting shot?

What is past is done; it can't be changed. That was so much a part of her experience, it rarely even needed to be said. How did a person make peace with the power to change the past, even only a few seconds of it?

Should she try to become some kind of hero, undoing every tragedy and accident she came across, giving back a suddenly orphaned child his parents again? If so, how should she live? Out patrolling all the time so she'd have a better chance of using the eight seconds to make things right? Or would she come to use the ring on a whim, playing with people like marionettes to get her way, or simply for sport, for the fun of it?

Wasn't life about accepting what came down the pike, both the joys and the sorrows, being responsible for what we did ourselves, facing it, making the best of it?

Like facing what had happened tonight?

She thought again of her grandfather, what her grandfather had written about her grandmother's unhealthy obsession with the ring. Lucy couldn't remember a single time she'd been with her grandmother and wondered if something was wrong with her. Had her father seen the obsession in his mother? Had he understood it? He'd known about the ring, but had he known what it did? She didn't think so, but it didn't matter now; they were all dead, there would be no answers for her.

Twenty-two years her father had protected his mother, and he'd protected her, too.

Twenty-two years he'd known his father's body was buried in the attic, waiting for the day it no longer mattered.

The strange thing was, it still mattered.

She thought it might matter forever. And she wondered again, had the stress of all of that killed him too young?

Her grandfather had believed her father wouldn't have wanted her to have the ring. But her father hadn't known the ring could have saved Claudine.

Coop snapped his fingers in her face. "Lucy? Are you with me?"

She looked blank, then quickly focused. "I was thinking about all the chaos — the local cops crowding around us to see for themselves what a mess the feds had made. Everybody knew she was long gone before they cordoned the area."

That isn't what you were thinking at all. She'd lied to him, nice and clean, but he decided not to call her on it. He grinned at her. "Yeah, we sure got to enjoy a lot of their jokes. The worst one I heard was from that young rookie — he looked about eighteen?" Coop mimicked him: " 'But I thought you guys were the best in the whole world!' "

Lucy said, "Yeah, well, we're supposed to be. Serves us right, I guess."

She hoped she'd never see anything like tonight's fiasco again. *The ring.* They'd been so lucky no one was killed. The two civilians Comafield had shot had suffered only minor wounds, thank God.

She said, "This was a learning lesson, and my father always told me learning lessons had to be painful to be worth anything. I'm afraid the price of this one is going to be too high.

"Where does Kirsten go from here, Coop? On a rampage? You know she's unstable, and now she's got to be enraged — at us, and at Sherlock in particular. Don't forget Savich gut-shot her boyfriend. What is she going to do now?"

Coop laid his hand on her shoulder. He could feel the bones. She'd lost more weight. Well, her father had died, and she'd remembered her own father and grandmother dumping her grandfather into a trunk. And now there was the blasted ring.

The bloody ring — he shook his head. He wanted to ask her, but more, he wanted to press her face against his shoulder and comfort her, maybe tell her a joke, but he didn't do either of these things.

He sighed, stepped back. "You're probably right. Look, we'll figure it out and we'll catch Kirsten Bolger." He paused a moment. She looked exhausted, from the inside out. It was worth a shot, and so he said, "Lucy, you were sitting here alone, your head down. What were you thinking about? Not about tonight, so please don't lie to me again. Were you thinking about that ring?"

She looked at him, saw the worry in his eyes. He was a good man, she knew that now, and he was a good agent, she thought; he could probably pry sardines out of the can without opening it. He saw to the heart of things, but even that didn't matter. She wasn't about to tell him anything about the ring; it wouldn't be fair to involve him, surely not yet, if ever. She touched her fingers to her shirt, felt the ring lying against her throat, warm and pulsing.

Lucy drew in a slow breath as she looked up at him. He looked tired, all the mad adrenaline drained out of him now, and he looked afraid. For her? She had to touch him. She laid her hand over his. "Don't be worried for me, Coop. All the excitement's over, and all of us survived tonight. We were lucky."

Coop took her hand between his. "Lucy, I want you to know, whatever you're going through, whatever is eating at you, I don't want you to think you're alone. Listen, I'd really like to be there for you. Actually — I want to be with you." There, he'd said it, for the first time in his life, he'd said those words to a woman, to Special Agent Lucy Carlyle. Who knew?

She looked at him for a long moment and

seemed to consider what he'd said. She pulled her hand away, giving a slight shake of her head as she rose. He watched her fill a paper cup with water from a water cooler and raise it in a toast. He watched her give him a bright smile. "Hey, here's to Mr. Spicer and his handy bat. Who knows, without the bat, maybe we wouldn't have Comafield. Excuse me, I've got to hit the bathroom." And she was gone in under two seconds.

He stared after her.

CHAPTER 45

Savich said to Ruth as he slipped another hospital pillow under Sherlock's head, "When Mr. Maitland got off the phone with Director Mueller tonight, he said the director wasn't pleased, and that's a whopper of an understatement. He can't figure out how it all got so screwed up. I told Mr. Maitland I was having a hard time figuring that out, too, except then a huge herd of drunk people stampeding around flashed clear in my mind. Luckily, Mr. Maitland said he wouldn't let the director reassign the case."

His heart nearly stopped when Sherlock said clearly, "I should have taken her down in the bar."

Not in this lifetime. Savich smiled, leaned down and kissed her cheek. "Next time I'm thinking knockout gas for the whole bar, everyone down and out, including Kirsten and Comafield. How do you feel, sweetheart?"

She thought about it. "Like my throat is on fire and someone hollowed out my stomach with a big scoop. What'd they do to me?"

"A little bit of this, a little bit of that," he said. "Go back to sleep, okay? You'll feel fine in the morning." To his surprise and relief, she did. She whispered something, but he couldn't make out the words. He'd wanted to ask her how she could drink that beer, knowing it was drugged, but that could wait.

Savich left Ruth to keep watch over Sherlock and walked to the waiting room to talk to the agents sitting there, drinking coffee and looking flat-out depressed. He said, "Look, guys, there's no reason for you to hang around any longer. It's after two in the morning. Go home and get some sleep. I'll see everyone tomorrow at the office. Don't forget to make all your bedtime prayers for Comafield's continued existence on this planet. He's our one precious lead. We'll discuss the operation tomorrow."

Jack Crowne said, "The plan was fine, except for that mob of people, most of them so drunk they barely realized they could have been shot dead."

"We couldn't have worked it any worse," Ollie Hamish said.

Jack's cell blasted out toe-tapping salsa. It was his fiancée, Rachel. He was smiling a little as he said hello to her and walked out of the waiting room.

No one left. They spent the next hour going over every detail of what happened, what they could have done differently, until all of them were so tired they couldn't think of anything intelligent to say.

At three a.m. Dr. Oliver Pendergrass, his green scrubs dotted with blood, strode into the waiting room. In a surprising British accent, he said immediately, "He made it through surgery."

There was a collective sigh of relief.

Dr. Pendergrass continued: "It amazes me what damage a single small bullet can do to the human body. That scrap of metal caused a great deal of injured bowel, I'm afraid, and I had to remove a good length of it. We'll see how he does. The major risk now is overwhelming infection, in his belly and in his blood. The next few days will tell."

"Thank you, Doctor," Savich said. "You and your staff should be aware there will be police at his door and in the hospital during his stay."

Dr. Pendergrass said, "Yes, I thought as much. By the way, the anesthesiologist said Mr. Comafield was involved with this woman I've seen plastered all over the TV — Ted Bundy's daughter?"

"That's right," Savich said. "I know it's tough to get your brain around that one."

Dr. Pendergrass said, "Involved how? Is he related to her in some way?"

Ruth said, "Not related but involved, I guess is the best word, and that's why it's so important he live — we're hoping he can tell us where to find her."

Savich asked, "When do you think he'll be able to talk to us, Dr. Pendergrass?"

Dr. Pendergrass turned to him. "Sorry, Agent Savich, but he's been in recovery only five minutes." He looked down at his over-sized watch. "I'd say he might be fully conscious soon, but I doubt he will have his brain together enough to answer your questions. Why don't you get some sleep and come back here maybe six hours from now?"

Savich wasn't about to leave Sherlock, but he ordered the rest of the agents home. He had no worries about Sean, who was sleeping at Simon and Lily's house.

One by one, they rose and shrugged into their coats. "Go home. I want you guys fresh tomorrow, your brains in gear. Don't come back here, go on into the office about noon. I'll be there when I can. Coop, you and

Lucy meet me here at nine, but call me first to make sure Comafield is still breathing."

Savich walked back to Sherlock's room, listened to her even breathing for a while, then eyed the big chair beside her bed. No reason he couldn't snooze for a while.

He fell asleep immediately, her hand lying limply in his.

CHAPTER 46

Thursday morning

Sherlock's voice was raw. "I'd planned to pour the drugged beer on the floor beside my bar stool. There were so many people weaving around, dancing, singing, I thought I could pull it off. But then I saw Comafield staring at me, not only that, but Kirsten moved closer to me, no more than six inches away. I couldn't toss it. If I'd tried to lip it, she'd have seen, so I had to drink it, no choice, but I didn't drink very much."

Savich wanted to tell her she should have called the whole thing off, simply left, but he kept his mouth shut. She'd made a judgment call. If they'd all done what they were supposed to do, her decision would have led to catching Bundy's daughter.

Sherlock continued, "I was feeling pretty bad by the time we got outside. I don't know if you saw me, but I hit her as hard as I could, pathetic though that was. At least I caught her by surprise, knocked her down, pulled my gun, and then everything went south. Where does that expression come from, Dillon? Then I remember being on the sidewalk, throwing up and wanting to die. I realize now that only a few seconds passed, but I'll tell you, it seemed like hours. What really happened?"

Coop and Lucy stood on the opposite side of the bed, not looking too bad, considering they'd had maybe four hours of sleep. Coop gave her a running commentary on the havoc and the mayhem, until he got to where Sherlock had refused to drop her gun, even with Billy the Cop hanging all over her and feeling like she was going to die. He paused, wiggled his eyebrows at Sherlock.

"Spit it out, Coop, or I'll deck you, maybe tomorrow. What happened then?" She rubbed her throat. She sounded like a frog, but the soreness was down and the hospital tapioca had settled nicely in her empty stomach. A nurse had told her cheerfully that she'd had her stomach pumped. So stomach lavage was *the little bit of this, little bit of that*" her husband had told her about. She suddenly wasn't so sure about the tapioca.

Coop told her about the gunshots after

Comafield blew out of the alleyway, protected from return fire by the crowd, and how Savich had managed to put the bullet in his belly while on the run.

Sherlock felt her body creak with effort to push the stupid button that raised the bed so she could look at everyone straight on. When Savich would have helped her, she shook her head. She could do this. Once she was sitting up, she said, "What happened to Billy the Cop? I remember he was yelling at me, waving a Beretta around."

Lucy said, "Full name's William Benedict, and he's a longtime homicide detective with the Baltimore Police Department. The Texas Range Bar and Grill is his neighborhood bar, been going there for years. He went after you, Sherlock, because you had a gun on Kirsten, but then, thank goodness, he realized what was happening. He took a bullet instead, but he'll be fine. I heard him laughing this morning as I walked down the hall, talking about Gator and his freaking bat. What a story he has to tell his buds."

Savich glanced at his Mickey Mouse watch, patted Sherlock's hand. "It's nine o'clock. I'm off to see Bruce Comafield. Coop, Lucy, I've given it a lot of thought, and I think it's best I speak to him alone. You guys stay here — if I need you, I'll call."

When Savich saw they would both argue, he raised his hand. "Look, we need information, and we need it now, with no messing around. I'm going to question him. Trust me, okay?" He didn't tell them that he'd already asked Dr. Pendergrass to cut down Comafield's morphine, told him exactly why. Savich wanted him awake and on the edge, if possible.

Bruce Comafield was in a small glass-fronted room in the ICU on the third floor. An FBI agent was seated at his door, his legs crossed, a magazine unopened on his lap.

"Hi, John," Savich said to Agent Frish. "Anything interesting?"

"Nope, if by that you mean Kirsten Bolger waltzing by, maybe to shoot him to keep him quiet."

Savich smiled. "Yeah, that's what I mean."

"Nope, not a whiff of her."

"Keep a sharp eye, okay?"

"You'd better believe it. I wouldn't want to get taken down by that crazy-ass woman."

Savich stood in the doorway for a moment, staring over at Bruce Comafield. There were lines running into his arms, a line running under the hospital blanket. He had an oxygen clip in his nose, and he was awake, moaning, his eyes closed, turning his head back and forth on the flat pillow.

He wasn't in happyland. *Good.*

Savich didn't say anything, simply walked to his bedside and looked down at him. Slowly, Comafield became aware of him, turned his head back, and opened his eyes to look up at him.

Comafield whispered, "You were one of the agents at the Willard, to speak to Lansford."

"Yes, that's right. I'm pleased you recognize me. If you forgot my name, it's Special Agent Savich, FBI."

"You shot me."

"Yes. I'm pleased you're still alive, Bruce."

"Not for long. They're going to let me die of pain. If I turn my head I can see all the nurses out there at that big counter. I keep ringing for a nurse, but none of them come. Dear God, it's horrible. Tell them I need some pain meds."

Savich leaned down close. "Tell me where Kirsten is, and I'll make sure you get more morphine."

Comafield tried to spit at him, a stupid thing to do, since he didn't have the strength to lift his head, and it hurt even to try, and the spit ran down his chin. He cursed the spit, cursed Savich, cursed fate. "Kirsten knows who you are, too, you bastard. She's going to kill you; she's going to execute you. It was a little promise we made to each other. Whoever brought one of us down is not going to live. So, you're a dead man. She's going to watch you die, count on it."

"Where is she, Bruce?"

"Look over your shoulder if you want to find her. She'll be looking for you."

"That's not going to cut it, Bruce."

He closed his mouth and stared toward the pale green wall opposite his bed.

Savich leaned close, watched Comafield's eyes dance madly with pain. "You want more morphine, Bruce? The only way you'll get it is for you to tell me where Kirsten is hiding."

Comafield's dark eyes turned black, rage boiling up. He whispered, voice shaking, "You can't do that. You think I'm stupid? You're the law; you can't torture me."

"You let Kirsten torture all those women she butchered. Did you help her jerk a wire around their necks, pull it tight while your victims were helpless from the drug she'd fed them?"

"That's different! How'd you even know about me?"

"A very sharp guy in New York described you very well. You know, the guy Kirsten set up to take the fall at Enrico's Bar?"

Comafield knew; of course he knew.

Savich leaned close again. "I liked you better with hair. I've got to say, though, you fooled me. I never saw you go in the bar, and believe me, I was looking."

"Yeah, I stuck myself right in the middle of a happy group, and hooked up with this little blonde. We waltzed right in. I'm always careful now — real careful after New York."

He managed to preen through the pain. Savich leaned close. "Now that you had your little rush, I can see the pain's really getting to you. Tell me where Kirsten is, and I'll get you a ticket on the morphine express."

At Comafield's silence, Savich turned away from him. He walked over to the single window and looked down into the parking lot. It was nearly full at a little after nine o'clock in the morning. It was a gray day, clouds swirling low, the wind blowing fiercely. He was glad he'd put up the Porsche's top. He began whistling.

He admitted to himself that he felt great relief when Comafield cursed him again, finally nodded, and whispered, "All right. Morphine, get me morphine."

He gave Comafield a long look before he got Nurse Harmony, a lovely name for a nurse, Savich thought, and she nodded, said she'd just as soon leave the killer to rot. Comafield watched her hook up an infusion device to his IV. Every fifteen minutes he could press the button, she told him. When she left, he was frantically pushing the button, his eyes closed.

Savich walked back to the window, and waited.

It was Comafield who spoke first. "Like I said, you'll never find her; she'll be the one to find you. So, it doesn't matter that you know where we were staying — at the Handler's Inn on Chestnut. Hey, the room is one-fifty-one. Go search our room to the rafters, you won't find anything, and believe me, Kirsten won't care, she'll be long gone."

And he gave Savich a malicious smile, proof that the morphine was kicking in. "Why do you care, anyway? You're going to be dead."

"The two of you didn't discuss where you were going after Baltimore?"

"Nope, she hadn't decided." Comafield actually gave Savich a small grin. "She told me her daddy was guiding her steps. Then she'd laugh and say, well, mainly it was her daddy."

"What did she mean by that?"

"I don't know exactly, but sometimes she'd talk on her cell phone, never told me who she was talking to."

"Did you hold down the women while she strangled them with the wire?"

"No, that was her deal. She said her daddy always worked alone, and so would she, at least at the denouement. That's what she called it — *the denouement*. She liked to say she not only wrote the scripts, she was the lead actress, and she wasn't about to share that with anyone, even me. The denouement was always just her and the pathetic female she'd chosen to dance with.

"When I was working for Lansford, she'd call my cell, tell me where to meet her." He shrugged, but it hurt and he grew very still.

After several minutes, he spoke again. "I met her in New York on Sunday, checked out Enrico's that night. We left Monday night, after Kirsten was done with Genny, to drive here. We only had two nights together, and now she's gone from me."

Genny — Comafield had called Kirsten's victim by her first name, like she was a friend.

"I really tried to hate Lansford, because Kirsten did, but when he finally accepted his political future was wrecked, I kind of felt sorry for him. The old bastard. She told me how he was terrified of her, she could see it in his eyes, and she'd laugh."

"Is that how you met Kirsten? Through

her stepfather?"

"It was back three years ago." He stilled a moment, then said, "I'd seen her before, at his office once or twice, but never met her. She didn't live at home, but she crashed there occasionally, for the fun of it, she told me, to think about her mother going into her old room and wondering.

"But one time I couldn't sleep even though it was really late. I looked out the window, saw Kirsten unlock the back door and slip inside. I snuck down to her, saw she was covered in blood and she was smiling so wide I could see her molars. And you want to know what? All she had to do was say my name and we ran back to my room. I tore those bloody clothes off her, and we had at it until I heard people moving around the next morning."

"Do you know who she killed that night?"

"I know her first name was Arnette. Kirsten kept saying it over and over, said it sounded tasty on her tongue. I think her last name had something with a rug — Carpenter, that was it. She was a model, like Kirsten, and a pretend artist, Kirsten said. Kirsten despised her because she was a fake and a snob, said she had put her lights out right and proper, and she deserved it.

"We were together whenever possible from then on."

"Did you know when she killed other women? Did she come to you afterward?"

"If she killed anybody else, she didn't tell me. I never got to see her come in fresh from a kill again until — well, until she left San Francisco. I realized I missed it, missed the planning of it, watching her work the woman at the bar, watching her change her hair and her role whenever she stepped in to put her name on another lady's dance card. I was her front man, always checked things out, kept an eye on what was going on while she was working. She never made a mistake until last night, with that redhead. I thought when she hooked up with that redheaded girl, she'd really hit the jackpot. I've never before seen her so involved; she was nearly thrumming with excitement —"

"With the thought of killing her?"

"Of course."

Savich held himself still as a statue, couldn't trust himself not to rip the IV lines from Comafield's body. To listen to him talk so calmly about murdering Sherlock. He said very quietly, "The redhead is my wife. They had to pump her stomach."

Comafield stared at him for a moment, then grinned. "Go figure that. That girl really is your wife? So she was in on the setup, too," and he fell silent again.

Savich smoothed himself out. He didn't know why he'd even told Comafield; it had just come out. He said, "Since you worked for Lansford, you couldn't see her all that often when she left San Francisco."

"Yeah, since I had to stick with him, it was difficult to get away to join her." His voice trailed off, and Savich feared he'd fallen into a drugged stupor, but then he whispered, his eyes tightly closed, "I remember one night we were together in Cleveland. She told me she sometimes warmed her hands over the fires. 'What fires?' I asked. 'In hell,' she said, where she was sitting cross-legged next to her daddy while he told her what he did to have the most fun. And he'd ask her when she was going to get serious about her own work, when was she going to hit the road, like he did?

"Then she'd talk about how sexy her daddy said dead people were, but only when you were the one who put out their lights. Then that made them yours, and it was a fine thing to come back to visit your works of art and enjoy them, over and over, until they fell apart, and then they weren't art anymore, they were trash. I didn't want to know exactly what she meant, but deep down, I knew."

Comafield's words were slurring. Savich knew he didn't have much more time before he was out of it. "Of course you knew, since I'm certain you've read everything written about Ted Bundy, including his taste for necrophilia."

"Yeah, lots of it. Maybe it scared me a little, and then she'd shrug and look at me like she was —" He closed his eyes again — from the pain or the image?

"Like she was picturing you with catsup?"

That snapped Comafield's eyes right open. "No, you bastard!" He swallowed, and Savich knew the morphine was slurring his brain as well as his speech. "Well, maybe, but I knew she'd never hurt me. Do you know, after her kills, she'd come back to our hotel and she'd always be flying high? She'd want sex and booze, and she'd want to dance and hoot. You know what else she did? She always dressed up like the woman she'd just killed. She liked to play that role as well as play the lead, she'd say. She had all these wigs, and she'd put on the one most like her woman-of-the-hour, she called them. And she'd sometimes let me play the kill and she'd —" His voice faltered.

"Yes?"

"— pretend to strangle me with the wire.

But she never really hurt me —" His voice was fading.

"Bruce, were you her acolyte?"

Comafield's eyes focused on Savich's face. "Her acolyte? That sounds like I wore a black robe and chanted. No, you've got it all wrong, damn you. I didn't wear robes and chant Latin. I was her rock; I tethered her to the world so she wouldn't fly off the planet. She needed me. She loved me."

"Did you love her?'

Comafield whispered, "Oh, yes. She could do what I never could. She was a whirlwind, always racing to catch her daddy. She was doing a countdown. I asked her how many women she had to kill to catch up to her daddy, and she said one hundred. She never told me how she came up with that number.

"Now it doesn't matter. I won't ever see her again." His eyes were suddenly hard on Savich's face. He whispered, "At least I know she'll kill you. Wherever she was going, it's off now, because she's coming to kill you. Sweet Jesus, I'm going to die and I'll never see her again."

"You're not going to die, Bruce."

"Yes," Comafield said very quietly, his voice nearly singsong with the morphine. "I know I am. I feel it. I wish I could see

Kirsten just one more time, but I know I can't."

And Bruce Comafield turned his head away.

Savich went back to Sherlock's room, ordered her to stop moving around and lie still, no arguing, and listen. Then he said to her, Coop, and Lucy, "Let me tell you about a very strange and sad couple."

CHAPTER 47

They spoke to Mr. Ricky Levine, skinny and tall, standing at attention behind the small reception counter of Handler's Inn. Savich thought he could still be in high school, with the acne on his chin, his belt pulled tight to keep his tan uniform pants up. He was so nervous his hands shook when they introduced themselves. He kept chewing on his lower lip, and had a hard time meeting their eyes. No, he told them, no, really, he didn't know a Mr. Bruce Comafield. He'd remember a dude saddled with a name like that. He offered to let them see that he wasn't registered in the computer.

Lucy sidled up to him, all friendly face and sweet smile, so he wouldn't drop over in a dead faint with Savich and Coop standing over him, that or start babbling nonsense.

"Mr. Levine, who did you give room one-fifty-one to late Monday night?"

Mr. Levine's nervous fingers worked the computer keyboard. "Here it is — Mr. Cane. He checked in, said his wife was joining him later. Cane — Comafield. I see, that's pretty close. Well, he seemed like a nice guy — young, you know? Yuppie-looking, had a gold credit card, I saw it in his wallet, even though he used cash to pay for the first night. I remember I asked him how long he was going to stay, and he said two, maybe three, days."

"How late was it Monday night when he got here?"

"Wow, it was nearly one o'clock in the morning."

Lucy nodded. So he and Kirsten had driven directly here from New York City. And she started partying the very next night.

Coop kept his mental fingers crossed. "Does the Handler have a policy of getting the license plate number?"

"Yes, we do, but I always go check myself, since guests never know. Mr. Cane drove a light blue Chevy Cobalt. Look here, the number's by his registration. It's a Maryland plate, that's white, with black lettering, CTH six-two-five. That's good, isn't it?"

"That's fantastic, Mr. Levine," Lucy said and beamed at him.

Coop asked him, "Did you ever see his

wife, Mr. Levine?"

Mr. Levine nodded. "They ate breakfast together the past two mornings here in our dining room. I eat when I come on duty, that's one of my perks, and so I saw them. That's how I know. She ate a bowl of prunes and a load of muffins. I remember that because she was so skinny and those muffins are loaded with fat. Go figure. As for Mr. Cane, he ate cereal, I believe, and a banana. More healthy. He looked really fit, a sharp dresser. I heard several of the waitresses talking about how cute he was, with his thick hair, and especially in his aviator glasses."

"How did she look? How was she dressed, Mr. Levine, do you remember?"

"She had long blond hair, real thick, sort of curly, hanging down her back. She was wearing blue jeans and one of those skinny knit tops. That's how I could tell she was so skinny. I thought it was kind of chilly out for that getup. She looked, well, arty, I guess you could say. She was wearing bloodred lipstick, I remember thinking exactly that, and her face was real white. I think it was makeup."

Lucy said, "Do you remember anything else about them, Mr. Levine? Anything they did that was out of the ordinary?"

Ricky thought about that, then slowly nodded. "It was the oddest thing. I was doing a double shift last night. I happened to be looking outside and saw him walking to his car. Like I told you, most times I saw him, he was dressed really sharp. But last night he was dressed more like my brother the nerd, you know, down to the black thick-framed glasses, pants too short, showing his white socks, and this crappy tweed jacket? And he had this dorky hat pulled down low over his head. Then she came out; her blond hair was gone, so I knew it was a wig. Now her hair was all short and black, and she was wearing a red blazer. I wondered if they were going to a costume party —" Mr. Levine swallowed, looked like he was going to throw up.

"And what, sir?"

Ricky leaned forward on the counter. "Well, before they left, they came in here to buy some gum, and she looked me right in the face. I'll tell you, that look of hers was real hinky, and then she licked her lips, like she wanted to stick a fork in me. It scared the bejesus out of me."

Ricky Levine wasn't stupid, Coop thought. "Did she say anything to you?"

"No, but when they left to go to their car, she looked back at me, and then she started laughing."

Lucy said, "Have you been watching the news on TV, Mr. Levine?"

He nodded slowly. "Some, you know, when I get a chance, the way you do when people are always interrupting, with kind of half an ear. Why?"

"Did you hear about the shoot-up last night at the Texas Range Bar and Grill here in Baltimore?"

"Yeah, I heard there was some trouble." Then Ricky shook his head. "Didn't hear what happened, though."

"Did you happen to see a woman's photo shown on the news?"

This was clearly a stretch, then Ricky said, "Yes, wait, I do remember seeing a woman's photo on the tube."

Lucy said, "She's the same woman who stayed here. She's Mrs. Cane. She's Ted Bundy's daughter, Mr. Levine. If the opportunity arose, she would have stuck a fork in your face."

Mr. Levine's fingers went to his cheek. Then he cocked his head to one side, looked at her blankly. "Who's Ted Bundy?"

Savich was putting out an APB on the blue Chevy Cobalt while they walked down the hall to room 151.

Coop said, "So they stole the car here in Maryland. I hope they didn't kill anyone."

"We'll know soon enough," Lucy said. "I hope it doesn't occur to Kirsten to steal another car just yet."

Coop said, "I wonder where Daddy is guiding her steps now?"

"To Dillon, that's what he said." Lucy added, "And that scares me to my toes."

"Did you believe him, Savich?" Coop asked him.

Savich said, "No, not really."

Lucy frowned at him, then said, "Do you think she guessed Bruce would rat out where they stayed?"

Savich said, "I believe him when he told me it didn't matter if he told me, because Kirsten was long gone. Still, let's not take any chances."

Lucy said, "And who is this other person Kirsten is calling?"

Savich shrugged. "Comafield didn't know."

Savich slammed the door inward when he unlocked it, and they went in, fanning their SIGs around the room, though Kirsten hadn't been there for hours now. Her fingerprints, sure, but that wouldn't help them.

Kirsten hadn't left anything, not even a

comb, but who knew if there'd be a stray hair from one of her wigs? Savich called in a forensic team.

When Savich got back to Sherlock, they let him take her home with orders for her to rest — in bed — today. She stepped into the wheelchair without any trouble at all. "I'll be ready to go once my stomach has some real food in it," she said.

"Yeah, but you'll do as you're told. I'm your boss. Suck it up. I'm thinking some chicken noodle soup might be a start, then we'll see." He grinned at the leap of interest in her eyes.

Chicken noodle soup. Sherlock's mouth watered. She looked at his profile, laid her hand lightly over his on the handle of the wheelchair. "We'll find her, Dillon."

Yes, he thought, they'd find her, but how many more women would die because of the mistakes he'd made? Where would Kirsten go next?

Savich was wheeling her down the hall when Dr. Pendergrass called out to him, "Agent Savich, I'm sorry to tell you, but Bruce Comafield has died. He developed sudden sepsis and then abdominal hemorrhage. We did everything we could, but he didn't make it. He was a young man, and I believed he had a chance. I'm sorry."

Sherlock saw Savich flinch, only a small movement. He said, his voice emotionless, "Thank you, Dr. Pendergrass."

Dr. Pendergrass nodded, then turned to walk away. He turned back. "Agent Savich, don't think your method of interrogating Mr. Comafield had anything to do with his death. It didn't."

Savich only nodded, then turned to look at his pale wife. "Nothing more to do. Let's get you home."

CHAPTER 48

Maryland
Midday Thursday

Lucy drove her Range Rover out of the hospital parking lot and headed for 95, Coop behind her in his blue Corvette. She was still smiling at what he'd said when he'd walked her to her car. "I know this really good Chinese restaurant near Dupont Circle, best Szechuan in town. How about dinner Saturday night?"

Dinner with Coop. A date, he was asking her for an actual date? She started to kid him about working her into his busy dating schedule, but that joke fell right out of her head. That wasn't what she wanted to say at all. She said with a smile, "Actually Chinese is my favorite, especially Szechuan." She paused for a moment. "Isn't there some bureau rule against agents in the same unit socializing?"

"Savich and Sherlock are in the same unit,

and they do, I imagine, a great deal more than mere socializing."

It was the strangest thing, but her heart speeded up, and out of her mouth came, "You want to get me alone so you can jump me, right?"

He raised an eyebrow. "What a thing to say. It'd only be our first date."

Her heart thudded to her feet, and her voice flattened. "Oh, I see. You want to talk to me some more about what I'm — feeling."

He lifted his hand, touched his fingers to her cheek, then dropped his arm. His eyes roved over her face. "Do you know, I happen to find myself worrying about you at the oddest times — like when I'm shaving or drinking nonfat milk out of the carton or singing in the shower, and wondering how we'd sound in a duet? The thing is, Lucy, I want to get to know you better, and talking isn't such a bad idea, now, is it?"

She laughed, thrumming with energy. "Okay, then, but all I've got to look forward to is talking?"

"Certainly not."

"Then you might as well think about what you'd like to sing with me in the shower, too."

He tapped his fingertips to her chin. "I'll

think about that, too, although that's an awful lot of thinking."

Lucy tossed him a little wave and got in her car.

Coop was whistling when he followed her onto 95 south and back to Washington. Cyndi Lauper's "Girls Just Want to Have Fun" would make a fine duet for the shower.

Lucy wanted very much to have dinner with Coop, Szechuan or not. She had gone to sleep thinking about what he'd said the previous night at the hospital. She knew he cared about her, and that was the rub. Whatever she told him or didn't tell him about the ring, she wasn't going to let the blasted thing take over her life, or keep her from being as close as she wished to people she could love. She refused to choose between telling someone about the ring and loving them, or not loving them at all. Besides, how could a girl turn down a Chinese dinner with a hunky guy like Coop?

As she wove through thickening traffic, she felt the pull of fatigue — far too little sleep, and too much excitement. She turned on the radio to a soft-rock station and sang along, hoping to wake up. The traffic on 95 got messy around Peterborough, so she turned off onto 35, a nice two-lane country road that led west, made a couple of turns, and headed back again south, roughly parallel to 95. This lovely country road was her own private find, a road few people knew about, and a straight shot to Chevy Chase. From there she'd follow her usual commute to the Hoover Building. She hadn't seen Coop turn off. Had he gotten ahead of her?

She rolled down the window and let the chill air blow over her, hoping the blast of cold would get her to full alert. There was not much out there to help her focus, mostly green pastures, some horses and cows, and lots of trees with scattered houses interspersed. An occasional car heading north passed her by.

She glanced back in her rearview mirror, hoping to see Coop's Corvette, but she saw only a white commercial van about the size of a FedEx truck behind her, and there was only the driver. She noticed the van was holding steady behind her, neither speeding up nor turning off. She slowed down to see if he wanted to pass, but the van kept the same distance between them for several minutes. She wondered if the driver had gotten himself off 95, as she had, and was content to enjoy the quiet ride into Chevy Chase.

The van behind her speeded up, closing to within about twenty yards of her Range

Rover. She looked up, saw another white van that looked identical to the one behind her pulling out about a hundred yards ahead. Only thing was, he was driving backward, the driver hanging his head out the window, his dark hair blowing as he looked at her. She felt a spurt of adrenaline as her heartbeat spiked. She drew a breath, kept her own speed steady. She pulled her SIG from her waist clip and put it under her leg.

What on earth was the guy doing? Was he going to smash into her with his rear bumper so he wouldn't get hurt himself? Then she realized they wanted to smash her between them.

She speed-dialed Coop's number.

"Yeah? Lucy, what's up?"

The van behind her was coming closer. She yelled, "Coop, I'm on Country Route Thirty-five, south of the Peterborough exit off Ninety-five. Two white vans have got me between them, and they're going to try to smash me. I think they want to kill me!"

A bullet slammed into the Range Rover's back window, shattering the glass.

She heard Coop yelling her name, heard the screech of his tires. She swerved into the oncoming lane, but the van in front swung over with her, keeping her trapped

388

behind him, while the van behind moved closer. There was no one else on the road, not a vehicle in sight except the vans. More shots crashed through the car's shattered back window, the bullets slamming into the back of the front passenger seat, shredding it. There was no doubt they were trying to kill her.

A bullet whizzed by her head and spider-webbed the windshield. She ducked automatically.

She looked down at the butt of her SIG tucked under her leg, but she knew it was no good to try for a shot at the driver of the van behind her. She had only seconds.

She jerked the steering wheel sharp left, stomped her foot on the gas. Her passenger-side fender hit the rear of the van in front of her, bounced off as she kept turning hard left, tires screaming, and spun the car into the sharpest U-turn of her life. The van behind her chickened out from hitting her head-on and swerved to the right. The metal screamed as he clipped her front fender, but she was free.

She hit the gas, quickly took the Range Rover to its limit more or less down the center of the road, going the opposite direction.

There was blessed silence.

She looked back and saw that both vans were racing after her, one in each lane, both drivers' arms out the windows, firing wildly. She prayed they were too far away, but still the bullets flew all around her, hitting the pavement and the metal frame of her car. She knew she couldn't be lucky forever. How many more bullets would miss her? She heard her own wild breathing, tasted fear dry in her mouth.

Where was Coop? She grabbed her phone and dialed 911 — "Officer in trouble" — and gave all the information to the operator.

The operator, bless her heart, didn't ask for more, said only, "Godspeed, Agent Carlyle. Help's on the way."

She couldn't wait for Coop or the cops; she had to fight back. Lucy grabbed her SIG, reached her arm around herself, and fired back through the shattered rear window first at one van, then the other. One of the vans swerved, then straightened again. At least she'd gotten their attention.

One guy went nuts firing at her, emptying his magazine. It would take him a moment to shove in a new magazine, but the man in the other van kept firing, and she heard pings and smashing glass, then felt a slap of cold against her head that knocked her sideways. She straightened as a bullet struck her windshield, shattering the glass. Shards struck her face, her arms, but without much force. She was thankful she was wearing a jacket.

Her beautiful Range Rover was a wreck, but if any car could save her, it was this one. She was still going more than eighty miles per hour down this country road.

She would die this way, or some innocent driver ahead of her would. She had to act.

Lucy stood on the brakes. Her tires screeched. As she skidded, she leaned out the driver's window, took careful aim at the closer van, and fired. She saw the gunman's arm jerk, saw his gun go flying. The van began weaving all over the road, out of control. She thought he'd smash into her, but the van behind rear-ended him first, sending him flying off the road toward a wide ditch. The van twisted and rolled over and over until it flipped and finally came to a stop on its back at the bottom of the ditch.

There was dead silence for a moment; then the other van backed up, screeched into a U-turn, and roared away. She stopped the Ranger Rover, shoved open the driver's-side door, and jumped out.

The van in the ditch exploded.

A ball of fire shot into the air, hurling her

backward, the blast concussion pushing the air from her lungs. She saw black smoke billowing up, smelled the stink of burning rubber, saw pieces of the white van blasting into the air. A part of a metal door slammed down six feet away, skipping over the asphalt with a loud grinding noise. She staggered to her feet and lunged beneath her car. She sucked in air, but there wasn't enough. She knew the shooter was dead inside the van, and there was nothing she could do for him.

Coop screeched to a halt behind Lucy's Range Rover, saw her car was a mess, all the windows shot out, dented beyond redemption.

"Lucy!" He was out of the car in an instant, running to her. He saw her struggling out from beneath the car, grasped her beneath her arms, and pulled her the rest of the way out, then helped her to her feet. "Good God, woman, what happened?"

A siren blasted in the distance.

Two police cruisers pulled up alongside Coop's Corvette.

They both held up their creds, Lucy shouting, "There's a shooter in the other white van, headed south!"

But there was no sign of the white van on the road now, nothing except an ancient pickup truck lumbering slowly toward them, strapped-down furniture filling the bed.

Two cops got out of the lead car, guns drawn, while the other headed south, siren blasting. Lucy was still holding up her creds. "I'm a federal agent! The man in that van tried to kill me!" She pointed to the burning van in the ditch. "I guess there's not going to be anything left of him."

One of the cops pulled out his radio. "You all right? You need an ambulance?"

"No, no, I'm okay." The cop nodded to her, looked at her creds again, shook his head, and strode to where the van still sluggishly burned.

"Lucy, dammit, you're not okay, you're shot." Coop grabbed her, pulled her close, examined her head. He pulled out a handkerchief and pressed it on the wound. "All right, okay, it must have bled like mad, but it's not deep. Good thing, or I'd really be pissed."

"No, I know it's not bad, Coop. I'm okay, really." She touched her hand to her face, and her fingers came away bloody. She stared at them, as if trying to take it in. "This is very odd," she said, and looked up at him. "I suppose we should have someone look at this."

Coop spoke to the cops, shoved her into the passenger seat of his Corvette, got behind the wheel, and headed back to 95. He made sure she kept pressing the handkerchief against her head. She felt a bit light-headed now, but who cared? She'd survived, she'd beaten them. She was alive. She heard Coop on his cell. "Yeah, Savich, I'm taking her to the hospital."

He was speeding, the Corvette hugging the road, as he pushed it hard for the first time. "Coop," she whispered, "you're going to get a ticket."

He laughed. "Hold yourself still, Lucy, and don't move. Our ETA to the hospital is about ten minutes."

Lucy touched her head again, lifted away the handkerchief. The cut was still oozing. The blood was red, and it was coming from her. She pressed the handkerchief hard against the wound. It hurt.

"The bullet grazed you. You'll be okay." He sounded like he was convincing himself.

"Then why are you racing like I'm bleeding to death?"

"Because I'm scared." He speeded up.

"I hope the cops get that other van. The guy left his partner to die."

She sounded strong, she was talking and she was making sense, but it didn't matter — Coop's heart was still pounding. "Lucy, tell me what happened."

"They sandwiched me between them." She told him about the trap they'd set, about her U-turn, and how she'd finally had the chance to fire and shoot one of the drivers behind her.

She gave him a big grin. "My Range Rover was a hero, getting me out from between those two vans." Then her face fell. "I didn't have a chance to name him, though, and now he's totaled. That's not fair for a hero, Coop, it's not fair."

They heard sirens behind them. They would have an escort to the emergency room. He looked over at Lucy, her bloody face and palms. She could so easily be dead.

CHAPTER 49

Whortleberry, Virginia
Thursday afternoon
Kirsten frantically turned the radio dial of the stolen Silverado to the next station, and heard it again. *The male accomplice of Ted Bundy's daughter, Kirsten Bolger, died after extensive surgery during the early hours of this morning from gunshot wounds in a shoot-out in Baltimore with the FBI. . . .*

She smashed her fist against the radio until it went silent, and pulled to the side of the country road. She laid her forehead against the steering wheel, the horrible truth playing over and over in her mind. Bruce was dead, really dead. But he'd managed to save her, and now those fed jerks were chasing their tails again.

She slammed her foot down hard on the gas, and the Silverado shot forward. Soon she was flying, singing Springsteen's "Born to Run" at the top of her lungs, hooting and hollering, trying to drown out her thoughts.

Who would she talk to now about her daddy and what he did with his lady loves? She remembered how after she'd gotten back to him, she'd dress to look like her own lady love for the evening, and they'd watch lovely raunchy porno and Bruce would grab her and they'd tear the sheets off the bed. No one would ever understand her like Bruce did; no one else would listen to her tell how it felt to jerk the wire one last time and know, know all the way to your soul, that this life was gone, forever. And he'd hold her and tell her how much he loved her as his thumb rubbed away the dried blood on her hands.

How had Bruce missed that setup? How had the cops even known they'd be at that dive? That big-haired waitress, she'd bet on it. She'd seen Big Hair looking at her, but she hadn't paid her much attention because she was just an old hag with tons of brassy blond hair who worked in a bar. Who cared what she thought about anything? Kirsten wished she'd told Bruce about her, but she hadn't.

Even that smart-mouthed redheaded girl was a fed. The redhead had played her, played her really good. She got hold of herself. With any luck, the redhead was dead now, like Bruce was dead, a tag hanging off her big toe. Kirsten hoped she'd died in her own vomit. Not that it mattered much. It was the FBI boss guy who'd shot Bruce, the guy on TV Bruce had told her about, whatever his name was. *I'll put him down, Bruce, like I promised you. Wherever you are, you can count on that.*

Kirsten heard a sob. It was from her, from deep inside her, and it surprised her.

Bruce was gone. She was alone again, and she couldn't bear it.

You never had anyone, did you, Daddy? You were always alone, weren't you? If only you'd known about me, if only we could have been together, you could have told me how clever I was, how right I was, to kill those snotty girls in high school. But like you, I had to learn alone, and practice until I was pleased with what I'd done, until I was ready to take a road trip, just like you.

But I had Bruce. I'll bet even when you were with my bitch of a mother, you felt alone. You knew she wouldn't understand, knew you couldn't ever confide in her, share your plans and triumphs with her, not like I did with Bruce. He loved me, he admired me for what I was, what I did, just as you would have done if only you'd known about me. You could have taken me away from that bitch. What fun we would have had. I bless Aunt Sentra for finally telling me about you. I would never have realized, never have felt what I could share with another person. Most of those ridiculous books I read about you, those writers were idiots, they didn't understand, didn't know what it was like to be so full of life, so full of power.

But I understand. And now I'm like you. Alone.

She'd crossed into Virginia on a narrow country road with few cars on it. She'd stolen a big Gold Wing outside Baltimore, but she'd felt way too exposed, so the first chance she got, she revved it off a cliff, watched it bounce into scrubs and trees on its way down to the bottom, smashing itself to pieces. She'd watched the wheels spin in the early dawn light. She'd hot-wired the old Silverado right out of a driveway on a cul-de-sac near Pinkerton, and started driving.

She saw a diner up ahead. *What an ugly piece of crap,* she thought, plunked down by itself on the edge of a podunk town called Whortleberry, a long name for a dot on a map. There wasn't a single car parked in front — no surprise there. The diner was long and narrow, old and weather-beaten. It reminded her of that big-haired waitress who'd called in the feds on them. What was her name? Kirsten didn't know, but she could find out, if she ever wanted to go back to Baltimore and pay her a visit. She looked again at the diner, still didn't see anything going on.

What a dump. Burgundy vinyl-covered booths lined up along the long window that gave out onto the empty parking lot. It was good nobody was around; it seemed like it was meant to be, a diner here, just for her.

She felt the chill wind against her face when she stepped out of the Silverado and pulled her leather jacket closer. A stupid tinkling bell rang when she pushed open the door. Sure enough, the place was empty except for a single woman sitting at the counter, hunched over, reading a paperback, a cup of coffee at her elbow. She turned to see who'd come in, her long streaked blond hair falling straight to her shoulder. Kirsten realized she wasn't a woman, she was a girl, real young, and she was wearing a dippy uniform.

Kirsten pulled off her driving gloves. "Get me coffee."

The girl looked her over, rose, straightened her red uniform with its stupid white handkerchief sticking up out of her single breast pocket, and walked behind the cheap laminate counter to pour some obviously old coffee from a nearly empty carafe into a chipped mug.

Kirsten said, "Bet you don't get much business here."

"Enough," the girl said, and shoved the mug toward her. "But not today. You want anything else?"

You're rude, little girl. Kirsten shook her head. Five minutes passed, and no one came in. Kirsten timed it. She had to admit, it made her consider the possibilities — that sweet young thing lying at her feet, making her journey to the hereafter, the sullen, rude little bitch. She watched the girl return to her seat and the novel. She ignored Kirsten.

Kirsten said, "You got a cook in the back?"

That broke the dam, and the complaints burst out of her. "The putz went home, sick to his stomach, he said, from stuffing down too many nachos last night watching a dorky football game. He made me stay even though all the regulars know I can't cook and they won't come in until he's back."

"I guess you made the coffee. It sucks."

"Yeah, I did. Hey, it looks like you've got crappy taste, since you drank all of it. You want a refill?"

Kirsten had to laugh; the girl had a mouth on her. *Like the redhead last night, like Suzzie with two z's.* This girl was pretty, fine-boned, with the greenest eyes Kirsten had ever seen. *Nice,* she thought, *succulent,* the way her daddy preferred them. *Young,* she thought, *and probably dead broke.* Kirsten bet she had a yearning to do a whole lot else that wasn't this. Kirsten shook her head, put her palm over the top of her mug. "No coffee. Why aren't you in school?"

"I graduated last May. I'm saving to get out of this dump. Hey, I'll get you a piece of pie if you promise to give me a good tip."

"What kind of pie, and who made it?"

"Strawberry. It's fresh. Dave made it this morning before he got sick and went home. How about an extra-large tip for an extra-large piece?"

Kirsten smiled at her, a scary smile, but she didn't know it. The girl took a step back and tried to mask her alarm with a shrug.

Kirsten said, "Sounds good to me." It did, indeed. Kirsten realized she was starving, hadn't eaten since — when? She couldn't seem to remember. The past hours were a blur of panic and pain and rage. But life had to go on, that's what her daddy would say, and so she'd eat a slice of strawberry pie, and then she'd see.

Ann Marie Slatter felt something cold slither through her when the weird woman smiled at her. The knife she was using to cut the strawberry pie slipped out of her nervous hands and dropped to the floor. She picked it up, wiped it on her apron. She gave the woman nearly a quarter of the pie, left only a sliver so Dave could complain about it when he came back, whenever that would be. He loved strawberry pie, particularly his own, and she knew he was looking forward to eating it when he got back.

"That big enough?"

"That's very nice of you." Kirsten cut a bite and ate it. Delicious. She ate steadily until it was gone. She sat back and rubbed her stomach. She said, "You won't believe the size of the tip you're going to get."

Ann Marie shrugged again, tried to act blasé, but realized she was frightened to her bones. She wanted to run out the door and never see this woman again. She stared at the woman's red hair, in thick, short spikes, and her face, it was dead white, like — something nagged at her, something just out of reach, but she couldn't remember what it was.

The door to the diner opened, and Ann Marie was so relieved she nearly shouted with it.

Kirsten watched two older men stroll in, shrug out of their jackets, and slide into a booth. Hayseed farmers, one paunchy, the other skinny, both wearing faded jeans, flannel shirts, and boots older than she was. The bald guy, skinny as a windowpane, called out, "Hey, Annie, two coffees for Frank and me. I hear Dave's living in the bathroom." He said to Frank, all jowly, with a full head of stark white hair that looked weird with his dyed ink-black mustache, "I told Dave what those leftover nachos would do to him, but he ate a huge mound without stopping, even with the cheese cold and hanging in strings off his chin."

Frank laughed.

Kirsten kept quiet, watched Ann Marie take them two mugs of coffee, these mugs not chipped, and the coffee was from a full pot in the back, nice and fresh, the little bitch.

The bald guy thanked Ann Marie. "Hey, I was telling Frank that the guy who was shacking up with Bundy's daughter, you know, that crazy chick who's killing women all over the country? He's dead. The FBI shot him outside a bar in Baltimore. At least one of those crazies is dead and gone."

Frank was stirring sugar in his coffee. "Talk about crazy — that guy had to be a lunatic to hook up with that nutty broad. As bad as her father, that's what everybody says. Hey, what's the guy's name? The guy who was shacking up with her?"

Bald Guy said, "It's something strange — I can't remember."

Kirsten said quietly, "His name was Bruce Comafield."

"That's right," Frank said. "He worked for her stepdaddy, you know, that rich guy who wanted to run for Congress from California until it got out who his stepdaughter was?"

Bald Guy said, "Big surprise for him, I bet, both his stepdaughter and his aide. I'll bet Stepdaddy's glad the guy's lights are out. What's his name? Oh, yeah, Bruce."

Kirsten couldn't breathe. She watched the bald guy wag a skinny finger at Frank; why, she didn't know.

She heard a soft keening sound, realized it was from her, from a wound deep inside her she thought she'd die of. Like Bruce had died.

She said to the two men, "That guy you're talking about who was traveling with Bundy's daughter? Bruce Comafield? Well, he wasn't crazy."

Both men were staring at her now. Ann Marie was, too. It came out of Ann Marie's mouth in a wild burst — "I remember now, I've seen your photo. You're her! Oh, sweet Jesus! You're Bundy's daughter!"

Frank and Bald Guy froze.

Kirsten smiled at all of them as she rose slowly, reached into her leather jacket, and pulled out a small 340 S&W revolver. She shot Frank in the middle of his forehead; then, still smiling, she turned to Bald Guy, whose mouth was open to scream, but no sound came out, because she shot him in the heart. They both fell forward on the table, sending their coffee mugs flying, blood mixing with the coffee.

Ann Marie Slatter screamed and screamed, but she couldn't move, couldn't do anything, shock holding her frozen. Her eyes never left Kirsten's face. She heard a whimper, didn't even realize it was from her.

Kirsten studied her dispassionately. "Hey, kid, I left you a big tip. I hope you get out of this podunk town," and she left.

CHAPTER 50

Coop pulled into a parking slot in front of an older three-story red-brick building, beautifully landscaped with grass, bushes, and trees, already hunkering down now for the coming winter.

He looked over at Lucy, felt a slap of anger seeing the bandage over her temple, knowing too well she could be dead if the bullet had slanted only a bit inward. Her eyes were closed. He hoped she wasn't still in pain. "Lucy? You awake?"

She opened her eyes and slowly turned her head to face him. She smiled. "Yeah, I'm okay. Don't worry." She looked around. "I've always loved this area. Did you know your neighborhood was developed in the 1920s, one of the first communities from a master plan in the country? So many beautiful properties here, you're lucky."

Coop said, "This building — I wanted to live here the first time I saw it four years ago."

She said, "I want to go home, Coop."

"One more time, kiddo — Savich ordered a guard for you until we get our heads around what happened. I'm not going to let you stay in that big house by yourself. Let me speak very slowly here, since your brain doesn't seem to be plugged in — two guys, probably pros, tried to execute you today. Going home ain't gonna happen."

Lucy needed another pain pill onboard. It wasn't only her head, it was all of her. Her muscles ached, and she had bruises everywhere. She felt exhausted, the aftermath of all the adrenaline that had rocketed through her.

He opened her car door, stood looking down at her. Finally, she gave him her hand, and he pulled her out. He saw she wasn't all that steady on her feet, and supported her along the walkway. He unlocked the front glass doors, the panes, she saw, a colorful display of Art Deco, and led her into a good-sized lobby with a bank of mailboxes along one wall and three healthy-looking palm trees in Italian pots along the other.

He got his mail, took her elbow, and

escorted her to the elevator. He pressed four.

The hallway was wide, covered with a stylish dark blue carpet with green splashes, but the track lighting was too bright, and it made her head hurt worse.

"Hang in there, Lucy. I'll give you some water when we get inside, and you can take another pill. I'm thinking a nice nap would be a good thing for you; then I'll order in our Szechuan."

She nodded, but nothing was okay. On the other hand, she was alive, and for now, that was enough.

She'd been trying to think, of course, as best she could manage. Coop was right, it had been a pretty well-planned execution, and she should be dead. *Pros?* But who would hire pros to murder her? She shivered. No one had ever wanted her dead before, not she herself the target. And why should that happen now, today, if not because of the ring?

Of course, Dillon and Coop and everyone wanted to know everything, but what could she say? She couldn't be sure who had tried to kill her, though, she had to think of her Uncle Alan. Did her grandmother tell him about the ring and what it could do? Did he or someone else who knew about the ring so many years ago find out her grandfather had left it for her? But how? And had the killers been told she kept the ring with her? And to take it off her dead body? Another big-time shiver.

She thought of the letter from her grandfather, tucked away in a book in her grandmother's library. Did someone in the law firm know what her grandfather had left her? Surely not Mr. Claymore. Or had someone found the letter in the library? The McGruders had the key, and so did Uncle Alan. The painkillers still in her system tumbled and tossed the thoughts in her brain.

Coop unlocked the door at the end of the corridor and helped her inside. She felt like falling over, but she forced that aside and walked into the square entry hall with its red-and-blue Gabbeh carpet on the polished oak floor. He walked beside her into a large rectangular living room with huge windows on both open sides, with more Gabbeh carpets in yellow and green scattered over the polished oak floor. The furniture was solid, kind of Spanishy, she thought, and the pale lemony walls held vivid oil paintings, again, many of them Italian landscapes. The room felt peaceful, a strange word to come to her mind just then, but it was true.

"This is beautiful, Coop."

"Thank you. I, well, I've put some time and thought into how I wanted it to look. The building went condo about two years ago, so I own it now. No yard work, and that means I go to Savich's house to play basketball with Sean."

"The paintings, they make me feel like I stepped into Tuscany."

"I spent some summers riding through Italy, picked some of these up in little out-of-the-way towns whenever I could afford them."

"A motorcycle?"

He led her to a big overstuffed chair, lightly pushed her down. "Nah, motorcycles are too dangerous."

"I suppose you speak Italian?"

"A bit. I wave my arms around a lot while I talk, makes me more fluent. I'm getting you a glass of orange juice, that's what Dr. Mom recommends for anything from a sprained ankle to a bullet in the head."

He spoke Italian, he had great taste, he wasn't a playboy — she fell asleep.

She felt fingers lightly stroking over her forearm, and heard a low voice. "Lucy?"

Her eyes flew open, and she grabbed for her SIG.

He touched her hand. "No, it's okay. It's

411

only me. Here."

Once she took a pain pill and drank half the orange juice, she laid her head back against the chair. She watched him walk to one of the windows and stand silently, looking out, his arms loose at his sides. Time passed, and she realized she was beginning to feel better, except for the light throb where the bullet had kissed her scalp. She suspected her other aches and pains would get worse as the day went on.

She said, "Dillon told me Kirsten dumped the Chevy Cobalt. Now she's driving a motorcycle."

"Hopefully the cops will see it and report it."

"She'll drive it in some bushes soon, anyway, and steal another car." Lucy drank the rest of the orange juice.

"Probably. Bedtime for you now."

She slept throughout the afternoon. When she awoke, she smelled Chinese, and smiled.

She walked to his kitchen, yawning. He was laying out plates and silverware. "Thanks, Coop, for taking care of me."

"You're pretty easy. Sit down, and we can eat."

"I guess you're right, going home wouldn't be such a good idea."

"I wanted you to see my place, anyway,"

he said, and handed her the carton of fried rice. Lucy saw there was Szechuan beef, her favorite moo shu pork, pot stickers, everything she liked. While she spooned up hot-and-sour soup, Coop said, "While you were asleep, Savich and I discussed who could have tried to kill you. Forensics is still at that van we left on Country Route Thirty-five. You know we're going to trace the van, and sooner or later ID the driver. Then we'll be able to find the other van and the guy driving it. The two men have a history, that'll make it easier to find him."

"I agree they were pros, Coop. They knew what they were doing."

"Can you think of anyone from a former case who could be behind this attempt on your life?"

She slowly shook her head.

He took her hand. "Hard as it is to think about, there's always family. We have to start there. We're thinking your uncle as well as your cousins, Court and Miranda, would stand to inherit a big chunk of money if you died, wouldn't they?"

"I suppose so, since I don't have a will. But I could make a will tomorrow, leave everything to an animal shelter if I want. Listen, Coop, my uncle is very rich. I can't believe it's about my money."

He sat back in his chair, crossed his arms over his chest. "The gorilla in the room, Lucy, is that you found your grandfather's murdered remains in your attic five days ago. Could someone be trying to hide something about that murder, something they don't want you to find, or something they think you could possibly know? And what about that strange ring your grandfather left you?"

So, it's obvious, even to Coop, Lucy thought as she slowly chewed a moo shu pork pancake. She knew to her soul the ring had to be the key. Someone knew she had the ring, and they knew it was important enough to kill her for it. How could she hope to prove that; how could she protect herself or anyone else around her if she kept the letter a secret from everyone, even Coop? She had to tell him some of it; it was the only way to move forward. The letter, then, and what it said. But she wouldn't tell anyone now about what she could do when she held the ring and said that word; maybe she never would.

"Coop, there's something I haven't told anyone yet, something I thought was private, between my grandfather and me. There was more than the ring in that safe-deposit box, there was a letter written to me by my grandfather, probably not long before he was killed. I think it's time for us to speak to Uncle Alan."

Ten minutes later, Coop followed Lucy out of his condo, his hand beneath her elbow, just in case.

CHAPTER 51

Washington, D.C.
Thursday evening
Huge yard, Coop thought, when he pulled into the Silverman driveway. *Way too much work.* Evidently, Mr. Silverman agreed, since the yard as well as the flagstone walkway were covered in six inches of sodden leaves left to rot from the last rain.

At least it wasn't raining now.

Coop scraped wet leaves off his boots on the front porch.

Lucy rang the doorbell. She waited nervously, knowing Coop had told them only that she'd had an automobile accident, but they shouldn't worry, she was okay and wanted to come by to visit. Even Savich had agreed that an impromptu visit with her aunt and uncle might knock loose a lead or two, if Lucy felt up to it. More important, he wanted the Silvermans to know the FBI were looking at them and knew about the

416

ring. He thought it might protect her. She hated this, hated that it had to be done, that her family's involvement had to be faced.

They heard the click of heels. Her Aunt Jennifer opened the door. "Lucy, my poor child!" And she enfolded Lucy in her arms and rocked her. "Agent McKnight promised us you were all right, but I'll tell you, we've still been worried sick. Oh, you've got a bandage on your head!"

"I'm all right, Aunt Jennifer, really."

"Come in, sweetheart, sit down, and I'll get you some hot tea. And you are Agent McKnight?" A lovely arched dark brow shot up. "Oh, yes, I remember you from Josh's funeral. It's hard to believe he's gone, but Lucy, you're what's important now. Come in, come in. Thank you, Agent, for calling us before we heard it on the news."

Lucy's cousin Court was standing in the living-room doorway, smiling toward her.

Lucy had told Coop about Court Silverman — that he was thirty-six, had never been married, owned vitamin stores, and was quite successful. He was tall, buff; he looked sleek. *Yes, that was the word, sleek — like a freaking otter,* Coop thought, and nearly smiled. He looked closely and saw the arrogant tilt to Court's head that seemed to go naturally with his soft white shirt and expensive gray wool slacks. With his hands in his pockets, jiggling change, he looked sort of bored and weary, as though it was no big deal his cousin had almost been killed this afternoon. *You're a conceited little prick, aren't you, Court?*

Coop saw Mrs. Silverman was beaming at her son. He shook Court's hand after he extended it, almost unwillingly, Coop thought, as if Coop wasn't worth the trouble.

Coop said, "You guys aren't first cousins, you're what, once removed or something?"

Court said, "Something like that, but unfortunately never kissing cousins, right, Lucy?"

"I'm too staid and boring for you, Court; always have been." She turned to Coop. "Court likes to play on the wild side — bungee jumping, skydiving, skiing the Alps, you name it. If there's a chance he can break his neck, he'll try it."

When they were all seated, Court opposite the rest of them in a beautiful French antique chair, swinging an Italian leather loafer, Jennifer Silverman said, "I'd hardly say you're boring, Lucy. I mean, you're a federal agent and all. But tell us what happened today! Agent McKnight said you lost control of your car and you were hurt? I told your Uncle Alan when you bought that monster that it wasn't for a single girl, it didn't make sense."

Lucy smiled. "Actually, my Range Rover was a hero, Aunt Jennifer, executed an amazing U-turn to save me. Unfortunately, he was totaled, so I am now officially without wheels. I was thinking about buying something really different from a Range Rover, something to help make me a little less boring. What do you think of a snazzy red Corvette?"

Court stirred, and a dark brow went up. "You're a cop, Lucy, but even you would find out you can't drive a car like that without other cops stopping you for blowing your nose, just to get up and close and personal to it. You'd spend your time wiping their fingerprints off the hood."

Coop heard a kind of slimy charm in that. He decided he never wanted to play basketball or drink beer with Court Silverman. He said, "I gave you both the impression that Lucy was in an accident. We wanted to tell you in person that wasn't what happened. Someone tried to kill her. But she was smart, took care of business. One of the men involved is dead; the other turned tail and ran. We're looking for him now." Coop looked straight at Court.

There was a shocked silence until Jennifer said, "How many times did I tell both you and your father, dear, that being an FBI agent was a ridiculous choice for you, and it's no big surprise that criminals are after you. I've always felt the only reason you went into the FBI was because your mother —"

Lucy felt a flash of pain, then calm. "No, not at all, Aunt Jennifer. I applied to the bureau before Dad even told me that my mother had."

"I thought I heard voices. It's you, Lucy. Thank God you're okay."

Jennifer jumped to her feet. "Oh, Alan, do come in. Lucy and her friend are here. They say it wasn't an accident —"

Alan Silverman raised his hand. "Yes, I know, Jennifer. I called Agent Savich, Lucy's boss, and he told me straight up what happened." He leaned over her, eyed the bandage on her head, and carefully hugged her. "I have no doubt the FBI will find out who did this. Mr. Savich assured me they would protect you until they do. I'm so sorry, Lucy. I hope it's not too bad?"

"No, a bullet just took off a bit of my scalp, nothing serious," Lucy said, smiling up at him. "We'll find out the truth." She introduced Coop to him, then, "Where's

Miranda?"

Jennifer said, "She didn't know you were coming, Lucy. She was leading the discussion at her book club this evening."

Lucy asked, "What book is that, Aunt Jennifer?"

"She never tells us," Alan said easily, sitting back in the matching chair next to his son's, his eyes on her face. She saw deeper lines etched by his mouth. "I kid her about the club reading erotic novels, but she denies it."

Court laughed, a false, practiced sound that got to Coop like fingernails on a blackboard. "I caught her reading *Portnoy's Complaint* last week. You might be right, Dad."

Jennifer slapped her hands together. "Stop it, both of you. What will Agent McKnight think of us?"

Agent McKnight thought the book club sounded pretty interesting. He said, "Your daughter lives here?"

Jennifer said, "Why, yes, she moved back maybe three months ago, but only until she finds a place she likes. They're hard to come by in the right neighborhood — too much crime elsewhere."

Coop looked at each of them in turn. "Do any of you have any ideas about who tried to kill Lucy today?"

There was a babble of voices, all of them horrified, all eyes soon turning to him. Alan said, "How would you think we would know anything about such a thing? We're the only family Lucy has left. We love her. Hurt her? That's ridiculous."

Coop said easily, "It's what we do, sir, ask questions until the answers fit together to solve the puzzle. It seems probable the attempt on Lucy's life is directly tied to finding her grandfather's remains."

Alan said, "For heaven's sake, Lucy, you don't think finding your poor grandfather had anything to do with these madmen trying to run you off the road today, do you? I mean, why?"

"Actually, they didn't seem like madmen, Uncle Alan. They were organized, both driving identical white vans. They tried to accordion me between them, and they shot at me." She lightly touched her fingertips to the bandage. "They were pros, and someone hired them to kill me."

"Two white vans?" Court frowned at her, confused. "Who on earth would try to run you down with two white vans? Postal workers gone berserk?"

Coop wanted to send his boot into Court's right kidney.

Lucy said very seriously, "That doesn't seem likely, Court."

Coop said, "Like I said, the other guy turned tail and ran. We'll find out soon who owns the white vans."

Court said, "I think I'd like a cup of coffee, Mom, if you don't mind."

Jennifer flew to her feet. "Of course, sweetheart." She patted Court's arm, saying over her shoulder, "I'll bring everyone some. Anyone for a snack?"

She's talking cookies when Lucy nearly got murdered today? Coop said, "No, thank you, Mrs. Silverman. Why don't you leave the coffee for the moment? I would appreciate your telling me what you thought about Lucy's murdered grandfather. Surely all of you have some thoughts about that."

Jennifer walked slowly back to the sofa and sat down, her eyes on her clasped hands.

Alan said finally, "We've already discussed that tragedy with Lucy, and at length with the police. I suppose I must accept the unavoidable truth that my sister was involved, as was my nephew, Josh. It is painful, but there is no other conclusion. Helen killed her husband, and we may never know why."

"Do you know why, Mrs. Silverman?"

"My sister-in-law, Helen, she was — quite emotional, often depressed, after Lucy's mother died. There was anger in her, too, that erupted from time to time. But killing Milton? No, that isn't possible. I have to believe someone else was responsible for Milton's death."

Coop studied Jennifer Silverman's lovely pale face. She was frankly beautiful for her age, with high cheekbones, good cosmetic surgery, no doubt, and a long, fit body — she would still be beautiful when she was ninety.

Court said, "No, Mother, no one else was responsible. It had to be Aunt Helen, and it was murder, not a simple death. I mean, Uncle Milton didn't tuck himself into that steamer trunk. You found his body yourself, Lucy. Maybe Aunt Helen discovered he was cheating on her. Dad, you think something like that would drive her over the edge?"

Alan said, "I remember at the time — goodness, that was twenty-two years ago — I simply couldn't understand why Milton had just up and left without a word to anyone, without a message, anything. He was simply gone. I can't remember that his behavior was any different, not really. As for your grandmother, Lucy, when Milton disappeared, she was distraught. She said she couldn't understand it, either, any more than I did. I remember comforting her, or trying to. Then she shut herself off, became remote. I was very worried about her for a long time.

"As for your father, Lucy, he was tight-lipped, didn't want to speak of his father. I remember he'd leave the room when we brought up Milton's name, you know, to try to figure out why he'd left." Alan sighed. "Helen killed him. Why? I don't know. I strongly doubt it was because Milton was unfaithful. He wasn't that kind of man. It's been twenty-two years since that awful time. He's dead, Helen is dead, Josh is dead. So, what's the point? I think whatever happened should stay buried with them. They were our family, and they deserve at least some discretion from us. I don't see that we need to discuss it further, Agent McKnight, unless you think that the men who tried to kill Lucy were somehow connected to her grandfather's murder? I confess, I don't see how."

Coop said, "Actually, we know the killers were after a ring Lucy got from her grandfather."

Alan Silverman looked bewildered. "Ring? What ring, Lucy?"

"Grandfather left me a ring, Uncle Alan."

"That makes no sense. I don't know about any ring. Where is this ring?"

Lucy smiled as she slowly stood up. "It's in a safe-deposit box at the FBI. It seems someone thinks it's very valuable. Why? To be honest, I don't really care why. What I care about is that someone is trying to kill me for it."

Alan rose as well. He studied her face. "I hope you don't suspect us of having anything to do with these two men trying to kill you, Lucy. For a ring your grandfather had and left to you? It makes no sense to me. Jennifer?"

Jennifer shook her head.

Alan continued, "This has been an upsetting day for all of us. If that's the only — official — business you have with us, Agent McKnight, I'd like to get some rest now. Lucy, I would like you to stay with us. We can protect you."

She said no, thanked him, kissed them all, and left. Lucy's head was pounding. Coop took her hand, helped her into Gloria's passenger seat. She slept during the entire drive back to Coop's condo in Wesley Heights.

CHAPTER 52

Savich tossed the kid-size Redskins football to Sean from the living-room doorway across the entry hall as he ran toward the front door. He caught the ball with both hands, then pulled it close to his chest, just as Savich had taught him.

"Way to go, champ."

Savich had moved the small entry table to the dining room, so there wasn't much left to destroy. It was dark outside, and it was, after all, football season, so what were he and Sean to do? He laughed at Astro, who saw his job as getting the football away from Sean if Savich wouldn't give it to him. He was leaping up, trying to grab it with his teeth.

Sherlock said, her voice low, since Sean seemed to be all ears since his fifth birthday, "Ann Marie Slatter is saying when Kirsten

427

heard those two men mocking Bruce Comafield's death, she just pulled her gun out of her jacket and shot them right there in the diner."

Savich said after he tossed another football to Sean, "There's something she didn't do that I'll admit surprises me —"

"She didn't murder Ann Marie, and Kirsten knew she'd talk to the cops as soon as she got herself together again."

"Exactly." He caught Sean's wobbly pass and tossed it back. Sean dropped it, probably on purpose, and Astro went nuts, trying to kill it, barking his head off. Soon the two of them were rolling around on the floor, fighting for the ball.

Sherlock said, "Do you think it's possible Kirsten left Ann Marie Slatter alive to send us a message? Felt like thumbing her nose at us?"

"I don't know," he said, but he was thinking, *Sending me a message?* Sherlock had been the one who played Kirsten and sucked her in, nearly bringing her down. Even though Comafield had said Kirsten was coming after him, all he could think about was that insane psychopath coming after Sherlock, and it terrified him. He rose, scooped up his son and the football, wet with Astro's slobber, hauled him over his shoulder, and trotted up the stairs with Astro at his heels. "I'll take care of Sean; you give Coop and Lucy a call, see how she's doing and how their visit to the Silvermans went, then finish your soup. You need to get to bed; you need to rest as much as Lucy does."

A half hour later, with Sean finally down for the count, Sherlock took her final drink of the tepid tea Dillon had made especially for her — spiked with his favorite supplements — and ate the rest of her chicken noodle soup. She felt fine, really, only a bit of rawness in her throat where some sadist had shoved down the tube. It made her shudder to think about it.

She leaned her head back against the chair and closed her eyes. What would Kirsten do now? She was worried for Dillon, because Kirsten had undoubtedly seen him on TV, maybe even saw him shoot Comafield outside the Texas Range Bar & Grill in Baltimore, and she was crazy enough to go after him. The thought scared her spitless.

But she slept deeply that night, her head on his shoulder, her arms wrapped tight around his chest.

CHAPTER 53

Wesley Heights
Thursday night

I'm lying on cement. Well, maybe the mattress wasn't quite that hard, but with her bumps and bruises and aching muscles from being thrown around her Range Rover, it sure felt like cement.

She finally got up, stiff and hurting, and went into the bathroom to pop some aspirin and move around a little. After she'd taken three aspirin, she managed a few stretches from side to side until she felt a zing of pain in her shoulder and had to stop. She stood straight again and, unfortunately, happened to look in the mirror. She saw a woman with ratty hair, her skin the color of oatmeal, with a big purple bruise on her jaw. Where had that beauty come from?

Lucy hadn't unbraided her hair before she'd fallen into bed. She did so now, and finger-combed her hair, not bothering to get her brush from the small overnight bag she'd quickly packed at her grandmother's house. At least the butterfly strips Coop had pressed down over the cut on her scalp looked better than the bandage she'd worn home from the hospital. Her eyes kept going back to the bruise on her jaw.

Of all things, she'd forgotten a sleep shirt, and so she was wearing one of Coop's white T-shirts. She'd never before worn a man's T-shirt, and thought she looked rather cute, at least from the neck down.

She said to the pasty-faced pathetic woman staring back at her, her eyes stark and hard, "You're alive, so no more whining. At least you look kind of sexy in Coop's T-shirt."

"I'd say you do. I like the way it falls off your shoulder."

She turned slowly to see her host standing in the open bathroom doorway, shirtless, wearing only a pair of slacks, zipped up, the top button unfastened. How could she see all that in a millisecond? She'd never seen Special Agent Cooper McKnight without a shirt before, not even at the gym. He had a nice chest, really nice abs and pecs, and that open top button on his pants —

Stop looking at his open trouser button.

"Hey, you want your T-shirt back? Looks

like you're in need here."

He absently scratched his chest. "I heard you moving around. You in any pain, Lucy?"

"I took some aspirin; it'll kick in soon. Look at this bruise on my jaw. Was it there before?"

He walked to her, lightly cupped her jaw in his hand, and lifted her face to the direct light. But he didn't look at the bruise, he looked at her, and he knew immediately it wasn't a good idea.

Who cared?

He leaned down and kissed her.

Lucy forgot about her bruises, forgot about the pain in her head, forgot about every sore muscle. They'd been circling each other for months now, despite what she'd heard about him, despite her distrust of him, and, to be honest with herself, she'd thought about this kiss for a long time. It wasn't the right time to come in for a landing, but here they were in the guest bathroom, of all places.

Who cared?

She was here and he was here, kissing her with lovely enthusiasm, and she had her arms around his back, her hands stroking him, learning how he felt, and she discovered he felt quite wonderful.

Not a single red alert flashed in her mind.

When he tried to pull back, she held on tight, kissed his chin, his nose, his neck, and went back to work on his mouth, hers open now, and so was his, and she poured herself into this awesome madness.

"I'll let you have your T-shirt back."

Where had the words come from? Surely from her own mouth, but wasn't her mouth in very close contact with his?

"Yeah, that's a fine idea," he said, and he pulled it over her head. There was a good thing about beginning not more than a dozen feet from the bed, Lucy thought. When they fell on it together, Coop cushioning her as best he could, she let out a yip of pain, and laughed. "I guess it's going to have to be easy going tonight, Agent McKnight. I'm still a mess."

When she at last fell into a dazed sleep, pressed against his side, her head on his shoulder, her palm flat on his belly, she slept deeply, without nightmares, without pain, and with a sense of rightness she didn't think she'd ever felt before in her life.

The mattress felt as soft as a cloud.

CHAPTER 54

Friday morning

At exactly seven o'clock in the morning, Lucy danced barefoot into the kitchen, already showered and dressed, her hair still damp and tucked behind her ears to hang loose down her back.

Two people had tried to kill her yesterday, but today she felt buzzed and happy, thinking of the huge smile on her face when she'd looked at herself in the bathroom mirror thirty minutes before. She smelled coffee, nearly shuddered with pleasure at the thought of it, and laughed, marveling at how the most special moments in life came at you out of left field. It took nearly getting herself killed to finally take the big step with Special Agent Cooper McKnight.

She called out, "You're a coffee god. I will worship at your feet if I can have some."

He was speaking on his cell. He looked up at her and smiled, but it wasn't the kind

434

of smile she was expecting, it was a distracted, perfunctory smile, one that didn't say anything like *Wowza, that was great, let's do it again, right this very second.* He was saying, "Sure, Savich. Hold on a second."

He picked up a pen from the kitchen counter and scribbled on his grocery pad as he listened. When he punched off his cell, he said, "Savich said they traced the VIN of the burned van to the last registered owner, a woman named Claudette Minsk. She lives in Welling, Maryland — actually, just about four miles from your grandmother's house in Chevy Chase. She was a florist, owned several shops, but her family is selling them now. She's seventy-nine years old, and unfortunately, she's developed Alzheimer's.

"The son said he sold the van and one just like it to two men he'd never seen before a couple of days ago, for cash. The vans still had his mother's florist logo — a big bright sunflower with MINSK'S MARVELS in gold script written beneath it — so they must have painted over them."

"What about the dead man, Coop?"

"Forensics got a hit on his partial fingerprints, and then matched some tattoos on his neck to the same man's mug shots. His name was Ben Eddy Dukes; he'd been in jail for attempted murder, so why not step up to first-degree? He was thirty-seven, on parole out of Briarwood State Prison for a couple of years, and had been suspected of a spate of robberies in upscale neighborhoods in cities all over Maryland.

"Savich is getting his photo over to Welling to confirm he was one of the men who bought the van. It sure looks like they were hired to kill you. Ben Eddy Dukes was a real badass professional. As for the other man, they're trying to get a description of him from Minsk."

Lucy said, "Yeah, we knew that was the case. It will be harder to find out who hired them. It's progress, though."

His eyes were fixed on her face. He reached out his palm and lightly cupped her bruised jaw. "I don't think I've ever seen your hair down before last night. I like all the cool shades. No more bandages on your head. You almost can't see those little butterflies covering the wound, and the bruise on your jaw looks like it might be fading. I think you look good to go, Lucy."

He dropped his hand, turned, and said over his shoulder, "Here's your coffee, no cream, no sugar." He waited until she took a sip, and asked, "How are all your sore spots doing this morning?"

Sore spots? You voodooed them right out of

me. "A little sore here and there. Better, though. Ah, the coffee's delicious, maybe as good as Dillon's."

"I worked at Starbucks when I was a teenager, got my addiction there. You've got to taste the mean nonfat mocha latte with just a touch of cinnamon I learned how to brew. My parents assure me it classifies as ambrosia."

Who cared about tasting fricking nonfat mocha latte — with cinnamon — when he was standing not five feet away from her, and she could cover that distance with a nice long jump and end up with her legs wrapped around his waist?

He turned away to put two slices of wheat bread into the toaster. "I'm making scrambled eggs. I only use half the yolk, so your arteries won't clog."

You want to eat? "That'd be good."

She drank some more coffee, sat down at the kitchen table where he'd already set out plates and silverware. The kitchen was large and bright, even in the dismal gray morning light.

"You've got lots of gadgets. Do you use them all?"

He said over his shoulder, "Not really. My parents are the real cooks and like to give me these things. The panini press is their

437

latest gift. I haven't used it yet. Maybe if we're here at lunch, we can give it a try."

"Coop?"

"Yes?" He didn't turn away from his skillet. She smelled frying bacon.

"Did Dillon want anything else?"

"Yeah," he said. "He'd like to see your grandfather's letter. So would I, for that matter. We can stop at your grandmother's house after breakfast, take it with us to the CAU."

As he spoke, Coop walked over to her, slipped his hand into her blouse, and pulled up the chain holding her ring. Lucy froze. He said quietly, "I saw you take it off last night. I remember you said you had no clue what these symbols mean. And this single word — how do you pronounce it?"

Her heart nearly stopped when he whispered the word closely enough.

"SEFYLL."

She waited to see a reaction, just as she'd waited, frozen, when Dillon had said the word, but she already knew nothing would happen when Coop said it. She was right; everything continued as it was supposed to.

She lifted his fingers from the ring and put it back inside her shirt.

"I've been trying to figure out how anyone knew I even had this."

He turned to face her, looking very serious. "Before I made the unforgettable decision to see if you were okay last night when I heard you moving around, I was lying awake in bed, asking myself that same question. If this ring is the reason your grandfather was killed, then someone must want it very badly. Maybe they were tipped off by somebody who knew you'd opened that box, or they could have been following you, or even have your grandmother's house bugged."

"I thought of that, but I wondered if I was getting too paranoid. I think you made a fine decision last night, Coop. After all, I'm your guest, and you had to make sure I was all right."

He stared at her — no, at her mouth.

She said, "All right, all right. We can go over right after breakfast. It will be interesting having a conversation knowing we might be bugged. What would you like to talk about?"

He lifted the skillet off the stove, gave her a slow smile as he leaned back against the counter and said, "We don't have to go right away. Come here."

CHAPTER 55

Whortleberry
Friday morning

Ann Marie Slatter watched the gorgeous TV reporter with the streaked blond hair climb back into her van, never once teetering on her stilettos, the cameraman behind her. She was still shaking when the young guy with the bad complexion drove them away. She'd made sure her makeup was perfect and the pretty yellow tunic she wore over her leggings looked hot. And she'd made sure they used her whole name, because adding *Marie* made it sound more sophisticated. Her boss, Dave, had told her some magazine or cable talk show might pay for her story if she played her cards right.

She didn't relish going back inside her parents' house. Her mom and dad wouldn't stop telling her it was a miracle she was still alive, and it was past time she went back to church, because the good Lord had surely saved her yesterday, hadn't He?

Ann Marie jumped into her ancient Mazda SUV and peeled out of the driveway. She'd rather spend some time with Dave and the sheriff than listen to that. She hadn't cried during the interview, didn't want to ruin her fresh eye makeup and look bad on camera, but now she teared up and got the shakes so bad she had to pull over. There wasn't a soul around, so she let herself cry.

She heard a car coming behind her and looked at the rearview mirror. *Great,* someone would see her crying her eyes out on the side of the road.

The car came closer — no, not a car, it was a dirty white Silverado, and Ann Marie's heart stopped. She knew who was driving it. She'd watched that crazy woman stroll out of the diner yesterday after murdering Lou and Frank, and drive away in that Silverado.

It was Ted Bundy's daughter, she didn't have a doubt. The tears froze on her face.

Ann Marie gunned her Mazda, but she didn't get far. It only took a second for Kirsten to pull ahead of her car and block her in.

She threw the Mazda into reverse, but

Kirsten simply pulled a gun out of her pocket and shot both the front tires. Then she strolled over to the driver's side and tapped on the window, and tried the door. At least Ann Marie had locked all the doors. She stared at Ted Bundy's daughter and saw her own death in the woman's crazy eyes.

"Hi," Kirsten said. "I've got you blocked right in, baby, and now you've got two dead tires, so you aren't going anywhere. Hey, you like all the attention you're getting from surviving the massacre at Dave's Diner? I heard a newscaster call it that — it sounds so hokey, but that's the media for you."

Ann Marie whispered, "You — you said you hoped I'd get out of town, you said —"

"I can't hear you, sweetcakes, you've got your window up. Roll it down so I can hear you better."

Ann Marie shouted, "You wanted me to get out of this town —"

"Yes, yes, I know, but you see, my daddy didn't ever do the expected thing, and I remembered that. And I really didn't like what you've been saying about me on TV, calling me scary crazy and a monster. You should have been a little more grateful, don't you think? But this isn't about you, really; you're not that important. This is about showing those fed bastards I can do whatever I want.

"Come on out now, little girl; it's time you and I did our dance."

"No!"

Kirsten kept that scary smile on her face as she slowly pulled a length of wire from her back pocket. "Remember all Frank's brains exploding out of the back of his head? That really cool red dot on his forehead — it looked so innocent until you saw all his brains splatted on the vinyl booth behind him. Hey, at least you won't have to clean that off now. Come on, little girl, time to get this show on the road. Open the door!"

Ann Marie scooted across the front seats, opened the passenger-side door, jumped, rolled, and came up running. She ran for all she was worth across an open field, gunshots sounding behind her.

CHAPTER 56

Savich listened carefully to what Ben said, then sighed. "Mrs. Patil having an affair — I wish I could tell you I'm surprised, but I'm not really. Why can't people behave like they're supposed to? Why can't they ever be what they appear to be? You're positive about the affair?"

Detective Ben Raven of the WPD said, "I guess I'm not surprised, either. Yes, we're sure. Like I said, I had her followed, Savich, for want of anything better, since the case wasn't going anywhere. Sure enough, she and Krishna Shama — remember, he's the nephew of Mr. Patil's lifelong best bud, Amal Urbi — met at a Holiday Inn just south of McLean. They spent two hours in room three-thirty-five. I doubt it was a prayer meeting for Mr. Patil. Then they went to a restaurant for a late lunch. Mrs.

444

Patil came trotting home at five o'clock yesterday evening, in good time to head out to the hospital to see her husband. We checked. Mrs. Patil and Mr. Shama have visited that particular Holiday Inn a dozen times over the past several months."

Savich thought about this. "You know, Ben, lots of people have affairs that don't even lead to divorce, much less attempted murder. We have no idea if this has anything to do with Mr. Patil's shooting. Why not hold off awhile until we can get more? I sure wish I had more time to help out, but what with Kirsten Bolger wreaking havoc, I'm up to my neck in alligators."

Ben said, "Not a problem. I was thinking I'd wait awhile anyway, keep even closer tabs on Mrs. Patil. Now I'll add Krishna Shama to the active surveillance list."

Savich punched off and stepped out of his office to see Lucy and Coop heading toward the CAU conference room. As he walked in behind them, he heard Dane Carver saying to Ruth and Ollie, "Our girl ran her feet off and managed to escape Kirsten. Sheriff Stovall said he couldn't get over it."

"She what?" Lucy asked.

Dane nodded to Coop and Savich, then turned to her and smiled. "Good to see you walking around, Lucy. You don't look too bad. That bruise on your jaw adds color."

"If purple's your thing, I'm the girl of your dreams. Now, Kirsten went back to kill Ann Marie Slatter?"

Dane said, "She did, indeed, and Ann Marie managed to survive the encounter intact. Sheriff Stovall said Ann Marie was on the high-school track team; he remembered her as a strong middle distance runner. Well, that girl ran her heart out. Kirsten couldn't catch her; all she could do was keep firing at her, but she missed because Ann Marie was too far away and she was juking around. She ran a couple of miles, flat out, all the way to the sheriff's office. He and his deputies were after Kirsten right away, but of course she was long gone."

Coop said, "I want to meet this girl."

Dane said, "I do, too. Ann Marie insisted she wanted to stay in a locked cell until they caught Kirsten, told Sheriff Stovall she'd never talk to him again if he didn't let her curl up on a jail cot."

Ruth said, "Smart girl."

Savich waved Dane to continue. "Sheriff Stovall is getting ready for more news vans to roll into town pretty soon. Ann Marie Slatter is going to be quite a celebrity now, the heroine of Whortleberry. Since the sheriff decided he couldn't let her take up residence in one of his two cells, we're taking Ann Marie and her mother, Libby, to one of our apartments on Mulberry Street, keep that poor kid safe until we get Kirsten. Talk about the resilience of youth — she's thinking about getting an agent to sell her story to the movies."

There was some head-shaking laughter at this.

Then Dane said, "By now Kirsten has dumped the Silverado, probably somewhere near town. Sheriff Stovall has his deputies asking everyone around town to check their vehicles, help them with finding the Silverado. Bottom line, Kirsten's dropped her MO, and she's killing at will, or trying to, to show us she can. She's a danger to everyone now, including us, but particularly you, Savich. You're the face of the people after her."

Savich nodded. "Thanks, Dane. Please keep us posted. We'll all watch our backs." Savich turned to Lucy, studied her for a moment, and seemed satisfied. He asked Coop, "Okay, let's get to Lucy now. What have you guys got for us?"

Coop said smoothly, "Along with the ring in the safe-deposit box, Lucy told me there was also a letter addressed to her from her grandfather. We went by Lucy's house to get the letter, Savich, and guess what? It was gone."

A letter? You never told me about a letter. A sin of omission is still a lie, and I hate lies. What Savich was thinking was as clear to Lucy as if he'd spoken aloud, pointing a finger at her. How could he ever come to trust her again? When he spoke, though, his voice was smooth and calm. "So, your grandfather wrote you an explanation of the ring. That makes sense. Okay, so the letter has disappeared? Where'd you leave it, Lucy?"

She said, "About the letter, Dillon, maybe I should have told you when you came to my house —"

He raised a hand, cutting her off. "I know about it now. Tell us where you left it."

"I folded it carefully and slipped it in the back of a book on UFOs on a shelf near my grandmother's desk two days ago. It never occurred to me it wouldn't be safe there. I don't think anyone had looked in there in years."

Savich tapped his pen on the table. "That means someone knew the letter existed, or maybe suspected it existed. They took it before the attempt on your life. If you had died, Lucy, then there would be no evidence there ever was a letter, so there would be no possible clues leading to them. Either that or the people were looking for the ring, and when they found only the letter, they assumed you had the ring with you."

Coop said, "We didn't see any obvious evidence of a break-in. It occurred to us someone might have bugged the house, since they seemed to know so much."

"We'll get a countersurveillance team over there to check for bugs, look more carefully for signs someone was poking around your grandmother's study. Lucy, can you think of anyone who could have known about the letter?"

"Maybe someone at the bank or the law office. Otherwise, I only told Coop about it yesterday. We didn't mention it to my relatives last night."

Savich leaned forward now, and looked at her dead-on. "Why did you take so long to admit there was a letter, Lucy?"

Coop took her hand, squeezed it, a simple thing, really, but it steadied her, kept one of her endless apologies from popping out of her mouth. She said frankly, "I believed I should keep the contents of the letter private, since it was about my family and the events happened so long ago. Since there wasn't any question about who killed my grandfather, it was no one's business."

Savich nodded. "Okay, Lucy, point taken.

But now it's a different ball game. Tell us all as close as you can what the letter said."

She looked at each of the agents in turn, then said, "The bottom line was that my grandmother told my grandfather about the ring right after the death of my mother. He wrote about how she kept talking about the ring, about if only she'd had it with her, the ring could have saved my mother, and then she showed him the ring. He wrote that in her grief, my grandmother became obsessed with the ring and he feared for her sanity, and so he stole it. He said he couldn't destroy it since it was my birthright, but he knew my father wouldn't want me to have the ring, and so he was leaving it to me along with this letter to open after my father's death. Of course, he never realized my father would die so young. He believed I'd be reading his letter when I was middle-aged. That's about it."

"He called it your birthright," Ruth said. "A birthright implies it was something incredibly special, and only for you."

Ollie asked, "What exactly happened to your mother, Lucy?"

"She was struck straight on by a drunk driver. My grandparents were in the car behind her."

Savich said, "If your grandmother had

only had the ring with her, she could have saved your mother? How could a ring stop a drunk driver from hitting your mother's car? Did your grandfather's letter tell you what those supposed powers were?"

"He wrote I wouldn't believe him if he did."

And then, of course, Savich asked the most important question of all. "Do you have any idea now what those powers are?"

As far as I can tell, I see absolutely nothing at all special about the ring. Or, if there is, I can't figure it out. Believe me, I've tried to find out why anyone would want this ring badly enough to want to kill me for it.

Lucy wished she could say that whopping lie out loud, but she couldn't bring herself to do it. She looked at him, mute for a moment, white as her shirt, the purple bruise on her jaw in stark relief. She said slowly, trying to lie clean, "No, I have no idea why the ring is so special. As I said, my grandfather didn't tell me because he said I wouldn't believe him. But someone believes the ring has some sort of power, and that someone believes he may know what it is."

She knows, of course, and it scares her to her heels, Savich thought, but he only nodded. He didn't expect her to say any more, and she didn't. Maybe she couldn't; maybe

451

she was forbidden to. He shook his head at himself. His imagination was running away with him. He said, "Lucy's right. Someone thinks he knows what the ring can do, and it's worth killing for. Do you still wear it around your neck?"

She nodded.

"May we see it?"

Slowly, Lucy pulled the gold chain out of her shirt, the ring threaded through it. Every eye in the room went to it, as if pulled by an invisible wire. She took the ring from the chain and handed it to him.

Savich rolled it around in his palm and passed it to Dane to look at. He said, "You'll see there's that single Welsh word etched into it — *SEFYLL* — it means to stop moving, to become stationary."

"Stop moving what?" Ollie said.

"I don't know," Lucy said.

Dane said the word aloud, and again, her heart seized for a moment, but nothing happened. All the agents had to repeat the word, and some of them got it close. Ruth said it right on the button. Lucy jerked, couldn't help it, and she knew Savich saw it. As for Coop, he held her hand and said nothing at all.

Lucy took the ring back from Ollie, slid it onto the gold chain, and slipped it inside her shirt. All of them looked at the small bulge where the ring lay warm against her flesh.

"Your relatives," Ruth said, "the Silvermans. They all know about the ring?"

"They denied even knowing about the ring; they didn't show any interest when I told them last night. I know they have to be our first suspects, given what's happened, but it's hard to accept that. I grew up with them in my life, and they're the only family I have left." She looked around the conference table as she spoke.

Families, Savich thought. *They were the very devil, if you wanted to be objective.* "Lucy, I know how hard this is for you, but you need to keep an open mind. Now, you're butt-deep in the swamp here. I want you to stick with Coop. Consider him another pair of jeans."

Lucy saw Coop's pants lying on the floor next to her bed, saw that Coop was grinning at her. She said, her voice cool, "I think that's an excellent idea."

There was a good deal of laughter.

Savich looked at Lucy again. "I could bring the Silvermans in for an interview, either together or separately, but the fact is, you and Coop have already found out what they had to say. We have no evidence yet of any complicity between them and the two men who tried to kill you, or the theft of the letter, so we don't have enough probable cause to get a search warrant. They probably wouldn't even speak to me without a lawyer at this point. So I'll treat them as your family unless we find something definite to talk to them about."

He paused for a moment, searching her face. "However, I've already done some checking into Alan Silverman's financial dealings, and his longtime presidency at the Washington Federated Bank. You said you thought he was very rich, and retired from banking?"

"Yes, he retired nearly two years ago. As far as I know, he's always had a great deal of money."

"Lucy, he didn't retire from the Washington Federated Bank like you were told. The board voted him out for gross mismanagement. He lost the bank a great deal of money in the recent financial crisis. The bank may be insolvent, and if the FDIC closes it, he will lose all the equity he has left. There's even the possibility of an indictment. So, we can't write off financial motives on his part, if he's involved."

How could he use the ring to fix this? It was odd, Lucy thought, but she wasn't all that surprised. Ever since their visit to Uncle Alan's house last night, she'd begun to see him with new eyes. Aunt Jennifer and Court, too. Now she wondered if she'd ever really known Uncle Alan, or his family. Her heart pounded. She'd never known her own father, either. She said, "I guess I understand why no one told me the truth about it. Maybe Court and Miranda don't know what really happened."

"One more thing, Lucy," Savich said. "Whoever tried to kill you failed spectacularly. They're going to be afraid now, afraid and maybe desperate. I want you and Coop to be very careful. Remember, close as a pair of jeans."

CHAPTER 57

Georgetown
Friday night

Savich felt the length of his wife's body beneath him, all loose and relaxed now. He breathed in the scent of her as he nuzzled her neck. He finally managed to lift himself off her and rest his weight on his elbows, but he couldn't resist kissing her again. He loved her mouth, her tongue. It made him crazy. "Do you remember way back when you were staying with me so I could protect you? Like Lucy and Coop? And you had that very fortuitous nightmare?"

She hummed deep in her throat. "And you came galloping in on your white horse to save me. No, wait, it was white boxers. And you stayed, to my everlasting gratitude. Goodness, what a time that was, Dillon." She hugged him tight. "The luckiest day in my life was when I shot you in Hogan's Alley."

He kept kissing her, then said, "Do you know I still have those pants I ripped that day?"

"I've seen them hanging in the back of the closet. Do you want to get them mended?"

"Oh, no, it would be like destroying a wonderful memory." He laughed, rolled over on his back, and brought her against his side. "More than six years we've been together. Now we've got Sean, and another big honking mess on our hands, just like we did then."

"Big honking messes — nothing new in that." She kissed his neck, lightly rubbed her palm over his chest, then rested her face against his shoulder. "Our lives, I suppose, aren't what you'd call exactly normal, are they? Not like the Perrys next door, for example, an accountant and a paralegal."

"Would you want us to be in those types of professions? To be nine-to-fivers?"

"Since it's never even been a consideration, I'd have to guess no. The thing is, Dillon, both of us are a perfect fit for what we do, a perfect fix for what we are, and that makes us really lucky. Sometimes I wonder what I'd have become if I'd never met you. I don't think it would be a pretty picture, Dillon."

He ran his palm down her hip, pausing here and there to knead. "Have I ever told you that you've got a lovely, twisted brain? I love to watch the way you figure your way through the murkiest problems. Let me add that when you take chances, it scares the bejesus out of me."

"You're not alone in that, but I guess it's part of the job description. It's what we are, Dillon, and I pray every day it's what we will continue to be until we're too old to aim our SIGs."

"I find myself thinking it'd be nice to go fishing in a nice mountain lake somewhere — we're eighty or so — and when we finally manage to row back to shore, there'll be Sean and his family waiting for us, and all our grandkids."

"What a lovely thought. Only thing is, I really hate fishing."

"I'll do all the dirty work for you, not to worry."

She grinned against him, and he felt it. She leaned up to look down at him. "I know a couple of wives married to cops, and they're always stewing about danger, and I've seen the fear of something happening to their husbands come to define their marriage."

"The reason for so much divorce," Savich said.

"At least both of us are together, to help each other, to look out for each other. I think we're right where we need to be, Dillon, as long as we feel we make a difference."

"Yes," he said quietly. "I hope we do make a difference."

She sprawled again against him. "Dillon, do you think Coop and Lucy are sleeping together? I mean, they do remind me a bit of us, and look where that led."

"They don't dislike each other any longer, that's for sure."

"And it's you who put them together because they weren't getting along. Coop's reputation — I guess that isn't a problem any longer. Now it's like a red beacon glowing whenever the two of them get within six feet of each other."

"I never believed his reputation, anyway," Savich said. "It didn't fit the man."

Sherlock sighed. "This whole ring-and-letter business — at least she did tell Coop about the letter, so that's no longer a big secret."

He said, "It's driving me nuts trying to figure out what the blasted ring can do. How could it have saved Lucy's mother? If it could have, somehow, then it's something miraculous, I know it in my gut. But what?"

She said, "That word — SEFYLL — it means to stop, to be stationary, right? What does that mean? What stops?"

"I don't know."

"Maybe it'll come out."

"Maybe, but I don't hold out much hope. Lucy's a clam, and maybe she has to be — or maybe she's supposed to be."

"If they get married, do you think they can stay in the unit together?"

"That'll be up to the director and Mr. Maitland. I'd have no problem with it. It would be pretty weird if I did."

"Can you imagine the jokes? We'd be known as the dating service of the bureau." She added, "I forget to tell you, I got a call from Dane before I came up to sing a bedtime duet with Sean. Dane thinks he's got a bead on the guy who may have driven the other white van. He's betting his name's Andrew 'Hoss' Kennen, a two-time felon, spent time in Briarwood with the dead guy, Ben Eddy Dukes. The two of them got paroled about the same time."

Savich heard her voice slow, knew she was about ready to hang it up. So was he.

He kissed her, said against her temple, "I heard the weather's going to be great tomorrow. Why don't we ask Coop and Lucy to go to the park with us tomorrow morning."

"That'd be good," Sherlock murmured, tucked herself closer, and went to sleep.

CHAPTER 58

Delaney Park
Saturday morning

Savich flicked the Frisbee to Sean, who yelled as he caught it, then whipped it off to Coop, who, surprised, had to back up ten feet to snag it out of the air.

Lucy whistled. "Great throw, Sean. You had Coop on his heels."

"Looks like another champion Frisbee player," Sherlock said, and promptly dropped the Frisbee Coop sailed to her.

"Mama, you dropped it! We've got to start over!"

Sherlock apologized, promised to pay attention, and sent the Frisbee toward Lucy. They got into a nice steady rhythm until it was Sean's turn to miss one. He picked up the Frisbee, hugged it to his chest, and did a little dance. "I dropped it, but it doesn't matter. We broke the record. Twenty-one catches without dropping it. I counted real

462

careful, Mama. Marty won't believe it. You'll tell her it was twenty-one times, won't you?"

"Yep, I swear."

Marty Perry wouldn't be happy, she thought, ruffling her son's dark hair and smiling into his glowing face.

At least the weatherman hadn't lied — it was a lovely morning, bright sunshine, the temperature hugging sixty. Another dozen Frisbee throws and all of them would be tossing off their jackets. The small meadow in the park was empty except for the five of them. Soon, though, Sherlock knew, more families would show up, excited kids in tow, and the Frisbee circle would steadily grow larger as Sean, always ready to make new friends, invited kids and parents to join until it was a zoo. The adults would then diplomatically excuse themselves so it was a kids-only Frisbee fest.

But for now, Sean wanted to throw the Frisbee farther and farther — okay if they missed now, since they'd broken the record — until Savich saw Sean was panting, his face red. "Let's take a break," he called out, flipped the Frisbee to Sherlock, and headed for the cooler set against a huge old oak tree. He grinned, hearing Sean announce to Coop and Lucy that Daddy was tired.

He'd just turned, smiling, with bottles of

lemonade in his hands, when there was a loud cracking sound.

Savich flew backward, blood spurting out of his chest.

CHAPTER 59

Lucy saw Savich hurled back, the bottles of lemonade flying out of his hands. *All the blood, a fountain of blood — oh, God, he's dead.* She didn't think, sprinted toward him as she grabbed the ring and yelled, "SE-FYLL!"

Everything stopped.

After an instant, she saw Savich standing near the cooler again, and she ran all out, knew she had to get to him before eight seconds ticked away. If felt as if she was running in a dream, her legs moving molasses-slow, as if she was stroking against the tide, as if time itself was pushing against her, and she fought desperately to outrace the passing seconds. She knew if she didn't reach Savich, he would die again. White noise filled her head, and every fiber of her strained to get to him before that eighth second clicked past, and the present would be past again, and Kirsten would shoot him in the heart. She wanted to scream at him to move, but she knew he couldn't hear her. So far away he stood, not knowing that within a second, he was going to be dead.

Now Savich was rising from the cooler again, the bottles of lemonade in his hands, turning toward them, smiling. Lucy screamed at him, and he looked at her, startled, just as she smashed into him, sending both of them flying backward to the ground. Not an instant later, a gunshot rang out over their heads.

There were shouts and more gunshots, fast and close. Savich flipped her under him, covering her as best he could. All Lucy could think was *I was in time; I got to him in time; thank you, God.* She felt him unclip his SIG and roll off her, returning fire. She marveled at how fast he'd reacted to keep her safe.

"Stay down, Lucy!"

But she rolled over onto her stomach, unclipped her own SIG, and fired. She heard the others firing as well, all of them in the direction of the trees at the far end of the park.

Would Kirsten try to kill Sean? No, Sherlock was protecting him, not firing back, covering Sean, keeping him safe.

As suddenly as it began, it was over. Lucy

heard no movement, no noise, not even from the birds, only her own heavy breathing. Then Savich was shaking her, his voice fast and impatient. "Keep behind that oak, Lucy. Thank God, Sherlock's got Sean; they're okay. I'm going to circle around after her."

She heard Coop speaking to the 911 operator as he crouched down behind a park trash bin. She saw Sherlock with Sean in her arms, rocking him as she looked out toward them from behind a tree.

She heard faint shouts from people walking toward the park, wondering what had happened, but they really didn't touch her. She was lost in a daze of numb shock mixed with such boundless relief she wanted to weep.

She looked up to see Savich trotting back to her, his SIG back in its belt clip, speaking into his cell. She ran to him, said over and over, "You're all right. Thank God, you're all right." She rubbed her hands over his chest, unaware that Savich was standing still as a statue in front of her, staring silently down at her. Finally, he pulled her hands away, held them in his.

She closed her eyes a moment to block out the enormity of what had happened — she'd succeeded, the ring had succeeded,

Kirsten hadn't killed him. But what if she'd been two yards farther away? What if she hadn't acted fast enough? Savich would be dead; his life would have been snuffed out by that psychopath.

"Yes, all of us are all right," he said, keeping his voice flat and soothing. "She's gone now, Lucy."

"Yes, she's gone."

"Lucy —"

She pulled away from him and leaned back against the oak tree. She began to laugh, and her laughter became wild, uncontrolled.

Savich heard that laugh, saw that she was shaking, her eyes dilated, her face dead white. He began rubbing her arms as he said very slowly, knowing he himself wasn't all that steady, "You were standing way over there, Lucy, Sherlock and Coop with you. I stood up with the bottles of lemonade, and suddenly here you were, smashing into me; then there was a shot. How did you get here so fast?"

Her laugher slowly died.

"Lucy, how did you know Kirsten was even here?"

"Thank God you're all right, Dillon," she said again, reached out her hand and cupped his face in her palm.

"Hey!" It was Coop, and he was panting, frowning at the two of them. "What happened, Lucy? I saw you plow into Savich. Did you see her? What's going on? You look like you're freezing." He shrugged out of his jacket and laid it around her shoulders.

Sherlock, clutching a crying Sean close, was on Coop's heels. She stared from her husband to Lucy, her heart pounding hard and fast, fear so thick in her throat she could only get his name out before her throat closed. "Dillon —"

He touched her, then lightly stroked Sean's head. "I'm fine, sweetheart. Hey, Sean, everything's okay." He looked at Lucy, who was staring down at her feet. He looked back at Sherlock, and a very clear, silent message passed between them. *This can't ever happen with Sean again.*

He held both Sherlock and Sean tightly against him. "Lucy knocked me flat; she was protecting me. I'm fine. Now, Sean, Mommy's going to take you back to the car, and I'll be with you guys in a minute, okay?"

But Sherlock wasn't about to leave him, and so Savich kept talking to Sean, who was still clutching his Frisbee tight in his hand. Savich looked over at Lucy. "How did you ever see Kirsten before she shot at me, Lucy?"

Lucy simply shook her head and turned at the sound of sirens, growing louder by the second.

Coop said, "Remember how Mr. Lansford bragged about how he'd taught Kirsten to shoot a rifle? Thank God she missed you."

"Yes, she missed me," Savich said, "but only because of Lucy." He hugged her to him. "Thank you, Lucy Carlyle, for saving my life."

If you only knew, Lucy thought. Savich slowly released her. She stood motionless, saying nothing, and she was staring down at the leaf-strewn ground, then over at the oak tree where the bullet had struck, hugging Coop's jacket around herself.

You're an experienced agent, Lucy Carlyle, but you're much more shaken than any of us. Why?

He walked to the oak tree, dug out the bullet casing. If Lucy had been a second later — a split second — he would be dead.

CHAPTER 60

Three teenage boys had told Coop they'd seen this jazzy woman, carrying something under her arm wrapped in a jacket, jump into a dirty dark blue Chevy Monte Carlo, with a ding on the back passenger-side fender.

They talked over one another until a tall, skinny kid won out because his voice was the loudest. "Short red hair, in spikes like a punk, you know. She was tall, and kind of skinny."

They'd nailed Kirsten down to the "jazzy."

"Dude, sir, she was flying. Ponce here yelled after her, and she shot him the finger and was outta here."

"She nearly clipped a fire plug, you know, headed out of the park on Clotter Street."

"Clotter's one-way, heads right to the Potomac."

"That old Monte Carlo, she floored the sucker, rooster-tailed gravel."

Coop, the dude himself, looked around now at the half dozen agents sitting at the CAU conference table. "Any ideas where she would go? She should be desperate, low on money, no supports left that we know of, having to rob or steal most everything she needs." Then he frowned. "Of course, we can't be sure of that."

Savich said without hesitation, "She isn't going anywhere until she kills me. Today she nearly did." He looked at Lucy, who was sitting silently next to Coop. She looked as if she wasn't there, as if she were far away, in a world no one else could see.

Ruth said, "Bruce Comafield wasn't just trying to scare you, Dillon. She must be fixated on killing you, given the chance she took trailing you to the park and opening fire on four armed agents.

"So, you're not going to be alone until we bring her down. No more playing Frisbee in the park. In fact, we all think you should camp out here in the CAU. We'll bring in veggie pizzas."

Like that was going to happen, Savich thought. Then he realized he hadn't eaten, and he was hungry. One of Dizzy Dan's pizzas sounded pretty good.

Dane said, "I still don't understand how you did it, Lucy, how you came to knock

Savich down the second before Kirsten fired at him. What did you see?"

She opened her mouth, then closed it. Beneath the table, Coop took her hand, squeezed it. Her skin was cold — not a surprise, given that death had crouched on her shoulder that morning. And what she'd done, knocking Savich down like that, had scared him just as much. Savich had flirted with shock as well when he was standing there digging out the casing in the oak tree, but he'd focused on his son, jollying him out of fright, telling him what an adventure they'd had, how Marty was going to be so jealous she might not speak to him for a day or two. Still, Coop knew both Savich and Sherlock had to be worried sick about Sean, about how death had brushed too close to their little boy.

"Lucy?" Savich said.

Eric Clapton sang out "Tears in Heaven."

"Savich here."

A brief pause, then he said clearly, "You're talking too fast, Kirsten. Say that again."

Ollie was out of his chair, racing to trace the call.

Everyone at the conference table leaned toward Savich. Savich's face, Coop saw, was red with rage, but that rage didn't sound through in his voice.

"How did you get my number, Kirsten?"

They all stared at Savich's cell, silently praying that she would keep talking until Ollie located her phone. They could hear her screaming at Savich, something about Bruce Comafield.

"Bruce died because he was with you, Kirsten. It's on your head, not mine."

More screaming.

"Truth is, I'm sorry he died. I was thinking I could put it out he was alive and lure you back to the hospital to try to save him. But he didn't make it."

More screaming, then a moment of silence before Savich said, "If you were me, you'd have thought about doing the same thing, wouldn't you?"

That was good, Coop thought, *keep her arguing.* He saw Ollie was nodding at them through the glass door. Dane and Ruth were out of their chairs, racing to the elevator, Ollie with them, still talking on his cell.

Savich continued after a moment, voice calm and slow, "Would you have come to the hospital to see Bruce?"

Coop heard cursing vile enough to curl his mother's hair. After she'd run down again, Savich said, "You're not going to have another try at Ann Marie Slatter. She's safe now.

"No, don't congratulate yourself on that, either. The redhead isn't dead; your drugs didn't kill her. She's very much alive, and she will stay that way, just as Ann Marie Slatter will.

"Listen, Kirsten, you need to stop this. What you're doing isn't about them, anyway. You need to meet me alone, and we can have it out. That's what you want, isn't it? Or do you want to hide and try to shoot me from a hundred yards away again? Yep, we found where you'd been crouched down, waiting to get a good shot at me. But you missed, didn't you? Why was that? I guess you're just not good enough."

There was more screaming, and Savich held the phone a bit away from his ear.

"You can try to kill me, Kirsten, but what makes you think you'll do better next time? How did you get my cell number?" After a pause, he said, "Yes, I did ask our unit secretary to give out my number to any woman who called. Again, wouldn't you have done the same thing?"

She didn't answer; she hung up. Savich pushed a button on his cell. "Dane, where is she?"

"She was moving in a vehicle near Arlington National Cemetery. We lost her when she turned off her cell. The cops are on their way. We've got to hope she's still driving the Monte Carlo."

Savich slipped his cell back into his breast pocket. "Now we wait." He added, more to himself than to the group, "Sherlock will be back later, after she drops Sean with his grandmother and Senator Monroe. We wanted him as far away from Kirsten as possible." He paused, remembering the park and how scared he'd been. He drew a deep breath. "Unless we're lucky, they won't know what she's driving, but she'll call me back after —"

"After what?" Coop asked.

Savich's voice was utterly emotionless. "She's in a killing rage. Someone in Virginia will die very soon now."

CHAPTER 61

Wesley Heights

Lucy sat cross-legged on the bed, her fingers twisting and untwisting the fringe on a bright blue afghan.

Coop said nothing, simply sipped at his coffee and watched her. Finally he said, "Kirsten's call to Savich this afternoon kept you from explaining what happened in the park this morning, Lucy. You've had time to think about it. Want to try out your explanation on me? I'll give you a fair hearing."

The light touch of sarcasm floated through her brain, then wafted away, not really touching her. She looked up, smiled at him. "What a day."

A dark eyebrow cocked up.

"You know, Coop, I'd rather haul you to the bedroom and take you down on that rock-hard mattress."

He eyed her, not changing expression. "As a distraction, that's a perfect ten."

She kept twisting and knotting the fringe, all her attention on her fingers. She drew a deep breath. "Okay, give me your fair hearing. I saw Kirsten, saw the glint of her rifle, saw she was aiming at Dillon. I ran my heart out and managed to get to him in time."

He rose and looked down at her. "All right, the verdict. That would sound plausible enough to anyone who wasn't there, but not to me, or to Savich or Sherlock, either. At that distance, there's not a chance in a million you would have seen enough to make that connection, or get to Savich in time. Did you have some kind of premonition?"

"I'm a fast runner, did you know? I ran track in high school, like Ann Marie Slatter. Not in college, though, too many boys." And she laughed.

His cell phone rang. After a minute, he slipped it back into his pocket. "Unfortunately, Savich was right. Kirsten's killed again, a young woman in her home in Fairfax. Strangled her. Her boyfriend found her body. We need to go."

He tossed her his jacket as he strode to the door, and said over his shoulder, "Saved again by a phone call."

CHAPTER 62

Georgetown
Saturday night

It was midnight when "Tears in Heaven" filled the silent bedroom.

"Hello, Kirsten. I've been waiting for you to call." Savich quickly pressed two buttons, heard a low "Got it," and switched to speakerphone.

Kirsten's voice was high and wild. "Yeah, well, I can't sleep, now, can I? Not with you still pulling air into your lungs, you murdering cop bastard."

"Me? Now, that's funny, Kirsten. Do you even know the woman's name you strangled today?"

"Yeah, something dippy, like Mary. Who cares? Suspicious little bitch, didn't want to let me in even though I was smiling really big and offering her a totally free trial of my company's new vacuum. I had to kick her backward, then she started crying, trying to run, but I caught her fast enough."

Savich felt the familiar feeling of dread pass through him — her madness, he knew, and now she'd lost any semblance of control.

Push her, push her. "You were too afraid to meet me, weren't you, Kirsten? So you went after another innocent who didn't have a clue how crazy you are. Does it make you feel powerful? Strong?"

"I'm not crazy!" She began cursing him again.

"What would you say you are, then?"

She fell silent. Seconds ticked by. Didn't she know he was tracing her cell?

"How about this — you're the daughter of one of the craziest, most perverted and depraved lunatics in history. Since your dad took the names of many of his victims to his grave, no one knows how many women he murdered. So how will you ever know when you match up to Daddy? Did you ever play with all those girls and women you murdered in San Francisco? Like Daddy did?"

"Shut up! Just shut up about Daddy! I'm going to make you suffer, suffer, suffer —" She was gasping for breath. "I should have nailed you right through your black heart at the park. I had you all lined up. I don't know what happened —"

"Yeah, yeah. So when are you going to come after me again, Kirsten? You want me to make it easy for you? Tell you what, tomorrow morning, real early, I'll go for a run in Deer Creek Park. You care to join me? Try to take me down again?"

"Do you think I'm stupid? You'll have the place crowded with cops, one behind every bush. No, I'm thinking I'm going to kill that little redheaded bitch next — you know, the one you told me survived? Like you killed Bruce? I know she's not just another one of your agents; she's your wife. You know how I know that? You're even on YouTube. Hey, why don't you hand her your cell. I'll bet she's listening, right?"

Even though Savich was shaking his head at her, Sherlock said, loud and clear, "Hey, Kirsten, when we were bellied up to the bar together in Baltimore, you sounded sane, like you were even fun. I can see how the other women thought you were fun, too. Boy, we were all wrong, weren't we? You're as crazy as one of those rabid bats that hang in the Ozark caves. You want to play with me again? What makes you think you'll have any better luck with me than you did with my husband? He's nice, my husband, but I'm nasty, Kirsten, mean as a pit snake. I'll kick your bony butt through your backbone, then I'll clamp my teeth in your neck and chew. When you're hollering and begging, I'll hold you down and jerk out all your teeth. Yeah, you keep cursing, it's all you know how to do. Why don't you come to Deer Creek Park, Kirsten? I'll be there, too."

Savich jumped up from the bed, turned the cell away from Sherlock. He looked furious, but when he spoke to Kirsten, he sounded calm as a judge. "I'll see you tomorrow, Kirsten. Don't let me down or I'll know you're not your father's daughter; I'll know when it comes to the sticking point, you're just a wannabe, a no-guts failure."

She hung up, cursing him.

A minute later, he got a call from Agent Randy McDowell. "She's moving, Savich, near Hightown, Virginia. I had local cops following her signal. She was heading toward D.C. I'll keep you posted."

Savich punched off his cell, rounded on Sherlock, who was sitting on her knees on top of the bedcovers, her hair tossed around her head, ready to fight, shaking her teacher's finger at him. "You mess with me on this and I'll take you down, you hear me?"

"Yeah? Like pull out my teeth?"

"Nice visual, don't you think? That's what

Kirsten's all about."

"You aren't going anywhere near her again, you hear me?"

"I'm fine physically, and you know it, so don't try that one."

"I'm your boss, so listen up. You are not back to one hundred percent, so don't lie to me. I said you're not going anywhere near that insane woman again. Even if I have to tie you down, you'll stay right here."

She had only a pillow at hand — a pity — but she threw it as hard as she could. He caught it out of the air.

"You try it, hotshot. Now, you listen up. The question is, did it work? Should we make arrangements to have people at Deer Creek Park in the morning?"

He growled at her and lunged. He landed against her, threw her back, and came down over her, jerked her wrists beside her head. She had no leverage, and he knew it. He stared down at her, at a loss for what to say. She looked ready to fight for a second, but then she said on a laugh, "How long are you going to hold me down?"

"As long as it takes me to think of something else. You're going to clamp your teeth in her neck and chew?"

"Yep. Another good image, don't you think?"

He was brimming with frustration, and she knew it. What she didn't know was that he was seeing her lying in the hospital bed after they'd pumped her stomach, so pale and still. The memory of it was too new, too raw, for him.

In that instant, intuition and experience mixed in his mind, and he realized that Kirsten wasn't about to wait until he was running all by himself in Deer Creek Park on Sunday morning.

He also realized Sherlock would demand to go after Kirsten even if she had to do it in a hospital nightgown. He hated it, but there was no hope for it. He kissed her hard, then helped her sit up. "Here's what I know in my gut she's going to do."

CHAPTER 63

The night was bright and clear, the moon nearly full, and cold enough that Savich was thankful for his heavy leather jacket. Sherlock was bundled up in her own jacket, a wool scarf around her neck, gloves on her hands. They were crouched down behind the thick yew bushes lining the flowerbeds in front of the house.

Savich was starting to get stiff when his cell vibrated. "Yeah?"

"Coop here. They found Kirsten's cell but not Kirsten. They tracked the cell again when she turned it back on in Fairfax, but the signal stayed stationary. She'd tossed her cell across the street from the house where she murdered Mary Cartwright. I guess she wanted to admire the crime scene tape."

Coop paused, then said, "You think she's coming after you, don't you? Right now. At home."

"We're outside waiting for her. It's a feeling I have; I could be wrong. It's very possible Kirsten won't show, and it would be a colossal waste of time for you to come over."

But the line was dead. Savich punched call back, but Coop didn't pick up.

Twelve minutes later, Savich heard them creeping up around the house behind him. He whispered, "We're over here, behind the bushes."

The four of them crouched down, pressing together for warmth. Savich told them about her call, about how he hoped he'd pushed her over the edge.

Lucy said, "After what you and Sherlock said to her, I think you're right, she'll come and she'll be crazy mad. I hope that gives us the advantage."

Coop, warm as could be in his shearling coat, whispered, "Yes, she's coming; my gut's with yours, Savich. I don't think she'll try using a rifle again, either. Kirsten likes to be up close and personal. I think that's what she'll do tonight. She'll come here to face you down."

Lucy asked, "Where have you stashed Sean?"

Sherlock whispered, "He's at his grandmother's, and that's where he'll stay until this is over."

Lucy forced her mind away from Kirsten's rifle shot in the park that morning. She said, "One thing I've learned about Kirsten is that she won't be straightforward about this. She'll have something planned, especially for you and Sherlock. She'll try to fool us somehow."

Coop said, "You're right. It's time we split up." Coop pressed a button on his watch, and a green light glowed. It was exactly two a.m. He started to move, then stilled, placed his finger against his lips. They barely breathed, just listening.

There was the sound of a light footfall coming up to the side of the house. None of them moved.

Savich whispered, "I turned off the alarm."

They couldn't believe it — the sound of a window breaking. Straightforward enough, and how could that be right? Wouldn't Kirsten expect the alarm to be set? But here she was, trotting right to the wolf's house. Had they built Kirsten up into some sort of invincible monster, since they hadn't managed to catch her until now?

Something wasn't right — Savich knew it. He imagined all of them did.

In the next instant, they were up and running around the side of the house.

CHAPTER 64

Coop grabbed Kirsten's shoulder and spun her around, his SIG against her throat. He heard a squeak, then a boy's high, trembling whisper. "Wait, don't kill me! I had to check out your security. It sucks, dude, it sucks; there isn't any. Please don't shoot me, I'm only doing what she made me do, I swear."

Coop whispered in the boy's ear, "Why?"

"She hit our mom, tied her up, and stuffed her in a closet. She forced us to come with her."

"Who's *us?*"

Savich shouted, "Down!"

Coop pulled the boy down with him as Savich shoved both Lucy and Sherlock back into the bushes. In the next instant, a half dozen fast shots cracked loud and sharp in the silent night. They heard bullets hit the side of the house, way too close.

They didn't return fire, since they didn't see her. The last thing any of them wanted was for neighbors to come out of their houses to see what was going on and step into the line of fire.

Savich whispered, "All of you, stay put."

The shots had come from somewhere on the other side of the street. She was close, probably had her car parked on the next block. Savich saw a shadow. It paused, then moved out fast. It was Kirsten, had to be.

Savich ran hard after her, all the while praying his neighbors would stay in their houses. *Another shoot-out,* he thought — that would be all their neighbors needed in their sedate Georgetown neighborhood.

She was running hard, bent as low as he was, and Savich thought she was heading toward her car. He heard Sherlock behind him, running all out. Kirsten didn't turn to fire at them, she ran.

He grabbed her around the waist and hauled her down. He flipped her onto her back and slammed down on her. She didn't fight him, didn't do anything. He pulled the gun easily from her hand. She still didn't fight, just lay there, panting.

"That's it, Kirsten, fun time's over." He came up over her. Something was wrong — she sobbed, then, "Please don't kill me, mister, please. Let me up, I won't do anything, please, let me up. This wasn't supposed to happen, it wasn't. She lied. Now she'll kill my mom."

Savich stared down into the face of a terrified young girl, maybe twelve, thirteen, tops. Sherlock came down on her knees beside them. "It's okay," she said. "Who are you?"

"I'm Melody. She made us come, swore she'd kill our mom if we didn't do exactly what she said, said she'd know if we screwed up. She told Bobby to break a window, then told me to fire the gun at you when I saw you get Bobby, and keep firing, then run away when the gun was empty. She said they weren't real bullets, so I shouldn't bother trying to shoot her with it."

Sherlock took the empty magazine out of the Glock 17.

Savich heard Coop running toward them, dragging Bobby with him, Lucy beside them.

Savich looked around but couldn't see any movement. Still, Kirsten could start shooting again at any moment, and they were all in the open. He wondered if she'd been the one shooting the real bullets at them, not this young girl.

It was quiet. Where was she? His skin crawled. "Let's get back to cover," he said, and they herded the kids back to the house.

Savich said low, "Lucy, I want you inside with the kids. No telling what she might try. Protect them."

"Where is she?" Lucy asked. "Why didn't she shoot us when we came running out?" There wasn't an answer to that. Lucy fanned her SIG around her as she pushed the kids inside the house, closed the front door, and told them to hunker down. She crouched next to them. "Give me your address so I can get people there to help your mom." When Lucy punched off her cell, she said, "You guys did good. We're going to wait right here until we hear your mom's okay." The little boy was sobbing. Lucy watched Melody pull him against her and rock him.

Outside, Coop said in a whisper to Savich and Sherlock, "Agents and police are on their way. They're supposed to come in silent. They know who's here, and that should make them real careful."

Sherlock nodded, her SIG trained on Coop as he juked across the street to take up position by the McPhersons' house directly opposite Savich's house.

Where was Kirsten?

CHAPTER 65

A car came slowly around the corner, headlights dimmed, a Crown Victoria, the first patrol car.

Coop hadn't expected anyone quite this fast. At least the officer had come in silently. The car slowed a good distance away from him, stopped. Coop waved toward Savich and trotted toward the car, his gun loose against his side.

He looked into the open driver's window to see a young man in a WPD uniform, a patrolman's hat on his head.

The patrolman raised a gun and aimed it right at Coop's face, and out of the young man's mouth came, "Well, now, isn't this the sweetest thing? You came trotting right over to me. Agent McKnight, isn't that right? For a moment there I thought you were the big dog himself, and I'd gotten real lucky. I saw you bring down whiny little Bobby, then the big dog caught Melody. The little bitch didn't run very hard, now, did she?"

Coop saw a shadow moving toward them. Savich?

He said calmly, "You sure fooled us, Kirsten; that Crown Vic you're driving looks just like a police cruiser, and the patrol hat you're wearing works. But you really should drop the eye makeup when you're trying to play a cop."

"I'd shoot you dead, Agent, but I need you to get out of here. Get in the car now, or I'll shoot you dead anyway, right here. Give me that gun. You're going to drive."

Her gun never wavered as she scooted over to the passenger side. Could he bring up his SIG in time? Maybe drop to the ground? No, she had the gun pointed straight at him, and she was too close. He got into the car, handed her his SIG.

"You and I are going on a little road trip, Agent McKnight. Get out of here, now!"

He couldn't stall. She was pressing the cold, hard steel of her Smith & Wesson against his temple. He pressed on the gas. He saw Savich clearly in the rearview mirror, his SIG drawn — but then an older man stepped out onto his front porch, and Savich lowered his gun.

"Go! Fast! Or I'll take down that old

codger."

Coop went. Fast.

Savich came to a stop in the middle of the street, kept his SIG pressed to his side. "It's okay, Mr. McPherson. You should go back inside now."

When Ollie arrived two minutes later, it was to see Savich's Porsche peeling out of his driveway, Sherlock beside him, speeding away.

Lucy was left with two terrified children, Ollie beside her.

They both looked up to see Mr. McPherson again on his front porch, watching.

CHAPTER 66

Early Sunday morning
If you don't survive, Cooper McKnight, I will be well and truly pissed.

It was nearly dawn when Lucy pulled Coop's Corvette back into his parking place at his condo in Wesley Heights. She was numb with fear because that madwoman had Coop. Had she already killed him? No, he was her hostage; there was no reason to kill him. *Yet. No, Coop's smart. He'll be okay.* It was now her mantra. She leaned her head against the steering wheel. Her cell rang, and she grabbed it up.

It was Sherlock. "Lucy, we haven't seen them yet, but we've got an APB out on the Crown Vic. We've notified every law enforcement agency in both states to watch out for the car but to keep clear of them."

Yeah, sure, like that's going to get any results. Lucy said, her voice flat, "You know she's changed out cars."

"Yes, it's very probable she has. But listen up, we have an ace in the hole. Kirsten hasn't taken Coop's cell phone, and it's on. The GPS location signal is moving south toward North Carolina, and so are we. We'll follow the GPS signal until we get to them ourselves. It will be enough, Lucy. Coop is well trained; he'll do what he needs to do."

Lucy started to say *But what if she takes his cell?* but she didn't — those words blighted hope. She said instead, "How can Kirsten possibly expect to control him for long while he's driving? How many hours can they drive before she has to sleep? What will she do with him then?"

Lucy heard Savich say, "You're right, but like Sherlock said, we've got the GPS signal, and we're traveling faster than they are. Look, Lucy, Kirsten could drug him, tie him up, whatever." She could shoot him dead, but he didn't say those words.

After a moment of silence, Sherlock said, "I think Coop is more valuable to her alive. Lucy, there's no reason for you to follow us down here. Get some sleep. Ollie is sending Agent Keppel over to stay with you."

"I don't know him."

"Keppel's a woman. You'll like her; she's hard-nosed, funny. And she'll make sure you get into bed. You hunker down — I'll call you when we catch up to them."

"What if Kirsten doubles back? What if —"

"She won't. Have a cup of tea and rest for a couple of hours, okay?"

Lucy flicked off her cell, sat for a moment in Coop's Corvette, smelling the wonderful new-leather smell, and tried to dial up some optimism.

There was a tap on her window.

She hadn't heard anyone come up. Agent Keppel? She whipped around to see Miranda smiling at her through the closed window.

"Lucy?"

Lucy pressed the down button. Because Miranda was a Silverman and because Lucy wasn't an idiot, she kept her SIG under her right hand.

She looked up at her cousin. "Miranda? What are you doing here at dawn? Is something wrong?"

"Oh, no, nothing's wrong. What happened to your bodyguard?"

"He's tied up."

"Well, that's dandy, isn't it?" Miranda brought up an old Kel Tec nine-millimeter pistol and shoved it into Lucy's face. "At last you're alone. I've been waiting here for the past couple of hours. I nearly gave it up, but his car wasn't here, and I knew you had to be with him, and sure enough, you drove right in, all alone. I see you've got your gun. I want you to throw it over on the floor. If you don't, I'll have to shoot you right here."

Lucy had known Miranda all her life; she meant it. She threw her SIG onto the floor in front of the passenger seat.

"That's good. I see you're not wearing the ring, but I wager you have it with you. Whether you do or not, if I think you're trying to get it out, I'll shoot you before you can touch it, you got that?"

The ring? "Why do you think I have the ring? Why would you care?" Lucy stared up into her cousin's face in the early-morning light. She was hunched over in a black wool coat. Her dark hair was pulled back, fastened with a clip. She said, "You look like a nun, Miranda, I've always thought that. What is this all about?"

"A nun?" Miranda laughed, but she shoved the Kel Tec against Lucy's nose. "Yes, well, nuns serve God, other people, and the greater good. I personally can't imagine anything more boring than that. I'm here for the ring, Lucy. My ring. And you'll give it to me. First, though, we have to get out of here. We're going to drive to a lovely little motel tucked into the middle of

498

Cumberland Street in the warehouse district.

"I'm going to walk to the passenger side. If you so much as whisper or move a finger, I'll kill you. Keep your arms around the steering wheel. That's right, hug it close and don't move."

"But why do you want the ring? Is it for Uncle Alan? What is going on here, Miranda?"

Miranda laughed. "What? Get the ring for my father? What would he do with it? You know very well why I want the ring. Do what you're told, Lucy, and only what you're told, or you'll be very dead."

Miranda, her arty, eccentric cousin, was responsible for all this? Miranda, with the magical name and the slouchy clothes and no interest in making her own way in the world? Lucy nearly laughed at herself — she had stopped trying to really engage Miranda years ago, simply because Miranda had resisted any personal attention from her. If Lucy hadn't finally stepped back from her, she might have realized what Miranda was capable of.

She felt the ring's now familiar warmth against her throat. If she grabbed it through the material of her shirt, was there time to use it before Miranda shot her? Would it even work if she couldn't clutch it in her hand? Even if it did work, Miranda was already holding a gun to her face eight seconds ago. It was a huge risk, and it would accomplish nothing.

She looked at Miranda, at the steel in her eyes, and kept her hands on the steering wheel. She had not a single doubt Miranda would kill her.

Miranda slipped in beside her, closed the door. "Nice car. I love that new-leather smell. Your boyfriend's, right?"

"Yes."

"And where is Agent McKnight?"

"He's out checking into something, with another agent. They'll both be here anytime now."

"Here you are a federal agent, Lucy, yet you're a crappy liar. Now, let's get out of here before someone comes out."

The Corvette roared to life. She backed out of Coop's parking place.

Miranda gave her directions in a low, intense voice, her Kel Tec aimed at Lucy's head.

When she pulled in front of the Allenby Motel on Cumberland Street, Miranda directed her to the back. She pulled a key out of her pocket. "We're going to the second level, to room twenty-two. You're going to stand in front of me, and you're going to take the key. Here."

As Lucy turned to face her, Miranda grabbed the golden chain and ripped it off her neck. Lucy cried out, grabbed at her hand, but Miranda shoved her Kel Tec into her ear.

She smiled, clutching the ring and the broken chain in her hand. "You gave it your best shot, Lucy. Don't try anything else, or I'll have to shoot you in the head. I thought I saw something pushing out from under your shirt. Be a good girl, do as you're told, and you might get out of this alive."

CHAPTER 67

Outside Fort Grant, North Carolina

Coop was more tired than he was afraid, and he knew that meant his brain wasn't as sharp as it needed to be. The sun had been up for two hours, and an hour before, Kirsten had directed him off the highway to pull into a 24/7 drive-through. They'd eaten breakfast biscuits, and he'd drunk a ton of coffee. Coop had been afraid she'd hurt the kid who took their orders, a smart-mouthed, freckle-faced little idiot who wondered why Kirsten was wearing a cop uniform with her black hair spiked up like a punker, but she'd laughed and told him he was stupid as spit.

She'd insisted on hot-wiring a ratty Dodge Magnum out of the parking lot of a shoe repair shop across the street from the drive-through, switching out the license plate for a rusty old Virginia plate she'd stashed in the Crown Victoria trunk, and left the Ford around the corner on the street.

Even though she could shoot him in a moment of time, Coop was still filled with hope — Kirsten had forgotten to take his cell phone, and as long as it was on and in his pocket, Savich could track them. All he had to do was keep himself alive until the cavalry showed up.

Kirsten had to be tired, too, and he figured that made them about even. He looked over at her and gave a start.

She was staring at him — her eyes fixed, her black mascara smudged a bit — didn't she blink? She kept his own SIG pressed against his side; though it was a heavy gun, her hand stayed steady. The white makeup she liked to wear was nearly gone now, along with the bloodred lipstick. She looked older than her years in the harsh morning light.

"Hi, there, handsome. You haven't said a word in a long time. You're staring at me. Like what you see? Bruce loved to look at me, and he'd touch me, you know, like he was stroking a cat, and I'd arch my back and purr for him. It's kind of nice having a man look at me like that again, having someone easy to look at to talk to instead of driving around all on my own.

"Hey, why don't I call you Coop? That's what I heard that little-girl FBI agent call you. You two sleeping together? You are, right? I got that vibe loud and clear. What, you playing at being a gentleman, not saying a word?"

"You're welcome to call me Coop, Kirsten. I'm glad you're enjoying this."

"Why wouldn't I? You need a shave, but that black stubble is pretty sexy. You thinking about your girlfriend?"

"I'm wondering where you're taking us, Kirsten. It seems to me we're getting pretty far away from Savich, if there's where you want to be."

"I've got all the time in the world for him. Too many people up there looking for me right now, partner." She laughed. "I guess you can think of this as a little pilgrimage, back to my daddy's roots down south. I was slowly heading down the coast, anyway. Daddy always tells me I've got to be fast on my feet, be willing to change my plans on a dime."

"He'd be proud of you, then."

"I like to think so." She frowned. "He was smart that way. Remember, he escaped that time in Aspen, jumped from a window two stories up."

"Yeah, but he got himself caught again because he was driving crazy, weaving all over the road. Why do you figure he was

504

doing that if he was so smart?"

"He was exhausted and probably so hungry he couldn't think straight, that's why." Kirsten pressed the gun harder against his side. "It wasn't his fault. They had the whole hick town out looking for him. He didn't have a chance."

"Why are we traveling south, Kirsten? You said something about a pilgrimage to Daddy's roots — are we going to visit Starke Prison in Raiford? You want to see your daddy's cell on death row? But why would you want to see where your daddy got strapped into Old Sparky and had two thousand volts shot through his body?"

She breathed in hard and knuckled away the tears in her eyes, smearing her mascara even more. "It was cruel what those animals did to him, and you know they acted all solemn and moral when they did it.

"Old Sparky! Can you believe that name? I'd like to strap all those animals down and fry them but good."

"Well, a lot of people agree with you. Old Sparky got retired a long time ago.

"They're more humane now; with the lethal injection, you're out and gone in an instant. Still, some people complain the needle hurts going in, and that's still cruel and inhuman. Go figure."

She poked him hard with the SIG in his ribs. "Do you honestly believe for a single minute your fed buddies are going to catch me? Do you honestly believe you'll see me on death row?" She was shaking her head back and forth as she spoke. Then she laughed. "Not in your lifetime, boy."

"I guess you're in control of my lifetime right now, Kirsten. I wasn't the one who flipped the switch on your daddy. Take it easy, okay?"

She laughed again, then turned reflective. "You know, Coop, I always believed it would be nice to visit Daddy's grave site, say some prayers, since I'll bet no one else ever has. But he wasn't buried, they cremated him. They fried him, then they burned him!"

Coop slowed a bit to let a sports car rocket past him. Too bad it wasn't Savich's Porsche. He shot a quick look in the rear-view mirror. Traffic was getting thicker now, but there wasn't any sign of a Porsche. Or a police car, for that matter. He had to be patient. He just had to stay alive.

He asked her, "What did they do with his ashes?"

"I couldn't find out for sure. Some say his ashes were scattered in the Cascades, but I don't believe that for a minute. They probably made it up, one of those media myths.

Yeah, if anything, they threw away his ashes."

She was angry now, breathing hard, and he didn't want to get shot. He kept his voice low and calm. "You read all about your daddy on the Internet, right? That's how you know all about him?"

She turned empty eyes to him. "Yeah, I'm an expert on my daddy, but it wasn't the same thing as really knowing him, having him hug me, tell me how much he loved me, admired me. I thought about what he and I could have done together, and I got to where I'd ask him his advice, you know, should I put out the lights of that little bitch who disrespected me? Sometimes it was like he answered me; I'd see exactly what to do. But he wasn't ever really there for me, thanks to my mother." She paused for a moment, never looking away from him. "I'm thinking maybe we'll go to Starke Prison, maybe hang out in Raiford; then again, maybe we won't. I'll figure it all out; I always do. I'm real lucky that way, lots of brain power. From my daddy, not my bitch of a mother."

He gave her a smile. "I've never been to Starke Prison before. Maybe that's not a bad idea."

"You think some of those bozo guards are

going to rescue you? Fat chance." She grunted, shoved the SIG against his side again. "I'll bet you the cell where they locked Daddy was cold and damp, and you couldn't breathe right, you know?"

"No, I don't know, and neither do you. Kirsten, you're going to have to sleep soon, and so am I, or I might wreck us."

"We'll take our chances on that, Coop," she said, looking at all the traffic around them. "We're going to put some distance between us and that parking lot in Fort Grant. I wouldn't want any of you feds getting lucky."

"How could anyone know about this car?"

"It seems to me this Savich guy knows stuff he shouldn't."

That was true enough.

She was silent, never looking away from his face. "It was so weird, when I had Savich lined up in my sights, and then your girlfriend slammed into him. It doesn't make any sense. He was standing there alone, none of you near him, asking for me to shoot him, and I did, but down he went, and my shot was high."

"Kirsten, you simply missed him, okay? We all thought you'd want to get in his face when you killed him."

She shrugged. "Shooting him seemed like

a decent idea at the time. Hey, I know where I want to go. Did you know I've got a little sister? I figure she's nearly thirty now."

"Yes, I read about your half sister."

"I don't know where she is. When her mama took her away from Raiford way back in the mid-eighties, I'll bet she changed her name. I always wondered what my sister is like, whether she knows who her daddy was, or whether her mama erased him like mine did?"

The words were out of his mouth before he could stop them. "For your sister's sake, I hope she did."

His SIG slammed hard into his ribs, and he felt pain steal his breath. His hand jerked the steering wheel to the left. Kirsten jerked the steering wheel back, to the sounds of a dozen sharp car horns. "Watch your mouth, boy, if you don't want me to put three bullets in your side."

"If you do, I'll kill both of us. I promise you that, Kirsten."

"Yeah, you would try that, wouldn't you? You'd kill both you and me for — what is it? — oh, yeah, the greater good." Then in the next breath, she said, "I wish I could find out my half sister's name. Her mama named her Mary Lou — boy, is that ever a stupid name. But like I said, I'll bet she

509

changed both their names when she left Raiford.

"I'd like to see how Mary Lou turned out, you know? Does she have four little kiddies, live in a dopey house in some stupid suburb, and have a boring accountant for a husband, like that Arnette Carpenter did? What a loss that guy was. I know that for a fact; I had drinks with him after I took care of his wife."

Coop pictured Roy Carpenter as he'd seen him — *was it only a week ago?* — how devastated he looked three years after his wife's murder at this psychopath's hands, the deep abiding pain in his eyes. "Tell me about Arnette Carpenter."

"Yeah? She was a talented little cow, conceited, full of herself, always lording it over me, adored that loser husband of hers."

"Where did you bury her, Kirsten?"

Kirsten laughed. "A freebie for you, Coop. I planted her on the VA hospital grounds, under a huge old oak tree facing the ocean. A great view. Too bad she doesn't care anymore." She tapped her fingers against her leg, frowned. "You know, it kind of pisses me off that Daddy married that stupid woman but not my own mother."

"I understand she worked with your father."

"Yeah, I know. Maybe he worked with my

mother, too; she wouldn't tell me, wouldn't even say how she met him. He must have known Mary Lou's mother even before he knew my mom. Can you believe that weird Florida law, though — they allowed Daddy to declare in court they were married, and whoop-de-do, the deed was done. They even let him sleep with her in prison lots of times. So my little sister came along in 1982, four years after I did. I really want to find them both. Do you think I'll like them?"

He kept quiet.

"Well, do you?"

"Sure. Why not?"

She chewed her bottom lip, the last of the dark red lipstick long gone. "I'll bet you she'd tell me more than my mother ever told me, which is a big fat zero."

"What would you like her to tell you? That he used a hacksaw to cut off people's heads?"

She only shrugged. "Who cares? They were dead; they didn't know."

"Do you know he confessed to cremating one of his victims' heads in his current girlfriend's fireplace?"

His SIG jammed against his ribs again. He managed not to grunt in pain, but it hurt, really hurt.

"He was having some fun, that's all, just a

little fun, and like I said, what did those girls care? They were dead and gone."

"How many women have you killed, Kirsten? I believe your daddy confessed to thirty-five."

"After I drop-kick your butt out of here, Agent McKnight, that'll be one less I'll have to go."

"Nah, I won't count. I'm a guy."

"You keep driving, you punk. I've got me a call to make."

Coop watched her hit speed dial. Bruce Comafield was dead, so who was she calling?

She never took her eyes off him. "Yeah, it's me. I wanted you to know I'm heading to Florida. Can't talk right now, but I'll call you from there. I'm having fun, got me a big FBI agent driving me. He's my own personal chauffeur."

She listened, then said, "Yeah, sure, I'll be careful. Bye."

"Who was that?"

"What do you care? I've got lots of friends."

"At least there'll be someone to scatter your ashes after you're dead. Who was that?"

"Bruce could have scattered my ashes, if you hadn't murdered him. He loved me, do you hear?"

"Maybe, but he's gone now."

"Shut up! All right, my mother would scatter my ashes, and so would — never mind. Take this exit, and get us out of sight — no cars, no houses."

Was she going to kill him?

He took the next exit off I-95, drove past a couple of gas stations and fast-food places on the access road. Soon they were in the boonies. There were flat tobacco fields on both sides of the country road, harvested stalks were a golden carpet to the horizon, the few houses and barns set far back from the road.

"Pull over. You and I are going to pee."

Coop's heart slowed down a bit.

He knew she was watching him from behind, but he didn't care. When he was turning, she struck him hard on the back of his head.

When he came to his senses, she was standing over him, whistling "Country Road."

"Unlike a guy, a girl's gotta have both hands. Come on, it's getting late. Let's get going."

She had his SIG in her hand, but she knew he was hurt, and she was looking around, checking things out. It was his chance. He started to kick up at her, and she shot him.

CHAPTER 68

Allenby Motel

Lucy froze. "Give me back the ring, Miranda. Grandfather left it for me."

Miranda laughed, slipped the ring off the chain and into her pocket. "It wasn't his to give to you. He stole it from Aunt Helen."

When Lucy unlocked the motel room door, Miranda shoved her inside with such force she fetched up to the bed and sprawled over it. Miranda stood far away from her, the gun pointed at her chest. "I've never disliked you, Lucy, at least not until recently, even though you were always everyone's little princess. You were too young to be jealous of, and then after Uncle Milton and the ring disappeared, it didn't really matter, anyway. You stayed my little cousin, and I watched you grow up.

"Even now I don't really dislike you; this is simply necessary. And necessary means I will kill you if I have to. Stay put."

She pulled two loops of skinny rope out of a big black tote with a bookstore logo on the side. "I want you to sit on that chair."

Lucy knew in her gut she didn't have a choice. She didn't want to die. She wanted to be here to welcome Coop when he got back. She sat down in the single chair.

"Put your hands on the arms of the chair, I'm going to tie your wrists to the arms." She carefully pulled the ropes taut and knotted them, always watchful. "I've heard Court talk about all that martial arts stuff you do in the gym, so I'm not taking any chances with you. Hold still."

When she moved to Lucy's right wrist, Lucy made a fist, which lifted it a bit from the chair arm when Miranda tied the rope around it. It worked, the rope ending up not all that tight, not like her left wrist. Lucy immediately began working it, slowly, easily, so as not to draw Miranda's attention.

Miranda placed her black tote onto the bed, shrugged out of her black coat, and sat down facing Lucy.

"Miranda, tell me what this is all about. What do you mean the ring is yours?"

Miranda didn't answer. Lucy watched her pull the ring out of her pocket and caress it like a lover. She pressed it lightly against her chest, then brought it down again to study it. She whispered, "It's been so long since I've seen this ring, since I've touched it, more than twenty-two years now since my Uncle Milton stole it and went walkabout — that's what my father called it. I wonder if he ever really accepted that Uncle Milton simply walked out, left his son, his wife, his precious little granddaughter. I was a teenager at the time, all into myself, the way teenagers are, but I remember Dad saying over and over, 'But why? It doesn't make sense. Why?' My mom and Court believed he'd just left, and so did I, simply because it was easier to believe he'd run away instead — instead of what? You were too young to know anything. Turns out Dad was right, it didn't make sense, and Uncle Milton never left.

"When I found out you turned up his skeleton in Aunt Helen's attic, we all realized the supposed walkabout was a big whomping lie. Aunt Helen hadn't driven him away, she'd murdered him, and your father must have helped her hide his body. They lied about all of it. I wonder what else was a lie? Aunt Helen told me your grandfather had stolen the ring and taken it with him when he left. All those years I thought I had lost the ring forever, and then suddenly anything was possible.

"I started searching your grandmother's house for the ring as soon as the police left, and whenever I saw you leave for work. Father told me you'd been looking around in her study, and that's where I found Uncle Milton's letter to you, his precious grand-daughter, in one of Aunt Helen's books."

"Miranda, you took the letter?"

"Of course. Who did you think did? My father? Court? They never had a clue about the ring — Mom, either. When I read the letter, I knew for sure you had the ring and that you'd never give it up, not after you discovered what it could do, and that's when I hired those idiot felons to take it from you. Congratulations, Lucy, either you're very lucky or you're very good. You got away, and you even killed one of them. I knew then the FBI would identify him and it was only a matter of time before you traced him back to me. I got everything ready to run, but I wasn't going anywhere without this ring."

"Miranda, how much do you know about the ring?"

"I know everything."

Lucy said slowly, "But how?"

Miranda laughed. "Your mother's death broke Aunt Helen's heart. She was always secretive, at least that's what I heard my father say, but after Claudine's death she got really depressed; she'd stare off into space, saying nothing, looking at nothing in particular. You were too young to notice, only two. I'll never forget the day she took me into her study and we huddled together. I had just turned twelve. She took out the ring and told me it was a special ring meant for only one girl in each generation of our family — one girl, not a boy — and I was her niece, and it would be mine someday, when she thought the time was right. At first she didn't tell me any more than that, but every time I visited, she would show me the ring and tell me stories about it, stories passed down that her own mother had told her, stories about how she'd used the ring, and all the while she was speaking, she was darting glances around the room to be sure no one was near.

"Aunt Helen said now she was passing all the stories down to me. She said it had to be our secret, that no one was to know or she couldn't imagine what would happen. Maybe the ring would disappear, maybe it would even stop working. That was a lie and at first, I didn't understand. I thought she was crazy. She scared me, but the ring didn't ever, even when she showed me what happened when she held the ring and said

the word. She could always tell me if something strange was about to happen, things
she had no way of knowing otherwise. It
was a game she played with me. But she
wouldn't let me use the ring myself; she said
I wasn't ready for it.

"I felt such power, and I was only twelve
years old. I knew it would belong to me, no
one else, only me. I asked her over and over
when that would be, and she smiled at me
and said we'd have to see.

"And four years later, Uncle Milton was
gone and so was the ring. We felt such
anger, such despair, both of us together, an
unbreakable bond between an old woman
and a teenager."

Lucy said slowly, "I am my grandmother's
direct heir, not you. I think if she hadn't
been so distraught when my mother died, if
she hadn't lost her bearings, she would
never have spoken to you about it, shared
its power and secrets with you, and you
know it. She would have waited and given
the ring to me."

"Dream on, Lucy. Who cares why she
picked me? The fact is, she did, whatever
her reasons. You were Uncle Milton's
choice, but he had no right to decide
anything; the ring wasn't his. I was Aunt
Helen's choice. You read the letter; you

know everything he wrote was true. Aunt Helen was strange, it's true, she was obsessed with the ring, and if that sent her to me, then so be it.

"Maybe you were too young to remember, but I was always over at your house after school so she could spend time with me, teach me about the ring. I've thought about this ring for over two decades, thought about what I could have done with it, how it could have changed my life.

"I'm thirty-eight years old now. I think it was fate you found Uncle Milton because it brought me back this ring. Now, finally, it's mine as it was meant to be."

"You were twelve years old when grandmother showed you the ring, showed you what it could do. You never said anything to your parents? Your brother?"

"That's right, I never told them. Why should I? I don't think Father even knew about it, or if he did he paid no attention. He and Court, it'll be a grand surprise to them when I leave with the ring, since they have no idea what I can do with it. As for my mother, she always cared about only two things in her life — being my father's wife and looking like a million bucks. She's the perfect wife for my father, since all he ever wanted was to make more and more money and have a beautiful woman on his arm." Her eyes went sharp and cunning. Lucy wondered if she was thinking about humbling both of them, proving she was the superior one.

Lucy kept gently working her wrist back and forth. The rope was loosening.

"I dreamed, Lucy, I dreamed for years about what I would do with this wonderful ring." She squeezed the ring tightly in her hand. She frowned. "Is it always cold? Odd, but I don't remember it being hot or cold."

Cold? What was this? Lucy said, "Yes, it's always cold. Miranda, what do you plan to do with it? You have only eight seconds. That's very little time to change much of anything."

"What did you do with it, Lucy?"

"I saved my boss's life when a psychopathic killer shot him. I had just enough time to shove him down away from the bullet."

"That must have been exciting. And your boss didn't even know he was dead." Miranda smiled at her. "Lucy, you are such an innocent. I bet if you had the ring you'd go through life trying to right wrongs, fighting your never-ending battle for truth and justice. Ms. Superwoman. Do try for a little imagination. Do you realize how much money I will make with this ring? Think about a trip to Las Vegas, think about playing blackjack. The croupier deals out the card and you say 'SEFYLL,' and you know exactly what the next cards in the deck will be. Think of roulette or poker, any game you wish. With a little imagination you could win at all of them at will. Can you imagine how rich you could become? And if you were careful, no one would ever suspect a thing, would they?"

"I didn't think of that," Lucy said honestly. But would she have thought of that after some time? As Miranda had?

"I've had years to think about all the things I could do." She paused, closed her eyes, and squeezed the ring tightly. She looked, Lucy thought, radiant.

"Yes, I'll be getting a lot of people to do most anything I want them to do — it won't take hardly any effort at all."

"What do you mean?"

"How often have you wished you could take back something you've done or said? I'll be able to do just that, whenever it suits me. If things aren't going my way, if someone doesn't react the way I want them to, I'll simply say 'SEFYLL' and try something else. Henry Kissinger couldn't have out-negotiated me, because I'd know what he was going to say before he said it, or realized he would say it. You see how easy it is?"

Experimenting with people, manipulating them — "It wouldn't really be living your life, more like living your own personal video game."

"I know what I want, Lucy, and I'm smart. I know no one in my family thinks I'm worth much at all — you included — but I am smart, do you hear me?"

"You're practically yelling it at me; of course I hear you."

"I've seen my father look at my mother and shake his head. This last time I moved home, he offered to find me a job, and he has before, boring jobs that were a waste of my time and my talents. How could I care about a payroll account or checking some idiot's job benefits after holding this ring in my hand?

"Yes, I'd sit there while Dad went on about his stocks and bonds, preening at his own brilliance, and all the while I was thinking about what I could do with eight seconds — eight whole seconds to buy or sell. I could be the richest person in the world, if I wanted to be." Miranda kissed the ring, then thrust it up in a victory signal, and took a waltz step around the small room.

She laughed.

Lucy watched her as she continued to work her wrist. *Another minute.* She wondered what Miranda could have become if Lucy's grandmother had never shown her the ring. "Miranda, since you ordered those men to kill me and take the ring, you obviously didn't think you needed me. So why did you even bother to bring me here?"

Miranda still clutched the ring in her hand. "Do you know, I regretted having paid those men to kill you. All I really wanted from you was my ring. But they said you were an armed FBI agent, and no matter what I wanted from you, they weren't going to leave any witnesses. I should probably have done it myself.

"Do you realize, Lucy, that the real magic of the ring is that no one — absolutely no one — ever knows that anything has changed in those eight seconds? To them, time is time and what happens simply happens. You have this extraordinary power, yet no one knows you have it." Miranda paused for a moment and frowned, then she squeezed the ring again and a blazing smile lit her face. "But you will know, Lucy, when I make it work, won't you? You won't experience it with me, but you'll know, and you will believe me when I say it, because you've

525

done it yourself. You're the only other person in the world who'll know, and understand the power of it.

"What do you think my first experiment should be? Should I shoot you, and then undo it? You won't know, but I will. And when I tell you that you were dead eight seconds before you died, you will believe it."

Yes, she would, indeed. Lucy swallowed. "Why not try another experiment, Miranda? Like crashing that clock to the floor and saying 'SEFYLL,' and then see if it's back on the nightstand again?"

"Shooting you would be such a glorious proof." She sighed. "But all right, it'll be my first time, best try something easy. All right, the bloody clock." She threw it to the floor and yelled, "SEFYLL."

Chapter 69

North Carolina

She'd shot him. Coop yelled with the shock of the sharp punch of pain in his side. He lay there panting, trying to get hold of himself. He felt blood spreading over his side, through his shirt, onto his shearling coat. He had to slow the bleeding or he'd die, since he couldn't picture Kirsten hauling him to an ER.

Kirsten was smiling down at him. "Not such a big mouth on you now, Mr. Agent. All laid out and bleeding. Here, get the bleeding stopped, I don't want to drive." She threw him a black T-shirt from a pile of clothes she'd heaped on the backseat. "Lucky for you I kept some of Bruce's clothes. That T-shirt ought to do it. It's clean enough. Too bad. I was going to keep that shirt."

Coop pulled up his shirt, eyed the wound. Thank God it was through and through, and shallow, but it was still bleeding. He folded the T-shirt, pressed it over both the entry and exit wounds, and fastened his belt around himself. That should hold it. He drew a deep breath, getting his brain to accept the pain and set it aside. There was blood on the inside of his shearling, but somehow no bullet hole. Realizing he'd even thought about his coat made him smile.

"What are you smiling about? I shot you, you moron! Come on, move! You don't drive, then you die here, your choice."

Slowly, Coop got to his feet. He could function, but he knew it wasn't enough. At least she'd proved she didn't want to kill him yet; she wanted to use him as a hostage, or at least as a driver. But it was up to him to stop her, there was no one else to do it. "I'll drive."

"Thought you would. Let's go, haven't got all day, now, do we? In a couple of hours, we'll stop at a motel, get some sleep."

When they reached the highway again, Coop saw a flash of black. It was a Porsche, Savich's Porsche.

CHAPTER 70

Sherlock saw them merging into traffic ahead of them. "That's Coop. In the Dodge!"

Savich quickly eased the Porsche behind a big SUV. "I see them. We'll hang back, wait for Coop to stop again."

Suddenly a silver North Carolina Highway Patrol cruiser, with its distinctive wide black stripe and State Trooper logo, pulled out around them and sped forward.

"Not good, Dillon. I'll bet they've spotted Kirsten."

The cruiser was a missile headed right for the Dodge. They saw the officer holding his radio in his hand, speaking into it, his partner, his head out the window, probably shouting back that the license plate was too dirty to read.

Savich accelerated. Drivers all around them were staring now, rubbernecking, and traffic was slowing down.

The cruiser's siren came on.

Sherlock got on her cell to the North Carolina Highway Patrol.

They watched, helpless, as the Dodge sped up, weaving in and out of traffic, trying to lose the highway patrol. *Good luck with that.* They could see Coop clearly now, and Kirsten, looking back at the cruiser, then at Coop. They saw her waving a gun, pointing it back toward them. Then, suddenly, the highway patrolman in the passenger seat began shooting.

CHAPTER 71

Kirsten slid down in the seat and shoved her gun hard into his ribs again. "Those idiot cops are shooting at us! How did they know about this car? You get us out of here, now! Move!"

Coop pressed his foot on the gas pedal. He saw Savich coming up behind the highway patrol cruiser, both of them closing on the Dodge, and all the while Kirsten screamed curses. Suddenly, a bullet struck the back window, shattered the glass. Another bullet, then another, striking the rearview mirror on the passenger side. They were aiming at Kirsten, not at him. He prayed they were good shots.

Coop saw her twist around, get her window down, and then she was leaning out, firing back at them.

He'd never have a better chance.

Coop jerked the car hard right, skidded across the shoulder gravel, and rocketed through a fence into a tobacco field, plowing through the harvested stalks. The impact sent Kirsten flying backward, striking the back of her head against the dash. It didn't knock her out, but she was dead silent for a moment, her face a white mask, her eyes glazed, and then she was up and firing, not at him but out the window again at the highway patrol car that had followed them into the field. She grabbed the chicken stick as they bumped and tore through the wide rows. She realized he kept mowing through the stalks on purpose to slow them, not letting the car pass between the rows, and she turned toward him, his SIG leading. Where was her gun? He shot out his fist and struck her jaw with all the strength he had.

She lurched away, hit her head against the glove compartment, and was thrown back again, her head bouncing off the seat. Then she slumped over, unconscious.

Coop brought the car to a sliding stop in the middle of the field. He saw his SIG on the floor where Kirsten had dropped it. He was looking for her gun when he heard the highway patrol cruiser pull to a stop right behind him, heard the cops shouting at him.

He had to respond or they'd probably shoot him. The pain in his side ripped through him, but he ignored it and shoved his door open, one eye on Kirsten. He raised his hands.

"You the FBI agent?"

"Yes. Cooper McKnight. I hit her; Kirsten Bolger's in the car, unconscious."

Coop was never so happy in his life to see Savich and Sherlock cruising toward them, Savich careful to keep the Porsche between the mown rows of tobacco stalks, so as not to scratch up that perfect paint job.

"Don't shoot at the Porsche. They're FBI!"

Coop waved, then turned to watch one of the cops answer his cell, nod, then say, "You sure she's out of it, Agent? Hey, what's wrong? Geez, you're shot!"

Coop waved a hand and looked back into the car. He couldn't believe it, but Kirsten was gone. He ran around the front of the car and saw her crawling through the rows of tobacco stalks several dozen feet from him. "She's headed toward that house! Kirsten, stop, or I'll shoot!"

Kirsten looked back at him over her shoulder, lurched to her feet, and started running toward the house in the distance.

Coop took off after her, his side forgotten, two highway patrolmen behind him, both firing toward her. He heard Savich shout, "Coop, we'll try to cut her off before she gets to that house! Don't hesitate — bring her down if you can."

Yeah, Coop thought, breathing hard, feeling his blood slick on his skin. *It was enough, it was more than enough.* He paused, aimed his SIG, and fired.

CHAPTER 72

Allenby Motel

Lucy and Miranda stared at the smashed electric clock on the ancient rag rug that lay next to the small nightstand.

"You didn't break it twice, did you?" Lucy asked, though she almost yelled out with relief.

Miranda was shaking her head back and forth. "I don't understand. Nothing happened. Aunt Helen swore to me it would happen for me. I'm her direct relation, just as you are. She's my father's sister; it has to work, it should!"

Miranda grabbed a pillow off the bed and hurled it against the door. She yelled, "SE-FYLL!"

Please don't let it work, please don't let it.

Both women stared at the pillow, still on the floor against the motel room's door.

Lucy nearly wept with relief, though like Miranda, she didn't understand why nothing had happened. *Thank you, Sweet Lord, she didn't shoot me.*

The ring is cold for Miranda.

Miranda was moaning deep in her throat, pacing, cursing, shaking the ring, saying "SEFYLL" over and over.

Lucy had the rope loose enough now to slip her hand out of it. Miranda still held the gun in one hand, the ring in the other. But she wasn't paying attention. Lucy knew she had to act, with the ring or without it, or Miranda would likely kill her out of jealousy and despair.

She whirled to face Lucy. "It has to work for me, Aunt Helen promised me, so that means I'm not doing something right. Tell me, Lucy. Tell me what I'm doing wrong."

Lucy stared at her. "Miranda, when I hold the ring, when it lies against my throat, it feels warm. Very warm. I don't do anything different than you did."

Miranda said slowly, "You said it was cold for you, very cold."

"It seems I'm not such a crappy liar after all."

Miranda howled. She flung her tote against the far wall, screamed, "SEFYLL!" Miranda's tote remained on the floor.

Lucy said slowly, "I can think of only one reason the ring doesn't work for you, Miranda. It's not meant to."

Miranda stared at her. She began shaking her head back and forth. "No," she whispered. "That's not possible. I am Alan Silverman's daughter!" Miranda ran toward her, waving the ring, beyond herself, beyond reason. "I am Alan Silverman's daughter!"

When Miranda was close enough, Lucy jerked her right hand free, roared up out of the chair, and smashed Miranda in the face.

She fell hard, and Lucy turned to frantically work the rope loose. She heard Miranda stir just as she pulled her wrist free. She didn't see her SIG, didn't see Miranda's Kel Tec, either, but she saw the ring. She grabbed the ring off the floor and ran out of the motel room.

She heard Miranda screaming after her, ordering her to stop or she'd shoot her.

Lucy ran. She was surprised by the crystal-clear sunlight that nearly blinded her as she ran.

Down the motel steps. She shot one look at Coop's Corvette, but she didn't have her purse. A bullet tore through her arm. She whirled around, yelled, "SEFYLL!"

Time stopped, and then she was closer to the motel again, Miranda screaming after her, and she ran again. This time she veered left, behind a steel trash container, and she heard more gunshots, but none were near. She didn't have her cell phone, but she had her legs, and she had the ring. She remembered Ann Marie running as fast as she could from Kirsten, and she did the same, the air crisp and sharp in her lungs as she ran, keeping her turns random past warehouses and across parking lots. She ran until she reached a rundown shopping district and came across a policeman in his cruiser pulled into a strip mall.

Twenty minutes later, Ruth Warnecki-Noble pulled up at the precinct house in her Silverado. She looked Lucy up and down. "I don't see any bullet holes, thank the Lord." Then sheer relief made Ruth hug her. "Sherlock called."

Lucy pulled away, grabbed her arms. "Have you heard yet, Ruth? Did Dillon and Sherlock catch up to them? Did they bring Kirsten down? Is Coop all right?"

Ruth saw a horrible shot of fear glass Lucy's eyes, imagined Dix, her husband, being driven around by a madwoman, and said without pause, "Yes, he's fine." Truth was, she didn't know that for sure, but Lucy didn't need to deal with that uncertainty right now. "Sherlock will call again with all the details. Don't worry, okay?"

"Ruth, dear God, we've got to get to the Silvermans' house right now!"

CHAPTER 73

There wasn't much cover, but Kirsten kept running, her eyes on the small white house no more than thirty feet away. Coop saw a bullet hit one of the mown stalks ahead of her, close to her head. He knew she was heading to that house. There'd be people there, people she'd kill without thought if they didn't do exactly what she told them to.

Bring her down, bring her down. Coop raised his SIG and fired again. She jerked a bit and grabbed her left arm but didn't slow down. He fired a third time as he ran, his side pulsing with pain with each stride, and he missed yet again. He was sweating. He didn't think, merely shrugged off his shearling coat. He could hear the highway patrolmen pounding behind him. They'd stopped firing, concentrating on getting close enough to her before she got into that house.

Coop's heart seized when he saw a small

boy and girl running through the rows, right toward Kirsten. He whirled around toward the cops. "Don't shoot. You see the kids?"

The kids were running right at her, shouting something to her. *What?* His heart sank when he realized the kids were seeing a poor bleeding woman being chased by three men with guns, and they were trying to help her.

He yelled, "Get away from her! Go back to the house!"

But the little girl didn't slow; she was running full-tilt at Kirsten, the little boy trying hard to keep up.

One of the patrolmen shouted, "We're police officers, get back!"

The little girl skidded to a halt, stared toward them, but it didn't matter now; Kirsten had her arm tight around her neck, and she was dragging her in front of her. The little boy was panting hard, shoving at her, kicking at her legs, but he was too small to do much damage, and Kirsten didn't slow.

Even from thirty feet away, they all saw the gun in Kirsten's hand.

"It's a Smith and Wesson," Coop said. "She'll use it, no hesitation at all." Had it been in the waistband of her pants? Didn't matter, it was his fault. He should have stripped her if necessary to find that gun as soon as he was sure the cops wouldn't shoot him.

The three men watched Kirsten swing the pistol's butt against the boy's head, saw him go down. One of the patrolmen was on his cell, calling dispatch for an ambulance, and more backup, and cursing.

She had the little girl, and she was dragging her, keeping her tight against her, and they were nearly to the house, only another twenty yards. Coop saw what Kirsten was focused on, an old white pickup parked in the driveway.

No, Coop thought. No, he couldn't let this happen, he couldn't let her get away, not with this little girl as her hostage this time. Coop took off running, firing over Kirsten's head. Kirsten turned, and he saw the little girl's face was turning blue, Kirsten's arm was that tight around her neck. Kirsten fired, then turned, dragging the little girl toward the pickup.

It was then he saw a flash of bright red hair. Sherlock's hair. She was bent low, moving toward Kirsten.

He heard a door slam, heard a woman's high, frantic voice. "Amanda! What's going on here? Who are you? Oh, no, you've got a gun! You're hurting my daughter!"

Kirsten fired toward the woman and

missed, but the woman fell to her knees and scrabbled behind a bush.

But she was up in the next instant. "You let go of my daughter!"

Kirsten took dead aim, but Amanda was jerking at her arm, twisting wildly, screaming, "Don't you shoot my mama! Don't!"

CHAPTER 74

Ruth gunned the Silverado through the Sunday traffic toward Chevy Chase. She eyed the ring clutched in Lucy's hand. "Listen, Lucy, I don't understand what it is about this ring that makes it so valuable, but don't you think it's time to tell me? Your cousin Miranda tried to kill you for it. Why?"

"Miranda wanted the ring badly, Ruth — she believed what my grandfather wrote, that it held some kind of power that belonged to her, and she could bring that power to life, but it didn't work out that way. I know in my gut she's going to confront her mother about it, and she's enraged. I don't know what she's going to do, Ruth."

Ruth tossed Lucy her clutch piece. Then she grabbed her cell and speed-dialed Ollie.

"No, Ruth, please don't call for backup, not yet."

She got a raised eyebrow from Ruth. "I

know these people are your family, Lucy, but I'm getting the cold, hard feeling these people are nuts. We're going to follow standard procedure, both of us." She called Ollie.

They were pulling into the Silvermans' driveway when they heard a gunshot.

Lucy was out of the Silverado in a second, Ruth shouting after her, "Don't you go in there alone, Lucy, you hear me? Stop or I'll hurt you!"

But Lucy couldn't stop. She shoved the front door open and ran through the elegant entrance hall to the living room. She flung the heavy wooden door open and skidded to a stop. Uncle Alan, Aunt Jennifer, and Court stood huddled together beside Uncle Alan's favorite burgundy leather sofa. They were frozen in place, Miranda standing in front of them.

Uncle Alan stepped in front of his wife. "No, Miranda, don't shoot that gun again, do you hear me? She's your mother, for God's sake, your mother!"

Miranda raised the heavy Kel Tec, aimed it directly at her father. "Dad, why would you protect her? She betrayed you. She got pregnant by another man. She cheated me out of what was mine. Don't you under-stand, she stole everything from me!"

Lucy said, "Miranda, stop now! You can't hurt your mother!"

Miranda whirled around. "Lucy, go away, I don't want you here. What? Are you going to shoot me, Lucy? And her? Will she shoot me, too?"

Lucy said very calmly, "No, I'm not going to shoot you, Miranda, and neither is Ruth. I want all of this to stop. Drop the gun, Miranda, and all of this can be over."

"No, it's not over. She destroyed everything that should have been mine; she made me into nothing, do you hear me, Lucy? I'm nothing!"

"You're much more than nothing, Miranda; we all are. Listen, it's only a ring, a stupid ring that shouldn't even exist. You lived without the ring a very long time. You did fine. You don't need it. Drop the gun and we'll talk about this as much as you want."

Miranda said in a dead voice, "Alan Silverman is not my father. I asked mother, and she told me the truth. She slept with some kind of artist she met in a coffeehouse — can you believe that? She said she was lonely then because my father — Alan — was working so much she hardly ever saw him. She said she wanted to protect me from knowing that, but she was protecting herself.

"And that's why the ring wouldn't work for me — I'm not a Silverman. Don't you think it's funny that I fell for an artist in a café myself? A real loser, like my own real father, I'll bet. Like me. I know that now. And look at you, all grown up, an FBI agent, and you have the ring, and it works for you, doesn't it? I would have sworn I hit you outside that motel, but then you weren't where I thought you'd be. Not that you deserve to die; you really don't. You're the one who has everything now."

She laughed. "And still you come back after me, Lucy? You think you're going to arrest me?" She laughed again, and then she fired the pistol.

CHAPTER 75

The little girl pulled and jerked at Kirsten's arm when she raised her gun to shoot again at her mother, and Kirsten clouted her. Savich's bullet caught her in her right shoulder. She staggered, screamed, and fell to the ground, taking the little girl with her.

"Sherlock, see to the mother!"

Sherlock ran to the woman, who had fallen, as Savich and Coop ran toward Kirsten, listening to the little girl's screams. She knelt beside the woman. There was a thin line of blood along her hairline. The woman looked up at her, confused and frantic. Sherlock said, "It's okay. I'm FBI. We've got Amanda. She's all right, too."

"But Taylor, Taylor? My little boy?"

Sherlock shouted, "The little boy — is he okay?"

Coop called back, "Yes, the highway patrolman said he's fine. Everyone's good."

"Taylor's all right. Let me get you cleaned

up. Thank goodness, it's only a graze, you'll be fine."

"When I saw that woman dragging Amanda toward me, and no sign of Taylor, I'll tell you —" The words fell into a hiccuping sob. Sherlock pressed a handkerchief to the bloody line on her head. "I know," she said. "You all did great."

The little girl had managed to wriggle away from Kirsten as soon as they fell. She'd stumbled away, then had fallen to her side, gulping in big breaths of air, rubbing her throat and sobbing quietly.

Savich saw Coop pull the little girl up into his arms. He rocked her, saying, "It's okay, your mama's going to be fine; so is your little brother. Taylor's his name?" At her jerky nod, he continued, "Yep, Taylor's all right." She clutched at him, and Coop kissed her forehead and kept rocking her. He saw Savich run past them to come down beside Kirsten. Blood snaked out of the wound, high on her shoulder, but she wasn't unconscious, she was moaning, her head twisting from side to side, her eyes closed. He picked up her gun, an old Smith & Wesson.

Coop kissed Amanda's forehead, gave her a last hug, and handed her off to one of the highway patrolmen. He walked to Kirsten, went down on his knees beside Savich, and leaned in close. "Kirsten, can you hear me?"

Kirsten opened her eyes, stared up at Coop, then over at Savich. "You," she whispered at Savich. "You freaking murderer. You killed me."

"Nah, you aren't going to die," Savich said. He tore off his shirt and pressed it hard against her shoulder.

She tried to spit at him. "You killed Bruce. It isn't right, it just isn't right. And you, I hope you're hurting bad."

Savich looked over at him. "What is she talking about? Coop?"

"She shot me in the side. No, don't worry, I'm okay."

Savich studied his face for a moment, nodded, then lifted his shirt off Kirsten's shoulder wound enough to see the bleeding had slowed.

Kirsten licked her lips. She was deathly pale, no more lipstick, no more of her powder. Savich knew she had to be in bad pain, but she wasn't making a sound. Finally she whispered, "What will Daddy say?"

They looked up at the sound of sirens. Two ambulances were whipping through the tobacco field toward them, behind them a half dozen squad cars.

CHAPTER 76

Lucy and Ruth both dropped and rolled. Miranda's shot went through a window, shattering the glass. Miranda had shot nowhere near them or her mother. Lucy shouted as Ruth pulled her SIG, "No, Ruth, don't shoot her!"

Lucy slowly rose to her feet. Miranda stood ten feet from her, motionless, staring at Lucy and back to her father, who really wasn't her father at all, and finally, she looked at her mother. She said quietly, "I know Dad loves you, and you're my mother, and that's why I can't kill you. I wish I could, but I can't." She looked at her father again, great sadness in her eyes, and gave a small nod. She slowly raised the gun to her mouth —

"No! Miranda! No!"

"This is what I want, Lucy — my choice, not yours. Don't you dare use that ring."

The shot was obscenely loud in the

still room.

Lucy ran to Miranda as she collapsed to the floor, Ruth at her heels. Jennifer screamed, tore away from her husband, and rushed to Miranda, who now lay on her side, the gun still in her hand. Neither her uncle Alan nor Court moved, as if they couldn't, as if the world they knew had ended, and in this horrible new world neither of them had any idea what to do.

Lucy reached for the ring, paused, then left the ring in her pocket. She stared down at Miranda's ruined face, at her hair streaked red with blood, at the blood splattered everywhere, even the wall behind her, all the way up to the crown moldings. Jennifer was rocking back and forth over her daughter, her limp hand clasped between hers, keening, not understanding, Lucy knew, why all this had happened, knowing only that if she hadn't slept with that man long ago, if Miranda hadn't been his seed, Miranda would still be alive. But Lucy couldn't ever tell her about the ring.

She heard Court say, "She came running in here, waving Dad's Kel Tec and demanding to see mother — 'that whore,' she called her. Mom finally had to tell her she'd cheated on Dad before she had Miranda. Mom begged for her forgiveness for not telling her, but Miranda was over the edge. She screamed Mom had ruined her life, stealing what was hers, making the ring useless to her, and then she shot Dad's Kel Tec into the ceiling. And then she laughed, a horrible sound, not funny at all, that laugh. I think I'll hear it the rest of my life. What did she mean? What has that idiot ring got to do with anything?"

Uncle Alan hadn't moved. He stood statue-still, staring at his dead daughter and his wife rocking over her, her deep tearing cries filling the silent room.

Lucy said, "I'm very sorry, Uncle Alan."

Alan Silverman shook his son's hand off his shoulder and looked toward Lucy. "This is your fault; you brought all this death and pain to us, you and that godforsaken ring." He walked to his wife, knelt beside her, and cradled her in his arms. Jennifer turned into him and wept.

Lucy couldn't bear it. Tears streamed down her face. Ruth pulled her close, stroked her up and down her back, trying to calm her, and said over and over, "He's overwhelmed with pain, Lucy. Of course it wasn't your fault."

Lucy clutched Ruth hard. She smelled death around her. She looked back to see Uncle Alan staring at her over his wife's head, his face ravaged, tears streaming down his face.

Aunt Jennifer pulled back and looked up at her husband. "It isn't Lucy's fault, Alan. It's mine, all of it. If only I hadn't slept with that man, if only — this ring, why did it mean so much to her? I don't understand."

Jennifer leaned into her husband again, sobbing.

Lucy heard the front door crash open, heard men's and women's voices yelling, heard their wild footsteps.

And Ollie's voice shouting, "Stop! All of you!"

She barely registered the voices swirling around her, some urgent, some weary, all of them were moving, doing their jobs. They weren't looking at her, not like Uncle Alan was. They were looking at Miranda's body.

CHAPTER 77

Washington, D.C.
Washington Memorial Hospital
Late Sunday night

Lucy laid her hand lightly on Coop's shoulder while Dr. Rayburn probed the bullet wound in his side. She looked at the line of black stitches in his bruised flesh, the traces of blood that had oozed from between the black thread until Dr. Rayburn covered it with a fresh bandage. It scared her to her toes to think how very close it had come to penetrating his belly. If only she'd been outside with him when Kirsten had taken him —

Dr. Rayburn straightened, gave Coop a toothy grin. "There you go, Agent. Except for some lingering soreness, you'll be good as new in a couple of days. Well, more like two weeks. You're a lucky man. No exercise until the sutures are out in seven days, well, more like no exercise for three weeks, and try to keep off your feet for a couple of days. No, er, strenuous activity, either. Don't want to pull those stitches apart." He shot a look toward Lucy.

"Indeed not," she said.

"What?" Coop asked.

Dr. Rayburn kept talking. "I'm happy to say the surgeon who saw you in that ER in North Carolina fixed you up fine — good, tight stitches, no signs of infection. Still, I'm glad you stopped here before heading on home, if only to be sure. You can see your own doctor tomorrow."

"Nah, not tomorrow, I'll give him a call on Tuesday. I feel fine, Doctor, thank you —"

"That's the narcotics you've got on board talking, Coop." Lucy patted his hand, and turned to Dr. Rayburn, who was no older than she was, bags under his eyes the size of carry-ons. "He'll do exactly what you've said, not to worry. I've got him well in hand."

"Only because I'm such a nice guy. But Lucy, we'll have to discuss this strenuous-activity business."

"Ah, are you both FBI agents?"

"Yes," they said in unison.

"You guys married?"

"I barely know him," Lucy said, kissed

Coop's cheek, and smiled at Dr. Rayburn.

Dr. Rayburn opened the curtain around the stretcher, shook hands with the waiting Savich and Sherlock on his way out, and then he was off in a fast walk, his white coat flapping.

Savich and Sherlock walked into the cubicle and examined Coop's face. "Lucy's right," Savich said. "You're happier now than you'll be for a good two days. Lots of rest, Coop. I don't want to see you at work until Wednesday."

"But —"

"Wednesday," Savich said very pleasantly, and turned to Lucy. "Lucy, we were so relieved to hear you're okay. We're very sorry about your cousin."

Lucy could only nod. The reality of Miranda's suicide crashed in again.

"I want you to take the time off, too, Lucy. Stay with Coop. You can help us get a better handle on what happened later. The police detective in charge, Mylo Dwyer, wants to understand what brought all this about, since he only saw the tragic ending. He told me it seemed Miranda became enraged because her mother told her Alan Silverman wasn't her biological father. There was also mention of a ring. He wants to speak to you again. One thing, though —

however did you get away from Miranda?"

"She tied my wrists to the chair arms, but managed to work one hand free. I couldn't get my SIG or her Kel Tec, but I could run, and so I did."

"Why did Miranda want the ring so badly?"

Lucy looked him straight in the eyes. "The ring is very old, and it may have been in my family for hundreds of years. She wanted it for herself."

Enough to kill you? Enough to kill herself? Savich shot a look at Sherlock, who was patting Coop like she patted Sean when he hurt himself.

He said to Lucy, "It looks like you're going to have your hands full with John Wayne here. Both of you regroup, take it easy, come to grips with the fact that all of this is over. You ride herd on him until Wednesday, okay? You're both going to need the rest, because I think you're going to want to go on a long trip on Wednesday.

"Coop insisted on calling Vincent Delion while we were still hunkered in that tobacco field, told him where Kirsten said she'd buried Arnette Carpenter.

"They found her. Roy Carpenter wants both of you to come to the funeral in San Francisco on Thursday, to thank you for finding his wife, but only if you're feeling up to it. There's a visit to Nob Hill you'll want to make, too, while you're there."

Coop said, "I'll be more than ready to fly out on Wednesday. As for Nob Hill, how did you know, Savich?"

"It only made sense. And we've had time to get a good look at the calls Kirsten made from her cell. By the way, Kirsten is out of surgery in North Carolina as of an hour ago. They say she'll survive her wounds fine, so now it'll be up to the state and federal courts to decide where they'll try her first."

"Amen to that," Coop said. He stood quietly while Sherlock buttoned his shirt. He gave Savich a big loopy grin. "I'm really glad we all made it out of this. I didn't like my chances for a while. And that mom, she was so happy her kids are okay she might forget to sue us. She and her kids sure have a story for a lifetime — bringing down Ted Bundy's daughter. Can you imagine how popular those kids are going to be in school?"

He stopped cold, swallowed. He realized he'd been babbling, when Lucy had almost died as well and had lost yet another family member. Like Savich and Mylo Dwyer, he simply didn't understand what had driven Miranda to try to kill Lucy, then to kill herself. So who cared if Alan Silverman wasn't her father? Did it matter so much to her? Evidently so. And that ring. He opened his mouth to speak, but Lucy interrupted him. "Smile, Coop, and relax, you're feeling all those meds they gave you. Enjoy not having any pain. That's a good thing."

Sherlock leaned up and kissed his cheek. "Well done, Coop. You brought Kirsten down." Then she clasped Lucy's shoulders and smiled at her. "I am so relieved you are all right." And she hugged her.

Sherlock looked after them as they walked to the waiting room, Coop flying high and happy. She could hear him humming from where she stood, his arm around Lucy's shoulders. "He looks like he should be punching cattle in Wyoming in that shearling coat. I'm glad he didn't ruin it, only the one little blood spot inside." She gave Dillon a look. "I'd have to say he looks nearly as hot in it as you do in your black leather."

He arched a brow at her, then called after them, "Lucy, if you want to talk to me about what happened, give me a call."

Lucy didn't slow, said over her shoulder, "I don't think I'll ever have anything else to say, Dillon, but thank you."

Coop stopped humming. "You'll tell me

all about the ring, won't you, Lucy?"

She didn't look at him — the horror of what had happened was too fresh, the utter waste of it all. Miranda's ruined face was clear in her mind; she could still see blind death in her eyes. She cut it off and looked up at Coop, hugged him to her side. "I want to tell you everything that's important to me, Coop. Always."

CHAPTER 78

Georgetown
Sunday night

Sherlock was giving a dishcloth a final pass over the kitchen counters when Jerry Lee Lewis sang out "Great Balls of Fire." "Oh, dear, I hate it when the phone rings this late."

"Savich."

"Ben here, Savich." He paused for a moment, breathed in deeply. "Mrs. Patil is dead."

"*What? Jasmine* Patil? Not Mr. Patil?"

"That's right. She was picking up some papers that needed Mr. Patil's signature in the office of the Georgetown Shop 'n Go. The clerk, Rishi Ram, a Patil cousin many times removed, heard a gunshot and ran back to the office, saw Mrs. Patil's head on the desk, her blood everywhere, covering all the papers. He said he called nine-one-one right away, then ran to the back door, which is usually locked, saw it was wide open. He said he ran outside, saw a car driving away."

"What kind of car?"

"He thought it was a Kia, black, didn't see the license plate or the driver. Then he burst into tears and said it could have been a Cadillac, for all he knew. His mom owned a Kia, and so he'd just said that. Go figure."

"Is Mr. Patil still in the hospital?"

"No, he went home yesterday. I was told he's recovering nicely. And now this. First him and now his wife." Ben drew in a deep breath. "He doesn't know yet. The cousin many times removed is still with the police. Will you come with me to tell him?"

"Yes, I'll come."

"Meet me there, okay?"

"Twenty minutes," Savich said, and punched off his cell.

Sherlock was squeezing his hand. "Dillon, Mrs. Patil was shot? She's dead?"

Savich nodded, but he was silent, staring toward the two pumpkins he and Sherlock had carved for Halloween. He saw a couple of pumpkin seeds on the floor, bent over and picked them up. "I'd hoped, even prayed, we were wrong, but I knew in my gut what had happened. But we didn't follow through fast enough; there was too much going on. That's why I asked Ben to assign a cop to Mr. Patil. I didn't see what was coming. I'm an idiot."

She lightly touched her fingertips to his cheek. "No, you're not an idiot. Just think about everything that's been happening — talk about a lot on your plate."

"Well, yes, but I should have given it more thought."

"Now you will, and now you'll act."

He nodded, smacked his fist against the kitchen table. The salt shaker did a small dance before settling again. "Sometimes I hate this job."

She hugged him fiercely. "You can't control what other people choose to do, Dillon. All you can do is set it right. Come home to us soon."

CHAPTER 79

Savich pulled his Porsche in behind Ben's pickup at the curb in front of the Patil home.

Ben stepped out of his truck, stuck his head in the open Porsche window, and said without preamble, "This sucks."

Savich leaned his head back and closed his eyes. "I didn't think this through logically. I'm really sorry about this, Ben."

"You're figuring this the same way I am, aren't you?"

Savich nodded.

Ben smacked his fist on the car window's ledge. "I'm sorry, too. The thing is, I can't think of a more likely scenario. I hate this; I hate this to my bones."

Savich was tired, so weary of death and how it tore apart the fabric of life of all those left behind to pick up the shreds. "Let's get it done."

Mr. Nandi Patil was sitting in a lovely red leather La-Z-Boy in the Patil living room, at

565

least a half dozen sons, daughters, cousins, and friends surrounding him. His color was good; he was nodding at something his friend Mr. Amal Urbi was saying. Mr. Urbi, Savich thought, looked more fragile than Mr. Patil, ready to topple over. His pants tonight were belted up near his armpits, his white hair even wispier than the last time he'd seen him. No, not quite two weeks, Savich thought, and simply looked at each of them in turn. He saw Mr. Krishna Shama was sitting beside his desiccated uncle, dressed casually in slacks and shirt, Italian loafers on his narrow feet, looking, to Savich's eyes, bored.

Mr. Patil looked up, beamed a smile. "Agent Savich, my very good friend, and Detective Raven, come in, come in. Jasmine will be home soon. I asked her to bring me a contract from my office."

"How are you feeling, Mr. Patil?" Savich asked him as he moved to stand in front of the fireplace.

"I am alive, still, something of a surprise, I must admit. I feel ever so much better than I did last week, Agent Savich. To what do I owe this honor?"

Ben asked, "Where is Officer Warrans?"

"Ah, the dear man is in the kitchen, eating some of Cook's delicious naan, fresh out of the oven. She is famous for her naan."

Ben said, "I am very sorry to tell you this, sir, but your wife was shot to death an hour ago at your store in Georgetown."

His shock was tangible, Savich thought, thick and hard and sour. Then came disbelief, heartbreak, questions, fury — the whole gamut of emotions.

Savich looked at no one except Nandi Patil. He would have sworn, as would Ben, that Mrs. Patil was the one who'd tried to murder her husband, and that he had retaliated.

But it wasn't so, Savich thought. No, not Mr. Patil, not this man who was suffering, his eyes blurred over with tears.

Suddenly, Mr. Patil clutched his heart and began wheezing for breath. They should have brought a doctor, he thought. Damn his arrogance for believing that since Mr. Patil had killed his wife in retribution, no physician would be necessary.

He was at Mr. Patil's side in a moment. Then a voice from the doorway said, "Move aside. I am a paramedic. I will see to him." A young woman, heavyset, her thick black hair in a long ponytail, ran to Mr. Patil and pressed a metal canister of medication to his mouth.

Mr. Patil finally sucked in a deep breath.

"He's having a bronchospasm. For heaven's sake, what did you say to him? What brought this on?"

"His wife was murdered tonight," Ben said matter-of-factly to the young woman.

"Aunt Jasmine? *Murdered?* What is going on in this freaking family!"

It began again, outrage, disbelief, fury at Mr. Patil's near-death right here in his own living room at the devastating news brought without warning by the FBI and the WPD.

Savich let it go on for a minute or two, until he was convinced Mr. Patil would be all right. He raised a hand until everyone fell silent.

"Mr. Patil, we are all very sorry about this. Now, I need all of you to listen to us." Savich nodded to Ben.

Ben said, "I regret to tell you, sir, that we believe your wife was involved in hiring those two people who tried to kill you, posing as robbers. Agent Savich killed one of them and the other is in jail, refusing to say a word. When the first attempt failed, we believe she herself came to the store at closing time and shot you in the back."

Nandi Patil stared blankly at them, shaking his head back and forth. "No, this cannot be true, it cannot. Jasmine has loved me forever, even more than I loved her, truth be told. She was a vivid light, no, she could not have tried to murder me."

"I'm very sorry, sir," Savich said. "When she was murdered tonight, both Detective Raven and I believed you were responsible, that you had found out she'd tried to kill you, and it was your vengeance."

Nandi Patil gaped at him. "No, no."

Savich turned to face Krishna Shama. "You and Mrs. Patil were having an affair, Mr. Shama. We are aware of that. Did you want to end it? Why? Because of the closeness of your uncle and Mr. Patil? Because Jasmine was so much older than you were? Why, Mr. Shama?"

Shama looked from Ben Raven back to Savich. "Yes, Jasmine and I were lovers, for nearly a year. I never wanted to end our affair; I never wanted to leave her. I loved her, but now she is dead. I think Mr. Patil killed her."

Tears rolled down Mr. Patil's face. He'd been rocked to his soul in the past ten minutes. His eyes looked blank with shock.

Krishna Shama said, "Listen to me. I did not kill Jasmine. I did not know she had tried to murder Mr. Patil. I did not know."

Savich turned to Mr. Urbi. "You and Nandi have been friends since you were children. You are older, though, aren't you, sir?"

"By twelve years. A lifetime of difference in our ages," the old man said. He was sitting perfectly still, not even blinking.

"You love Nandi like a younger brother, don't you, sir?"

"Yes, of course. He is very important to me. His near death filled me with grief."

"And then you discovered your nephew and Jasmine Patil were lovers. They had betrayed both you and Nandi. You were furious, weren't you, sir?"

"That is right. When Detective Raven questioned us after the robbery, he left me with doubts, merely suspicions — glances, phrases that had passed between Jasmine and Krishna that I realized I had chosen to ignore. And when Nandi was shot a second time, it all became clear to me. To be absolutely sure, I paid a large sum of money to that criminal, Mr. Wenkel, through his lawyer, to confirm to me privately that it was Jasmine who had hired him.

"Nandi isn't of my flesh and blood, but he is my brother in all ways that are important on this benighted earth. He did not realize, could not see what she had become. Had I told him she had betrayed him, that she continued to betray him with my own flesh and blood, this worthless jackal sitting here all proud beside me, Nandi would not have believed me. As you see, he will never believe she tried to have him killed for his money. She and the jackal would have won." He waved a veiny hand toward his nephew.

The room was utterly silent now. No one seemed to breathe.

Ben said, "You waited until Mr. Patil came home from the hospital, waited until you were certain he could survive the blow, and then you hired someone to kill her, to end it all, to avenge your friend's betrayal by his wife."

Mr. Urbi only nodded. He looked up and gave them both a very sweet smile. "I know what your district attorney will want to do with me, but I am too near to death now to worry about that. I am not worth spending the taxpayers' money on a trial."

"Uncle, no!"

"Be quiet, Krishna. You have dishonored me; you have dishonored my closest friend in the world. I will never speak to you again. Do you understand that you are nothing now to me? That you are as worthless as dung?"

Krishna Shama bowed his head.

Again, the room was perfectly quiet.

Mr. Patil said, "You, Krishna, how could

571

you do this? I don't understand. But, then, I am an old man. It is true that I have only the memory of lust and what it leads men and women to do that dishonors them and is so very hurtful to those they supposedly care about. Jasmine, I knew I'd lost her desire, but I did not mind all that much. Your uncle took vengeance, and I am sorry about that." Mr. Patil turned to his friend. "Amal, I would not have killed Jasmine for betraying me, even for trying to kill me. What I would have done is divorce her, made certain she did not have a single penny, and I would have kicked her out into the street. Honor, Amal? Killing her has brought me back my honor? Hardly. You have brought only death into my house.

"I would like to be alone now, if it is all right with you, Agent Savich and Detective Raven. I would like not to have to look upon either of these men's faces again. As it is, I will still see them in my dreams, and that is a great pity."

Savich took Mr. Patil's hands in his. "I am so sorry about all of this, Mr. Patil."

Mr. Patil raised pain-deadened eyes to Savich's face. "I know that you are. You are that kind of man."

CHAPTER 80

Nob Hill, San Francisco
Wednesday evening

Inspector Vincent Delion was curious but was content to sit back in an elegant wing chair worth more than his son's used Honda and stare out the huge glass window of Clifford Childs's living room at the view of San Francisco Bay. And watch Agents Cooper McKnight and Lucy Carlyle both turn their laser intelligence loose on Sentra Bolger.

Sentra Bolger sat on a lovely blue-patterned brocade sofa, her very nice legs crossed, a cup of green tea in her hand. She was wearing very high heels with open toes, showing off her lovely French pedicure. She looked expensive all over, Delion thought, in a long black gown that left one white shoulder bare, her dark hair pulled back in a polished chignon. She also looked like the queen of her kingdom, her consort guarding her back.

Clifford Childs stood behind her, his hand resting possessively on her bare shoulder. Childs said, impatience making his voice sharp as glass, "We agreed to see you on short notice, but we are expected shortly at Davies Hall. The symphony performs Mendelssohn this evening, and Sentra is very fond of Mendelssohn. I would like to know what this is all about, why you wish to speak to her."

Coop pulled a cell phone out of his pocket. The movement brought only a slight pull in his side, better every day now, thank the Lord.

Both Sentra Bolger and Clifford Childs looked at the purple cell phone, then at Coop's face.

Lucy said, "Ms. Bolger, Kirsten called you over a dozen times over the past two months. The last time she called you, Agent McKnight was in the car, as Kirsten's hostage. I understand you gave her some advice?"

Sentra's elegant white hands were still, her fingers relaxed. Her expression didn't change. She sighed. "I didn't say anything to Clifford, because I didn't wish to worry him, but the truth is, Agents, I wondered when you would arrive. I had thought about calling you to ask about Kirsten's real condition, since the media is spouting so much nonsense about her."

Childs picked it up, disgust thick in his voice. "Including interviews with each celebrity attorney who wants to represent her, pro bono, the jackals. Is that the truth?"

Coop said, "I will tell you exactly what I know, Ms. Bolger, Mr. Childs, and then we will speak about your conversations with your niece. As a matter of fact, Kirsten's injuries are responding well to treatment. She may be suffering psychologically, though. She hasn't said a word for several days. Our psychologists have tried, and can't get her to speak. Her being depressed would be understandable, what with getting shot and captured, her boyfriend, Bruce Comafield, dead. The last thing she said was to me in Florida when we captured her: 'I wonder what Daddy would say.'"

Sentra shook her head, and her voice was filled with sorrow. "Poor child. She idolized the man and started thinking she could talk to him at times. Perhaps it was her reaction to Elizabeth — her mother. How she never said a word about Bundy to Kirsten, indeed, not even telling her who her father was until, well, Kirsten already knew and confronted her."

Lucy sat forward in her chair. "You told

her, didn't you, Ms. Bolger? You're the one who told her about Ted Bundy."

Sentra nodded. "She was twenty-five. When she was a child, she asked Elizabeth who her father was, and Elizabeth made up some malarkey about his being a Navy SEAL who was killed in a training accident. In any case, yes, I told her the truth, she deserved to know. All the books talk about how handsome he was, how charming, but that doesn't begin to capture what Ted really was — a shining star, and so fascinating he could charm the tattoo right off a cell mate." She shook herself, smiled. "I told her how gaga her mother was over him, how much she wanted to marry him. Now, there's a dollop of irony." She paused for a moment, as if considering it, then, "I offered to date him, too, once they broke up, but Ted turned me down, said one woman with my sister's face was more than enough. I remember telling him he was missing out, big-time, that I was much smarter and more beautiful than Elizabeth, and he laughed, said, 'No, thanks,' and then he turned that wicked smile of his on me and said maybe he'd look me up someday.

"Of course, neither Elizabeth nor I ever heard from him again. He didn't know he left Elizabeth pregnant with Kirsten. I rather think it was a good thing he didn't come back. He was killing by then, you know, in 1977, for three years at that point, probably longer, but who knew? If he had come back, would he have killed her? Me?

"Neither of us knew what he was, what he'd done, until he was caught. We couldn't believe it, really — that Ted would kidnap young women, rape and torture them, then murder them. What he did to them after that, well, that's best not visited, is it?"

Clifford Childs said, "I tell Sentra she and her sister were very lucky. What if Bundy had turned on them, tried to murder them, as he had so many women?" He actually shuddered, tightened his hand on Sentra's shoulder. "I'll never forget when we got the news he'd escaped, somewhere in Colorado. It took them forever to catch him, but they did, thank God. When he was finally executed in Florida, I bought up the most expensive champagne in my wine cellar — Krug, Clos du Mesnil, 1980. Sentra, my darling, I remember you didn't wish to drink much of that precious ambrosia. It was hard for you, wasn't it?"

She nodded. "I realized the finality of it, Clifford, that he was truly gone forever. It's difficult, still, to come to grips with the fact of what Ted actually did to those women, and to realize that the man we knew felt nothing for those women he brutalized, he never saw them as people who just wanted to live, to enjoy life as best they could, to see a future. He lost his conscience, his very soul, I guess you could say, if he ever had either of those commodities in the first place. I would say the evil chemicals twisting his brain finally made him more monster than human. Toward the end, I suspect his wife must have realized that as well, and grew afraid for herself and her daughter. I was relieved when I read she left Florida all those years ago." She clasped, unclasped her hands, looked at them with finality. "There is nothing more to say. Poor Kirsten has his blood, the same insanity flows through her."

Vincent Delion spoke for the first time: "Did you know Kirsten had already killed at least six women here in the San Francisco area years ago, Ms. Bolger?"

"No," Sentra said without hesitation, and Coop wondered if she could be that good a liar. He let it go.

He said, "Kirsten knew all about Starke Prison, what happened to her father there. I think she was headed there when we captured her."

"Do you believe she will speak again,

Agent McKnight?"

"Yes, of course she will," Coop said. "All of us are hoping she will tell us where she buried the other women she murdered before she left San Francisco and went on her rampage. Can you imagine being the parents of a fifteen-year-old girl who is simply gone one day, who never returns? Perhaps you could speak to Kirsten, encourage her to tell you where she buried these women."

"I doubt she would tell me, Agent. Perhaps it is best to let them lie in peace."

Coop could only stare at her. "Tell me, Ms. Bolger, are you Kirsten's mother?"

"I? No, my dear sister is indeed her mother. Ah, I see. You're wondering why Kirsten and I were always so close."

Delion sat forward in his chair.

"She was a disturbed child, and she needed me. I believed I knew her very well."

Coop said, "How old was she when you gave her a ring to match Bundy's?"

"Ah, so you know about that. Those matching rings — Kirsten told me it was the best present she'd ever get in her entire life, she knew it. She never took off either ring, so far as I know. I gave them both to her when I told her who her father was.

"Now, about the girls here in San Francisco. I never had a clue she'd killed girls and women before she left. But looking back on it now, knowing what I know now, it doesn't surprise me. I knew soon enough she was the Black Beret, impossible not to. I did not, however, ever know where she was at any given time. Whenever she called, I counseled her to turn herself in."

She paused for a moment, to see if they'd believed that whopper. Fat chance. After a moment, she continued, "I mourned when the FBI released the news that Bruce was dead. I knew she had to be devastated. Kirsten counted on him, you see, couldn't really manage much in her life without him. They were like two halves of a puzzle that fit together, to produce — well, I suppose, you would have to say that together they produced monstrous evil. Do you think it odd she began killing before she even knew who her father was?"

Coop said, "You make it sound like an unusual quirk. She was only fifteen when she killed a classmate. We may never know if she killed when she was even younger. Ms. Bolger, it was your legal responsibility to inform us about Kirsten. Why didn't you? Why did it take us finding Kirsten's cell and coming to you?"

Sentra merely raised her hand and laid it

lightly over Childs's. He said promptly, "I have spoken with our attorneys." He walked around the sofa to stand in front of her. "He tells me you can't do anything to Sentra. As she said, she did not know where Kirsten was at any point in time; that is all."

"Her cell phone —"

"You will find nothing incriminating in Sentra's telephone records."

Sentra said from behind Childs, "Is there anything else you would like to know, Agents?" She looked down at the beautiful thin watch on her wrist. "The symphony does such a nice job with Mendelssohn. We really must be leaving."

"You could go see Kirsten, Ms. Bolger," Lucy said, "You could encourage her to speak again."

Slowly, Sentra Bolger rose. Clifford Childs clasped her hand in his. Over thirty years, Coop thought, these two were the age of his parents, but somehow so different — why hadn't they ever married? He turned to see that Clifford Childs's sons and their wives had filed quietly into the immense living room, as if summoned by their queen for departure. Did they all want to protect this woman? It was as George Lansford had told them: the Childs family seemed to adore Sentra Bolger. Coop imagined Childs himself would gladly kill for her as well, if it came down to it.

They rose.

"I am fine," Sentra said toward the group, then said to Coop and Lucy, "Kirsten doesn't need me. I know her. By next week, she will be speaking again, and she will be enraged. She will be judged sane, and she will go to trial and she will be given the death penalty, like her father, despite all the self-promoting lawyers who will demand to represent her. Her appeals will stretch on for years and years, probably for long after I'm dead and forgotten."

"You will never be forgotten!" One of the young men hurried to her side, a lovely cashmere shawl in his hands. She smiled up at him as he placed it over her shoulders. He looked the picture of his father. "That is very kind of you, Basil." She smiled at the knot of people around her. "Now, Inspector, Agents, I wish you a pleasant evening. Do you know, after this tragedy, I look around and realize how very lucky I am. I have the most wonderful family in the world." Her slightly mad smile took in all the people standing protectively around her in the vast living room.

CHAPTER 81

More than a hundred people stood grave-side at the burial of Arnette Carpenter, many of them members of the media. Her body had been found three days before, the autopsy showing that she'd been bludgeoned to death. They found her skeleton exactly where Kirsten had told Coop she'd buried her.

Lucy studied Roy Carpenter's face. There was a blank tightness around his eyes and his mouth, but there was something else, too — Lucy saw some measure of peace. Arnette had been found; she'd come home. They still didn't know where to look for the bodies of Kirsten's other victims. They were hopeful the profiler visits from the FBI would yield some results. Maybe Kirsten would eventually tell them to cut some sort

583

of deal. And they could finally be laid to rest.

A bagpiper, standing solitary on a small hillock at the edge of the cemetery, played "Amazing Grace" at the close of the service. Everyone turned toward the haunting sounds that always seemed to pull people deep into themselves. Then the last notes sort of drifted away, swallowed by the thick fog that was rolling in through the Golden Gate. Lucy realized she was crying, both for Arnette Carpenter and for her own father, gone so recently, and there was Miranda, who'd died for nothing. And she marveled at how her life had changed irrevocably. She held Coop's hand tightly. He looked down at her, and she searched his eyes for any sign of discomfort. He'd said nothing, but she'd seen him lightly rubbing his side.

She wanted the bagpiper to play more, but he, too, seemed to fade slowly into the fog and disappear. There was a collective murmur from the people standing near Arnette Carpenter's grave. Coop and Lucy laid a red rose atop the casket.

Coop pulled Lucy close to his side. Coop saw Sentra Bolger and Clifford Childs standing off at a distance, both in unremitting black, holding hands.

EPILOGUE

One week later

Lucy stood on the walkway of the Markham Bridge overlooking the Potomac. It was very early. The sky was overcast with heavy gray clouds, and the wind off the water was sharp, stinging her face. There was only one lone runner, and she was at the far end of the bridge. A single van drove past, then she was alone.

She stared down into the dark, slow-moving water, wondering how deep it was here.

She pulled the necklace from beneath her turtleneck, opened the clasp, and let the ring slide onto her palm.

She clutched the ring in her hand. It was hers, passed down to her from her grandfather, long dead. She was responsible for it now, she alone. She thought of Uncle Alan, Aunt Jennifer, and Court, devastated by grief, not really understanding, and they never would. They were refusing to speak to her, still blamed her for what happened. Uncle Alan hadn't left his wife. She wondered if Uncle Alan would ever come to see that Miranda's suicide wasn't her fault, if they could ever be any sort of a family again.

There hadn't been a formal funeral for Miranda, only a grave-side service that was small and private. Her aunt had invited her to the cemetery, but she'd stood back, just as Sentra Bolger and Clifford Childs had done at Arnette Carpenter's graveside service, and watched her remaining family grieve.

She opened her hand and studied the ring, felt it pulse warm in her palm. She whispered, "If you never existed, none of this would have happened."

Dillon would be dead. She might be dead, too, if she hadn't had the ring when she'd escaped from Miranda.

She looked at the three red carnelians, duller still in the gray morning light, and at the word *SEFYLL* — was it a curse or a salvation?

It had cost her grandfather his life, and Miranda.

Throughout the centuries, how many other lives had the ring taken? Had it changed history itself? For the better or for worse? She didn't know, couldn't know.

She had honored Miranda's wish that she not try to use the ring when she shot herself, however bloody and useless trying might have been. Miranda wanted to make her own choice, but she never seemed to realize that everyone should have that right, the right to make their own choices, and live or die by them. Miranda made her realize the future should be determined by everyone, not by any one person, whether a well-meaning person trying to do the right thing or a dangerous one like Miranda who could change the world in unimaginable and tragic ways. No one should have that much power.

She squeezed the ring tightly, then stared at the water flowing beneath her. "Goodbye," she said, and dropped it into the water. It didn't even make a ripple in the surface.

She turned to see Coop standing next to his Corvette some twenty feet away. He'd driven her here. She knew in her heart he wouldn't ask why she'd come. He would accept her and love her, and they'd build a life together, and hopefully it would be a good one.

She waved at him. She never looked back.

ABOUT THE AUTHOR

Catherine Coulter is the author of sixty-five novels, almost all of them *New York Times* bestsellers. She earned her reputation writing historical romances, but in recent years turned her hand to penning — with great success — contemporary suspense novels. Catherine grew up on a horse ranch in Texas. She graduated from the University of Texas and received her masters at Boston College. Prior to becoming a full-time writer, she worked on Wall Street as a speechwriter for a company president. She lives in Marin County, California, with her physician husband and her three cats. Catherine Coulter loves to hear from readers. You can e-mail her at ReadMoi@aol.com.

The employees of Thorndike Press hope you have enjoyed this Large Print book. All our Thorndike, Wheeler, and Kennebec Large Print titles are designed for easy reading, and all our books are made to last. Other Thorndike Press Large Print books are available at your library, through selected bookstores, or directly from us.

For information about titles, please call:
(800) 223-1244

or visit our Web site at:
http://gale.cengage.com/thorndike

To share your comments, please write:
Publisher
Thorndike Press
10 Water St., Suite 310
Waterville, ME 04901